THE THIRD PRINCESS

THE THIRD PRINCESS

Philip Boast

This first world edition published in Great Britain 2006 by
SEVERN HOUSE PUBLISHERS LTD of
9–15 High Street, Sutton, Surrey SM1 1DF.
This first world edition published in the USA 2006 by
SEVERN HOUSE PUBLISHERS INC of
595 Madison Avenue, New York, N.Y. 10022.

British Library Cataloguing in Publication Data

Boast,   Philip
    The third princess
    1.   Nero, Emperor of Rome, 37 - 68 - Fiction
    2.   Rome - History - Nero, 54-68 - Fiction
    3.   Detective and mystery stories
    I.   Title
    823.9'14 [F]

    ISBN-10: 0-7278-6322-3

Typeset by Palimpsest Book Production Ltd.,
Polmont, Stirlingshire, Scotland.
Printed and bound in Great Britain by
MPG Books Ltd., Bodmin, Cornwall.

Prologus

Rome, 11 nights before the Kalends of Januarius, AD *63*

The dead woman sprawled on silk sheets. She smelt beautiful. Her perfume was 'Poppaea', named for the wife of the God-Emperor Nero. Only the richest, most highborn women in Rome dared afford it; she'd died in the height of fashion. At her throat a necklace shone like fire.

Her gown was cinnabar red, hideously expensive, decorated with gold charms at neck, and sleeves, and hem. Her body looked about forty years old, her face older, yet smooth; great skill and attention to detail had been lavished on her in the hours before she died. She was dressed to kill.

Her neckline plunged to her chalk-white breasts, delicately etched with faint purple veins as though still fertile with milk. Where the paint had flaked, her flesh showed through as grey as old stone.

Her ice-white hair was piled high in the latest *Neroeia* fashion, intricately curled and twisted, held by long steel pins. The push-ends of the hairpins gleamed black against white, like a constellation of dark suns burning in ice. Brilliant work; hours of patient nimble-fingered labour by someone both skilled and conscientious.

Her head lay about halfway down the large bed, on a lambswool pillow. The walls were hidden by wooden screens, riotously painted. Wine stained the Arabian rugs, the dropped lyre. Her bare left foot was propped over the bedhead; her right leg, still wearing the red leather sandal, hung to the floor. A Venus mask lay broken on her belly. The door was closed, bolted on the inside. No windows; the only illumination came from the gold candelabrum guttering on its side.

Her face, powdered with white lead, with wine-rouged cheeks and saffron eye-shadow, looked lively in death, seemingly interrupted in a laugh; only her fixed downward-staring eyes showed she neither slept nor lived.

1

One

The Opened Vein

Severus Septimus Quistus lay in his bath, naked as the day he was born.

His life had run its full circle, from birth to death. Only a few thousand heartbearts remained for him.

The Nubian princess, dark as night, heaved herself on tiptoe. For the hundredth time tonight she shoved her eye to the spyhole, one of many picked through the wall-mosaic by previous generations of slaves, peering into the steamy darkness of the Villa Marcia's *therma* where her master lay soaking. A few watery reflections rippled along the dimly seen murals; the last lamp-flame was dying down like a life going out. It must be as hot as the Hell of the Christians in there by now, but still the ex-Senator remained awake. What sleepless demons did such a man fight, who'd lost all he loved? Still his fist gripped the sword tight underwater.

She rubbed her eye, worried out of her mind for him. What if—

Suppose he—

It wouldn't be hard for him to die. Living was hard.

Omba pushed her eye to the spyhole, sweating, making him out through the steam. His body hadn't moved.

Standing, he was too tall, not enough fat on him. Lying, especially birth-naked, she reckoned he looked about right, fit to pass for any age between thirty-five and fifty-five. True, by the standards of the Oromos tribe his legs were too skinny for such a muscular chest, his head too big. A runner's legs, a fighter's body, a thinker's head. His hair was black, not short enough, curly; his mouth too small, his nose too large, and his eyes – his eyes were hidden, tight closed.

She thought: He's perfect. For a Roman.

Omba's noble, warlike features softened maternally; the

2

strong curve of her belly ached, childless. Look at him, his face calm and quiet as the face of a sleeping baby. Who knew what inner passions tormented his soul behind that Stoic mask, forbidden to show any feeling of pain?

She knew.

Tonight, she knew, he'd die like a Roman. His time had come. She'd seen his eyes this morning, no stopping him. At first she'd screamed at him. *No, no.* Then she was angry. Threats and grief failed, even reason and persuasion, his logic was harsher than hers. She mocked him, begged, wept. Fell silent. Stormed out. Stormed back, throwing things. Stormed out again, weeping. No good.

Finally, grew cunning.

All day she'd watched him like a hunter stalking her prey, not to slaughter but to save.

Not one word did he reply to her chatter. Ate not a mouthful of the lunch she prepared with her own hands, finest cheeses, beautiful fat olives, all wasted. Ignored supper. Undistracted by her small watchful kindnesses, staring past her with already-dead eyes. As darkness fell he retreated alone to his study, sat unmoving in his chair, a man fading into the shadows.

It was deep night, the fourth hour, when she found the household chest open. The wedding gift was missing, the sword that was so much more than a sword: an oath, a promise, a memory, a life.

That was when Omba understood he really would be dead before dawn. She'd run after the sound of his footsteps to the *therma*, but the door was already locked.

All night bad spirits laid siege to the house, moaning against the shutters, rattling the roof-tiles. Their cold breath gusted under the doors, terrifying her, but she kept her nerve. To confront him was pointless. Omba threw herself into her life-saving stratagem. By now the hypocaust hissed like an angry serpent, red-faced, demanding more wood. She fed it then returned to the spyhole in the eye of a water-nymph.

What thoughts passed through his mind?

Beneath the boiling-hot water Marcia's sword lay heavy across his belly. The blade's tongue licked his left wrist, sharp as ever, hungry as any man could wish. The water-wrinkled fingers of his right hand clenched the hilt tight, as they had for hours; the steel rose and fell beneath the steaming mirror

3

of the pool as he breathed in and out. Sometimes his eyes opened a little, one or both, dazed because of the heat, but now the last lamp flickered out, and even with both eyes staring wide he saw nothing but darkness, dark as death.

Quistus thought he heard a woman's gasp, but knew he was alone. Even faithful Omba, whose people practised a tradition of murder rather than honourable suicide, would have tired of warming his bed and fallen asleep by this hour.

Tonight was the night of his anniversary; this very night. Twenty-one years had passed since Marcia married him in this house – his father's house, back then – when they were fourteen years old. They'd been in love since they were children.

Four years ago, almost to the hour, he died here. Cold dawn – the first hour of the winter solstice – touched the Villa Marcia around this marbled, steaming, windowless room. When he pushed open the door that winter's morning to greet his family – seven boys, one girl, Lyra – the sun rising behind him had flung its light past him, revealing such a bloody horror that his mind still blinded him to the sight.

'Great Zeus our Saviour, help me,' he prayed in the dark. 'Holy Maiden, save me. Grant me grace. Let me be with them.'

The gods of the household watched without reply, seeing all, knowing his heart, silent. His whispers disturbed the steam condensing on the dome roof and drops fell suddenly out of the dark, plopping into the water around him. He felt them splash cold on his forehead, and blinked.

Decem, tenth and darkest month, tonight the longest darkest night, tenth before the Kalends of Januarius. Four years; even Volusia the Christian, saved by him from the Cross a handful of months past, had seen that without Marcia and his seven sons and lovely daughter Quistus was a dead man, only breathing.

Breathing in and out as though he were alive. But his heart had frozen that night.

All of them, dead.

No. Worse than dead.

Two of his beloved children – the twins – their bodies were never found. His two dearest children with no burial place, no home for their souls. Their spirits doomed to wander the earth for eternity.

But – he'd told himself – perhaps Septimus and Lyra were not butchered like the other children and their mother. Those

4

two could be alive. Yes, it was possible. There was hope. Desperate, imprisoned, enslaved, suffering somewhere, but still alive. Praying for their father to find them, to release them, to embrace them.

It kept him going. He observed their birthday, kept their rooms ready for their return. For four long, empty years. That was a long time not to lose hope.

He'd searched for them through all the world Rome knew, then roamed further, from Nubaeia to Ultima Thule, from India to the western lands. He'd shivered and burned. He'd seen the Walrus and the Dragon. He'd tracked each strand of logic to its bitter, bitter end and never found a sign. But a Stoic didn't know how to give up.

Yet the time did come when any sensible rational man looked into his heart and faced the truth: *They are all gone. There is only one way you will ever see them again.*

A sensible, rational choice. Death.

So hot in here, almost too hot for thought.

The sword stirred in his hand, the steel rising from the water like a blood-red flame, as though dawn came early. He saw his own pallid face, white as a death-mask. A relief to slide the point into his dull heart, peace to slice the edge across his scarlet jugular, or his blue-veined wrist, or the artery thudding in his groin, and bleed to merciful oblivion. Kind, gentle, Roman suicide. He heard the suck of an indrawn breath.

It was not dawn he saw, only a lamp reflected.

Quistus stayed motionless for a long heartbeat, then moved the blade until it showed the face behind his own, dark as night despite the light she held. A cold hand gripped his heart. But it was no ghost, no lemur of dead Marcia. The door, which he had locked, hung crookedly from its hinges.

'Omba.'

Omba, once First Princess of Kefa, now his slave. His power over her was total. By law he could shout at her, strike her, whip her, change her name, put her to death, give her freedom. He'd done none of these things. In return she infuriated him.

'Who else cares about you,' she rumbled from deep in her belly, 'but I?'

Yes; infuriating.

Solid gold tattoos glinted on her shaved head, midnight-black, her massive breasts swinging like gourds of finest polished

5

jet, their points fancily gold-tasselled in one of her character-istic gestures at modesty. There was a ring of dust around her right eye, probably from a spyhole. She splashed into the water and crouched close behind him, her great round face swelling in the blade. 'Who did you expect to find here tonight, Master? Did you really believe you'd find their murderer?'

No, they both knew what brought him here. Omba feared nothing that lived and walked the earth, but sometimes Quistus terrified her.

'Their murderer?' He stared into the blade, his mind – which was his heart, the source of all hope – still desperately gnawing for answers. 'No, it could have been murderers. It could have been—'

'Quistus the logician,' Omba snorted contemptuously, then mangled her Latin, which always cheered him up. 'Could have been anyone did them. Any reason, no reason. Robbery gone bad. Ransom, botched kidnap. Barbarians. Zealots. Christians – remember, Prefect of the Jews, remember Jerusalem? Political enemies. Soldiers with a grudge. Desperate slaves. The wrong address. Escaped gladiators. The Emperor Nero himself.'

'What? Why?' That got him. 'Do you really think so? What evidence—'

'Senator, it's the only crime you'll never understand.'

'There's always a reason, Omba. We just have to find it.' He added, 'Senator no longer.' He'd resigned all his titles after that day: ex-senator, ex-prefect, ex-praetor, ex-tribune, ex-quaestor, almost ex-Roman, all gone, rejected, a man travel-ling like a ghost, without baggage. Three years ago that was how he'd found Omba – or perhaps she found him, certainly their need was mutual – staked out as she was in the Nubian high desert, her back arched over an anthill, her mouth held open by thorns and honey on her tongue.

'Perhaps—' She stopped. She'd never known Marcia, only seen her self-portraits on frescoes and screens around the house. Striking-looking, powerful, small, like most Roman women. *Perhaps your beloved wife had a lover and a secret life and she tried to end the affair and somehow it all went wrong . . . or the children found out . . . and she—*

Omba knew her master well enough to be sure that his logic had already taken him to that dreadful place.

She said: 'Don't blame yourself.'

He felt her sweat drip from her chin to his head. He knew Omba's cunning. By now the pool steamed like a cauldron, hot enough to make a salamander sleep. No doubt she'd sent the rickety boy-slave who tended the fire early to his straw, and spent the night stoking the hypocaust white-hot herself, her eyes pressed to the various spyholes to check on him. He'd never really been alone. He noticed her eyes gleam in the sword.

'Did you really watch over me all night?'

'Did I have anything better to do?' He stood and she fetched his towel, standing thigh-deep on the slippery marble steps to drape it around him, hiding his sword. 'Come, master. Sleep. Forget.' He nodded, childlike. Just then a loud bang echoed through the house. His foot slipped on the step. 'Ah!'

He looked startled. Dark blood trickled through the towel. 'Master!'

The banging that echoed from the street door of the house was repeated, urgently. A high shout carried faintly, a girl's shout. They heard Cerberus, the old slave who kept the door, shouting back. No *ostiarius* accepted visitors at this hour, waking his master and getting him into trouble.

'It's all right, Omba.' Quistus held up his hand. Blood slid down his wrist from the opened vein. He laughed, wonderingly. 'It was an accident!'

Two

A Cry in the Dark

The girl's shouts and frantic knocking woke Cerberus so suddenly that he leapt to the door still half asleep, falling off his three-legged stool into a heap.

'What? Who?' he muttered thickly. He hauled himself up against the double-faced statue of Janus, guardian of door-ways. Not dawn yet.

'Help!' came her voice again through the thick iron-bound door, then more banging.

'Shut up! Go away!' He pulled his sleeping-cape around him – an *ostiarius* slept sitting up, hands on his knees with his lamp beside him, ready for duty. Strictly speaking he was supposed never to sleep at all. The dark told him it was still 'the end of the old day', not yet the first hour of the new day, late though that came with dawn at this time of year. Whoever she was, she'd better have a good excuse.

'Help! Severus Septimus Quistus!'

Oh yes, a shouter all right. He'd heard them all before. Fire, rape, murder. All trying to sell you something, any trick to get the door-hatch open, then it was buy my lemons, nice fresh lemons. Or broccoli. Or anchovies. Just let me see Cook, keep something for yourself. Sometimes a saucy look to go with it too. But not at this hour.

He raised the lamp, snapped the hatch open, shouted, 'Shut up! Get off home!' and snapped it closed.

He thumped back to his stool.

Her frantic looks, white fists upraised. What a nice one she was, eyes wild by the flash of lamplight, cheeks flushed, just the right age by the look of her. And fists had nothing to sell.

He thought about her.

'Please,' begged her voice through the door, muffled.

Cerberus's tunic was scratchy old rams' wool; pickings had been lean lately. He was a short red-faced man with white hair, not much left, but filthy. The maids thought he looked like one of those ugly *gorgoneia* rainspouts you saw on the corners of public buildings, because his lower lip hung out. Especially when something troubled him. His lip hung now, dribbling slightly. He pinched the soft flesh between finger and thumb, undecided.

Still beating away. He heard her gasps. Hurting those pretty lily-white hands that had never done a day's work. Not only a stunner, but a lady.

Except a lady knew how to behave. Strictly didn't let her feelings show.

A ruse, no doubt about it. Four or five Subura heavies round the side with clubs behind their backs, waiting for him to open up for the pretty one. She looked too innocent for that sort of trick, but they all did.

Like every house along the Vicus Armilustri, the Villa

Marcia had only one entrance, and no windows in the outside walls. It was safer that way.

He thought some more. Something about her worried him. He knew what fear smelt like.

Terrified, was she? An even worse reason for letting her in.

Cerberus was a slave born and bred, a *verna* of *vernae*, proud of his servile dynasty. His father, Cerberus *secundus*, had been *ostiarius* for old Tiberius Quistus until the day he died. Doorkeeping ran in the family blood, and a good life it was too. Better any day to be a slave in a good home than poor free trash, who sold their souls to a *patronus* for protection, paid the cost of living through the nose (*he* got all he could eat for nothing, and wine perks too, and a cuddle from the cook on festival days – maybe), bled money for rent and taxes. Free to get kicked out by landlords, free to lose the lot, free to sell their brats into slavery and sink to the bottom of Rome's *cloaca*, the sewers where all the ordure falling down landed on their heads, they died lucky if they'd pinched enough for their funeral. Stuff freedom. Cerberus knew better; best to belong.

But lately his confidence had taken a knock.

Slave or not, a senator's *ostiarius* was an important man. People took notice of you. You checked who came through your master's only door, and kept your eyes open, and valued each visitor to the last penny. A lifetime judging faces meant you never got it wrong. Your beady eye examined them through the hatch, your hand swept the door wide to ambitious upstarts who slipped you a shiny *denarius*, less sweepingly for shuffling *clientela* who only afforded a copper, reluctantly for tradesmen who offered a bare plum or a pear, but you fawned for nothing on old blood, old money, old land. You knew your place.

All that had stopped. Since that terrible day – Cerberus had seen it himself, the blood in the bath-pool, the hacked bodies of the children and their mother floating in blood – the master had given up everything except his senatorial status, which no man could give up, unless the Emperor stole it, and that was only for treason. Everything else worth having, gone. No bowing clients queued at Quistus's door for patronage. He wandered Rome's streets alone, a lost spirit, a nobody; he lost face, ceasing to be a great man. But that meant the whole slave *familia* of the Villa Marcia lost face too, and more importantly the good pickings that went with it. Senators, lawyers, generals, thinkers, stopped calling. The master rejected even Rome herself and took off to faraway lands, leaving the Villa Marcia rotting in limbo for his occasional return, and Cerberus with nothing to do but twiddle his thumbs or snore, dreaming of the glory days.

Now Quistus was back home, but changed. Diminished. People knocking at his door were bad types more often than not. Word was getting about. There was a smell of death clinging to the Villa Marcia. Sometimes people came for help who shouldn't be helped.

Dangerous people. Desperate people. Lots of those in Rome.

Listen to her. Wear her fists out she would. Must be hurting. What frightened her so?

Screaming the master's name again. 'Severus Septimus Quistus, help me!'

She'd wake the whole street if Cerberus didn't shut her up. The neighbours and his *ostiari* brethren knew what to say about noise.

He pulled his lip, deciding, then stuffed his face in the hatch. My, even sweeter on the second bite, all pale and panting. Those wide terrified eyes, so vulnerable, who could resist such naked fear in a girl? Small, but the hint of a lovely figure under her plain tunics; shiny, curly blonde hair. Any man could see she didn't add up, sweaty from running, dirt on her bare feet, hardly more than a child, perfect milky skin, yet her long nails well cared for . . . a young lady, except a lady didn't walk the streets of Rome at this hour, and not at any hour barefoot. She didn't beat on respectable doors with her fists. And she didn't scream.

She wasn't a lady.

'That's enough of that,' he said. 'You! Who do you belong to?'

'You must let me in at once.'

He pulled his lip. *Sounded* like a lady.

She spoke Latin as good as his, born to it, but her tongue had a classy edge. She hadn't denied she was property, but one slave smelt it on another. 'Ooh, must I let you in,' he mocked her. 'Must I, my arse.'

'I must see him. I know he lives here. Let me see him or you'll be sorry!'

'Ooh,' he repeated, but mockery sounded weak the second time. The lamp was fading; he studied her seriously in the growing dawn. 'What's it about?'

She took a deep breath. 'Something terrible has – my mistress—' Her eyes brimmed. 'I found – you must believe me!' Her tears overflowed. 'He *must* come.'

'You should be on the stage.'

She opened her mouth wide. She screamed at him. No holding back. Screamed to wake the dead, fists to her temples, eyes wide, staring, crazy.

'All right!' he hissed. 'Keep your hair on.' That was a good one; a slave giving herself airs with blonde curls like a lady, whatever next. 'You're a strange one,' he grumbled. 'I know your sort. Stay there. No more racket from you, right?'

She stared at him through narrowed eyes. 'You don't know me,' she said.

He slammed the hatch, shaking his head.

Quistus called from inside the house, 'Who is she?'

Cerberus straightened his tunic. *Who is she*; not much the master missed even now, he'd still got his sharp ears. Holding his lamp high Cerberus strode at his professional pace from the vestibule, along the entrance hall, crossed the atrium which was open to the sky, skirted the rainwater pool with the eel swimming in it, and stopped respectfully at the study archway without passing through. And stared. Quistus was leaning wearily against the desk by a window, his pale left arm stretched out flat on the lacquered wood, dark blood welling from the slit across his wrist. He wore only a wet towel, blood-stained. Cerberus gulped.

Quistus spoke without turning. 'How many names does she have?'

The darkly glittering African warrior-woman, Omba, tore a bandage with her teeth and wrapped the strip tight around the cut. One of the Nubaei, she was, one of the half-mythical tribes from over the edge of the world. She tore another strip and tied it tighter than the first. Cerberus licked his lips. She looked like she could squeeze a man to death from loving him too much. Death by ecstasy. She gave him an angry sneer, seeing his thoughts.

Cerberus realized he could hear the girl shouting again,

11

they never kept their word. 'She's no one, sir. It's a trick. Probably selling—'

Quistus turned his head one inch. He didn't ask a question twice.

'I don't know who she is, sir.' Cerberus could have kicked himself. 'No one. I didn't ask.'

'No one's no one,' Quistus said in a low voice. 'While I live.' His eyes moved to the hearth that was the heart of the house. Cold, choked with ash. In a raised alcove the ornamental bed stood on its end, empty, the holy *lectus genialis* that was the soul of his marriage, his family. No more.

Quistus said: 'Tell me her name.'

The *ostiarius* bowed, sweating. The walls and floor were too hot despite the season and the hour, he heard the heating flues roar like madmen. He returned shaking to his door, mumbled through the hatch, and came back swallowing nervously. 'She says she's called Docilosa, sir.'

Quistus knew many in Rome were not who they claimed to be. The Emperor Nero had a great many eyes, though not as many or as great as the fear of them. Even friends could not always be trusted, and never strangers.

'Let her in.'

Cerberus swallowed with an audible click. 'But she's a one-name, sir. She's someone else's property. You can't—' He flushed bright red. A master couldn't talk to another man's possession, taking her as his client without a by-your-leave, any more than he'd steal his couch or wife or table. It was unthinkable.

Quistus looked at Cerberus. A tiny drop of blood squeezed through the bandage. He had a way of looking.

'Now, Cerberus.'

'Yes, sir.' Cerberus ran as fast as he could. They heard his footsteps thumping through the atrium, then the bang of door bolts. 'Hey, you!' came his surprised shout. 'Stop, you!'

Running on bare feet the girl made no sound. She simply appeared in the archway and threw herself on her knees, shoulders heaving, head bowed. 'Sir, our mistress is dead. She died peacefully in her sleep!'

Three

The Virgin's Tale

'**Y**our mistress died peacefully,' Quistus murmured. 'Don't tell me her name. She died peacefully while she slept? Yet here you are rushing to my house, breathless, with dirty bare feet, bruising your hands on my door.' He glanced at the circle of blood on his bandage; two drops. 'Why?'

The moment the girl ran at him Omba had pushed her body protectively between them. Her hand hovered by her ornate gold belly-band. Concealed in the frills and ornamentation was, he was quite sure, a knife-blade no longer than his thumb. Death under the *lex Julia* for a slave, or even a citizen, to be caught with it, but where Omba came from such devices were considered useful – when time ran short for slow, subtle tortures and refined dismemberment – for settling family squabbles. Since he saved her tongue (indeed, all her internal organs) from the fire-ants her devotion to him was total. He was all the family she had. She was as protective as a doting mother.

Omba's tongue was her favourite body-part. She rarely stopped using it. More than saving her life, he'd given her a complete, noisy reason to go on living. She'd jabbered thanks in Nubaean, tracking him between the mountains and the river. That was only the beginning. Not all the way downstream from the fork of the Nilus (by which time she'd already learnt to speak continuous Latin), not when the Coptus innkeeper sold them both into slavery, not when the Aryans tied stones to their feet and threw them into the Pontus Euxinus, not when the Norvaaks shot arrows at them on the iceberg, not when the snow bear came sniffing to their cave, not when the Barbarikons of India roasted them on funeral spits and the silk traders of the Subtle Road stole them to the Imperial Court of the child-emperor of China, not once did she ever stop talking.

'Don't trust her,' she muttered. 'It – she – could be a trap—'

He pointed out, 'What harm can she do? She's barely more than a child. Let her speak.'

Omba stood aside, staying alert. The girl burst out in a high desperate voice, 'Sir, they sent me because they say you are the only man in Rome who is not afraid!'

Quistus stared at her, remembering those exact words from the lips of Volusia Faustina the crucified Christian, in this very room.

'Oh, you poor darling! She's out of her mind with worry!' Omba turned impulsively to him, her mind changed in an instant. She had a soft heart, a heart of gold, a heart of stone; she was a woman. 'Look at her! You can see someone forced the poor kitten to come because they didn't have the guts to do it themselves.'

He watched Docilosa closely, kneeling as she was, her slim young body bent in submission. Her cream woollen tunic, long-sleeved, cut slightly smaller than her linen under-tunic. Her face hidden, bowed over clasped hands. Cared-for hair. She looked perfectly innocent, perfectly truthful. He wished he could see her face – more importantly, her eyes.

He asked gently, 'Who says I am not afraid, Docilosa?'

Her shoulders shook, weeping. He murmured, 'Omba, fetch me some of your *kefa*, would you. And hot water.'

'But—' Omba hesitated warily. She liked to eavesdrop, but she liked interrupting too.

He added, 'And honey.' She growled and left the room.

Alone with him Docilosa raised her head shyly. Her eyes gleamed topaz brown, golden, breathtaking. Her pale skin glowed with youthful good health. No powders, no paste, no colours. Dark eyelashes and eyebrows contrasted with her blonde curls that alone looked artful. Her fingers, all bare, showed she was untouched, a property of rare value; such an innocent blameless gaze. A virgin slave, although she must be fifteen years old at least, perhaps sixteen.

Her eyes widened. He'd forgotten the bloodstained towel that was all he wore. His bandaged wrist oozed, darkening. She pressed her hand to her mouth.

'An accident.' He cleared his throat. 'Getting out of the bath.' She stared him in the eye. He had the feeling she already knew too much.

'What they say is true,' she whispered admiringly. 'You are

14

the man they say you are. You do not fear death because your life has already been taken from you. You live without love, seeing clearly.'

Again she bent her head over clasped hands. It looked very like a way of praying. Women had as many gods to care for them as men did, or more; and certainly more mysterious in their ways.

Omba called from the next room, 'She's a clever one!'

He repeated: 'Who says I'm not afraid, Docilosa?' Did this girl know Volusia?

But Volusia was a thousand miles away, safe; he'd saved her from Nero's profane, upside-down Cross even though she begged him for mercy, for him to let her die to go to her 'God' and somehow live after death. He'd refused. He asked, 'Was her name Volusia? Was she Volusia Faustina?'

'Sir? No sir. A simple girl told me, but truthful, as are we all, and I believe her.'

'How has she heard of me if she's so simple? I'm not a fashionable figure.'

'She's my friend, sir. A slave, Protia, my mistress's *ornatrix*, as am I. You helped . . . people . . . some people Protia knew.'

Quistus smiled, showing his teeth. Christians. The business with which he'd started the day – death – might yet succeed. Omba was right, this girl was a dangerous trap, designed for his death. Certainly she was clever. He watched her clasp her hands devoutly to her forehead, her wrists pulled slightly apart over her lips, making the keyhole shape of the Egyptian *Ankh*: a message, mysteries to be unlocked. Was she a blasphemer against the good gods of Rome, a hate-filled terrorist, a secret Christian? Or only a good liar, paid to test his loyalty to the God-Emperor? Could someone so lovely be his nemesis?

Yet she could be telling the truth. Volusia had shown him the forbidden gospel books that spread the word of Chrestus, their Christ. Paul the thinker had told Quistus that Christ lived in everyone's heart, Peter the fisherman that he could only be seen with the help of a 'Church', whatever that was. The banned cult appealed to women more than men, making as it did a virtue of poverty, chastity and submission to male priests, a single male god, and the god's son; the gospels promised believers a happy place called heaven and eternal bliss for the poor, the meek, the downtrodden, a message pitched more to slaves than their owners.

But Christians prayed standing, their arms outstretched *orans*, mimicking the shape of their Cross. He wondered if Docilosa's was a new style of silent prayer, less publicly expressive, more suited to covert worship kneeling in cramped cellars and sewers where discovery meant death.

'So your fellow slaves, when your friend Protia the *ornatrix*' – a skilled maid, a dresser – 'suggested that I was a man you could trust, elected you to fetch me because you'd discovered the body, and knew most?'

'Yes, sir. That's why Narcissus chose me.'

'Narcissus?'

'Our *dispensator*, sir.' The chief steward lording it over all the other stewards and slaves, responsible for the smooth running of a house.

'Obviously a great and important household, to require the services of a Greek *dispensator*.'

'Yes sir, though Egyptian not Greek. There's thirty-three of us in my mistress's household, her slave *familia*.' One of the greater houses of Rome, then, though not the greatest. Docilosa added, 'And another one thousand two hundred and eighty souls, sir, approximately, on my mistress's country estates.'

Quistus blinked. 'You said how many?'

'One thousand, sir, and two hundred, and eighty.' Someone, probably Narcissus, had made her memorize the number. 'MCCLXXX.'

Quistus studied her. 'You are speaking to me for one thousand three hundred and thirteen slaves?'

'Narcissus sent me, sir, as I said, on behalf of us all. Our *domina* was like a mother to us, she often told us so. I myself am a foundling, she took me up from the crossroads where I was dropped. Her own children died as babies.'

'Did you love her like a mother of your own, although you were only her property?'

'I never knew my mother, sir. I don't know what love would feel like.'

Every year in Rome thousands of unwanted newborns were dropped in doorways, on temple steps and rubbish tips. Sometimes little gifts were left in their clothes so that they were taken in by someone poor, if they were lucky, rather than left to die. Collectors employed finders to roam the streets at night and made a business selling the best-looking or strongest finds into slavery. Docilosa had been very lucky to catch her mistress's eye; she must have been as lovely as a child as, now, she was beautiful as a young woman.

'What were your duties in the household exactly?'

'General tasks, and I helped Protia dress my mistress. Protia fetched any small pieces of jewellery, she was *ornamentrix* in addition to her other duties. My speciality was as my mistress's *tostrix*.'

He glanced. A hairdresser. That explained her smart blonde curls. A hairdresser must be a good example of her skills.

'The girl who does her mistress's hair usually knows her quite well.'

'Yes sir, as I said, she cared for us like a mother.'

Quistus said gently, 'Did your "mother" really die peacefully? Did your *dominus*, her husband, kill her? What really happened? Was it justice?' A man had power of life and death over his wife. It would not be murder, or even a crime, if the woman had deserved to die, only justice.

'No sir! Her husbands are dead, they're all dead. My mistress was a widow three times. The last died one and one-fourth olympiads ago.' Three marriages was not unusual, and accounted for the woman's substantial wealth, if she'd chosen husbands wisely. 'My mistress swore never to take another man to her marriage bed but to live out her old age in chastity and devotion to the gods.'

'Still, it appears to me, Docilosa, that Narcissus fears foul play.'

'Oh no, sir!' She was horrified. 'Nothing could be further from the truth. He is *certain* she died in her sleep. Oh, you should see her, sir, her calm sweet face, her crossed hands, so peaceful! Death is merciful to the good, and none was better than our mistress. The fire in her heart cooled, or her brain overheated, or the gods—'

'Narcissus feels there's some small doubt, and wants to ask my advice?'

'He just begs you to confirm that she died in her sleep, sir.' Her eyes filled with tears. 'She was the kindest mistress, sir, frugal, virtuous, admired, beloved. We all loved her. She was stern and devout, an example to all. She never wore makeup. She was like a god to all of us. She never told a lie nor coloured a truth. She lived simply and soberly although she was the richest woman in Rome—'

17

Startled, he said, 'Aunt Censorina? Amanda Censorina is dead?'

'Dead in her bed, sir, this very morning!' The tears of grief overflowed from her eyes. More than grief. Terror. She was crying from sheer terror.

Omba returned. She placed a tray on the low table. Next to the steaming jug a handful of dark brown balls, like powdered nut rolled in fat, lay piled on a small platter. Quistus helped himself, chewing thoughtfully.

'*Kefa*.' Omba offered one to the girl. 'Coffee. It makes my people strong and stops weak weeping.'

Docilosa nibbled. She made a face at the bitter taste without realizing it, her attention focused completely on Quistus.

Absentmindedly he sat in the tall *patronus* chair, unaware of Omba folding a toga around him so that he looked, in her opinion, proper. 'Let him think,' she whispered to Docilosa.

Amanda Censorina was dead. He did not know quite what to feel. He knew the Censorina, of course, everyone did. As a child he'd been given to her to hold, he remembered her cold hands, fierce features, tightly coiled black hair. Probably he'd cried. But he'd been allowed to call her Aunt, and that was an important blessing, and later, for an up-and-coming young man, an important connection.

You could think of Rome as a spider's web with the Emperor, the spider, at the centre. You were born into Rome's web, you fought for it, married into it, gave your children to it, and struggled up and down its sticky rungs all your life, thread by silken thread. You never really saw the spider, only felt movements trembling in the threads, and sometimes glimpsed frightening shadows. You struggled as your parents had struggled, as your children would struggle after you. You gave your life to Rome. That was all.

His wrist felt cold and heavy with blood.

The Censorinae were ancient paragons, impoverished old blood proudly tracing their line to the glory of the Republic and their formidably righteous ancestor Cato the Censor. On her fourteenth birthday her father Censorinus had burnt his daughter's childhood toys in front of her and arranged a good marriage. Her sons by her first husband, Annius, a hugely wealthy importer of Indian spices, died before him. Her second spouse drowned tragically off Ostia, going to the bottom with a fleet of his own grain ships from Egypt, and his young sons too. She was the last of her line. She reverted to her fabled ancient family name after the death of her final husband, Porcinus, reputedly impotent or at least uninterested and thus acceptable to her morals and pious religious beliefs. Porcinus had made a vast fortune supplying the army, spent a million a year on imported delicacies and fine wines, and died within the twelvemonth choked on Alexandrian shrimp.

Amanda Censorina's life was a golden tragedy, the pain of all she'd lost leading her to renounce pleasure and devote herself body and soul to good works. She swore she'd never marry again. She gave public gardens and drinking-water fountains to the poor. Like any wise matriarch, she bound Rome's best and greatest to her with the usual web of family adoptions, lapdog politicians, public donations, religious devotion and moral example: she was an honorary Vestal Virgin and godmother of Nero. She devoted her twilight years to restoring decrepit temples to the sternest gods. Quistus had endured her hospitality, a grim stoical supper with vinegar for wine, no silverware, no music, no conversation, and the stoniest Lucanian sausage he had ever encountered. A Vestal Virgin in her fifties who employed only virgins, unbroken boys and Egyptian *castrati* did not need to talk in order to dominate her pleasureless surroundings.

'I'm sorry she's dead,' he said, watching Docilosa closely.

'We all are, sir,' she said, bright-eyed from the coffee. 'She was a wonderful example to us all.'

'I don't doubt it.' He nodded to Omba, who offered the girl another coffee-ball, gratefully accepted. Quistus dissolved honey and coffee in hot water, stirring thoughtfully. 'Tell me how you found her, exactly. This morning, I suppose?'

Docilosa said brightly, 'May we go to her now? Everyone's so anxious and upset. It would be such a weight off our minds if you would just see—'

'What were your duties? What hour was it?'

'The start of the twelfth hour of the night, sir. I awaken my mistress in good time for her to pray at the temple of the goddess Anna at dawn—'

'Wait.' Quistus sipped thoughtfully. 'You wake your mistress, but who wakes you? Presumably you don't stay awake all night, counting the hours down?'

'The boy Tempus wakes me, sir.'

19

'Who wakes Tempus?'

She frowned impatiently. 'The *horologium ad aqua* in the private atrium, sir. A water-clock. With the passing of each hour a mechanism operates, sending a silver ball rattling against a bell.' She chewed, smiling, on a fresh ball of coffee.

'Go on.' Quistus's eyes, which were wide apart, were grey-green as the Tiber, and as opaque.

'You should understand, sir, that my mistress sleeps in a locked room, for obvious reasons.'

'What obvious reasons?'

'So that she is not despoiled, sir.' Docilosa turned to Omba, trying to make her understand. 'Intruders. Rapists. Men.'

'She's been married three times,' Omba growled. 'Surely she—'

'Her last marriage was not . . . completed,' Docilosa murmured, colouring. 'Amanda Censorina had already left the world of men behind her and attained female perfection.'

'I see.' Quistus put down his cup. 'Please continue, Docilosa. Your mistress was asleep in the locked room where she felt safe. What of windows? Were they shuttered? Padlocked?'

'There are no windows. They wouldn't be safe.'

'What of ventilation?'

'The room is large and high, warmed in winter by small flues under the floor, cool in summer because it's so deep in the centre of the house.' She called the house *domus*, the socially acceptable word for a palace. 'It's too large for bad humours to accumulate.'

'The room is nearly soundproof, I suppose?'

'She did not like her contemplations to be disturbed by the outside world.'

'Locking her in her room was your last duty of the night and first duty of the day?'

'Yes, sir.'

'Then you were the last person to see her alive, as well as to find her.'

Docilosa gave a sudden laugh. 'Well, yes, I must have been!'

Omba pushed the coffee platter across the table. 'Help yourself.'

'Thank you.' Docilosa munched, smiling helpfully.

Quistus asked, 'Did she seem in good health last night? No sweating, nausea, aches and pains?' He was talking of slow

20

poison. Under the *lex Cornelia* all poisons were illegal, but that only made them more expensive, not less common.

'None sir, she was her usual self. She ate alone. All her food is tasted, and wine, even the water that goes in her wine. Last night her *praegustatrix* was Clio.'

'So there you are, somewhat over an hour ago, putting the key in the lock – a revolving key, I presume?'

'The best, sir, from Elidus's workshop under the seventeenth arch of the Pons Caligulae. My mistress always had the best.' She nibbled the fresh coffee-ball, her hand trembling slightly. 'I knocked loudly and turned the key but the door wouldn't open.'

'Did you hear the lock operate?'

'I heard it unlock but the door wouldn't open. It was bolted on the inside.'

'Was it usual for her to bolt herself in?'

'She felt safer like that, sir. She'd open the bolts when she heard me.'

'But not this morning.'

She shook her head.

'What did you do next?'

'I knocked again, sir, then called her name through the keyhole.'

'The keyhole goes all the way through the door?'

'Yes sir, the lock can be operated from both sides. She kept her own key in case of necessity.'

'So she could have used it to come out during the night – perhaps for the latrine, or to meet someone, or for whatever reason she wished – and then she could have locked herself back in, and closed the bolts?'

'No sir, not unnoticed. Hardalio sleeps outside her door.'

'Hardalio?'

'A boy, his voice as yet unbroken. A very light sleeper, her night-servant.'

'Hardalio heard nothing untoward from the room?'

'No sir, he slept until I arrived as usual with the key, an hour before dawn.' She swallowed. 'When our calls went unanswered I knelt, looking through the keyhole.'

'And saw your mistress lying dead.'

She nodded, trembling.

He said, 'But it was night, and no windows, totally dark in there.'

21

'Oh no sir, she feared the dark, what men might hide there, what monstrous men. What happened to your family, sir . . . everyone knows Rome is not safe . . . she ordered a gold candelabrum to burn all night, always.'

He felt blood trickle warm on his wrist, and covered it with his toga.

'You saw her clearly by the light of the candles? Where was the candelabrum?'

'Standing on a table by her bed, sir, its light falling plain on her face. I saw at once she was . . . so peaceful, but I could tell . . . I cried to Hardalio, run, run! Fetch Narcissus! And he ran, and Narcissus came running, and the whole household awoke—' She sobbed, 'We could see she was dead!'

'Did Narcissus order the door knocked down?'

'My mistress's door? Never, sir! The keyhole showed us enough.'

'You thought that if you broke violently into her room you might somehow be blamed for her death?'

'We could see how suspicious it would look, sir. My mistress was the friend and relative of so many rich and powerful people. By entering the locked room, despoiling it, we would all become suspects if there was even the slightest chance her death was suspicious. While it remained locked none of us could possibly be anything but innocent.'

'Because you were absolutely certain, from your peerings through the keyhole, that she had died peacefully in her sleep.'

'Obviously that is the only possible explanation, sir. Violence is impossible.'

'And to this very moment, the door remains locked?'

'Narcissus has forbidden anyone to touch it, sir.'

Quistus leant forward reassuringly, his elbows on his knees, hands folded under his chin. He searched her eyes. 'Docilosa, before we walk to the house and I see for myself what happened, I need to ask you the very obvious question that lies at the heart of this matter.'

'Yes, sir.' Too much coffee had made her excitable. 'Anything!'

'If all you thirty-three slaves of the household loved your mistress so much – I might almost say, from your manner, worshipped her – why should her apparently perfectly innocent death, though admittedly sudden, fill you with such very obvious fear and guilt?'

She bowed her head over her hands. Her voice, when it came, was muffled.

'The terms of her will are well known to us, sir. She would let small hints and promises slip, temptations. You see, by her death we are no longer slaves. Since this morning we are free people.'

Four

In the Locked Room

'Freedom!' Quistus spat the ashy, peppermint-tasting paste. 'They had a reason to kill her.'

Omba rinsed the splintered end of the stick and again brushed it over his teeth, removing the last traces of paste. 'Who'd want to be free, master? They'd have to leave the fine house where they'd spent most of their lives and scratch a living on the streets.'

'You forget she's my aunt, I knew her. She was no fool. There'd be a little money. Not quite enough.'

Omba sponged his face with cold water. The hypocaust was dying down but it remained infernally hot in the Villa Marcia. 'She can't have thought such a will would make her popular with her high and mighty friends,' she pointed out. 'Over a thousand slaves suddenly off the market, and with a bit of their own spending money, too. Less for everyone else. Could be a lot less.'

'Maybe she didn't care. She'd be dead. Some folk like the thought of causing trouble when they're gone.'

'Was she one of those?'

'Maybe. Maybe I didn't know her as well as I thought I did.'

Omba wrapped a fresh bandage over the old one, knotting it so tight he grunted.

Cerberus coughed from the doorway. 'It's another one, sir. Pretty as a peach.'

Quistus thought for a moment. 'Protia?'

'Saucy little thing, sir.' Cerberus reddened under Omba's gaze. 'Couldn't help noticing.'

'We'll be out shortly. Take Docilosa to her and overhear what they say.' Quistus dropped the towel and held up his arms for his tunic. 'Quickly, Omba, now. We must hurry to the Domus Censorina.'

Omba combed the back of his hair hurrying after him through the atrium, then gave up. Cerberus was shouting through the door-hatch. He turned, flushed. 'There's more of 'em, sir, and more coming.' He added, 'Our girl didn't say much to t'other one, just *all is in good hands*, she said.'

'Anything else?'

'Well, sir, the boy, his face—'

'That would be Hardalio.'

'Red as a red-cheeked plum when he saw Docilosa.'

Quistus glanced through the hatch. 'The one hanging back?'

'That's him, sir.'

'Did he kiss her?'

'Not him, not even a hug.'

'Very well, Cerberus. Open, please.' Omba pushed forward to clear a way, but the half-dozen youngsters in the street, chattering eagerly, swooped easily past her. Their skin – except for the blushing cheeks of Hardalio – was pale and sunless, almost transparent in the chilly dawn light, but all seemed well cared for. Yet so young.

Docilosa called, 'Friends, Severus Septimus Quistus has agreed to help us!'

'Quiet.' Quistus held up his hand; they drew back obediently, watchfully. 'I have agreed only to give my opinion on what has happened. If any of you have anything to tell me, spit it out now.'

'Sir, it's obvious what happened!' Hardalio burst out. 'She died, that's all! There's no need for this, it just makes it worse—'

'Hardalio sleeps so light a feather wakes him!' Protia was dark-haired, full-fleshed, marble white, with pouting lips. 'That's all that matters, isn't it? No one could go in, no one could come out.'

Quistus drew her aside. His pleasant manner evaporated and his voice was harsh. 'Are you a secret Christian, Protia? Do I have to search you for the sign of the fish? Where are you tattooed?'

If it was possible for her skin to be paler, she paled. Then she denied it, shaking her head from side to side. He left her standing where she was.

She ran to catch up as Quistus strode quickly along the Vicus Armilustri, past the sleeping white houses. He cut down a dirty alley, the youngsters gaggling excitedly around him like geese, their cries echoing between walls and shop-fronts. Yawning women strung washing between the balconies. A working-man's tavern was already open, if it ever shut. 'You'll see, sir!' the children cried – that's all they were, just children, even fat little Clio the food-taster. 'We loved her and respected her!'

Quistus turned to Protia as he walked. 'Don't be afraid. Your mistress, was she too a Christian? Did she worship Chrestus as well as all the other gods?'

Protia said, 'You don't understand, sir. God called her to his side peacefully in her sleep.'

He said: 'Which god exactly? Her "God"?'

'Sir, she was a *Sanctus.*' What a strange word to use of a person. Saint. Undoubtedly blasphemous. Only Nero in his religious role as *Pontifex Maximus* was *Sanctus.* To be sanctified, made 'Saint', would be an ordinary human's promotion halfway to being a god. Only the Holy Roman Emperor, on earth, was a god; only Nero. No wonder he hated the Christians.

Quistus lengthened his stride, murmuring to Omba, 'I must see the house exactly as it is now, before word gets out and everything's trampled on.'

'Yes, master.'

'No visitors.' His mind worked busily. 'Today's Mercury's day. Amanda Censorina was a *patrona* of the temple of Mercury so winged messengers are bound to call, perhaps even priests offering *adulatio.* Keep them out. Half the senatorial class call her Aunt, so on an average day I'd expect a couple passing by to pay their respects. All ordinary enough, but send them away too.' He added, 'Politely.'

'I shall, master.'

They blinked in the cold winter sun by the vegetable market, then crossed into the shadows between factories and granaries, coming into the sunlight again by apartment blocks, tumbledown *insulae* at first, but quickly white and high-rent as they climbed uphill. As always the rich enjoyed fine comforting views over the squalid rooftops below, and each turn of the Palatine revealed a finer house than the last. The street was quieter now, wider as they climbed past the Domus Q. Lutatii Catuli towards the Domus Augusti. The Pons Caligulae – the murdered Emperor Caligula's private footbridge from his palace above to the temple below – swept past them downhill. The road turned again, rising. The youngsters hurried with him up white marble steps to pillars, a portico, a tall double door that opened. No *ostiarius* greeted them.

After a heavy-breathing moment a hand, plump and pale, beckoned them inside.

'I am Narcissus! What a dreadful day!' In the stark marble vestibule the tall eunuch bowed over his cupped hands and quivering belly, dark-eyed, bald-headed, beautifully dressed, in despair. 'Senator, forgive the hour, I begged them to fetch you. Wit's end, you know. Terrible business. Still, nothing to worry about. Perfectly obvious what happened. Natural causes.'

Quistus ignored the lickspittle false title and attempt at friendship. Narcissus, sweating, gestured at the youngsters to go about their duties. Most of them huddled in corners. The *ostiarius* allowed the door to shut with a bang, shooting a dark look at Narcissus for stealing his job.

'A dreadful day, Narcissus?' Quistus murmured. 'It's hardly started. Nothing to worry about? We'll see. When did you call the doctor?'

'It's too late for a doctor, I assure you.'

'Send a *puer a pedibus* for her physician at once, running. Much can be revealed by a dead body.'

A boy was woken and sent scuttling. Quistus stared. This entrance hall was vast, yet heavy in style, and too plain. He'd been here before as a guest, surely, but he didn't remember such a confusion of dark doorways behind the tall marble statues. Not a clue which might lead to Amanda Censorina's bedchamber. 'Narcissus, stay with me.'

'We're all at your service, sir.'

'You sent Docilosa to fetch me because she was first to see the body, or because she's beautiful?'

Narcissus hummed. 'My mistress died tragically in her sleep, sir. That's all there is to it.' He unclenched his fist, revealing the key. 'The room is untouched.' He clicked his fingers and

26

two heavy bodyguards with shaved heads stepped forward, naked but for oiled muscle, leathers, loincloths. One held a road-hammer. 'They can do the door, yes? They're awfully good at that sort of thing.'

'Wait.' Quistus called them back. The two Egyptians looked to Narcissus, who nodded. Quistus examined the taller bodyguard on the left. 'Name?'

He kept his mouth shut.

Quistus pushed the man back suddenly, forcing him backwards until his shoulders slapped the wall. He pushed one elbow against the man's throat, reaching down, then lifted the studded leather flap of the loincloth. Only a stitched scar between the girlish shaved thighs, a tortured white centipede of puckered flesh.

'Narcissus, this man sits to pee.'

'My mistress valued her privacy,' Narcissus explained smoothly. 'Before you ask, they not only have no balls or tail, they speak no Latin, only the old tongue. Except they have no tongues.'

The bodyguard closed his loin-flap. He could have crushed both Quistus's hands in one of his own. Quistus looked him in the eye. The mute looked away. He smiled.

'No tongues tell no tales,' Narcissus said. 'No balls—'

'She didn't like men much, did she,' Quistus said.

Narcissus said, 'Who does?'

'I'll examine her door before they break it down,' Quistus said. 'Where's the boy Tempus?'

Narcissus bowed and led the way. Omba watched them go. She leant back against the door and crossed her arms, glowering. The *ostiarius* looked miserable.

Their footsteps echoed. Quistus remembered some of these one-after-the-other boring rooms from earlier visits, cheerless and plain, with low ceilings and walls of grey and white, sometimes dark red like the tiled floors. Docilosa walked on soundless bare feet at his side, head down, saying nothing. Protia kept well to the back, still flustered. In the atrium staff with dull faces were lined up for his inspection, yawning cooks, cellarers, bakers still with flour on their hands, *fullones* from the laundry, an earnest *rogator* with his guestbook, which Quistus examined briefly. Narcissus recited the slaves' names in a bored monotone as he walked past; mostly Roman.

27

'Pavo. Valus. Celerus.' Not a brain between them, but all afraid.

With polite mutterings Narcissus contrived to lead Quistus forward from behind, guiding him up steps to new levels higher and deeper in the house – the *domus* rose sprawling up the hillside. Sunlight streamed through the tall windows, gleaming off the lines of soldiers parading in the Campus Martius below.

Quistus looked round, impressed. These private quarters were like a different house, bright with mosaics – original works of the highest artistic standard, not cheap pattern-book copies. Fresco landscapes fooled the eye, stretching the walls apparently into the distance, the great Musicus's trademark style. Lifelike portraits and characterful street scenes – so real he almost expected the figures to move, to hear the market cries – these could only be from the hand of 'The Aquitaine', Annaeus Atticus; Quistus recognized some faces he knew well enough to greet, trapped youthful in paint while their owners grew old. 'My mistress did not like this part of the house,' Docilosa said severely.

Narcissus explained, 'She considered the decorations frivolous. Her late husband made the purchase. The glutton choked before he could enjoy it.' He reeled off the names of more staff, mostly Greek at this level, all anxiously whispering, all following behind once Quistus passed, their whispers and shuffling bare feet rustling like mice in the increasingly magnificent rooms. Some areas were roofless, turning suddenly into gardens, clipped geometries of hedge and shrub, some designed with grottoes and thatch Romulus-huts with low rustic doors, as though the great founder of Rome still lived here and might return at any moment. Coming past a sumptuously decorated upper atrium, its long pool swirling with carp between fountains and sunlit colonnades, Quistus heard the soft classy ring of silver against a bell. 'Ah,' he said.

In a vaulted side room the water-clock stood taller than a man, one of the most intricate mechanical contrivances in the world. Water dripped like a heartbeat. Its guardian, Tempus, small, his hair like a mop on his stick-thin body, was about twelve years old. He crouched by the clock with his head sunk between his arms, pretending not to see them. Quistus knelt. 'You know who I am,' he said.

The hair nodded miserably, then the boy's white face peered up. 'I didn't do nothing wrong.' He pointed at Docilosa. 'Don't kill me, I did my job, that's all.'

28

'Why should I kill you, Tempus?' The boy looked so terrified that Quistus joked lightly, 'Why should I kill time?'

'I wake her when the clock says so! That's all I do.'

'How do you know the clock's accurate, Tempus?'

'Accurate, sir?' He sounded astonished. 'That's my job. I
set the hour by the sundial every day at midday, if it's sunny.'
He warmed to Quistus's obvious interest. 'It's an art, sir, time
is. Night-time's tricky, no sun, see? Never. Sometimes the
moon though. The thing is, sir, hours is all different lengths.
A day's always twelve hours long, and starts at dawn and ends
at sunset, but that means summer day hours are longer and
night hours shorter. But in winter, like now, 'tis t'other way
round, so each night hour's as long as an hour and a half of
day. Half as much again, right? But the clock's clever, knows
how to make up for that.' He pointed proudly at the six water
containers, one for each month before or after a solstice, finely
marked with a slightly different scale to account for the
changing length of day and night. 'Perfect, it is. Ultimate.'

'You're absolutely certain you woke Docilosa at the twelfth
hour?' Hours were counted from the start.

'I always do, sir.'

'And you did this morning.'

'Of course he did,' Narcissus interrupted. 'My mistress was
most particular.'

Tempus added accurately, 'Actually, sir, I always wake Docey
at three-fourths down the eleventh hour, to give her time to get
from her corner where she sleeps, so she knocks on our mistress's
door at the exact moment the twelfth bell is struck.' He gave
a silly, proud smile. All his own teeth, and good ones too.

Quistus looked from the boy to Narcissus and back again.
'Thank you very much, Tempus.'

'That's all?'

'Yes, Tempus, for the moment. Where's Hardalio?' Quistus
pulled the plum-cheeked boy to Docilosa's side. He shuffled
his feet, embarrassed. 'You sleep outside your mistress's door?'

Hardalio glanced at Narcissus. 'Always, sir.'

'Where?'

Hardalio led them to a bright circular hallway with a dome
roof, statues standing along the curved walls, a doorway set
between each one.

'You slept here last night, all night?'

The boy looked at Docilosa. 'Of course he did,' Narcissus said.

'And a feather wakes you, Hardalio, but you didn't wake.'

The boy asked Narcissus, 'Does a feather wake me?'

Docilosa said, 'You idiot, Hardalio, Protia said so, it's a figure of speech.' Hardalio looked crushed.

Quistus turned to the doorway with the rumpled blanket nearby. 'That's my blanket,' Hardalio said.

Quistus studied the heavy bedroom door, impressed. Indian mahogany. 'Still,' he said, 'you look tired, Hardalio.'

'I'm not tired!' Hardalio said.

'How amusing it would be, in view of all this fuss, if your mistress was in fact still alive in there. All any of you have done is peep through the keyhole. Perhaps she's just sleeping deeply. After all, she's over fifty, she needs her rest – even a thunderstorm wouldn't wake her through a door this thick—'

Narcissus said tightly, 'See for yourself. She's dead.'

'Yes,' Quistus said. 'I'm sure she is.'

He folded the blanket, knelt on it, and pressed his eye to the keyhole.

Back at the Villa Marcia it was quiet again, just another day. As usual Cerberus sat on his stool. Years of faithful duty had worn the seat into the exact shape of his backside, so it was completely comfortable. Just as his body had changed the shape of his stool, over the years the stool had changed the shape of his body, growing him a pot belly and thin, scrawny legs; his sharp ears he owed to the thick, muffling door. He nodded sleepily as he sipped his herb tea. Often his ears identified passers-by without him bothering to open the hatch: the soft thump of horny-footed sedan-chair slaves from Vitellius's mob, the shuffle of old Lupula on her way to market, the slapping sandals of busy young men, the slow click of a walking-stick, the running feet of a thief followed by cries. And this sound. This new, steady sound that stopped his snores and made his eyes pop wide.

It was the sound two soldiers made tramping on hard soles of cured leather, marching in time, and his ears even picked out the lighter slap of ordinary sandals between them.

Cerberus dropped his cup. He sat with a dry mouth, waiting for them to go on by.

They halted, and there came the unmistakable sound of a sword-hilt striking the door of the Villa Marcia.

Quistus knelt at the keyhole. It took his eye a moment to adjust to the candlelit gloom of the room beyond.

Docilosa was right. The richest woman in Rome was dead, no doubt about it. She lay on a single bed, very low and simple, her feet towards him raising two bumps under the drab coverlet. Her hands were crossed on her chest, her head resting on a hard linen-covered bolster. Her face was grey and lined, her eyes staring straight at him between her feet, tooth-less mouth gaping. Death had taken her as it took most people, at least the lucky ones; by surprise.

'Dead as a doorpost,' he confirmed.

The room made her body look small, for it was very large, its corners flickering with shadow. Three candles of the gold candelabrum beside the bed had burnt out, the other four wavered, dying. Seven in all; more than a candelabrum, a menorah. He'd seen them in Jerusalem, where they were considered holy.

He moved his head from side to side, but the keyhole was too small to reveal more. He snapped his fingers at Docilosa for the key. The mechanism turned easily, locking. Turned back, unlocked again. He pushed the door with his shoulder. It creaked against the bolts inside, immovable.

'You see?' Narcissus said. 'Died in her sleep. You are our witness, Senator.'

'They're not here,' Cerberus said nervously. 'No, not here. All gone.'

The praetorian guard, his chest-plate stamped with the sign of the scorpion, pushed his face against the hatch-hole. There were two Scorpions but this was the one who liked to ask questions. His helmet grated against the wood. His jutting chin looked like it was chiselled from stone. 'You, you piece of dirt, what's your name?'

Cerberus collapsed in terror.

The Scorpion pulled back, armour gleaming, greasy purple cloak swirling in the sunlight. He spat. The other guard, the one who did the rough stuff, looked eager.

An impatient voice ordered, 'Stand back.'

31

A new face appeared in the hatch. Cerberus knew this face. 'It's you, sir,' he whispered. This man had been here before, not one of those you forgot. Never tipped. Wore his toga angrily and slightly wrong, letting the upper classes know its clever folds and foppish intricacies didn't fool a simple blunt man of the people like himself. Always arrived in a bad mood and always left in a temper, something broken, trouble, threats, shouting, the door slammed.

Quiet like this, he was even more dangerous.

'I never forget a name, Cerberus.'

He was about forty-five years old, squat, broad-shouldered, powerful, with straight black bushy eyebrows. Thick grey hair crimped tightly across his forehead. His square face was intelligent, callous, sweaty, debauched. Most of all, he looked determined. His eyes were cold and unfeeling, olive black, hard as stones.

'You know who I am, don't you, Cerberus.'

'Yes, sir, I do!' Cerberus fawned eagerly, but his master's worst enemy held up his hand for silence.

'Where is he, that's all I need to know.'

Cerberus pointed a shaking finger uphill. 'He's gone up there, sir. They've all gone there. It's the Domus Censorina, sir. Something terrible's happened.'

Quistus stepped back. The two bodyguards struck together at the hinge side of the door with road-hammers, and again. The hinges broke before the mahogany or the bolts. The door fell in loudly and Quistus stepped on it. 'The rest of you stay outside.'

The children stared white-faced. Narcissus shushed them importantly behind his robes, but they gazed round. 'Look, sir,' he gestured indulgently, 'you see how much they love her.'

Quistus ignored him. It wasn't love he saw in the children's tired faces, simply fear.

'More light,' he called. He looked around carefully. No windows, true. The floor was a midnight-blue mosaic of the seven planets and constellations of stars, standard enough for a sleeping-room. The sapphire moon set in one corner, the golden sun rose in another. The walls were painted with dull murals, the usual religious scenes, nothing exciting; a rather small she-wolf suckled two adult-looking infants, Romulus and Remus, watched over by the god Jupiter Lucetius with a thunderbolt in each hand, making the golden sun rise beneath his feet; and all the rest of the gods, one after the other around the walls, gazed down with watchful eyes. A woman supremely confident of her holiness and virtue to encourage such company to overlook her bed. She'd even included herself, a woman with striking eyes wearing a black cloak, a ruby necklace at her throat, a cherub at her knee.

He walked to her body in a straight line, stared down, then touched her face. 'Amanda Censorina, can you hear me?' Her cheeks were cold as marble. So was her neck.

'You see?' Narcissus called, stepping inside. 'Dead. And you saw the door knocked down. Thank you for coming.'

Quistus glared. Narcissus stopped, looking awkward, then walked backwards in his footsteps.

Her skin was pallid, not black as it would have been from suffocation. Her grey hair was coiled into a simple bun above each ear, secured with two plain bone pins – that would be Docilosa's work. Her downward-staring eyes were dry, her ear-channels clean, unswollen. He bent, peering into her mouth. Her tongue had fallen back in her throat, the tip grey not black. Her gums showed small sores where she wore teeth of wood or ivory during the day; he rubbed them and sniffed his fingertip, only the usual odour of dried spittle, no poisonous bitterness. He lifted her arm and let it fall back.

He pulled down the coverlet. She'd slept like a woman laying herself out perfectly for death – could it be suicide? Heels touching, knees together, her nightdress smoothed decorously to her ankles. She had neither turned in her sleep nor stirred in her dreams.

He sat her up, her head lolling against his shoulder, and hauled her nightdress off her body. Narcissus said, 'No, that's not right!' There was no other sound from the doorway.

Amanda Censorina's belly, breasts and thighs were stone-coloured, bloodless, like her face. He turned her over. Her shoulders, back, buttocks and the backs of her legs were almost black, gorged, livid with heavy blood. 'It's normal,' he said. 'Cold blood sinks, lifeless.' He flopped her on her back and slipped his fingers between her legs, dry as sand. He pressed his hand between her breasts. Even her heart was cold, cold and unflickering as a hearth whose fire has gone out.

Her head slipped to one side on the bolster, hanging down.

A clear drop trickled from her right nostril, and a little saliva that had pooled in her cheek oozed from the corner of her mouth. He examined the fine grooves of age above her top lip, then called to Docilosa for a pin. She took one from her hair as she walked to him and he pushed the tip into one of the grooves, scraping out brittle white scale.

He said thoughtfully, 'You said she didn't wear makeup.'

Down in the vestibule Omba leant back against the tall double doors, her gold-chased arms crossed over her gold-tasselled breasts, a frown on her face. This *ostiarius*, whose name was Clumens, was not talkative enough. The more she told him her life story, the more frightened he looked. The lower he cringed, the deeper she frowned.

A knock sounded behind her. She turned, but Clumens leapt to the door. They were all the same, they all had their pride.

'You sent for a *medicus*,' a haughty voice announced. 'I am Eos the Greek, a citizen, I am he.'

Omba clicked her fingers for a footboy. 'Lead our good doctor upstairs,' she growled.

'All women wear makeup,' Docilosa explained. 'Immediately a girl is fourteen, she's a woman, a *matrona*, under a man. As soon as a woman sees there's nothing more to life than being bedfellows with men, she struggles to beautify herself, pinning all her hopes in the delight her appearance gives. It's a delicate subject, not suitable for a man's ears. It's wrong to talk of women's secrets.'

He said, 'You don't wear makeup, and I reckon you're nearer sixteen than fourteen. I suppose you're different.'

Her cheeks blushed, very beautifully.

Quistus changed tack. 'But then, she was fifty or more. Did she apply the stuff herself, from her own *unguentaria* bottles?'

'Of course not, she was a lady. It's a skilled job. Protia and I do it. Protia knows the recipes, but I have a lighter touch. They're so disgusting but they work.' She looked back to Protia for support. 'We use a whole chemist's shop, don't we?'

'She was wearing night-salve,' Protia confirmed. 'We put that on her, didn't we, Docilosa? To stop wrinkles.'

'And make the skin soft and youthful,' Docilosa said.

'*Oesyspum*,' Protia said. 'The best, Patrimonus's from

34

Attica. Grease from sheep's wool. Bean flour to remove lines and make the face smooth. Lupin powder. Illyrian irises to cool the eyelids. Of course our mistress used them. Who doesn't? It's not the sin of pride, it's femininity.'

Vanity. So the old woman was human after all, with human foibles. Quistus warmed to her for the first time, a little. But still, not to wear makeup at all was, it seemed, the sign of real beauty. He touched the pin to his tongue, grimaced at the metallic taste, then shrugged. 'I'm sure it doesn't have anything to do with her death. Who's this?'

'It is I, her physician.' Eos pushed through self-importantly. 'Oh! Dead.'

'She was found this morning. I'm a friend helping the family. Have you treated her recently?'

'My dear fellow, she was always in the very best of health. Quite amazing for her age.' Quistus's wrist oozed a drip of blood. The doctor stared.

'Would you examine her, please?'

Eos tried to concentrate. 'But she's dead.'

'I've had some experience of death, Doctor. It's taught me that dead bodies talk.' Quistus took him by the elbow. 'I would like you to examine her and listen to what she tells you about her death, if you can.'

Eos stiffened, outraged. 'It's illegal to examine the organs of a dead body, it's an obscene suggestion. Only criminals, crucifixions—'

'You'll be paid.' Quistus beckoned for a stool. Eos put down his medical bag with shaking fingers and sat in the textbook posture of medical men, with a straight back and his knees together. While the good doctor started his examination of the body at the head, working towards the feet, Quistus examined the room by taking his sandals off and walking around, hands behind his back, humming. Docilosa watched him. He seemed unimpressed by the murals. The smooth gold arms of the menorah gleamed. The three flames danced in Docilosa's eyes; she looked away with a shiver. Protia yawned. After a while Quistus stopped and lifted one foot, picking something from between his toes, a small wooden rod about the size of his little finger. A mark on a single mosaic *tessera* near the end of the bed caught his attention; six long strides to the other side of the bed took him, as he expected, to another mark. The two girls yawned.

'You must be tired,' he called, smiling.

'No, sir.' They shook their pretty heads.

'What am I talking about?' he agreed. 'You've been awake only three hours. It can't be later than the second hour of the day.'

'The second hour and one-fourth,' Tempus called precisely.

'Thank you, Tempus. I, on the other hand, have been awake all night.' Quistus yawned, stretching. He strode close to the wall by the bed, stared between his toes, and seemed to see what he expected. He walked round to the other side of the bed, stood close to the wall, looked down, and nodded.

'You may know that I am a Stoic,' he told them. 'A Stoic believes in reason. Logic. The world is reasonable and logical. Evidence enters through our senses into our heart. Our eyes don't see, our flesh doesn't feel, unless our heart sees and feels.' He pinched the dead body's hand, hard. It didn't move. 'We Stoics believe life is fire, heat. That is why the dead are cold and unfeeling. Their fire is gone, departed.'

Eos examined her wrist, pressing softly. 'The veins and arteries contain only air after death.'

Quistus called to Narcissus, 'Have her *unguentaria* bottles and jewellery case fetched in here.' The *dispensator* clapped twice, sending boys scampering.

Quistus turned to speak to the doctor, but his toe sent a tiny black ball rolling across the mosaic. After a search he found it lying in the corner by the painted entrance of the Romulus-hut. He squeezed it between finger and thumb, holding it close to his eyes. He turned it round slowly. One side seemed to interest him particularly. No one asked him what it was. He returned to the doctor. 'Well, Eos? Your diagnosis?'

Eos sat back. 'It is my considered opinion that Amanda Censorina undoubtedly died of cardiac arrest.'

Quistus said, 'The heart ceasing and falling cold is always a symptom of death. But not necessarily the cause of it.'

Eos sighed. It was impossible to argue with a Stoic, they were all logic-slicers. 'Very well. The cause of death was *apoplexia*.' He explained, 'Apoplexy, a blood vessel burst in her brain. Afterwards the brain is no longer able to cool the blood, the heart overheats, and death follows from overexcitation.'

'Slowly?'

'Unconsciousness instantly. Death very soon.'

'When did this happen, in your opinion?'

'It must have been during the night, after the girls Docilosa and Protia left her. She did not even have time to cry out before death took her, so the boy Hardalio naturally slept on.'

'I see. That makes excellent sense. Thank you, Doctor.'

Eos stood, closing his medical bag. 'I trust you will see my fee is paid.'

Quistus watched him go. 'Just one thing, Doctor.'

Eos turned.

'Her body was stone cold, Doctor.'

'Obviously. It's winter.'

'Still, a body takes time to go completely cold, especially one lying in bed under a coverlet. Even if she suffered the apoplexy immediately after she was left alone, twelve hours ago at the most, I would expect her to be cool rather than cold, wouldn't you?' Quistus smiled helpfully. 'Correct me if I'm wrong.'

Eos said haughtily, 'Since she *did* go cold, that *must* be what happened.' He nodded, pleased with his logic. 'Now, if that's all . . .?'

'Just one very small point. You see how limp her muscles are.' Quistus lifted her arm and let it fall. 'No *rigor mortis*. How do you explain it?'

'That's easy. Rigor sets in perhaps four hours after death and is gone within twenty-four or so. Obviously, therefore, she has been dead less than four hours.' Eos headed for the door.

'But we established that her body is utterly cold,' Quistus said. 'She has not been dead for more than twenty-four hours, has she?'

'I think the doctor covered everything,' Narcissus interrupted smoothly. 'Thank you, doctor.'

'I'm sure he's done all he can.' Quistus held up the tiny ball between finger and thumb. 'Anyway. Look what I found.'

Narcissus gave an impatient sigh but Eos asked, 'Well? What?'

Just then the house echoed with a thunderous knocking from below. They heard voices, shouting, a cry from Omba, then silence.

'It's a black pearl,' Quistus said.

Five

The Emperor's Special

'It seems we have unexpected guests. I'll send them away.'
Narcissus hurried out. He came back very shortly, walking
backwards, his arms outstretched in submission. 'Sirs. Officers.
Welcome. You find our house in sad disarray.' Despite his oily
suntan Narcissus was pale as a fish's belly under a gutting-
knife – perhaps literally, for though the first praetorian saun-
tered with his thumbs hooked in his belt, the second drew a
sword. The handle was notched with kills. Quistus watched
them without moving. Scorpions, the Emperor's guards, killers
all. 'Helmets off, men,' he ordered. 'You're in the presence
of death.'

The two soldiers stared at the body, then tucked their bulky
helmets under their left arms. The second man kept his sword
out, sweating slightly. Both men breathed heavily. Some children were sobbing.

'I'm Bellacus,' snorted the first soldier, with the chin. 'This
other mean bastard's Ursus. Shut up, you lot. What in Hell's
happened here?'

Quistus heard the slap of sandals. A new voice demanded,
'What's going on? Where are you going with those bottles?'

Quistus called, 'I ordered them to be fetched, Stigmus. Come
in.' He scratched his hair wearily. Sometimes it didn't seem
possible for things to get worse. 'What can I do for you,
special prosecutor?'

People called Stigmus the Emperor's Special. Special times
demanded special measures. The Christians were getting out
of hand; everyone remembered how their God had killed
Matrusus. Stigmus would round up God if necessary. He was
a popular man.

'Severus Septimus Quistus, by order of the Emperor—'
Stigmus's black eyes fixed, seeing the blood trickle from

38

Quistus's wrist to his elbow. He pushed through the children, his eyebrows drawing together in a single dark slash. 'This is Aunt Censorina's bedroom. What—'

'Dead, as you see. Has the Emperor sent you to arrest me? For what crime?'

'Great Jupiter preserve her. I saw her only last week.' Stigmus shook his head. 'Crime? No, it's another matter between you and the Emperor, much more important. Goodness. Aunt Censorina.'

'She was your aunt too?' Quistus saw Omba in the hallway with a swelling cheek and bloody nose. He waved her quietly out of sight with his little finger.

'The old frump was everybody's aunt,' Stigmus said irritably. 'She was in perfect health, never seen her so happy. What happened?'

Narcissus said as smoothly as a man saying it for the hundredth time, 'Died in her sleep.'

Ursus prodded her with his sword-point. 'Dead'un.'

'Yes, in her sleep,' Quistus said obligingly. 'No doubt about it.'

'I don't believe it,' Stigmus said. That was all it took. Bellacus drew his sword too and both armed men moved quickly, herding everyone into the room. 'Nobody leaves,' Stigmus said. 'This crime is under imperial investigation.'

That was inevitable. It was certain that the Emperor would be willed a large portion of the Censorina's fortune. That was the way it was done. In return her memory would be lauded in the temples of the Imperial Cult, her assets wouldn't be seized, and her assigned heirs would receive their cut.

Quistus said, 'There's no crime, Stigmus.'

Stigmus glared at Docilosa and Protia. 'Who are they?'

'Probably the last people to see her alive.'

'Arrest them,' Stigmus said. Ursus pushed them into a corner, forcing them to their knees. He stood over them grinning. He liked girls, especially when they squeaked. 'Leave us alone!' Docilosa cried.

The boy Hardalio shouted, 'I was the last one to see her, I shut the door—'

'Him too,' Stigmus said, and Hardalio was chucked in the corner. Docilosa crouched at his side. He pretended his knee hurt, looking dazed but happy.

'Stigmus, these people are innocent.' Quistus whispered urgently. 'There's nothing for you here.'

'You say so?' Stigmus was interested. 'That makes me think there's something. You know who I saw downstairs, come to pay his Mercury's day respects, being held at bay by your enormous harpy?' He finished happily, 'C. Cassius Longinus.'

Quistus closed his eyes. 'The lawyer.'

'Wrong, Quistus. *The* lawyer. More fully, *her* lawyer. You remember the magistrates down in Puteoli half a dozen years ago, accused of corruption—'

'Rightly so.'

'Longinus settled that.'

'The same magistrates are still in power, as corrupt as ever.'

'Yes, but the people making all the fuss were executed and peace was restored. That's the important thing.'

Quistus said, 'You're saying it's not the legal process that matters, or justice, it's the penalty?'

Stigmus clapped Quistus on the shoulder like a friend, but it was a hard blow. 'Just the result. Justice, eh? We're both men of the world.' He called to Narcissus, 'You, get Longinus brought up here.'

Quistus said, 'We're not men of the same world. You aren't me.'

Stigmus exclaimed theatrically, 'Why do you Stoics all hate the Emperor so? You all do, don't you?'

'I didn't say that. I don't hate Nero. I worship him.'

'Be careful,' Stigmus whispered. 'Be very, very careful. He, Nero, personally, commands your presence at the seventh hour. The seventh exactly, today. Perhaps you should make your own will.' He squeezed Quistus's bloody wrist. 'Try not to do yourself *before* you meet him, won't you?' He turned with a cry of greeting. 'My dear Longinus! What a terrible business!'

Longinus was tall, grey, thin and old. Quistus shivered at the touch of the lawyer's hand, nearly as cold as the dead woman, and explained, 'She died of an apoplexy.'

'You must be utterly certain,' Longinus said in a cold grey voice. 'Are you?'

'My investigation will be thorough,' Stigmus assured him. 'I loved her, Longinus, loved her. We were related, you know.'

Longinus, of an old family, gave the prosecutor a scaly look. 'I understood you were a freedman.'

'Very distantly related, through my father.' Stigmus coloured, not from embarrassment but anger. Everyone was always doing him down however hard he struggled up. Everyone he treated as his friend was his enemy sooner or later. Best to stab first.

Longinus's time would come. One day he would no longer be Nero's friend and confidant. Then it would come suddenly.

'The doctor,' Quistus said doggedly, 'will swear it was an apoplexy.'

Longinus's grunt dismissed every doctor in Rome as a charlatan. He went off to find her will in her desk, stepping aside for the large cabinet of bottles being carried through, its base lined with drawers for powders, the top with holders for pestles and mortars of various sizes, and grinding and cutting tools.

'You see, Stigmus?' Quistus said. '*Unguentaria*. Perfectly ordinary.'

'And this is her *ornamentarium*, her jewellery box,' Narcissus said. Quistus had expected a small casket, but this was a chest carried by four bent-over slaves.

'We don't need to see that,' Quistus said.

Stigmus said at once, 'Open it.'

Protia said, 'I keep the key.' She wiped her cheeks and crawled fearfully past Ursus. Kneeling, she used the ring-key on her finger and lifted the lid. Stigmus said, 'Well?'

Almost at once Protia started to shake. The inside of the chest was organized into boxes that could be lifted out, revealing compartments of various sizes beneath, like a maze. Necklaces, rings, brooches, pins, torcs, gold and silver pieces, jewels, sapphires to the left, rubies to the right. Stigmus muttered, 'These can't be hers. Whose is this? It's a treasure chest.' He turned angrily on Quistus. 'What's this about? My Aunt Censorina never wore anything but plain silver, religious symbols, dowdy stuff. What's going on here?'

'I don't know.'

'This isn't right!' Stigmus said.

Protia's white fingers flashed among the jewels, overturning them. Her head twisted from side to side, she gasped for breath. 'Not here,' she muttered. 'The Phoenix. Not here!' She jumped to her feet, white hands pressed to white cheeks, hair tumbling. 'Gone—'

She turned, running. Someone shouted, 'Thief!' There was a

41

scream. Ursus grabbed her hair, dropping his helmet. 'If I'm a thief,' she screamed, 'kill me.' She screamed again, hysterical. 'I swear!'

Ursus stuck the sword through her, pushed with his foot to get it out, then slashed her neck as she went down.

Everyone stared. Nobody moved.

'So there was a crime, I knew it,' Stigmus said. 'Theft. What sort of a person would do that from a dead woman?' He shook his head, disgusted.

Ursus had dragged Protia's body out before anyone fell over it but the room still smelt of blood. The children were mopping up the streaks. They sobbed with terror as they mopped. Quistus could feel their fear like a solid force invading the house. Narcissus stood unmoving – he had remained utterly motionless – the fingers of one hand pressed tight over his lips, his eyes bulging.

Docilosa curled weeping in the corner. Quistus beckoned Omba to go to her. The African wrapped the girl in her big comforting arms. Hardalio looked from Docilosa to Quistus and back again. He'd been sick on his sleeve.

'A most successful morning,' Stigmus said breezily. 'No doubt we'll find the jewelled bird hidden in her room or some pathetic corner somewhere. All part of the estate. I reckon the old girl probably left fifty mill, don't you, Quistus?' For the second time this morning he clapped Quistus's shoulder like a friend. 'I'll go and find Longinus, get the good news from the horse's mouth, eh?'

Quistus murmured, 'I'll be along.'

'Don't leave it too long.' A third clap on the shoulder and Stigmus departed in search of Longinus, followed by the two Scorpions. Ursus had relaxed since he'd cleaned his sword. He walked with a swagger.

Quistus waited until the echo of their footsteps was completely quiet.

'Shut the door,' he told Narcissus. 'I'll tell you what happened.'

Narcissus muttered a word in a foreign tongue. The two Egyptian *castrati*, the oiled-leather bodyguards who'd hidden at the first sign of violence, propped the door in its frame as best they could. They listened silently, arms crossed.

42

Docilosa hiccuped. She couldn't stop. The youngsters watched Quistus with large eyes. He sat calmly on the end of the bed, the old woman's foot against his hip. Her stare, too, seemed fixed on him.

He began, 'You see, when a distraught girl beats on my door at an unsocial hour to gasp that her mistress has died peacefully in sleep, obviously my first thought is it's murder, and that she is the murderer.' He sighed. 'But almost at once Docilosa claimed that Narcissus, and all the rest of you, *chose* her to come. Why all of you? I'll come to that. Why Docilosa? Perhaps because she was the last to see her mistress alive.'

'No, I was the last,' Hardalio claimed. 'When Docilosa left the room, I closed the door and saw my mistress still alive, lying in bed just as you see her.'

Docilosa hiccuped.

'That is certainly a lie, Hardalio,' Quistus said. Hardalio shut up.

Quistus continued, 'Perhaps, I thought, Docilosa was chosen to come for her particular beauty. Such a beautiful virgin.' No one contradicted him. 'After all I'm a man, not blind. Narcissus was not to know that in my heart I'm still married.' He rubbed his wrist. 'Very soon she blurted out a motive for murder – that the old woman's slaves were all made free by her will – yet she insisted they were all innocent. Why? How could she know surely enough to swear it? What was I missing?

'Or, I wondered, was she a trap of another sort? Almost at once I smelt Christians. Was this a larger conspiracy, with Docilosa the tool of the Emperor's henchmen – Stigmus sprang to mind, but there are others – to trap me into some admission of guilt? After all, he knows I helped Christians before.'

Docilosa hiccuped, 'Sir, I'm no Christian.'

'Protia was.' He patted the old lady's foot. 'And I think *she* was, too. I think this rich, powerful old *dominatrix* liked to mock the gods of Rome with her secret Christianity.' He gestured at the male gods lining the walls. 'She hated them. But that asks the question: why did she surround her bedroom with them?'

Narcissus took his fingers from his mouth. 'I promise you, we knew nothing of what went on in this room. Nothing. I swear it on my mother's tomb.'

'Then she's turning in her grave, Narcissus. You knew every

little thing that went on in here. There are spyholes, I don't know where exactly, but there always are. You knew everything, you arranged everything for her, and don't you deny it.'

Narcissus groaned and rubbed his face, streaking his eyeshadow.

'Amanda Censorina was a hateful old woman,' he hissed. 'She hated everyone. She sucked in light and spat out darkness.'

'Whatever happened, you were all involved in her death, all you tired-looking slaves. All of you couldn't kill her, of course, and you didn't. Nevertheless, she was murdered in here.'

'But – I thought – the doctor, apoplexy—'

'It was murder. And you were all accomplices afterwards, accessories in the cover-up. Why? Why not just push the murderer forward for justice?' Quistus smiled unhelpfully. 'I'll come back to that later, too.'

He stared into the dead woman's eyes, wondering if from whatever Hell she inhabited she saw him.

'Amanda Censorina was the paragon of Roman modesty, female honour and virtue,' he murmured. 'Not quite. I think she was a very disturbed woman, right from the day of her fourteenth birthday. We'll never know what really happened to her first husband, Annius, and the sons his insatiable lust forced on her – I think that's what happened – a wife may not refuse her husband in the bedchamber. He died with them. Or her second husband and her babies by him, who all died with him. Her life wasn't a tragedy, it was a design. As for her third husband, poor rich Porcinus, he needed merely to be immensely wealthy and completely uninterested in anything but food. The marriage almost certainly wasn't consummated.' He glanced at Narcissus. 'You're wrong, eunuch. She didn't hate everyone. Just men.' He looked around the faces of the boys. 'As soon as their voices broke, she had them castrated.'

He stroked the old woman's lustreless grey hair. 'But she certainly loved herself. Here in secret, closed off in her private quarters with her chosen ones, she was a different woman. The real woman. Thirty-three slaves, the finest creams and salves, an *ornatrix* to drape her in jewellery – Protia – a *tostrix*, Docilosa, for her hair. Docilosa is very, very good with hair, aren't you, Docilosa. You could do better than this.' He pulled out the grey coils. 'Much better. And you *did*.'

44

Docilosa hicced. Omba held her gently. 'Hold your breath,' she murmured, 'they'll go away. Master,' she said reproachfully, 'you're bullying her.' Since Protia's execution she was firmly on Docilosa's side.

'Yes, I am,' Quistus said.

'Leave Docey alone!' Hardalio jumped in front of Quistus, fists bunched.

'As for young master Hardalio here, his voice hasn't yet broken, fortunately for him, but his plumbing has started working just fine. You're in love with her, aren't you, Hardalio?'

Hardalio sank down red to the tips of his ears, and covered his head. He wouldn't look at Docilosa. But she stared at him with a small smile, her hiccups forgotten. He said something muffled. Her eyes gleamed, then she returned Omba's hug. 'Oh, it's a love story, they're so sweet,' Omba said.

Quistus said coldly: 'I searched this room thoroughly. I found a few things, but not the one thing I expected to find. Docilosa told me the old woman kept her own key in the room in case she wanted to leave during the night for any reason. That's what I didn't find. That key.'

'So what?' Hardalio recovered a little of his cockiness.

'Either Amanda Censorina had left the room and dropped the key outside – but then how did she get back into the room to lock it, and how did she not wake Hardalio? – or someone else removed the key.'

Omba said, 'But that's impossible. The bolts on the inside—'

'Oh, no, there's another door in this room, Omba, somewhere. Some very, very nasty things happened in here. There has to be a secret way in and out – something incorporated into the outline of a god, for example, or a temple, or perhaps the painted door of the Romulus-hut is a real door.'

'But why should someone go to all the trouble of breaking in to take a key?'

'It was taken by mistake. It was cleared up along with everything else.'

Omba said, 'Cleared up?'

Quistus nodded at the menorah. 'Look how smooth the gold stalks are. If that's been burning all night, where's the wax?'

Narcissus gave a low groan.

'You thought of almost everything,' Quistus said. 'You even replaced the burnt-out candles with nearly burnt candles. But the wax was one little detail you didn't get quite right, Narcissus the Egyptian. Narcissus the Copt.' He glanced at Omba. 'Yes, listen to his accent, he's from Coptus. You remember the town on the Nile?'

'How could I forget.'

'Narcissus the Christian. The young god that Christians worship was schooled in Egypt. Plenty of Christians in Egypt, very few in Galilee.'

Narcissus spread his robes. He dropped to his knees, clasped his hands in the *Ankh* of prayer. 'For God's sake help us, sir. We're all guilty. We're all sinners.'

'I know,' Quistus said. 'I know. So, there you were, all of you, a murdered woman on your hands, and a big situation to deal with. Never mind how it happened: you had to deal with it. Not a mark on her, so you reckoned your best bet was to make it look like a natural death. But her bedroom didn't look like this, not then. There was a big double bed, very big, very heavy, very soft, utterly out of character for the modest virtuous Amanda Censorina we thought we knew. That had to go.' He walked round, pointing out the four cracked *tesserae* of mosaic where the four massive bed legs had stood. He reached in his sleeve and showed them the piece of wood as long as his little finger. 'It's called a dowel. A dowel holds pieces of wood together. It gets dropped when they're dismantled.'

Narcissus winced. He closed his eyes.

'Wake up!' Quistus snapped. 'Oh, did I forget to mention that this didn't happen last night? No, she died the night before, *eleven* nights before the Kalends of Januarius – last night was the tenth night, the winter solstice. That's why you're all so tired. You needed a day to think, to make plans, to get rid of the evidence. All the evidence that Amanda Censorina was not a saint. I suppose it was an orgy-bed for after Protia and Docilosa had left . . . young studs invited to pleasure the old woman. Dancing. Drinking. You had to dismantle such a huge bed to get it out through the secret door.'

'It's a small door.' Narcissus pointed without opening his eyes. 'Yes, you're right, it's the Romulus door.'

'That's why the body was stone cold, because it took you all day to clear up such a mess, and probably half last night

46

too. And then you sent Docilosa to fetch me, so that you could try and fool me.'

'There's more to it than that.'

'Let's stick with you clearing up for the moment. It was a *lot* of clearing up. But the really difficult bit was the body. Whatever Amanda Censorina was wearing, it wasn't this plain chaste nightdress. You stripped her naked and cleaned her. But she was wearing thick makeup – white lead, I tasted it – and that's hard to get off. She was wearing a wig as well as her own hair, something sophisticated, gorgeous, Docilosa dealt with that.' He showed them the black pearl he'd found. 'At first I thought it was from a necklace. But look carefully. The hole doesn't go all the way through. It's the push-end of a steel hairpin. Amanda Censorina was wearing black pearl hairpins. Her wig probably cost more than a working man earns in a year.'

'In a lifetime,' Narcissus said bleakly. 'You don't know what she was like. You really don't understand.'

'And then you left the room for me to find, looking just as it was supposed to for the saintly woman we thought she was. A natural death. A windowless room locked and bolted on the inside. It couldn't be anything *but* a natural death.'

Still in Omba's arms, Docilosa said, 'May I speak?'

Quistus said, 'Do you think you should?'

'I don't think I have anything to lose.'

He spread his hands. 'Then you should.'

The girl pulled herself gently from Omba's arms and stood.

'No, it's all right,' Omba said. 'Don't say anything. Don't tell him.'

'It was I,' Docilosa said. 'I killed her.'

Quistus glanced at the door as a shadow moved. 'No, Protia killed her,' he said quickly. 'It's all over. Docilosa, be quiet! There's nothing more to say.'

'I'm glad she's dead.' Docilosa looked him in the eye. 'I'm glad she's dead, Severus Septimus Quistus. She was the devil.'

Quistus called, 'No! Protia killed her, she's dead, justice is satisfied.' He held his finger to his lips, moving so fast on his feet that even the children stared, grabbing the girl's wrist so hard that Docilosa yelped. 'Say it was Protia—'

'Thank you, my dear Quistus.' The propped door fell open between the *castrati*, who melted away. Stigmus stood in the

47

doorway looking pleased with himself. 'How interesting. Couldn't help overhearing. So it was murder as well as theft, and the murderer was Docilosa, by her own confession.' The prosecutor stepped smiling into the room. 'What satisfactory progress for a single morning.'

The water-clock tolled the third hour. Stigmus rubbed his hands. 'Don't forget, Quistus, my dear fellow. The seventh hour, by the Emperor's command. I'll fetch you myself.'

'I haven't finished here.'

'It's over. Murder's so much more prestigious than natural death, and I've solved it already. Docilosa, eh?'

Quistus said, 'Stigmus, I promise you, none of the others knew anything.'

Stigmus grinned. 'In the eyes of the law ignorance is no excuse. They all failed to defend their mistress. That's as good as murdering her.'

Docilosa, instead of pulling her wrist away, pressed forward against Quistus. 'I know you're not afraid,' she whispered. 'Let the truth come out. I trusted you. Deserve my trust.'

He stared into her wide-open topaz eyes.

'This girl is my client,' he decided. 'Let her speak the truth as she sees it.'

Six

1313 Clients

'We're all damned anyway,' Narcissus groaned. 'We've nothing more to lose. Speak, Docilosa.' He pulled his collar over his head like a man already dead. 'Sweet Lord, let us live through this day. Forgive whatever sin we have done to others. Grant us our daily bread—'

Quistus said loudly to Stigmus, 'His prayers are to Nero, of course, our source of all mercy and goodness in this world.'

'Indeed,' Stigmus said. 'Now, the girl.'

Docilosa wept. She gave way to a storm of tears, her body twisting, her head in her hands, tears and saliva leaking

48

between her fingers. It was the most oddly dreadful sight. Omba, angrily watching the men's stares, forced herself between them and took the girl to her bosom. 'It's all right.' She cuddled her tight. 'Let it come.'

Stigmus sighed through his nostrils. Women should, above all, be honoured for their modesty, quiet good manners, deference and self-respect. The girl's yelling self-indulgence appalled him. She just wanted to draw attention to herself and the black barbarian was helping her, they were in it together. They should both be arrested.

Docilosa took her hands from her face. She gazed at the two Romans. She looked awful, tearful, snotty, her lips swollen, eyes reddened. Both men took a startled breath at her beauty. Narcissus blithely continued his prayers, but he didn't have any balls.

Docilosa slumped on the bed. She wiped her face on her tunic. 'Protia didn't kill her. Nobody did. Anyway, Protia liked it.'

Stigmus said, 'Liked? What?'

She stroked her knees. 'What happened.'

Stigmus cleared his throat. 'What happened?'

'I can't tell you.'

'You have to tell me,' Stigmus said, 'or I'll torture you.' He'd torture her anyway, soon.

'It was disgusting,' Docilosa said dully. She examined her hands, wiping them. 'She'd learned to like it. It happened to Protia since she was so young, I don't think she knew anything else. It seemed natural to her however disgusting it was. She lapped it up.'

Stigmus swallowed.

'You don't need to tell me this,' Quistus said. He stood by the wall, almost sure the god looking over his shoulder had the face of Amanda Censorina's first husband, Annius.

'Go on,' Stigmus whispered. 'Tell me, you foul creature.'

'There were never any men, only girls. Girls. Not women. You know. Girls under fourteen. Girls who'd . . . never been touched. Sometimes little boys, children, like babies. They were supposed to be the old woman's babies. I never saw . . . Protia and I left them after we had done our work preparing our mistress, dressing her. Makeup, hair. We made her like a doll, thirty years younger. She would be their mother.'

Omba said throatily, 'What sort of mother?'

'Everything mothers are.' Docilosa brushed cobwebs off

her knees; they couldn't see anything. 'Kind. Strict. Playful. Angry. Sometimes she suckled them, even gave birth to them. So Protia said. Sometimes she went in.'

'What do you mean?' Quistus called.

'To the womb.'

'But your mistress didn't call you in too, did she?'

'She wants to, Protia says. I'm special to her, she says. Different and special. Always. At the crossroads my mistress saved me from death, she's always been saving me for this special moment. It's time to show my gratitude.'

Stigmus said, 'And you came in to her of your own free will.'

'Protia says come on, there's extras. You know. Food. Wine. Fun. You can laugh, you can do anything you want. She wants you to. She loves you. You're her little baby and you can kiss Mother like her baby. Mother wants you to love her. And suck her for milk. And she can give birth to you, you can go right up and come all the way down, being born.'

'Stop,' Quistus said.

'I need to know it all,' Stigmus said tersely. 'All these lies.'

'It was me she really wanted.' Docilosa smiled. 'Yes, me. She loved women, but she loved me most of all. She saved me all these years, innocent, I worshipped her. But last night – no, Severus Septimus Quistus, you're right, it was the night before last. She wore a mask such as actors wear to tell lies on stage, or women in childbirth, to hide their contortions of pain. I had prepared her hair – oh, it took hours! When I came in Protia left me, smiling, knowing what would happen to me.'

'That's when Protia stole it from the jewellery box,' Stigmus nodded.

'Such beautiful silks in there, Arabian rugs, beautiful girls, clothes. No one resists. Indian herbs burning. Wear what you like, or nothing. They look so funny. The lyre player, a Greek *castratus*, with a smooth chest, very laughing. Naughty pictures painted on screens, *very* naughty. Someone gives me wine and it goes, oh, like this. Straight to my head. All swirly yet so clear. My mistress claps her hands. She commands everyone to leave, except me. Together . . . alone. I'm shy. She whispers that I'm so lovely, so precious. She wears the Venus mask to be beautiful as a god for me, her hair piled up so white and magnificent, all my work, my nimble fingers, she reflects my skill. She kisses my lips like hunger. Mmm.'

50

'Vile perversion,' Stigmus said. 'Lie.'

'It's easy to do, child, do it! No, no, stop, I don't like it. Yes, now your tongue, *here*! No, I won't. Yes, do this for me, be born for me, I am your mother! Disobedient child! Now!'

Stigmus touched her blonde curls. She shook him off, hissing.

He stepped back. 'So you killed her.'

'No. She was dead. If saying no is murder, I killed her. I screamed no. No! *No!* And she died.'

Stigmus turned, baffled. 'Quistus, do you believe this?'

'Do you see any mark on the body, Stigmus? Do you think a word made of thin air can commit murder? Whatever it is, it's not murder.'

'Killed by a spoken word,' Omba murmured. 'I told you, master, she's clever.'

'I never hurt her,' Docilosa said.

Stigmus looked at his feet, then said, 'Why are you protecting this girl, Quistus? I only want to get to the truth. To see justice done.'

From the doorway, Cassius Longinus interrupted. 'I know why,' came his grey dry voice. 'Because *he* knows, my stupid Stigmus, that if our dear departed Amanda Censorina was murdered, and one of her slaves is shown to have murdered her, then *all* her slaves are equally guilty of murder. Every one. If the suspect girl Docilosa is to be executed, as seems perfectly proper to me, then all must be.'

Quistus said, 'All one thousand three hundred and thirteen of them.'

'Indeed. Crucified. It's the law. You may remember I represented the estate of Pedanius Secundus a few years ago.'

'Ah, Pedanius,' hummed Stigmus.

'The pederast was killed by one of his boy slaves in an argument over another boy. I got the lot executed. About four hundred in that case.'

Quistus crossed his fingers. 'I believe if you consult the will, which I note you've unsealed before the magistrate's investigation has even begun, you'll find that Amanda Censorina's slaves became free at the moment of her death. Therefore immune from group reprisal. You can't touch them.'

'My expert opinion is that the relevant law is the senate decree *Silanianum*, which as you know applies equally to manumitted freedmen. I say the girl killed her mistress and the magistrate will accept my word and that's that.'

'I overheard her confess,' Stigmus said. 'She said she was glad her mistress was dead.'

'Then their fate is inevitable.' Longinus continued: 'Quistus, my friend, they're all dead. Legally they are *all* the murderer. They're slaves. They're the cesspool of Rome. Nobodies. You're one of us, not of them. Accept justice. You owe these scum no loyalty.' He unfolded the closely written parchment. 'Besides, she bequeathed them this rather large sum of money, money that should better go to the cream of Rome. I can't see the Emperor approving this as it stands. Best these vicious scum are dealt with simply and effectively, got out of the way. After all, we don't want to set a bad example.'

'But it wasn't murder,' Quistus said. 'Show me the wound. You can't. Show me the murder weapon. You can't.'

'I think it's time you decided something important,' said Longinus in a voice as dry as ash. 'Are you with us, or against us?'

Longinus spoke in a low voice with Stigmus. They were making plans. Quistus stayed by the doorway looking out into the hall. The house beyond the windowless room was quiet, sunlit, lovely; occasionally shouts and screams carried to them, the slap of bare feet running in the corridors. He thought he heard Clio cry out. Quistus didn't move whatever he heard. People were being rounded up. Omba stood with her back to him for a while, arms crossed, her round face squashed into a frown.

Hidden between them behind the statue of Amanda Censorina's first husband, Docilosa sat with her legs bent tight under her tunic, her face buried between her knees, as motionless as Quistus, exhausted. No tears. No hiccups.

A distant echo, a cupboard going over. The number herded to the strongroom downstairs must be growing steadily. Narcissus had accepted his fate with all the dignity he could muster, bare feet skidding, one cheek torn. Ursus knew how to treat a eunuch. Narcissus had grabbed the doorpost.

'Quistus.' He'd looked back for a moment. 'I'm sorry.'

After a while Omba muttered, 'It must be nearly full down there.'

Quistus nodded.

'Now,' he whispered. He moved smoothly, lifting Docilosa by her wrist, pulling her through the doorway. Omba's bulk hid them from the two men still talking. Quickly he tugged the girl across the domed hallway to the private atrium splashing with fountains, let go of her without slackening pace. Docilosa stood where he left her. She stared into the pool. The fish made patterns. He strode to the room where the water-clock stood and slapped both hands hard against the wall.

'Don't.' He rested his forehead on the cool marble. 'Omba, don't say anything.'

'I didn't say a word.'

'Don't.'

'I won't,' she said.

'I didn't know Stigmus was eavesdropping. Don't say it.'

'Everyone makes mistakes.' She glanced at the girl by the pool. 'He's an ant. Look, she still hasn't moved. I feel so sorry for her. I'd better go to her.'

'If you were me what would you do?'

'I'd bang my head against the wall. But *I* would go to her and smuggle her to Scadinavia, the Orcades, Nubaeia, even Kefa, anywhere furthest from here.'

The water-clock dripped.

'And leave the rest to die.'

'You didn't actually accept all of them as your client. Only her. Forget your honour, one life lived is better than none. Is it really worth your own life?'

'They're children. Did you see their faces?'

They watched Docilosa.

'You're right,' Omba said, 'you're stupid.'

'Don't say it again.'

'All because she said you aren't afraid. If you had any sense you'd be afraid. *She's* clever, she got you into this, and now you can't get out.'

He sighed, 'Well? What about her? Is she mad?'

'I think she was made mad.'

'I can't get through to her. Each time I think I know those thoughts burning in her heart, she slips away from me.'

'She isn't a man. She doesn't think like one.'

'She's guilty.'

'I believe her, master. When she claimed she said no, I believed her. *No!* And the old creature got so angry and

53

furious, so *contradicted*, that something burst in her head and she died.'

'I don't know if Docilosa said no. I do know what she actually did.'

'What was that, master?'

'She grabbed out one of the steel hairpins fixing Amanda Censorina's wig and she forced it up the old woman's right nostril into her brain.'

Omba breathed out. 'You're sure?'

'The brain exchanges heat into the water that bathes it within the skull. A drip came out of her nose. I saw it. Not mucus. Water.' He added, 'And I found the pearl that pulled off the pin as they struggled. The black pearl.'

'I preferred it the way Docilosa told it.'

'Do you think she was telling the truth about Amanda Censorina's behaviour?'

'She sounded convincing. I would have done more than just stick a pin up the old bitch's snout.'

'Yes, but how much of it was true?' He rubbed his face. 'Do such things really happen?'

'Surely you remember when we were shipwrecked on Lesbos, master. The Lesboeans.'

He frowned. 'I must have missed something.'

'I'm sure you did, master.'

He held up his arm. It was still bleeding. The wound wouldn't stop.

The water-clock trickled, glugging. A silver ball rolled down a complicated ornament and rang the bell.

'Two hours until I see Nero,' Quistus murmured. His mind was busy, Omba knew. She kept her peace. Quistus's deep thoughts were always followed by action, rational, stoical, logical; but that was not the same as wise.

'There's got to be a *posticum*,' he whispered in Docilosa's ear. The many rooms of the Domus Censorina were quiet now, and still. 'Think.'

'A *posticum*.'

'You know what it is. You want to live, don't you?'

'Left,' she said. 'Right. I don't know. Don't know this part of the house. It's not on my duties.' Then she said: 'I think Stigmus believes me, don't you?'

'The bit he overheard about you killing her. He believes that.'

'But that's not fair.'

'Sssh,' he told her.

The three hurrying figures moved from room to room, Quistus leading, the willowy figure of Docilosa swaying between them. 'Over here.' He tugged her wrist and she swung round, drawn limply after him. Omba prowled alertly behind.

Another doorway, another room bright-barred with sunlight. No outside windows downstairs, in case of thieves, but these openings upstairs were too high to jump from. The street below was basalt blocks, hard as iron, and Docilosa's legs were thin. He dreaded the thought.

She asked suddenly, 'Will they hurt us if they catch us?'

In due course the slaves would each be questioned by torture – though mercifully only whip and cane in the case of children, the law wasn't a monster – to establish the truth for the ears of a magistrate. But not yet.

'Just tell them the truth, Docilosa.'

A sense of exhaustion, of vacancy, had settled over the house. These rooms didn't seem to lead anywhere. He walked quickly, eyes flicking. The place was a maze.

'Where are you taking me?' she demanded.

'Anywhere but here.'

'Why?'

'She talks more than you do!' Quistus said. 'Doesn't she ever shut up?'

Docilosa tripped, sliding. Blonde curls fell over her eyes. It was impossible not to feel sorry for her.

'Omba, quickly,' he said. She swept the girl up in her arms and followed him with long, heavy, prowling strides. Quistus took a turn. At once he stopped dead, teetering. Omba almost knocked him downstairs.

He made a sign, inching back. The *ostiarius*, Clumens, sat down there by the tall double doors. Obviously he'd been suffered to stay at his post for the moment, but Bellacus scratched fleas and stood guard until the *vigiles* arrived. He looked bored but permanent.

The way in; no way out.

Quistus signed to Omba. From the gallery they retraced their steps deep into the *domus*, turning left not straight on, then straight on again towards the back.

The rooms were smaller now. Omba grunted and put the girl down. Quistus strode forward. 'Aha,' he said. 'A *posticum*.'

It wasn't quite true a house had only one door; it had only one public door. The others were private and secret. A *posticum* was a low outward-opening exit, usually somewhere on the side or rear, in case the master of the home wished to exercise his right to steal away from his wife and family, or back again, without them knowing. There were many reasons, all of them good.

Quistus kicked the rusty bolts loose. He shoved his shoulder against the planks. The hinges stuck, groaning, then gave way against a crate of figs. The three of them came crouching from behind a market stall, blinking suddenly in a busy sunlit street lined with more stalls, roofs flapping like sails in the breeze, stallholders crying out like gulls. Quistus melted into the crowd but Omba always stood out. Her walk slowed, entranced; shopping was her second love. Sweet Nile dates, oysters freshly shipped in ice from Parthia, spices of India and China, nutmeg and cloves from the Maniolai Islands on the edge of the world, fabulous and exotic. Quistus went back for the two enthralled women who'd so quickly forgotten the danger they were in. He grabbed Docilosa angrily. Omba made a face and followed. 'Where now, master?'

'Where they won't find you. Somewhere men don't go. Where you'll be safe until closing time, anyway.' He led them downhill, flowing with the crowds past the Romulan wall, to the crossroads on the Clivus Victoriae. Plenty of bath-houses down here, men and women queueing at separate entrances; other establishments were more exclusive, for men only, or admitting only women. Locusta's Healthy House of Pulchritude was known as the most reputable; no man ever set foot in there. 'Omba, if this goes wrong, you know the places I've hidden money. Get out of Rome, save yourself.'

'And her?'

'That may well not be possible.' He led his companions quickly up the steps, beneath the fake portico, into the shadows. The ante-room, gleaming with precious inlays, smelt like an Arabian perfume box. The long-fingered girl who took money and gave out towels looked startled. 'Sir! Ladies only at Locusta's.'

'Get her.' Locusta would already know he was here, the walls had eyes. Quistus handed over a couple of coins for towels. Quickly Omba pushed through the door at the back

56

and pulled Docilosa after her. A pair of older women came in, giggled at him, showed their wooden tallies to the girl, and went straight through. Regulars. He lost patience and followed them as the door swung. The room beyond was large, smelling of flesh, perfumes and steam.

'My dear, dear, *dear* Quistus!' The famous – or infamous – Locusta had never lost her honey-deep Gallic accent, by far the most attractive part of her; as small as a child, crippled in one leg, she still wore the hooded woollen *burrus* favoured by her Carnutian tribe, perhaps because she was so ugly, perhaps because she worked best unrecognized. He'd known her since she first arrived from Gaul, a penniless stranger, but carrying a priceless knowledge of herbs and remedies in her clever nasty head. If a woman were ever allowed to practise medicine, Locusta would be the most sought-after doctor in Rome. Since she wasn't, she'd made herself most sought-after at an even more lucrative profession – not beauty, or even passion, but murder. Her shadowed, sharp eyes observed Quistus quietly and carefully while peals of over-welcoming laughter burst from her toothless mouth. 'I am your client for ever, I will never let you renounce me, *patronus*!'

'I'm glad to hear it. I need you today.'

'We'll be lovers. Anything.' She embraced him, pushing her hood against him, kissing his cheeks wet-lipped, whispering, 'Who is she?'

'Her name is Docilosa.'

She eyed the girl, who seemed out of her depth. 'An innocent.'

'Obviously.'

Her breath was warm and sticky on his cheek, her lips almost touching his ear. 'Is she to die?'

'Look after her,' he said. 'That's all. A few hours. I don't know how long. Until the dust settles.'

She came down off tiptoe. 'From the Domus Censorina?'

'You already know?'

'In here everyone knows everything.'

The long busy room was a-buzz with chatter, greetings, laughter, gossip, echoing between the white-tiled pillars. A few heads bobbed in the steaming pool at the far end. Other figures splashed palely in the icy plunge-bath, hairstyles carefully wrapped against condensation. Quistus leant against the pillar near the Nymphaea oyster-bar. Sweating middle-aged women lay like soft pink lizards on rows of hard marble plinths, revealed by towels rather than covered. The beautifying process was highly organized, starting with rough bushy arrivals on the left and ending with shiny-smooth satisfied customers on the right: polite young studs and foxy milky nymphs with tweezers nipped, teased, twisted and plucked from top to bottom, eyebrows, lips, chins, armpits, pubes, shins, while scourers rubbed and soothed. Herbs, vegetables, pastes and packs were lovingly applied. Locusta called to Omba, 'Got a Lusitanian lad just in, circumcised for your extra pleasure?'

'Working,' Omba said. She was sweating freely. 'Strip 'em off, Docey, we'll blend in.' Docilosa stared wide-eyed. She wrapped her arms around her, holding her tunics on tight, and shook her head.

'Very young in heart,' Locusta murmured to Quistus. 'Don't tell me you have been so foolish as to become her patron. You *haven't*.'

'Not just her. All of them. All one thousand three hundred and twelve who will be accused and killed with her for Amanda Censorina's death.'

'Did she do it?'

'Mitigating circumstances, perhaps.'

'Just like me.' Locusta pretended not to notice Quistus's sharp glance. 'Did she use poison? Women always prefer poison.'

'Not that I found.'

'The whole point of a poison is not to be found.'

'I think she used a different sort of point.'

'A crime of passion then, without premeditation.'

'It seems so.'

'The colour of the body's tongue, ear-lobes, any smell from the mouth, cloudiness in the eyes, rawness in the throat, swelling?'

He shook his head.

'I could have done it,' Locusta said. 'You wouldn't know.'

After a while he said, 'Did you?'

'No. How could she afford me? A slave. Please. I've worked for—' Her hood bowed modestly. 'The very highest.'

It was true. Locusta Pulchra was who you came to when you needed someone to die of impeccably natural causes. All Roman women made fine poisoners – subtle, ruthless, patient, they had an innate sexual gift for it – but Locusta was a legend in her own lifetime. Within a week of passing through the gates she'd realized that any scorned Fury seeking revenge for years of abuse, absence and indifference wanted a lot more for her money than a quick blade in the heart of her ex-loved one or a stone through his worthless head from a high building. That wasn't the Roman way, or at least the way of Roman women. Wives and mistresses of any age by nature preferred horrible suffering to precede the inevitable death of the once-loved who had failed, spurned, struck or betrayed them; they looked forward to encouraging the thrashing helpless victim with comforting deceits, pretend panic, fake grief, a not-quite-hidden smile and eyes ice-cold. Best of all, the victim always knew. He'd struggle horribly against the poison, knowing he was dying, knowing exactly who was killing him, too agonized to do anything but feel his body fall apart very slowly, and be so very sorry. Slow, ghastly, mute, certain death. Perfect.

Locusta, at the peak of her fame, taught a hundred women in her class. Women rarely poisoned other females; and men, when an accidental death was required, came to Locusta.

No man in Rome was higher than Nero, and about nine years ago he'd made Locusta's reputation overnight. His brilliant young brother Britannicus, Emperor Claudius's real son – Nero was only adopted – was widely hailed as emperor-in-waiting. Britannicus suffered from epilepsy, alarming but not fatal, until Nero invited him to dinner. Britannicus's personal *praegustator* tasted the food and mulled wine unharmed, but Britannicus fell foaming at the mouth. How had Locusta administered the poison? Nobody knew. Anyway, her toxin mimicked the spasms and contortions of epilepsy perfectly, Britannicus was dead and buried within hours, and her name was made.

How had she done it? Quistus knew. A few years later when she was accused of poisoning a senatorial dinner party in which several ancient families fell extinct, Locusta had rushed to him, her patron, for help. Quistus uncovered circumstances that were more than mitigating and Nero hastily pardoned his old accomplice, no doubt hoping to use her again. Besides, people who failed Locusta rarely lived without distressing symptoms.

Quistus said in a neutral tone, 'You knew Amanda Censorina.'

'Of her,' Locusta said.

'You knew her professionally.'

'Certainly not. No woman in Rome was more virtuous.'

'Yet she was afraid of being poisoned. I know she employed a *praegustatrix*, Clio. Docilosa told me that Clio tasted her mistress's food and wine, and even the water that went in the wine.'

'Did she?'

'That made me think of Britannicus.'

'Perhaps it's best we don't say his name, old friend, even in here.'

'It made me think that Amanda Censorina knew how the poison got into Britannicus – not in his hot wine, but in the water that cooled his wine. Not very many people know that.'

'What are you saying exactly?'

'Amanda Censorina knew how Britannicus died because you told her.'

'Even if I knew, why should I tell her?'

'As I said, it was a professional relationship. You were selling her your services. You had to show you really are the best. After all, she could afford it.'

'These rumours get about. Rome's a gossip-mill.'

'I couldn't help thinking of poor Porcinus. How did he die? An Alexandrian—'

'That was a shrimp!' she exclaimed. 'He choked. Am I guilty of every accident? Am I to fly to Alexandria like a bird and back again?'

'I'm not asking how you did it.'

She muttered, 'Sea-snail poison. *Conus magus*, specially shipped from the Indicum Mare. They cost a fortune.'

'I think you knew Amanda Censorina quite well. She led such a tragic life, didn't she?' Locusta didn't reply. Quistus continued, 'Or was she just the most evil woman who ever lived?'

'No one who is rich is evil. People look up to them.'

'It's just that I was thinking of her second husband, who went down with the flagship of his grain fleet.'

'How can that possibly be the fault of his wife, or me?'

'Most of the crew swam to shore.'

'So?'

'He didn't. Neither did his children. Any of them. Poison has that effect.'

'If what you are saying were true then, yes, she would be the evillest woman in the world, to kill her husbands and children too.'

'I forget what happened to her first husband. No doubt he died a natural death.'

'Yes, he did.' She added, 'Though agonizing.'

'They say those who live by the sword die by the sword. Perhaps those who prosper by poison live in fear of being poisoned.'

'I've never worried about it myself.'

'You're not the richest woman in Rome, only the most feared.'

'One thousand three hundred and thirteen?' Her clawed hand slipped from her sleeve, gripping Quistus's fingers. 'Really? It would be an atrocity.' They watched Omba lead the girl between the laughing women into the shadows. 'Why throw your life into such danger for her?'

'I may be asking a great deal of you too, Locusta.'

'I owe you a great deal.' Then she murmured, 'You see Lyra in her? Is she what lies behind your foolishness?'

'No. No.'

'I know you do. I see her. I knew Lyra. She's Lyra.'

'Lyra's dead.'

'She's not dead until you believe it.'

'Lyra was fifteen when she died.'

'Oh, you know she died? For sure?'

He put his hands in his hair. 'She'd be nearly twenty by now. Changed. Different. Less. Would I even know her? I don't know. I can't think. I can't imagine what she's suffered.'

'Poor Lyra. She's so terribly alive in your heart. Give her peace.' Locusta looked at his hand. 'You're still bleeding for her.' The shadowy line of her lips stretched, smiling. She loved nothing better than a doomed conspiracy of the heart. 'Very well. I can do until sunset. No longer.'

Seven

The Emperor's Pleasure

Noon, the seventh hour. Stigmus, no Stoic, felt his bowels creak. His fingers ached with nerves, his stomach filled with sick cold fear. It was the old, familiar fear of failing. At

61

dawn this morning the imperial messenger, flanked by the two praetorians in unnecessary reinforcement of the message's importance, had brought him the order spoken word for word from Nero's lips. *'Bring Quistus to Us at the seventh hour. Do not tell him of Our suspicions.'*

Stigmus stood like a man who carries a heavy invisible load on his back. You couldn't see the load but you could sense its weight in the hunched set of his shoulders, his bent head, the strain in his legs.

The sunlit plaza in front of his tiny figure was one huge sundial. The shadow of Jupiter's pointing finger fell from such a height that it inched visibly across the minute markers as Sol circled Rome. *Almost* noon, but not quite. Still time for Severus Septimus Quistus to turn up. Just.

The idol of the god could be moved on wheels to take account of the season and the varying height of the sun. No one was late for the Emperor and lived. Even Seneca ran – well, hobbled – when Nero clicked his nail-bitten fingers. Yes, even Seneca the stinking-rich old *consiliarius* was here from the country, recalled from self-imposed (but very wise) exile. Everyone was here.

Except Quistus.

Nero always kept plenty of people about in case he wanted anybody. But today he wanted Quistus, so they all did – the whole Neronian *amici* of hangers-on and suckers-on and kissers-on jabbering and jibbering like deadly echoes. Where is he, Stigmus? He's here, isn't he? He *will be here*, won't he, Stigmus? The Emperor's depending on you, Stigmus. Don't fail.

Stigmus shook. No such thing as not being here. You came. You crawled on your knees if that got you here.

He'd promised: 'He'll be here.'

Then he'd fled the rarefied air of the palace, their sly looks and jibber-jabbering gossip in the golden vaults, and sought peace down here; or at least time. Time to think.

Stigmus gave a dry swallow. His mouth was spitless. In an odd way he trusted Quistus. Unthinkable that the snooty cold-hearted bastard wouldn't turn up, somehow, in the nick of time, towing the girl behind him, casually spouting some genial contemptuous upper-class story you were supposed to believe. He'd done it before. She tried to escape, Stigmus. Some improbable chase through the streets. 'Caught her in the end!'

he'd grin insincerely. Good, Stigmus thought viciously, clap them in irons. In fact clap them both in irons.

But that didn't happen. Nothing happened. Stigmus stood alone on the bottom step. At his feet the shadow of the fingertip quivered beside the giant VII, midday, as a tiny cloud crossed the sun; then it steadied again.

He wasn't coming.

That arrogant, unbelievable bastard. Stigmus's hatred boiled from his heart into his blood, turning him to fire despite the cold wind, curling his stubby fingers into fists. When the moment passed it left him colder than before. Icy cold. His belly moaned. Behind him, one after another, ever higher godward, the stairways of white marble climbed, shrinking, to Nero's rambling palace across the hilltop, the Domus Transitoria. Stigmus felt the weight of the great building and the wonderful prestige it represented pressing on the back of his neck.

Stigmus had been born a great man, almost. His path from privileged birth to greatness in the Senate was almost granted him from childhood, almost expensively educated in all the skills a great man needed, almost climbing the silk ladder from *quaestor* to *aedile* and so on to greatness in the magistracy and law. Everything handed to him on a plate. Almost.

Almost was all the difference in the world.

Stigmus was a magistrate's son, but by his father's laundrymaid not his wife. Since it was best Dicero's wife Domilla never knew (or at least, kept up appearances), the laundrymaid was sold on to a fuller's in Minturnae where she died worn out, and Stigmus was brought up in his father's house as the slave of his clever half-brothers. Of course *they* knew, they smelt the shared blood, and they made sure *he* knew he stank like an overflowing latrine. And perhaps his misery was part of Domilla's revenge, too, on her husband: the torments his base son endured at the hands of her own true-borns must have given her pleasure extra zest.

Nothing in a slave's appearance showed he was different from a free person; you mingled freely in the streets, shops, baths. You didn't wear a badge or different clothes, the Senate forbade it. Stigmus, *Specialis* of the *a Cognitionibus et Fides*, the Chancellery's Office of Investigation and Faith, scourge of Christian blasphemers, now knew why: it was so that you didn't see there were so many like you, so very many. The number was terrifying. Of six million people in Rome and Italy, two million were slaves. Had they known how many they were they would have been the masters.

Too many slaves were Christians. They drank the blood of their god and, drunk, ran riot in the streets and scrawled graffiti and were killed. That was the easy part. Worse, the infection of the Fish, the secret network of believers uncovered by the late, lamented Matrusus, had spread to people of breeding, thinkers, artisans, people who should have known better. They must be flushed out. No man had been more suited by birth to this vast cleansing task than Stigmus, none more eager or more thorough at eradicating the disease of Christianity and punishing the vermin he despised – his social superiors. He had so nearly been one of them.

Stigmus had crucified his own brother. Nero had seemed rather impressed with his loyalty.

Stigmus had no childhood. He was never a child, only a machine for revenge. At his father's house he'd learned to write so that he could record every insult, however small, like a water-clock patiently accumulating water until one day there was enough weight for the balance of power to tip. He drank the contempt of his smart-talking older brothers, their mockery, loathing and, yes, he knew their secret fear of him too, because soon they all knew he had only to tell their mother the truth – tell her in a certain way, in public, in front of her friends – to destroy her socially; and, being Dicero's wife, her social standing was her life. Stigmus watched his back, and kept close to his father's protection, and bided his time, knowing the day would come. Drinking every drop and keeping his mouth shut.

By the age of fifteen he was indispensable, his father's shadow, hardworking, obedient, dogged, loyal, vicious, earning his freedom drop by drop. One by one brothers moved away from home, climbing the spider's web. Stigmus prospered without them. After their mother's suicide – by eating hot coals, Stigmus had been *very* truthful, and it turned out she had her own pathetic liaisons – he prospered still more. Finally the day came when his father lay dying. Due to some letters sadly lost by the messenger, his other sons didn't rush home to the deathbed.

Stigmus's father had written his will apparently in his own hand, giving freedom to Stigmus, his house to the Emperor, and not a penny to any of his other sons. All gone, used up, given away. The brothers were equal at last.

Stigmus, totally faithful, devoted, alone, had carefully watched his father draw his last breath. The chest slowly deflated, rattling. That was the moment Stigmus was free. He'd walked around the darkened house not knowing what to do, then ordered a heron for supper.

Freedom terrified him. In reality it was darkness, the abyss. He felt like a man who awakens to find his dream has come true, but that he's in a nightmare where he's clinging desperately to the mid-point of a high cliff, enormously high, terrified of falling but too scared to climb. In such a situation there was only one safe course of action: you used your contacts in the magistracy, established so patiently. You wangled a transfer to the Palatine where the real power was, and you made yourself indispensable, just as you'd practised on your father. Totally loyal, you asked no questions. You didn't think, you climbed. You kicked the heads below and kissed the backsides above, and did it better than anyone else. The more criminals broke the law and forced you to discover them and make them suffer, the more you hated them for being so stupid. The more you hated them the more stupid they were, and easier to find, and the more of them there were. Where there had only been a few, soon there were many. And so Stigmus rose competently higher and farther, discovering conspiracy everywhere, through the lower ranks of the dreaded *Cognitionibus et Fides*. He was now a citizen, promoted to *Specialis*, feared. Once he had actually spoken with the Emperor in person. Another time he had drunk a cup of warm wine with him, or at least in the same room.

There was one golden rule. You never looked down. You remembered where you came from, so far, far below, but you never dared look.

Stigmus looked at his feet on the lowest of all those steps rising behind him. The air felt suddenly chill and dull. 'Ho! Stig!' Quistus clapped his shoulder, breezing past. 'Come on, you'll be late.' Stigmus stared after him taking the steps two at a time. The sun passed behind a cloud. The finger cast no shadow on VII, time had ceased to exist; it was impossible to be late.

He'd done it again.

Stigmus ran to catch up, toga slipping from one shoulder,

dusty sandals skidding on the marble. 'Where've you been!' he hissed.

Quistus looked surprised. *Where* was as obvious as could be. His hair was combed, his cheeks shining with cleanliness, his gaze relaxed and his toga fresh. 'The baths. Got to look our best for the Emperor, haven't we?'

Quistus spoke in that patronizing way he never used with anyone else but Stigmus, needling him. But still he wore that dirty bandage on his wrist, blood spreading through. He wasn't so perfect after all. Stigmus controlled his breathing, falling in step as they climbed. 'So, where is she?'

'Who?'

Stigmus snorted, 'You know!'

'I've no idea what you're talking about. I've been at the baths.'

Stigmus caught up again. 'Docilosa. She's missing. I thought you—'

'Oh, the girl? Yes, Docilosa. She's probably with the other slaves, wherever you've put them.' Stigmus was sure Quistus knew perfectly well where they were, in the strongroom. 'I'm sure she's innocent, Stigmus, you know.'

'She confessed.'

'I think you misunderstood. Eavesdropping does that. I don't think anyone killed anyone.'

'You would say that.'

'You would say the opposite.'

'Why are you protecting her? She's nobody.' Stigmus struggled to understand Quistus but it was beyond him. 'Give her back.'

'Amanda Censorina died by natural causes. Apoplexy.'

Stigmus's blunt face went dangerously red as he climbed.

Quistus said, 'You did find that Phoenix? Probably a brooch in the shape of a bird.'

'The trinket?' Stigmus frowned. 'Protia stole it from the box after Docilosa killed the old woman, thinking no one would notice in the confusion. Yes, we'll find it. I don't suppose it matters now.'

'There must be hundreds of brooches called the Phoenix in Rome, it's a lucky name. I suppose you searched Protia's body?'

Stigmus missed a step. 'I gave her body to Ursus, he wanted it. Executioner's privilege. You know – for, ah, you know soldiers. It'll be burnt by now.' He bit his knuckle. 'We've been searching the house.'

'Probably just a trinket, I hope,' Quistus called down from the top step. 'For your sake, eh, Stigmus?'

Being a genius made One hungry. Nero held out his left hand when leaving the stage of his private theatre and someone gave him something to eat as he walked. Perfectly awful audience today, senators, client princes, Iberian generals, dog-faced women without a scrap of artistic sense between them. 'Greeks!' he shouted, and people went running for Greeks. Romans couldn't see genius if it smacked them on the cheek, you raised your music-poem to its final ecstatic note of lyrical perfection but they just sat like stones, pretending they didn't realize you'd finished. Not a single tear or cry of loss, not one call begging him to start again. Greeks were artists. One Greek's adulation was worth that of ten Romans. Greeks understood what he went through for his art.

Not only that, he had affairs of state to bother about. Important affairs. These, for an Emperor loved and revered by the people, generally came down to one important question: *Who can I trust?*

Who will do what needs to be done, whatever happens, to see it through?

You had to choose a man – perhaps, in this case, even a woman – who would follow his or her heart come what may. Nero was a good judge of hearts. When his mother survived two almost simultaneous assassination attempts and Seneca panicked, Nero had simply said to Anicetus the sailor, 'You know what needs to be done.' That was all that was necessary; yes, he was a good judge of hearts, in fact a genius at it, as he was at everything else.

There was another trick known to a lyre-player of his divine standard: never let your left hand fully know the tune your right hand is playing. The most perfectly original melodies resulted.

'Well, Polyclitus, has he arrived?' he demanded. His imperial secretary, a freedman who'd grown fat as a tick calming the Emperor's troubled waters, made soothing noises. Polyclitus had recently returned from Britain; still grim from the experience. Generals and civil servants didn't like being told what to do by an ex-slave smelling of patchouli, who chewed cardamoms to sweeten his breath if not his words.

Nero snorted. Someone wiped his chin. A mirror – these cursed rooms were rather dark, without even any holes to pee in, the Domus Transitoria was a hovel barely fit for a human. Someone ran backwards, holding up a circle of polished brass. His handsome features were satisfactorily flushed from his performance, just the right glow of divine perspiration, but his lips were rather pale. Some pretty thing's finger pouted them with red wax. Perfect. The front of his gown was cleaned where food had dribbled down it. 'Wine.' Wine at noon; an Emperor could live properly. He held out his right hand and gulped from the golden goblet. Twenty-year-old Falernian. Once you'd tasted wine from gold, you couldn't go back to silver.

Someone wiped his chin with white linen. Nero stopped, the back of his right hand to his brow, thinking ahead. Someone had to do the thinking round here. 'I have to make a proper entrance. What time is it, Vatinius?' Then Nero laughed, because Vatinius the shoemaker was such a funny fellow to look at, leathery-brown and bent-over as a toad, hunch-back, spy, informer, tittle-tattler, always terrific fun. Vatinius clambered on someone's shoulder like a mating animal, raising himself high enough to peer from the window. 'Can't see! Sun's gone in, time's gone!'

Someone – Petronius, master of ceremonies – murmured obsequiously, 'The seventh hour, I believe, Caesar,' but Nero only had eyes for Vatinius, who jerked his hips as though mating with the slave's ear, at the same time swigging wine through the spouted cup he always held in his scarred hands, saying he didn't like to spill any by mistake, except in his mouth. 'There he is!' Vatinius cried out, pretending an orgasm. 'Our senator reaches the top step at last.' He said the word again, *senator*, with a sneer. He jumped down then scuttled at Nero's gold-painted bare feet, rolling over like a dog for his belly to be scratched. 'I hate you, Caesar, because you too are a senator!'

'Keep your voice down, shoemaker.' Tigellinus the Sicilian gave the belly a playful kick, hard. Vatinius pretended to be hurt, and perhaps he really was, because he fell quiet after that, though no less alert.

Nero peered round the corner into the entrance hall, so high he'd once seen a cloud drifting against the domed ceiling. Hundreds of grovellers, time-wasters, self-important twits, beseechers, supplicants – among other duties he'd married Rome Herself, the Holy Maiden – offered up prayers and tiresome incantations for his good health along the walls, as usual, but the place was so big that it looked empty. Most of it, anyway, was taken up with himself, or rather, Himself: the statue of divine Nero, wise-looking, draped in an immense toga, stood well over a hundred feet tall beneath the golden dome, spiky gold rays shining from his head like the sun. 'Watch!' he chuckled, deciding. 'Watch his face! I'll amaze him!'

Nero walked out like an ordinary person and stood by his great marble foot, his head not much taller than His ankle. Behind him his adoring *amici* murmured polite applause from the shadows.

Quistus saw Nero at once, perched like a tiny human toy between the ankles of his own Colossus. 'It's *him*,' Stigmus whispered. 'What shall we do?' He followed Quistus's gaze upward. The statue's head was constructed much too large so that it didn't appear pin-headed from the ground. The sun came out, blazing through the circular windows around the dome, lighting the noble features. 'See, Stigmus,' Quistus said casually. 'Only the Emperor can stand in his own shadow, looking up his own toga.'

Stigmus stood fixed, immobile, sweating, wishing his name wasn't involved. The *amici* silently awaited Nero's reaction. Nero stared, wondering if he had been cleverly insulted or subtly complimented. Quistus reckoned Vatinius looked petulant – he liked only his own dangerous jokes, not other people's – but Tigellinus, an evil man, gave a calculating smile. Next to him Quistus made out lovely barefaced Poppaea in her stunning white-and-gold ankle-length gown, the empress slimmer than he remembered; he'd last seen her pregnant in Antium. She'd recently lost the daughter at four months old, supposedly killed by Nero to encourage her to conceive a son. It was the sort of strange but all-too-likely story people believed of Nero; he'd murdered his brother, mother and first wife, so killing his baby daughter (the rumour went) was merely acting in character.

Quistus frowned. The real Poppaea had put on weight and was never seen in public without a veil. He realized her part was played today by the boy Sporus, Nero's latest favourite, half a donkey lighter and bearing an unearthly resemblance to Poppaea in her prime. Like her, Sporus was blessed with everything but a virtuous mind. The *amici* gossiped that if Poppaea ever had one of those terminally unfortunate accidents, Nero would simply have Sporus castrated and marry him in her place. Again, it was the sort of story no one believed, except of Nero. Sporus, wisely, preferred power and wealth to a full scrotum and was said to be ecstatic at his proposed honour; Poppaea less so.

Nero still hesitated beneath the great statue of himself. He hated decisions, except artistic ones. Had Quistus insulted him or not? He looked over his shoulder, and Tigellinus nodded and smiled broadly, so Nero came forward with an equally broad smile. 'Quistus, you noticed my clever joke! I was standing between my own legs! Looking up my own toga!'

Quistus said politely, 'I'm sure your private parts are equally huge in the flesh.'

Nero said the only possible thing that came to his mind. 'Yes, actually.' He was wearing an odd belted garment, half dressing-gown half *burrus*, stained with wine and sauce. He called proudly to Tigellinus, 'There! I told you he'd be amazed!'

Vatinius scampered, seeking attention. He knocked Quistus with his cup. 'Bow to Caesar! Bow to great Caesar!'

Vatinius was from Beneventum, and the Beneventese never uttered an *ae* without making it sound like a sneeze. Quistus gazed into Nero's eyes, watery with wine, eerily blue beneath his fair hair. 'Caesar,' Quistus nodded seriously, pronouncing the imperial title correctly: *Kaiser*. 'You sent for me, Caesar?'

Nero was immediately vague. 'Ah, Sigma,' he said, noticing Stigmus.

'Great Caesar.' Stigmus knelt. 'My enquiries, following your instructions, led me to locate the ex-senator at the house of Amanda Censorina, where there has been a murder' – his voice rose – 'which Severus Septimus Quistus has tried to cover up.'

'I know Quistus, I trust him as a man who follows his heart, I will hear no criticism of him.' Then Nero frowned. 'Murder, you say?' He turned again to Tigellinus, who gave the smallest possible shake of his head. There was an awkward silence. Vatinius shook his head too. Nero said, 'We don't know about it, do we?'

'We're sad to hear of it,' Tigellinus said.

Nero repeated, 'Murder, you say? In *Rome*?'

'No,' Quistus said. 'Not murder.'

'Yes, murder.' Stigmus looked to Tigellinus for support, having often taken orders and assignments from the prefect of praetorians. But Tigellinus chose to avoid his eye rather than take sides, yet. He liked the winning side.

Nero said, 'She was terribly mean, wasn't she? Amazing no one murdered her before.'

'Terribly rich. And she was your beloved godmother,' Tigellinus purred, appearing as if by magic at Nero's shoulder, not liking him to speak to anyone without the conversation being overheard. The Emperor was over-friendly by nature and tried too hard to be popular, making promises that Tigellinus broke. 'Naturally the lion's share will go to you, great lion of Rome, once the slaves are disposed of. They're all guilty of murder of course. Once the girl is found guilty they'll be executed in one lot. The formality merely requires your signature.'

Nero's income was vast, but so was his spending; one-sixth of all the water flowing through Roman aqueducts came out through his fountains. There were rumours, too, that even the immense Domus Transitoria was too small for him, but there simply wasn't space in crowded Rome to squeeze in a bigger palace.

Quistus said, 'They're innocent.'

'No one likes signing these things,' Nero said. 'I wish I'd never learned to write, every time.'

Standing less than six feet from the Emperor, Stigmus grabbed his chance to make his name. 'Caesar, I have already instructed Longinus to examine her will. I am sure you will find it most favourable . . .'

Nero drank a cup of wine.

Tigellinus drew Quistus aside. 'I hear you're still searching for your family.'

'Do you have anything to tell me?'

'No. No one else cares. Yet you're unable to let go. It must hurt.'

'Yes,' Quistus said. 'It must.'

'A word of wisdom.' Tigellinus put his face close. 'Great Caesar likes senators no more than I, and he detests Stoics.'

'Then why am I here?' Quistus permitted himself a gamble. 'What's this about? Why do you need me so much that everyone is so very pleasant today?'

Tigellinus glowered; so, Quistus knew, it was true. They needed him, but even Tigellinus did not know why.

Sophonius Tigellinus, Prefect of the Praetorian Guard, was the second most powerful man in Rome and by far the most unpopular. A brutal, sentimental Sicilian who wore a thin but cultured skin of Greek descent, he was to Quistus's certain knowledge a rapist, arsonist and thief, cruel, jealous, shallow, devious, a sophisticated thug with, it was said, two memories: a short memory for friends and a long one for enemies. Tigellinus had survived the savage hurly-burly of imperial politics for more than a third of a century, his trick being simply to sleep with everyone important. Strictly only their importance mattered, not their sex or even, reputedly, species. Twenty-five years ago he'd been banished for sleeping with the Emperor Caligula's sisters Agrippina and Livilla, both individually and together. In return Agrippina, who'd given birth to Nero two years previously, made sure Tigellinus was recalled and found indispensable by Caligula's successor, her next husband-to-be, Emperor Claudius. Agrippina and Tigellinus persuaded Claudius to adopt Nero as his son ahead of his own Britannicus; Claudius, having thereby outlived his usefulness, was poisoned by Agrippina, Tigellinus and Locusta. Agrippina had then used Britannicus as a threat to control Nero, saying Britannicus even had the sweeter voice.

Since Britannicus had suffered his nasty fit and Nero's mother had been clubbed and stabbed to death (a collapsible ship failed to work properly, and Agrippina always had antidotes to poisons), and since the fall of Nero's wise but indecisive teacher Seneca, the Empire was ruled by the 'divine tripod' of Nero, Tigellinus and Poppaea. But only Nero mattered. He was artistic, not stupid. The tripod was a circle of one. The others were nothing without Nero, just powerful, wealthy, and as afraid of him as everyone else. Quistus whispered to Tigellinus, 'No idea at all what it's about?'

The prefect tried to look smooth and in control. 'Of course I do. News from Britain.'

'What news?'

'Disturbing news.'

'You don't know. I think you're closer to Poppaea than Nero. Is that wise?'

Tigellinus said: 'He knows of your visits to Britain.'

Quistus shrugged. 'The last time I visited Britain was fifteen years ago, when Claudius conquered the place.'

'I mean, he knows of your secret visits.' Tigellinus watched closely but saw no change in Quistus's expression. 'He knows you know people. You *know . . . people.*' Tigellinus added, 'People whom, perhaps, it's not advisable to know.' Still no expression. 'And even scum in Rome, down-and-out scum, we hear, come secretly—'

Quistus seized Tigellinus's wrist. He pulled the Sicilian behind a pillar. 'Did he kill my wife and children?'

Tigellinus laughed. 'Why?'

'*Did Nero order it?*' Quistus squeezed the wrist in his hand. White flesh came up between his fingers.

Tigellinus stood on tiptoe. 'I'll have *you* killed,' he grimaced.

Quistus tightened his grip. 'Not while the Emperor needs me so much.' A bead of sweat trickled down Tigellinus's forehead. 'Sssh,' Quistus said.

'I didn't order it, that's all I know!' Tigellinus clenched his teeth.

'*Did* he, Tigellinus? Did he, four years ago?'

A small gasp. 'Why should he?'

'I don't know. I don't know. Are Septimus and Lyra still alive?'

'You can break my wrist,' Tigellinus gasped. 'I don't know. I don't.'

'You don't know anything. You've lost control of him. Just as Seneca did.' Quistus let the other man go. 'You could be a Stoic, you know, Tigellinus. I could train you.'

'By breaking my wrist?' Tigellinus rubbed painfully.

'It's a start. There is no pain.'

Nero's voice called petulantly, 'Where is he?'

Tigellinus stepped out, smiling. 'Caesar, forgive us,' he called, 'we merely spoke of race horses.' He kept famous stud farms all over Calabria and Apuleia; racing was only for the richest as the winning horse, blessed by victory, was sacrificed in gratitude to Nero and the other gods. 'Great Nero is a master driver of racing chariots, four-in-hand, in the privacy of the Vatican valley,' Tigellinus boasted on Nero's behalf. 'I begged Caesar to compete before the people at the Circus Maximus, but everyone knows he'd win every race—'

'No, not you, it's Quistus I want,' Nero said. Immediately there was silence. The *amici* shuffled out of the way, drawing back from Tigellinus. 'Quistus, over here,' Nero commanded. 'Walk with me, my old friend. I've prepared a magnificent entertainment for your enjoyment. It's all part of my *Neronia*, a spectacle of games so wonderful and exciting that only my astounding mind could have thought of it.' He reached up a rather dirty hand and took Quistus's shoulder with a wide, excited smile. 'Nude dancing. Very tasteful. And there's more.'

Eight

Dance of Death Part I

Quistus stumbled. It was almost dark here in the theatre, somewhere very deep in the palace. Petronius, master of ceremonies, showed him personally past hastily moved feet and legs to a purple-draped bench illuminated by a lamp-slave. Rows of wooden seats rose steeply from the gold-painted revolving stage. The raised circle moved silently, water-powered, slowly turning around Nero at the centre, exactly as the whole world turned around Rome. The Emperor *was* Rome, made flesh. A finger of sunlight pointed through a hole in the golden roof so that Nero's figure shone in the gloom like a god. You couldn't take your eyes off him.

Every seat was full. Quistus dimly made out the audience, elderly senators, equestrian class, knights, squeezed in the shadows on each side, hands pushed in their laps by the crush, shoulders hunched. They sat without moving, chosen for their age or poverty; many ancient families had fallen on hard times and were forced, rigid with disgust, to watch their holy Emperor perform in public like a street-corner busker for his pleasure. So many people forced together made the theatre too hot despite the season, and there was an odd smell. Probably they'd been locked in here since dawn. The woman beside Quistus stared straight ahead. She trembled slightly, as if desperately uncomfortable. The old man on his left sat bolt upright, his hands knuckled over his stick. Quistus peered. 'Seneca?'

The old man bent his head a fraction. 'Wait. Too quiet to talk now.' He nodded at the stage.

Nero spat on his hands and rubbed them sensuously on his gown, preparing to play the lyre propped on his knee, a Greek ten-string instrument of turtle-shell, ox-skin and lamb intestines forged for him by the god Apollo himself. After a long period of tuning up he finally touched his fingertips in earnest to the strings and his cheek to the golden wood, closing his eyes, drawing breath. Some Greeks who'd been pushed around the walls drew breath in *sympathia*. The Emperor's virtuosity was legendary. On his recent visit to the ancient Greek festivals he'd been judged winner not only at the contests he played in but also all the others as well, making him *periodonikes*, an unheard-of feat. Nero had graciously awarded his crown to the people of Rome, making himself more popular than ever.

Today his audience just looked frightened. Quistus made out a pregnant woman arched in her seat. She'd bitten her fingers white. She made not a sound.

Nero spread the fingertips of his left hand across the strings; his right strummed backhand, with his nails. The music began, slow and low at first.

After a while Seneca whispered in Quistus's ear: 'He's not so bad, if he was anyone else. But the Emperor, *our* Emperor – playing on stage like a harlot from a Greek tavern! Ye gods. Since when did Romans believe anything good comes from Greece?'

Quistus nodded. The piece continued, becoming rather long. The audience, motionless, stared down at the moving stage. The effect was sickly; soon the mind could not tell whether it was the stage that moved or the whole auditorium that revolved around it in reverse, and several people clung to their bench afraid of falling.

Quistus put his mouth to Seneca's ear. 'Tell me music alone calls you from the country. Or do I hear the siren call of affairs of state?'

'I'm retired, a simple *rusticus*.' Nero's old tutor and adviser was worth three hundred million sesterces, an incredible and dangerously large fortune, which was why – a Stoic – he lived frugally, probably accompanied only by a cartload of slaves between his country villas in his old age. He added, 'I might ask you the same question. I hardly imagine you're here for pleasure.'

'I hear you've been in Rome for a week. Nero commanded me only today. You know more than I.'

The music finished and they covered their ears, deafened by the sudden tumultuous applause of feet stamping on the tiers of wooden boards. Many people took the chance to stretch their legs, making the applause even more prolonged, then settled back reluctantly. Nero bent over the lyre, and began again.

Seneca whispered, 'You want to know what the fuss is about? Really?'

'I've been distracted from political affairs. Educate me.'

'Queen Boadicea is alive.'

Quistus stared, listening to the song like a deaf man – Nero was singing with a deep tuneful voice, but a good deal less powerful than you'd expect of an Emperor.

Boadicea. Seneca spoke of her with respect. Most Romans contemptuously latinized the British Queen's name as *Boudicca*, a common nickname for little slave-girls – it meant victory, *victoria* – but Seneca pronounced her name correctly, as Brits did, with awe. Boadicea. He was taking the threat seriously.

Three or four years ago, after her dead husband's will was plundered (as was usual) in his *patronus* Nero's favour, Queen Boadicea of the client Iceni tribe was flogged for appealing for justice, and her two daughters raped. Closely watched by restless tribes along the Rhine, indeed along all the other vulnerable outposts of Rome's borders, Boadicea united the British tribes under her leadership with almost mystical speed. Her army, mostly women, burnt the capital town of Camulodunum, killed every Roman soldier and hanger-on, threw down the statues of the imperial gods, massacred the Ninth Legion, burnt Londinium, slaughtered the romanized inhabitants as collaborators, and all but succeeded in throwing the Romans out of Britain.

An army of women. That was what really stung. No wonder Romans sneered, calling her mere Boudicca; she'd frightened and humiliated them.

Governor Paulinus, with a vastly smaller force, tricked Boadicea's Furies into battle on his terms, in a valley between trees. His trained soldiers trapped and killed them by the tens of thousands. Tens of thousands more died of starvation during reprisals so fierce that even Nero recoiled. After an imperial investigation carried out in person by Polyclitus, too late, Paulinus was recalled to Rome.

Boadicea escaped, never to be found. Some said she took poison, others that she died of fever.

Quistus whispered, 'Alive?'

'So they say.'

'How can you be sure?'

Seneca shrugged. 'It's what our spies hear. The living Queen comes back to lead us, that sort of thing. Death to us. Britain for the British tribes.'

'It's poetry.'

'They're a poetic people. They believe it.'

'They're leaderless.'

'Not if she lives. Not if she really does. Since Paulinus left the tribes have got their nerve back under weak governors and lost none of their anger, believe me, or their hatred of us. Poems handed down from father to son, from mother to daughter, give people long memories. Even barbarians have culture, of a sort.' Seneca pushed his lips tight to Quistus's ear and murmured a heresy. 'Just because Brits won't – not can't, *won't* – read and write doesn't mean they're stupid, backward or even uncivilized, in their own way. Towns, roads and writing are our tools of government, not theirs.' He paused as Nero ended. More applause. 'I do believe that woman is going to have her baby. Last week a man had to feign death in order to leave.'

Nero, sunlit, glowing, held up his arms. 'Obviously the pupil has outstripped his master!' He called graciously into the wings, 'Terpnus, you are now my pupil not my teacher, but I will allow you a note or two.' He began yet another song, 'Canace in Labour', accompanied from the wings by his subservient muse, once his tutor, poor brilliant Terpnus. A woman dressed in filmy silks fluttered in the shadows, gradually emerging into the light. 'Ah,' Seneca muttered, interested. 'Calvia Crispinilla, Nero's *magistra libidium*. No, really, her official title. Mistress of the imperial libido. What a lovely belly.'

She fluttered around Nero like a moth on tiptoe, her bare feet thumping on the boards, the silks falling away one by one. The story was unimportant; incest, mother-murder, unnatural passion, the usual.

Quistus murmured, 'Paulinus herded all the British poets and priests on an island. A few days before Boadicea's rebellion.'

'Mona. The island was Mona, beyond the western mountains. Yes, Druids, priests, priestesses, thousands of them, all in black, chanting curses.'

'He slaughtered them.'

'Many. Not all. You're right, that was the cause of the uprising, the real cause. That's what rallied the tribes to Boadicea so quickly, Paulinus's affront to their religion. Idiot. A religious atrocity, the one thing that could have united them all against us.' He gazed admiringly at Calvia Crispinilla. 'Do you know how she's grown so powerful? I mean, apart from her beauty and depravity. It's because she has no children.'

'Perhaps she uses her body only to tease.'

'I assure you she does not! Nor does she simply conceive, bear and abandon offspring, as most women would, which would at least give her five good months out of every ten. No.' Seneca showed signs of life, clasping his stick white-knuckled. 'Contraception. She knots a string around her lover's tail before . . . before. Tight. A man may take her twenty times a night and still be full of lust. Yet leaves her in no risk of inconvenience.'

'Amanda Censorina also had no children, at least none who survived. She too derived her power from her childlessness.'

'I heard you are involved. She preferred her own sex. She hated all men.'

'So I gather.'

'Hand over her murderer to the authorities. Let matters proceed.'

'Hmm. Word travels fast.'

'I have big ears and keep them close to the ground for my own good. You have no choice, Septimus. You're making yourself an accessory to the crime. That gives Nero power over you. He has you on a leash he can pull any time he wants.'

'What else do your ears tell you?'

Seneca dragged his gaze from the dancing woman. 'Listen to me. Seven days ago, I again advised Nero to withdraw all Roman legions from Britain.'

They watched the dance.

'He nearly did before,' Seneca said. 'After the Ninth. And then Londinium.'

'That was your advice then, too? Withdraw?'

'Yes, and Tigellinus's,' Seneca said. 'Abandon it. Let the province slip back into the dark age. Britain causes us nothing but trouble, costs us legions we can't afford, is an island remote enough and large enough to be forever a seed-bed for generals dreaming they can subvert their troops and be Emperor, and provides nothing of value – well, some rather fine hunting dogs. That's all.'

Calvia Crispinilla lost her last silk and tumbled nude at the Emperor's golden toes. 'Shameful,' Seneca muttered. 'Magnificent. Appalling. No one can control him. The few great of Rome hate him, the lesser millions love him. I dread what will come next.'

'You know Nero's mind better than anyone. What will he do?'

'About Britain?' Seneca couldn't take his eyes off Calvia, now writhing her hips in time to the dying music. 'Nero will never, ever, give up the country his father Claudius conquered. He'll do anything to keep Britain in the Empire. Absolutely anything. He's an artist.'

Calvia rolled on her back with her legs apart, motionless, deathly. A tableau, a real baby slipped between her thighs as if newborn, death giving birth to life. Nero laid down his lyre, turned in a circle, and dropped a rose petal on her face. He'd worked himself into such an emotional state that he wept real tears, though Calvia's chest visibly rose and fell.

'Look at him,' Seneca said. 'I've never felt so degraded.' He sighed. 'He has a plan. I don't know it. When he speaks to you, you're in blue waters.'

'Tigellinus—'

'I think not even Tigellinus knows. Did you speak to him?'

'It's out of his hands. Under pressure, all he gave me was a single drop of sweat.'

'Good.' Seneca looked satisfied.

Nero walked to the front of the stage and let its movement sweep him slowly round in front of the audience.

Quistus whispered, 'Why me?'

'Nero suspects—' Seneca stopped. 'He has suspicions about you. He believes you are a ruthless man. That excites him. He believes – forgive me, Septimus, your father's seventh and most beloved son – he believes you murdered your family, your wife, your children, all of them. I'm so sorry. Nero believes that you are like him.'

The stage swept the Emperor slowly round, his arms upraised, swinging slowly in and out of the sunlight.

'He further believes,' Seneca said, 'that you may be a secret Christian.'

'Then why am I alive?'

Seneca shrugged. 'Still, he believes it. And so, paradoxically, he is all the more sure he can trust you.'

'Trust me?'

'To be yourself. To follow your heart. These Christian beliefs are certain death yet still you hold them, or at least tolerate them. And now you even shelter the girl Docilosa.' The whites of Seneca's eyes glowed as he glanced sideways at Quistus. 'He knows I'll tell you all this. Do you think we find ourselves sitting together by accident? Nothing happens by accident, nothing's as it seems in Caesar's court. It's a performance, a puppet-show, all Rome is a puppet. I told you, he's an artist.'

They watched as purple rose petals rained down on the stage from invisible apparatus in the roof, celebrating Nero's performance.

'Do you have any good advice for me?'

Seneca said, 'Do you have eyes in the back of your head?'

Quistus touched the back of his head without thinking, then felt like a tricked child. 'No. Of course I don't.'

'Grow them,' Seneca advised. 'Grow them.'

Quistus asked another question but Seneca shook his head firmly. The conversation was over. The stage, still revolving, sank into the floor on some sort of hydraulic lift, removing the Emperor from sight in the most dramatic and unexpected way. When the stage came back up, it was empty.

Quistus heard a trickling sound; the woman beside him relieved herself where she sat, pretending everything was normal. He looked back, but Seneca was gone. The audience broke up, people rising stiffly, shuffling to the door guarded by praetorians. Sudden sunlight spilled into the room, and with it a rank musty smell of dust, dung and sweet blood. It appeared the entertainment was moving to a new level. 'Senator Quistus.' A voice spoke respectfully at his shoulder, a *nomenclator*, whose duty was to match faces to names. 'I am commanded to bring you to him another way. My name is Epaphrodites.'

'Him? Who do you mean, exactly, Epaphrodites?'

'He prefers it to be a surprise, sir.'

Quistus, remembering Locusta's words, wondered what hour the afternoon had reached. How much longer would Nero take? *I can do until sunset. No longer.*

Nine

Dance of Death Part II

Without looking back the freedman cleared a path through the crowd to a door that had not been visible before, descending stone steps to a gloomy stone tunnel that stank of animals. Quistus, with an increasing feeling of dread, followed the *nomenclator*'s hurrying shoulders past barred cages, dark holes of iron and stone where pale faces turned towards him, not the faces of animals. Men, brutes, criminals. Children clung to women, staring. 'Quickly, sir!' Epaphrodites's voice echoed. 'He doesn't wait!'

Quistus followed the *nomenclator* through a vaulted doorway into a high room, its arched roof supporting the weight of the palace above. Steps led to a door at the far end. These guards were definitely not praetorians, each resplendent in black and silver – fabled *Augustiani*, the Emperor's personal bodyguards. Not a man under six feet tall, all with perfect teeth. Their body-armour shone like mirrors, polished steel intricate with manly musculature, full-face helmets high and Greek-looking, floor-length cloaks of brushed black rams' wool. They didn't move a muscle as Epaphrodites passed between them, but Quistus saw the mean glint of their eyes through the helmet-slits.

The door swung. 'Behold!' Epaphrodites cried. 'The Lion of Rome!'

In the room beyond a lion stood on its back legs, long tawny mane swinging ferociously. The skull had been hollowed out to make room for Nero's head; he stared through the gaping mouth, eyes glaring past the rows of lion teeth. The limbs had been strapped to his own arms and legs, the sharp claws curved like gutting knives. For a moment he looked perfectly mad, trapped, insane. 'If you aren't afraid of me, Quistus,' came his voice, 'I suggest you should be.'

'Indeed, great Caesar.' Quistus looked round for Tigellinus, Vatinius, the hangers-on, perhaps even Seneca, but they were alone except for the half dozen formidably silent *Augustiani* around the walls. He caught the faintest scent of patchouli, the Arab perfume favoured by Polyclitus. There were other entrances and exits, not all of them quite closed.

Talking with any other man dressed as a lion would almost have been funny, but Nero wasn't funny. He was wearing a lion's skin, so he was a lion.

The lion remarked, 'I hear you too are an artist, Quistus, like me.' He waited for adulation.

'My wife was an artist. I only play the lyre.'

'I shall show you how to become a true performer.' Nero scratched the shale table with his claws, tearing grooves in the stone; Quistus saw the claws weren't living nail, they were honed iron. 'I shall give you lessons. I warn you, you will never be as good as I.'

'The honour will be all mine.'

Nero frowned suspiciously. 'Yes, it will.' Then his face, as much of it as could be seen, smiled. 'I have another honour for you today.' He reached out his arm in a friendly gesture; but the claws caught briefly in Quistus's toga, slicing four strips through the wool. 'You enjoyed one dance. Now for the real fun.'

Quistus's mind raced. Nero nodded and a centurion snapped an order. Two *Augustiani* flung open the door and went ahead. The other four fell in step around Nero and Quistus, and as they passed, the two who had guarded the door took up positions to the rear. The corridor was short, widening suddenly, turning to sand under the open sky, and Nero held up his arms in the sunlit arena, claws gleaming, the lion's head thrown back to reveal his own. The crowd, which judging by patches of scuffed sand and a few bloodspots had been warmed up ready for this moment, roared in adulation and excitement.

'*Hoi poloi*,' Nero murmured in insulting Greek, but loud enough only for Quistus to hear, smiling contemptuously as he posed and strutted for the crowd. 'Observe my dear common people, low, vicious, expensive, essential. How genuinely they love me and share my interests. Unlike those stuffed faces in my theatre, unable to appreciate true art.' He scratched his claws in the dust, driving the mob to a frenzy of anticipation. 'My amphitheatre! Here is life and death! Here is reality.' Nero shrugged the lion's head over his own. 'Walk with me. Not too close. The glory is mine alone.'

Three paces back, Quistus walked calmly behind the lion-headed Emperor. *Augustiani* circled watchfully on every side. The arena was small as such places went, but high-walled, almost overhung with steep tiers of wooden seats for perhaps six or ten thousand people, more standing, who would be close enough to be spattered in due course. Beneath flags and banners the western curve of the oval fell into shadow as the short hours of afternoon rushed towards sunset.

Across the centre of the arena a line of tall dark crosses stood planted in the dust. Most of the crossbars were nailed high but the children's were smaller and lower, a thoughtful touch that brought an appreciative growl from the lion. A few of the full-size crossbars were mounted very low, so that the worst of the Christian terrorists could be crucified upside down in mockery of their saviour, their souls falling straight to their Hell. Mostly they hung dazed-looking from the nails. One ugly old woman turned her head, slowly making out the Emperor. 'We forgive you.' Someone whacked her with a sword-flat but a few more, dying, took up the chant. Nero snapped his fingers for the *impresarius*. 'You haven't broken their legs?'

'Certainly not, Caesar, we aren't Jews.' The *impresarius* was a short bulky man, mostly belly, with rings on his fingers. 'They don't have to die quick and be buried before sunset, do they?' He chuckled. 'Roman Christians are the worst, our own sort gone wrong, right? After the show we don't bury 'em, don't burn 'em, we plant 'em along the Via Appia to rot. A lesson to others.'

'No spear in the side, anything like that?'

'Criminal waste of entertainment.' The impresario was offended. His name was Lustrus.

The woman with the broken nose murmured, 'You don't know what you do.'

Nero turned to Quistus, excited. 'Don't you love it when

83

they forgive me and I haven't done anything yet, almost?'

Quistus said, 'Yes.'

'Christians. You see what they're like.'

'I see it,' Quistus answered.

'Ever thought of joining them?'

Quistus said, 'Rome has many gods, great Caesar, including you. I worship all of you.'

Nero rubbed his itching nose on a tooth. 'Many gods, yes, but that's not what these Christians say. That's why I hate them. Their intolerance. Their one "God", no others allowed. It's so arrogant.'

'Strictly speaking Christians have three gods, perhaps four, if those who believe the Virgin—'

'My mother was a virgin,' Nero said, interested. 'Believe me, I know. I stripped her body after her death, I pointed out every blemish. She was a virgin.'

The old woman mumbled, 'Go in peace, Satan.'

Nero pulled his claws down her belly. Her body bowed out, hanging limp. Quistus didn't look away. Nero said alertly, 'They call me Satan, the Beast, 666. What do you think, Quistus?'

Quistus said, 'You are the Emperor of Rome, great Caesar.'

'Here's a child.'

Quistus watched.

'It's not as though I don't give them every chance,' Nero complained. 'Before they're nailed they're given the opportunity to renounce "God" and make a sacrifice to me and the universal catholic gods. They refuse, they refuse. It's all forgiveness, *they* forgive *me*. They eat and drink their "God"—'

'They believe it's his son.'

'Yet they won't spill a drop of blood for me. So I'll spill theirs.'

Quistus listened to the crowd. They were getting bored, wanting more. Nero continued along the line of crucifixions with his claws, playful as a cat.

'Quistus,' he called.

Quistus walked through the blood without lifting his toga. 'Yes, great Caesar.'

'You're no fool. You know I have a little something in mind for you.'

'I know, Caesar. Seneca told me.'

84

'Seneca does not have the greatness of mind to know what it is. Only I know.' Nero stopped by a young woman. 'Listen, this one can pray and scream at the same time. I could teach her to sing. Sing, little songbird, sing. The last song is the finest and most poignant.' At last she fell silent and he moved on. 'Queen Boadicea is alive in Britain. Do you believe it?'

'I doubt it. But if Brits believe it, that's what matters.'

'She's alive to them. Yes. Alive to her people like Christ is alive to these folk. A god on earth come to lead them. Like I am a god to Romans.' Nero pondered, then smiled between the lion's teeth. 'You know some of these people, don't you. This one? You know him. Not a Roman citizen like Paul, unfortunately for him.'

Quistus glanced down at the head by his knee, one of the upside-down ones. 'Yes, great Caesar, I've met this man.'

'You even recognize him on his head? Great friends, I suppose?'

'His name's Peter.'

'He's their leader. One of the murderers of Matrusus.'

'I proved who murdered Matrusus, great Caesar. It wasn't Peter.'

'Pope of the Church of Rome, they call him. It's *my* title. *I* am *Pontifex Maximus*, I am the great bridge between life and death, I have claws to prove it. What do you think, Quistus? Shall I be merciful to this usurper?'

Quistus shrugged. 'He's a man of no importance. Only a simple fisherman caught by mistake in Caesar's net. A merciful god might throw that one back.'

'I could. I could, if you asked me to.' Nero watched Quistus's face, then shrugged. 'No? Perhaps I will anyway, for my mercy is greater than you can comprehend.' He turned away with a bad-tempered scowl, kicking paw-prints into the dust, then muttered to the centurion, 'Save that one for next time.'

Quistus followed him without a change of expression. In the low glare of the sun Nero suddenly threw off the lionskin, its itchiness revolting him. The crowd rose in acclamation of the revealed Emperor. Servants scampered alongside, dressing him in a tunic of Tyrian purple and a purple cloak with gold stars.

The lowest tier of the arena was stone faced with pure white Pisaean marble. Past a movable barricade a flight of marble stairs curved to the imperial balcony, standing on great legs of cypress beneath flying banners and a flapping linen roof. Girls, young men and food were laid out, but Tigellinus had been banished to the level below, from where his pale face looked up to judge Nero's mood. Quistus saw no sign of Seneca, not even an empty seat. Even lovely Sporus and dirt-brown Vatinius had been banished to the lower balcony, forbidden to speak. Down there Stigmus stood on his own, out of his depth, motionless as a man listening for orders who hears only silence. Polyclitus, smooth-faced, elegant, ate grapes that were skinned for him. Nero commanded Quistus to sit close. 'You'll enjoy this.'

'More enjoyment would almost be too much,' Quistus said.

'I failed to tempt you with Peter. Perhaps with this one I shall succeed.' Nero raised his arm in a sign, whispering, 'She'll make a better dancer than Crispinilla, I wager. A princess.'

Quistus showed no emotion. He crossed his hands in his lap. He thought Nero meant Omba. The First Princess of Kefa had been captured at Locusta's together with Docilosa, and they and all the slaves would be executed in front of him.

'Try these olives,' Nero said. 'From a small island in the Ikarion Sea, I'm not revealing which one, grown by female priests who polish them between their thighs for the unique patina.'

'Thank you.' Quistus helped himself to a couple. One *Augustianus* guarded the stairs. He held a spear in one hand, but his other hand was away from his sword-hilt. A second soldier stood to Quistus's left, his sword hidden from this angle. Often they were secured by a leather thong so they could not be pulled by mischief. Quistus lounged forward, chewing olives, gazing over the railing.

A gate was flung open below him and the mob roared. Two gladiators marched into the arena, each holding one end of a long leather tether. As it snapped taut they strained forward, dragging something struggling from the cells beneath.

Quistus took a fresh handful of olives. 'What's the name of the island?'

'I told you,' Nero said, 'I'm not telling you.'

The struggling object was a woman – a white woman, not Omba. Red hair, not Docilosa, though her skin was as sunless white as Docilosa's. Very red hair indeed, and very long – as long and red as Boadicea's, by all accounts. Quistus, his mind in turmoil, maintained an air of calm as he nibbled an olive.

Had Nero somehow captured Queen Boadicea after all? But he'd said *princess*. Could this be one of the queen's raped daughters? Could there have been a third, younger than the others, who'd escaped, and now been captured? Everyone thought the youngsters were dead, but—

No. This woman's age was wrong. Fit, yes, but no adolescent. She was about thirty.

Nero watched him, smiling. Quistus yawned.

The princess, if princess she was, choked. Her hair covered her face as she struggled with the strangling tether. The gladiators wrapped the leather around their fists, hauling it tighter between them, jerking her forward. Another tether was knotted to her left ankle, so she dragged a heavy wooden cross behind her with each staggering step. Its weight pulled her back and she fell, the cross bumping after her through the dust as the gladiators dragged her neck.

'Landing her like a fish.' Nero watched Quistus carefully. 'A Christian fish. Their secret *graffitus*, their sign. They think I don't know.'

Somehow the princess got to her feet, gripping the tether in both hands, very tall, strong, taking the pressure off so she could breathe, hopping after the gladiators on one leg, the other pulled out behind her by the cross. Her muscles stood out. She was naked but for leather and bronze on her loins, a leather sash across one breast. For a moment the hair was swept from her face by her struggles.

Quistus spat an olive pit. 'I know her. Her name's Claudia.'

'Princess Claudia,' Nero corrected, applauding as she was toppled. 'King Caractacus's daughter. Remember him?'

Caractacus was great King Cymbeline's greatest son. He'd led the British resistance for years, finally betrayed and brought to Rome, paraded in irons together with his daughter Princess Gladis. King Caractacus's noble manner and dignified bearing persuaded Emperor Claudius to defy precedent – enemies of Rome were invariably executed the morning after the celebrations – and allowed the family to live discreetly in exile on the Viminalis. So Caractacus and Gladis (who'd adopted the Roman name Claudia after the Emperor who saved their lives) exchanged the white cliffs of Britain for the white cliffs of Rome – as the great buildings and whitewashed apartment blocks seemed to them at first – and acquired Roman ways and Latin. By the time Caractacus died in his bed Claudia, already with a reputation for a strong will and independent mind, had married the well-to-do Roman thinker Rufus Pudens. On marrying a Roman citizen, of course, she ceased to be royal, and became simply Claudia Rufina.

There was more to it than that.

Pudens was one of the first converts to Christianity. Though a gentle, phlegmatic man, to the point of meekness – which made such a good marriage with Claudia's fiery nature – in his youth he'd come briefly to the notice of the authorities in the Christian riots about fifteen years ago, then sank again from sight. Claudia was a passionate woman, by all accounts, who undertook no project lightly or wantonly, and she embraced Christianity with the same fervour she embraced Pudens, marrying the religion as well as the man. His house was a church for Peter's priests, but she was one of the leaders of the Pauline movement preferred by many women, the 'In-Dwellers' who didn't believe in priests but in Christ alive within their own hearts. They didn't believe Peter's priests should even call themselves Christians, it was Paul's word. It was Claudia who gave food, shelter and money to Paul the Damascene when, betrayed in the Temple by James the brother of Jesus for preaching Christianity to the Jews, Paul was arrested for blasphemy and brought to Rome for trial as a citizen. Claudia paid for Paul's lawyers and the case was still going on, though the defence was futile. All these difficult matters came to light in the Matrusus affair, when Christians were suspected of murdering the Emperor's chief *Specialis*, as Matrusus was at the time.

Numerous others were arrested in the reprisals: Pudens himself, Claudia, her brother Linus, Peter, Timothy, Faustinus the British merchant, his wife Pedilla, their daughter Volusia Faustina who'd run to Quistus for help, and many more (though not Paul, who was already in trouble enough). Most were crucified sooner or later, but by a trick of disguise Quistus freed Volusia and helped her escape. The others were not so lucky; some, like Peter, still awaited their fate. Pudens had been executed not with the axe like a gentleman, or by being allowed to commit suicide (which his religion forbade), but by being chucked down the Gemonian Stairs to the Tiber like a common criminal.

Claudia, ceasing to be a princess with her father's death, ceased to be a citizen with the death of Pudens, and Nero could do what he liked with her. Even make her a princess again; Cymbeline and even Caractacus, finally, had been his clients. The death of a barbarian princess always went down well with the mob.

Quistus watched quietly. Her hair, grown wild and unkempt during her imprisonment, made her look not Roman but completely, barbarianly British again, the stereotype so familiar from mass-market mosaics and slave markets. The people loved someone to hate without thinking.

Claudia struggled to her feet, clawing her fingers under the tether, gagging for air as it was jerked tighter. She fell again to her knees, strangling, her spine arching until her long red hair touched her bottom.

Nero glanced at Quistus. He made a gesture. *Release her.* The gladiators dropped the tethers.

Claudia stayed on her knees. She looked slowly around her, realizing she was free. A tense smile spread across her wide, freckled face. The gladiators drew their swords.

Claudia worked her fingers under the noose, lifting it over her head. She stood. She threw back her hair then, hands on hips, stared straight up at Nero. Her left breast, the one not covered by the sash, quivered with her breathing.

Nero made a sign.

A gladiator tossed a club at her feet, then turned and ran.

Quistus understood at once. Choices. Nero gave her choices. Always the most exquisite part of any dance choreographed by Nero's dark artistry; an excruciating moral torture as well as first-class entertainment.

Claudia ignored the weapon. She bent and loosed the rope from her ankle, then lifted the cross that had been attached to her and embraced it. She kissed the wood, holding out her arms provocatively along the crossbar. Quistus murmured, 'She's inviting you to nail her up. She wants to die with her friends.' A few voices from the mob called rude suggestions. Patchy laughter.

Nero rubbed his chin. A gladiator whacked a whip across her back, pulled the cross from her, dragged it away.

Claudia turned to the crucifixions. She must have known them well, every one, her friends, fellow Christians. She'd prayed with all of them at her house, no doubt. They heard her calling out the women's names in farewell.

The mob watched, silent, thrilled, amused. They loved a good tear-jerker. Someone threw a cap into the arena.

Nero ate a small bird stuffed with its egg. 'What should she do?'

Quistus said calmly, 'She should pick up the club and beat her friends to death, quickly, before you can send men to stop her.'

'You Stoics care nothing for human nature. Real people aren't logical.'

'Then she kills herself, quickly, if she can, before you kill her slowly. She saves both her friends and herself from a long, agonizing, degrading spectacle, and she even spoils your show. By losing on her own terms she wins, in a way.'

'Christianity forbids both murder – even merciful murder – and self-murder. Besides, Quistus, she looks like a fighter to me. What choice does she really have, when you think about it, but putting up a good show?'

'She can choose to leave the club where it is. She runs to her friends. She pulls them down one by one, doing her best to save them.'

'Pulling them bodily off the nails. Imagine their awful agony.' Nero, frowning with concentration, chose between a robin's egg and a sparrow's egg. 'Is her heart strong enough? Could she bear their screams?' He looked forward to it.

Quistus said, 'If she does, will you let them go free?'

Nero chose a falcon's egg.

'It wouldn't be much of a climax,' Quistus said.

'Indeed.'

'The people wouldn't put up with it.'

Nero licked the yolk from his fingers.

'Her third choice is simply to pray for them,' Quistus decided. 'So, great Caesar, whatever she does, it isn't much of a show.' He added, 'But you've thought of that.'

Nero, wiping his lips, raised one finger. At once a chain clanked in the arena. Knowing what was coming the lonely figure of Claudia dropped on her knees in front of the line of crosses. She clasped her hands in the *Ankh* of prayer just as Docilosa had, bowing her head at the feet of her friends.

'Ah, yes,' Nero said. 'The power of prayer. I did think of that.'

Behind her a trapdoor opened like a mouth. Dust plumed like exhaled breath into the evening wind.

'Behold the power of temptation.' Nero grinned. 'She'll do exactly what I want. She'll fight.'

Strange creatures, yellow-furred, dark-muzzled, ran from below with terrified yelps. Exotic creatures, heavy in front and small behind, the size of large dogs, they'd been driven up the steps by whips or something even more terrible down there, unseen.

'Hyenas?' Quistus knew them from Africa.

'Assassins.' Nero pointed to an egg. 'Cowardly like all assassins, but believe me, starving. I ordered the whole pack but only these four survived. You can't imagine what each one cost.' He basked in the people's *adulatio* for the fortune he'd lavished on their entertainment.

Quistus chose another olive. The soldier to his left turned slightly, showing his sword-hilt.

Three hyenas circled the crosses, throwing long shadows, drawn to the blood-stench. The fourth scouted the outside of the arena, sniffing, then curved back to the others.

'Watch them close in,' Nero advised. 'It's an art. Almost military.' He glanced sideways. 'Ten thousand sesterces says my princess fights. I've seen what these vile creatures do once they start on people. Revolting.'

Quistus shrugged. 'My ten thousand says she dies a Christian.' He was almost sure he was right about Christians, but on the other hand he'd met Claudia. She'd been brought up in the pagan court of King Caractacus for the first fifteen years of her life, sheltered in hideouts, caves and sacred groves by Druid sages and priests during the years of the rebellion, then joined her father willingly in chains, and not come to Christianity until she was perhaps twenty or twenty-one, in enlightened Rome. How deep did a royal childhood in a faraway, savage, Druid land run in the blood of a romanized, christianized, urbanized, civilized widow now thirty years old?

Nero licked his lips. 'Your Christian will be torn apart while she prays. Any of her children watching?' Nobody knew.

Quistus wondered what Nero was really up to. Was Claudia just an entertaining distraction before he got down to the real business . . . or was she the business?

He knew that the hyenas, somewhat like dogs, would avoid the unfamiliar shape of the kneeling woman, at least at first, but the smell of blood and raw flesh held no terrors for them. They circled the crosses, drawn inwards.

'She's childless,' Quistus murmured. 'As you must know, great Caesar.' Otherwise Nero would have been tormenting her children too.

'Really? Is she? I suppose Pudens was more interested in prayer than his pudendum.' Nero took a sip of honey wine, then pretended surprise. 'Look, the devils aren't going for my princess after all. Tut. What terrible torture not to be torn to shreds before your friends are. Now she'll have to watch them die.'

Quistus said, 'Christians don't believe it's death.'

The hyenas moved straight for the crosses now, hunger growing with proximity. One hyena ran suddenly along the line, yelping with fear. When nothing bad happened it returned, head extended, jaws open, sniffing the bloody ankles, the thick blood hanging in slow drops from the toenails. One of the crucified men shouted. The hyena fled, crouched, eyed him. Then it slunk to the cross next in the row, where a woman hung, probably his wife. The man cried out her name, Maia. The hyena licked Maia's toes, the soles of her feet, her heels. Maia, her ankles nailed immovably, seemed to find this completely unnerving. She moaned, and tried to kick the beast away. That did it; the crowd roared with laughter.

Nero leapt to his feet. 'A bonus for Lustrus! Ten thousand sesterces!' A crowd-gasp, a fortune, and applause for the Emperor. Nero lolled back. 'Not my money, Quistus, yours. She'll fight. I guarantee it.'

Claudia's prayer was in trouble. Her forehead almost touched the dust, her hands buried in her hair. She was weeping.

The hyena nipped Maia's foot and fell back, crouching warily. Then it leapt gape-mouthed, seizing her leg muscle. It swung by its jaws, back legs kicking off the ground, comic-looking. More laughter. The leg tore. Nero watched Quistus, not caring what was happening below, he'd seen it before. The screaming of the Christians rose terribly, mingling with the grunting snarls of the hyenas. Still Nero didn't take his eyes from Quistus, not even when the mob gave a great shout.

Claudia had stood up. 'If she picks up that club, I win,' Nero said.

She took the club in both hands, swinging it over her shoulder.

'That's my win!' Nero said. 'And I don't forgive debts.'

Quistus watched Claudia run at the hyenas, whacking at

them, missing, trying to chase them away from her companions. There was no hope. The hyenas curved round the far side, splitting up. She ran after a couple but the other pair latched on to the jerking, suffering figures behind her. She turned back, bare feet skidding in the dust. A hyena ran close by, snapping at her, long bloody mouth and black eyes turned back over its shoulder, leading her on, while the other three fed hungrily.

The soldier on Quistus's left moved away to get a better look.

Claudia's forearm pushed back her hair. Her eyes were as blue as Nero's. Instead of running, now she advanced half-hidden by the crosses, inching forward. She threw the club, bowling one of the hyenas off its feet. At once she pounced with her bare hands, holding it under her knee, its snapping jaws inches from her face, and broke its neck before grabbing the club again.

The crowd stood as one, thundering.

Three hyenas circled her, snarling through bared teeth.

Claudia feinted right but jumped left, sweeping the club high. She brought it down hard. Two, now.

Quistus turned to Nero. 'It seems a Christian can fight after all.'

'I'm a good judge of people.' Nero appreciated himself. 'An artist looks into people's souls. Watch.'

Quistus wondered what thoughts Nero might glimpse passing through his own heart, and hid them completely.

'You too are an artist,' Nero said. 'It's why I trust you.'

Claudia pretended weakness, hurt. She crouched on one leg, showing fear. The third hyena leapt at her. She stood tall and swung the club.

'Seneca recommends you highly,' Nero said. 'Fearless, ruthless, the most dangerous sort of man, he says, because you are a man who follows his heart.'

'Seneca says the trouble in Britain is serious.'

'If Boadicea is alive, then where is she? Why do I hear nothing but rumours? There's no flesh to them.' Nero yawned casually, his teeth yellow with egg yolk. 'Our armies there are stronger than ever. On Polyclitus's advice I sent re-inforcements from Germany, an extra two thousand legionaries, eight cohorts of auxiliaries, a thousand cavalry.' He pointed into the arena. 'What of my dance? Tell me. What next?'

Quistus had covered his surprise. The numbers Nero spoke of were tiny, not even enough to replace the men lost, and two years too late.

Claudia and the last hyena, snarling, circled. She threw dust. The trapdoor stood open between them. Claudia kept the crosses behind her, feinting left, then right. Sooner or later the hyena would make a break for the meat. Quistus said, 'She'll kill it.'

Claudia dodged close to the trapdoor, swung the club, missed. Her foot skidded over the edge. She staggered, arms windmilling, almost falling down the steps. A great animal roar came from down there.

'My dear, poor Quistus. You still don't see my genius. All this is planned by me. The hyena will live, I have ordained it so. That is why I am an incomparably greater artist than you.' Nero clapped once. The chain clanked, the trapdoor flew wide. A whip cracked somewhere below.

Claudia gave a cry, backing, gripping the club in both hands.

The lion was a male. It lunged up the steps with a deep belly-rumbling growl, its tawny shaggy mane rising as high as Claudia's shoulder as it leapt into the arena. Its tail swished as it prowled. The hyena yelped and ran away. The lion ignored the dirty creature, padding towards Claudia. Its eyes, black at first, dark-adjusted, yellowed in the sunlight. The shouts of the crowd neither frightened nor confused it; it heard these noises every feeding time. Claudia, forced back by the relentless approach, raised the club. She shouted. The lion knew all these tricks. It yawned with hunger.

She ran straight at the lion's head. She swung the club with all her strength. The lion broke stride, batting her with its paw. Claudia sprawled, spreadeagled in the dust.

'Bravo,' Nero said, watching Quistus.

She crawled, holding her side. She'd lost the club. Blood came through her fingers. The lion brushed past her.

The Christians wailed, a forlorn sound like the night-wind. Only their children were strangely silent, past understanding perhaps.

Claudia lunged, grabbing the lion's tail. The mob erupted in a thunder of excitement. Everyone craned to see. One unfortunate man was knocked over the railing into the arena and the hyena, wild with shock, tore him before he could get up.

The lion roared, twisting. Claudia was thrown sideways, tumbling, rolling over in the dust. She lay still. 'Get up!' Quistus cried.

'I'm a greater musician than Terpnus will ever be,' Nero said. 'I'm a greater poet than Lucan or Veiento. I'm wiser than Seneca. Foolish, ruthless, dangerous you might be – to yourself more than others, I fancy – but, Quistus, only I see you as the man you really are.'

Quistus stared into the arena at the fallen figure. Beyond Claudia he saw the lion, ignoring her, leap up clumsily on its back legs, resting its paws on a crossbar like a kitten with a toy, but its weight almost pushed the cross over. A lion always went for the head. The scream stopped.

'You're a sentimental case,' Nero said. 'A merely emotional man. Who is it, your latest doomed cause? Some slave-girl, I hear?'

He said without thinking, 'Docilosa.'

'You sleep with them, of course.' Nero was excited. 'That's why you do it, isn't it? Is she a Christian? The thrill of it, putting your life in danger, demeaning yourself for a moment of peace worth a couple of sesterces – she'd probably do it for free—'

Quistus said, 'I'm married to Marcia. Marcia is my wife.'

'Married to a dead woman,' Nero sneered. 'Even I don't do that.'

Quistus looked at his hands. 'What do you want of me, great Caesar?'

'I want Claudia to live as much as you do. She's in no danger. Look, a dozen gladiators within forty paces. Why are they there? To look after her. She's too valuable to be killed.'

'Why?'

Nero leant close. 'You'll go to Britain. She'll trust you.'

The lion fed, lifting its bloody face from time to time.

'You'll make sure Claudia gets to Britain,' Nero said. 'Make sure she lives, Quistus. Make sure she arrives in the right frame of mind. Make sure she trusts you completely. Be her friend. Look after her. Keep your eye on her twenty-four hours of the day and night. You know people in Britain, don't you?' Nero waited a moment. 'Christians, even.'

So Nero knew of Volusia Faustina, whom Quistus helped escape to the safety of Londinium. It no longer seemed so safe.

95

'Why do you ask this of me, great Caesar?' Quistus had to raise his voice over the crowd's cheering; the lion prowled to the next in line.

Nero looked bored. 'You remember Procurator Classicianus, the one – together with Polyclitus – who persuaded me to recall Governor Paulinus.'

'Classicianus, yes. An honourable man.' A procurator held a province's purse-strings, which made him more powerful, in some important ways, than his superior the governor.

'He's dead. Died in Londinium.'

Quistus said, 'My commiserations.'

'Natural causes, of all things.'

'The Brits must be devastated.'

Nero said moodily, 'Governor Turpilianus, who replaced Paulinus, has been replaced by Trebellius.'

Why? What had gone so wrong? Quistus looked at Britain from Nero's point of view. Whatever it was, it was starting to look like a major problem. 'Marcus Trebellius Maximus, the tax collector from Gaul?'

'A tax expert. Brilliant. Not exactly a military man.'

Quistus savoured the moment. 'And Boadicea reborn. Or not.'

Claudia's head moved weakly. One hand flexed. She was waking.

Nero said, 'Princess Claudia is Caractacus's daughter. To the British, royalty are gods. They're like me. The tribes will listen to her. Whatever she says.'

Quistus shook his head. 'Great Caesar, she wants you to die. She wants Christianity, not you. You don't have anything to offer her. Life? She'd rather die.'

'She'll take Christianity with her to Britain,' Nero said. 'Britain is worth a Christ.'

Quistus stared at her lying in the arena. Which ran stronger in her blood, Christianity or barbarity?

Claudia pushed with her feet, lifting herself on her hands. She stood, staggering, then limped towards the lion. She'd even forgotten the club that lay in the dust. 'Stop her.' Nero, still watching Quistus, moved the back of his hand. At once a gladiator, sheathing his sword, ran after the tottering figure of Claudia. She'd fight the lion bare-handed. He grabbed her elbow just in time. The last of the sun glinted on the gladiator's slit-eyed helmet and the oiled muscles of his chest. He pulled her back.

Claudia half-fell against him then turned easily into his body, rolling against him and away, his sword in her hand. He grabbed the empty sheath but the sword was already through his chest. She twisted on one foot, freeing the blade from the falling body, and ran.

Not towards the lion. Claudia came sprinting across the grit towards the smooth marble walls rising to Nero's stand. Dust drifted from her footprints. She ran through the curve of shadow into the sun again. Quistus turned to his left where the black-cloaked soldier already freed his sword-hilt of the leather restraining strap, drawing his sword right-handed, left hand rotating around the spear to the throwing position. No haste, no great surprise even – and no tension in his wrist. He wouldn't throw. The man on the right, beyond Nero, was performing the same drill. Nero hadn't bothered to move. Gladiators were running, shouting. Claudia sprinted from sight below the stand; no one could climb the smooth marble. She was trapped.

The front of the stand shook as she used her speed to jump against the wall, throwing herself back and upward against the legs of cypress, clambering. Nero tensed, afraid for the first time. Quistus turned to him.

'Interesting,' he said. 'The blood's made her feet sticky.'

They heard her climbing up. A bowl of grapes fell off a table with a sudden crash. Claudia came over the rail with amazing speed. Her sword was bronze, finger-blunt along the bloody blade; only the end was pointed. The spears of the *Augustiani* were instantly at her throat, their sword-tips at her heart. Quistus thought her eyes were completely wild, as sea-blue and crazy as Nero's.

'Life or death,' Nero said. 'Does she die here, or does she go to Britain?' He raised his voice. 'Life for her, Quistus? Or death?'

Quistus could smell Claudia's skin. He could smell other people's dried blood on her. The scent of her own fresh blood, still trickling from her side. Dust. Sweat. Could hear her panting breaths.

Nero whispered in his ear. 'Christians believe in peace, don't they? She can bring peace. You can make her under-stand. She can unite the British in peace, and I will consent to adopt their Jesus as my son. You've had enough of death, my friend.'

Nero held out his fist for the crowd's judgment, his thumb pointing neutrally to one side. The crowd's roar swelled, the chanting began. Death. Death. Death.

Quistus was silent.

'What do you want?' Nero shouted. 'Even I can't give you your wife back, your family, not even I!'

Claudia blinked. Her eyes moved from Nero and for the first time she seemed to recognize Quistus. Her breathing grew less laboured and the blunt sword, though still upraised, trembled a little in her hand. She did not realize that behind her, in the arena, a whole threadbare pride of lions had already been let loose to feed.

She watched through narrowed eyes, held back by spears and blades, as for a moment Quistus bent his head, speaking privately with the Beast. Did the deluded ex-senator think a man could negotiate with a monster? She watched Quistus's lips move, then fall still. He'd spoken only one small sentence.

The Beast nodded assent. His pouting, eggy, wine-dribbling lips widened in a smile, as if amused by a short, brilliant performance from another artist – although one who, of course, could never be his equal.

Nero turned to the crowd. He thrust out his fist for all to see his judgment, and turned his thumb down.

Ten

Unscheduled Departures

'You bastard,' she said. 'You utter stupid idiotic *bastard*.'
He stood quietly at the window which, extraordinarily, was made of glass. Rome was always a different place after dark, but as he peered through the greenish ripples he saw the city oozing and bulging and bending into endless new shapes before his eyes. The great public buildings of the hilltops

melted into whorls and streaks, the dimly lit streets mere tangled string in the valleys. Above the looping city wall the Tiber shimmered at first, vivid with the last smears of sunset, then lemon-coloured, grey, nearly gone, gone.

The public rooms of the Transitoria contained not one latrine, apparently. Quistus's need to relieve himself was so great he had an erection. He controlled himself stoically, staring at his reflection in the almost total darkness of the glass, the great torches that burned at each crossroads making a map of sparks across his face. His eyes moved, watching the face behind his own. This room was some sort of unused dining room, forgotten. Claudia, wisely, stayed in the corner where the guards had thrown her. After a while she'd sat up with her hands around her knees, staring at the back of his head. Just stared. They'd got off to a bad start.

You couldn't blame her for being angry. He knew she'd been certain, absolutely certain, when she saw the Emperor's thumb turn downwards for death, that she'd die. She'd even drawn her last breath, eyes raised to the sky, her Heaven, in terror, exaltation, joy.

But the spears and swords were instantly withdrawn. To most provincials, a thumbs-down sign meant death; to the Romans, it was life. Nero's downward-pointing thumb meant that Claudia would live.

There would be conditions.

At first Claudia couldn't believe she'd been spared. Then she shook. Later she cried, shivering. Behind her the arena had filled with shadow, then gloomy evening where the lions finishing their feed moved as dimly seen shapes; finally darkness. Then they'd thrown her in here, where Quistus was waiting. She was calmer now. She'd begun to think.

'Did you sell your soul to the Beast for me?' she whispered.

Her lips, which in the arena earlier had seemed full and generous, were a thin straight line. The same went for her eyebrows – a darker red than her hair – and her eyes were hard as bluestones, nasty and demanding. She was feeling stronger, he could tell. When the *Augustiani* threw her in he'd knelt to murmur reassurance, examining the wound in her side, but she'd slapped him away with a hiss, and swore. That was when he came here and stared from the window, seeing Rome and himself and Claudia Rufina – Princess Gladis –

99

reflected all at once, intermingled. He didn't like what he was seeing, or hearing.

'What did you think you were doing,' she said bitterly. 'Didn't you think?' She went on and on, she didn't stop.

He interrupted, 'Would you rather be dead?'

'You think you're so clever, you fuck,' she cursed him. 'You've done a deal with the devil and aren't you just the cat's whiskers. My arse.'

He'd forgotten her accent was so strong, lilting, Britishly distinctive. Rustic, but her command of Latin vernacular was precise.

He said without turning, 'Cat's whiskers?'

'A cat knows a drain's big enough to crawl along if its whiskers just touch the sides. That's why so many fucking stupid cats get stuck up drains.'

'I didn't do it just for you.'

Her eyebrows bunched. 'You were at my husband's house. Once. Maybe twice. He called you the madman.' She said irritably, 'What d'you mean, you didn't do it for me? Who else matters but me?'

He shrugged. 'Who?' she demanded. 'Well?'

If only she'd just shut up for a minute. How could he explain to this proud, self-centred woman about Docilosa and Omba? It had been full dark for an hour. He'd already exceeded the terms of his agreement with Locusta, not known for her sympathetic treatment of unwanted visitors, those that survived.

'What am I doing here? What did you promise Nero?' Claudia's voice rose, echoing in the bare room. 'What's he going to do with me?'

'You're in my care, Claudia. It's official.'

'What of the others?'

'There was nothing I could do.'

She pressed her hands to her eyes.

She said very quietly, 'Quistus, why am I alive? It's worse than death.'

They heard footsteps. Epaphrodites arrived together with an older man carrying a portable flap-topped desk, a scribe. 'Good, good, getting on fine I see. Just one or two formalities.' The *nomenclator* consulted a list. 'As always the ship of state floats on a sea of paper, eh? And wax.' The scribe, smiling toothily, drew a blood-red candle from within the desk and lit it from the lamp. He wrote carefully on a small piece of linen paper and handed it to Epaphrodites, who read at arm's length. 'Release form. Yes, all in order. Wax please, Phaedrus.' The candle dripped. Quistus pressed his seal-ring into the hot wax. 'In triplicate, please. There. And again. That's it.' Epaphrodites examined a new sheet that was handed to him. 'This is your agreement with Caesar – technically with Rome herself, of course.'

'What agreement?' Claudia said.

'Your seal please, here . . . and here. And the two copies.' Epaphrodites snapped his fingers for a slave girl carrying a large greasy cloak, a *sagum*. 'A cold night outside. It'll keep our princess warm.'

'And you don't want her attracting attention,' Quistus said.

Epaphrodites just smiled. He didn't know anything.

'It smells of stinking soldiers,' Claudia sulked. 'I won't wear it.'

'Seal here please . . . and here. Everything to be accounted for, even a cloak.' Epaphrodites kept his smile, witnessing. 'And now the horses.'

'Horses?'

'The pair at your house, sir, on the left side. You'll ride tonight to the New Port, where the trireme *Pharsia* awaits with flags flying to take you across the sea to Gaul. We strongly suggest you head for Massilia, near the mouth of the Rhodanus river. Remember it's winter; it can be cold inland. Hire a wagon. Your discretion – secrecy, even – is essential. You have the Emperor's complete trust. The exact route you choose from Massilia is up to you.'

'You mean we go whichever way we want?' Claudia stood. 'Where to? What's going on? Are you sending me into exile?'

'If you'd just listen,' Quistus said.

'Your destination is Britain,' Epaphrodites said. 'Severus Septimus Quistus will ensure your arrival without undue delay.' He held out a parchment to Quistus. 'This is the Emperor's protection. None may hinder you.'

'You're sending me back home?' Claudia struggled to understand. 'But this is my home now.'

Epaphrodites said politely, 'Rome may have seemed that way, Christian. You'll be killed if you stay.'

The little slave-girl put the cloak around Claudia's shoulders.

Epaphrodites led them to the entrance hall and bowed farewell. Two burly slaves accompanied them into the starry night, down the marble stairs, now lined with flaming braziers, to the plaza of Jupiter Tempus below. Claudia stumbled, weak with shock and hunger. The slaves lit lamps from the flames and fell in step before and behind. Even the Palatine was dangerous at night, but Quistus stopped before they reached the Victoriae crossroads.

A blazing torch above a fountain threw rippling shadows over the shop-fronts and apartment blocks. He took a lamp from one of the slaves, tipped them both generously, and sent them back. Carefully he watched them return uphill, seeing no other sign of life.

He put his finger to his lips and took Claudia's hand, leading her through dark alleyways where they could not be followed except by another person with a lamp. He blew out his own lamp and waited, but no light came after them to disturb the darkness. The wall behind them was damp; he felt along it to a back door and gave an irregular knock. It opened at once.

'We'd almost given up hope.' Omba pulled them inside, crinkling her nose at the newcomer. 'Who's *she*?'

'Princess Claudia, Princess Omba. Princess Omba, Princess Claudia.'

The two women frowned jealously at each other by candle-light. 'I'm First Princess of Kefa,' Omba said. 'It's the greatest country in the world. I'm only his slave because someone's got to look after him.' She checked the street was clear, shut the door and barred it, speaking all the time. 'Docey's been half out of her mind with terror, master.' After a quick glower at Claudia she led the way like a dark mountain along narrow corridors to the deserted *tepidarium*. The long warm pool, motionless, stretched like a mirror between the pillars. 'Locusta said we could stay on until the, uh, night shift starts.' She nodded at an old hooded woman near the furnace, warming her hands like brown claws. 'She gave Docey something to shut her up.'

The slave-girl lay asleep on a blanket. The glow around the furnace door lit her peaceful sleeping face, making her even more lovely. She twitched, dreaming, her eyes moving beneath her lids, which half-opened. 'She tried to run away.' Locusta shrugged. 'A little something to calm her down, that's all. Sweet dreams.' She patted the couch for Claudia to sit beside her. 'My dear, that we should meet again like this, when you've suffered so much. Shall I call you Claudia – or Gladis?'

Claudia, shivering, held out her hands to the stove. 'You're well informed as always, Locusta.'

'You look exhausted,' Locusta said. 'You're bleeding.' She lifted the cloak and hissed, then fetched smelly salves from a cupboard. Quistus excused himself and followed the Triton signs to the sea-god's latrines. There was no man's wall, obviously, in such an establishment, so he urinated in one of the row of twenty or so holes normally covered by women gossiping and having their nails done. He leant against the tiles and closed his eyes for a moment. Claudia was talking. Omba was talking. Locusta was talking, and then Claudia said 'Ow!' and he heard the first laughter.

He returned to Omba and Claudia, who bit her lip as Locusta rubbed herbs and oil into the cuts. 'A lion did this,' Locusta said. 'You spoke with Nero himself for her?'

Quistus nodded.

'Why? Are you mad? Are you making a habit of this? First Docilosa—'

'Claudia is his idea.'

They all resumed talking at once. He sat and leant back against a pillar with his eyes closed, weary.

They stared at him, suddenly silent.

Locusta started again. 'She'll be bruised in the morning. A rib may be broken. I'll strap her tight.' She looked expectantly at Quistus as her hands worked. 'So? He sent his regards? What? Do I have to fall on my knees and beg you for news?'

'How much longer can you give us here?' he asked.

'I open for night affairs in two hours. My staff arrive before that to make ready.' She glanced at Omba. 'Limbering up.'

Omba was interested. 'Which ones?'

By night Locusta's establishment was – as, indeed, it was by day – a palace of female pleasure, though for the deep sensual delight of morally mature ladies rather than the shallow exploitation of young girls. Locusta's virile young men, all called 'Staff', loved nothing better than being exploited, especially by rich older women close to writing their wills.

'Two hours! We'll be gone very soon.' Quistus turned decisively to Omba. 'Go at once to the Subura, to Sandalmaker Street, the house of Vitellius the *facilitator*. Give my name to the strong big-bellied men who won't let you in. One or another of Vitellius's illegitimate sons will escort you to the house of one or another of his mistresses. Remind the old thief of me, as he will pretend to have forgotten, and how much he owes me, including his life, and also remind him that I say he is a rogue, a murderer, an incestuous mother-lover and a sausage-stealer. When he has given up denying these truths tell him I require two strong horses and a four-wheeled *carpentum* at' – he hesitated; anyone really travelling to the New Port would take the Via Portuensis – 'at the Aurelian gate. The Via Aurelia, do you understand? And another, identical in every respect, at the Flaminian gate. Both within the hour.'

Omba repeated the message, nodded, and left.

Claudia asked plaintively, 'What happened to the trireme?'

'No insult to our most helpful Epaphrodites, but I prefer to make my own itinerary.'

Locusta washed her hands and brought wine. Quistus told Claudia everything Nero had said. Docilosa's eyes fluttered half-asleep while he spoke. He finished, '*Could* Boadicea really be alive?'

Claudia said, 'Why fucking not?' The pain made her mood even worse.

'In Gaul,' Locusta murmured, 'we still find followers of the Old Faith. It was brought from Britain by Druids. They believe the immortal soul flies from the body at the moment of death into a child, an innocent.'

'In other words, it's not just possible she's alive, it's inevitable.' Claudia winced as the bandage was tightened. 'The Brits just have to find Boadicea in a child's body. Ouch!'

Quistus made a pacifying gesture. 'Nero needs peace, not war. He's chosen you to change their beliefs with Christianity. Jesus told Christians to give Caesar the things which are Caesar's, didn't he?'

Claudia breathed out through her nose, then nodded. Quistus said, 'You remember Volusia Faustina?'

'I haven't seen daylight for six months. She must be dead.'

'No, she's safe. She's in Londinium. Never mind how. A flour-ishing Christian community there. Nero will no doubt encourage its prosperity under the leadership of yourself, a princess, and Volusia as . . . what do you call your chief priests?'

'Peter's bishops?' Claudia looked staggered. 'Us? You mean

us? *Women*? But bishops are men – Timothy says women can't possibly—'

'In return Nero will adopt Jesus as his own son.'

Claudia stared at him round-eyed.

'After all,' Quistus said, 'Nero's already a god. You can see how it would work, the way it always works. The Imperial Cult welcomes all gods to gather under its broad roof.'

'No, Quistus, you don't understand. Christianity's different.'

'Nero's already made one exception. He permits the Jews their one God, doesn't he? Perhaps he'll do the same for the Trinity, if you can give him a peaceful Britain in return.' He leant forward. 'The Brits will never follow a man who preaches peaceful co-existence with the Romans. For twenty years they've tasted Roman freedom and still call it slavery. But you're Caractacus's daughter, daughter of a rebel, a legend. The kings and chiefs will listen to what Princess Claudia says, so will the women, the slaves. They'll hang on your every word. You want to lead them to your "God", don't you? What have you got to lose?'

Claudia opened the furnace door, warming her hands. She sounded overwhelmed. 'I don't know. It's so – it's impossible. The responsibility . . . it's so huge. I could just run away.' She pressed hot hands to her cold cheeks.

'Not before I get you to Britain, I'm not next in the arena feeding the lions. Do we have a deal?'

'How can we possibly trust Nero?' She shook her head. 'He's *Nero*.'

Locusta said, 'Excuse me. Gossip's such a big part of how I make my living, you know how it is, a penny turned is a penny earned. I mean, you know how important men's wives talk while their backs and everything are rubbed?'

Quistus said, 'I can imagine.'

'We hear everything first. Pardon my ears but they say – they *say* – that Governor Trebellius has lost control of the army in Britain. They say it's mutiny, some flaming row between him and General Roscius of the Twentieth. Now – so they say – no one knows for sure where Trebellius is. Not even Nero. Certainly he's not in Londinium. Where? The savage north? The fearsome west?' She stopped, her eye gleaming naughtily under her hood. 'In Germany!'

'It's an interesting story but it's impossible,' Quistus said. 'A governor's not allowed to leave his province.'

'Nevertheless.'

'Are you sure?'

'Their wives say, *say*, everyone's playing politics. So perhaps you stand a chance of success, if the dice fall your way.' She whispered, 'Even a god doesn't live for ever.' A log crackled in the grate, sending up sparks and the bitter smell of treason.

Docilosa gave a whimper, dreaming. Her eyes snapped wide open, staring at the flames flaring up. She drew back, trembling. Locusta soothed her. 'It's all right, little one. It's just the medicine.'

Docilosa dragged her eyes from the fire. She seemed confused, afraid of Quistus. 'What's he going to do with me? He'll send me back, won't he? Will they torture me? Will they make me scream?'

Locusta looked reproachfully at Quistus.

'She's coming with me,' he said. 'Docilosa isn't just one person, one life. She's thirteen hundred and thirteen lives.'

Claudia looked interested, wondering how a brainless slave-girl could possibly contrive to make herself so important.

They turned as a door opened. A naked young man plodded past them, yawning, then sat on the poolside painting his toenails.

'Time to go.' Quistus lifted Docilosa to her feet but she swayed, almost falling. He hesitated, then carried her in his arms. Locusta beckoned Claudia and led them to the door. The street was quiet. Quistus bent to whisper his thanks to the old woman.

Locusta gripped his left wrist, hard, deliberately reopening the wound. 'All for Lyra?' she murmured savagely in his ear. 'Fool!'

He didn't reply. She watched them steal into the night, shaking her head.

'Stigmus. Stigmus?'

'Great Caesar.'

'Come closer. Let me see your eyes. I knew your father.'

Stigmus stared at the candlelight; he could see nothing behind the flame. Dry-voiced he said, 'You knew . . . knew my father?'

'He was my faithful servant. And faithful servant to my father.'

Stigmus felt his heart would burst. 'No one could be more faithful to you than I, great Caesar. No one.'

'You know your orders? You are quite clear?'

'Yes, great Caesar.'

'The trireme *Pharsia* sets sail from the New Port at dawn.'

'Yes, great Caesar.'

'Moored nearby you will find the trireme *Phalusia*. Follow them. Discreetly.'

Stigmus hesitated. 'And then—'

'You follow orders, Stigmus. Wait until you're sure. No mistakes.'

'Yes, great Caesar.'

Nero dismissed the *Specialis*. He thought for a while, scratching his name in the desk, then said, 'Tigellinus?'

The prefect of praetorians slipped from the shadows.

'Tigellinus, send a phalanx of praetorians with him. And two good men.'

'Good men, great Caesar? I don't understand—'

Nero said impatiently, 'Men who follow orders whatever they are. Stigmus's orders.'

The toughs found them almost at once, heavy shapes melting from the shadows of the Subura to block their way. 'Metellus, sir,' the leader said. 'Father sends his regards. The woman warned you might need some help.' He clenched fists like melons in front of his chest to show which woman he meant. 'Black like night?'

'Omba.'

'This here's my brother Stichus. Take the weight, Stichus.' Docilosa was transferred from Quistus on to Stichus's back, her arms hanging over his shoulders and her face against his ear, which made him smile; he had no teeth. 'This one's my brother Aemilius, sir, and this is Cotus by our other mother, who makes up for his ugliness with muscle. Some of these streets hereabouts aren't too safe in my opinion.'

'People like you around?' Claudia said sharply.

'You're all welcome, gentlemen,' Quistus said. 'The Flaminian, please, as quickly as you can.'

'This way, sir, if you don't mind. Smaller and nastier is safer in our case.' The brothers guided them in almost total darkness through a maze of stinking, cluttered alleyways,

107

steps up, steps down, then up again. After a while Metellus's hand found Quistus in the dark and his voice whispered, 'One of our mothers keeps a fruit stall, sir, and another's married to a baker, so my brother Luca's bringing supplies like Omba asked. She's back at your house to fetch a few necessaries, she's got two or three sisters to watch her back.' Metellus led them left and right; once there was the sound of a scuffle. 'Lucky the night-wagons were just coming into the city, sir. We got you a four-wheeler at the Aurelian, but sorry, we couldn't do identical. A two-wheeler at the Flaminian was the best we could manage at short notice. They're parked up with half a hundred others waiting to come in.'

'Good work, Metellus. Two wheels is faster, anyway.'

'Mules though. A quick sneeze and we could get you something better. Arabs, now,' he said longingly.

'Attract too much attention.'

Metellus sighed. They passed under a torch. He had a white streak in his hair, some fighting injury. He paused, pointing out a complicated intersection where carts and people milled around. Beyond them in the massive wall were the twin one-way tunnels of the Flaminian, both set to 'Enter' at this time of night, both jammed solid with muddy carts supplying the city. He whispered orders to Cotus and Aemilius. Stichus moved quickly despite his burden, weaving forward between the stalled carts, followed by Claudia and Quistus. A fight broke out behind them. The road was thick with mud, splashing them to the knees with ox-dung and worse. Metellus got ahead and clambered on the high pavement by the wall, holding Docilosa steady while Stichus scrambled up, then offered his hand to Claudia, who ignored him and got up herself. Quistus used the steps. The moment they ducked into the tunnel the noise behind them stopped and the fighters melted away.

Outside the city was almost as busy as inside. Whips cracked as impatient incoming drivers pushed and shoved and locked wheels in the dark, blaming each other for not moving faster. Others slept, letting the animals pull forward when they could. Quistus lost sight of Metellus then saw the white streak.

Metellus beckoned from a staging area between the rubbish tips and a cemetery. 'Proper senatorial job this,' he bragged when they arrived, showing off the stolen cart. 'Got couches in, look. Wooden sides, spoked wheels. Luxury.' He pointed, and by starlight and the glow of torches along the city walls Quistus made out the high roof, linen stretched tightly over shallow hoops. Metellus couldn't hide his pride: 'Natural daylight, see, when the sun's out you could read a book in there.' Quistus tested the wheels with his foot; the hubs felt solid enough. 'There's a bow and a few arrows come with it,' Metellus added, 'just in case. You never know on the roads these days.' Whatever wealthy stable the wagon was stolen from, the mules came from somewhere else: they were mangy, stringy-looking creatures, but Metellus had even stolen their hay-bags too. Quistus grabbed him and gave him a hug. 'Not a bad night's work, young man.' While they waited he took Metellus aside and talked quietly, asking advice and making plans.

'Here they come.' Omba had thought to load up the two strong horses she'd found at the villa with supplies. Metellus helped his shy sisters throw everything in the back of the wagon while Quistus harnessed the horses in place of the mules. They heard Claudia explore the inside of the *carpentum*, swearing. 'Cramped until you get it sorted,' Metellus apologized. He slammed the door. It swung open and a loaf of bread fell out. He tossed the loaf back in and shoved the door closed with his shoulder.

Quistus swung up into the seat. Metellus handed him the whip. He didn't know how to say goodbye. Quistus called down, 'Don't rob my house while I'm gone.'

'I'll keep an eye on it myself,' Metellus promised. 'Rob it, sir? Us? As if we would!'

Quistus cracked the whip. Metellus stared as darkness swallowed them, then turned to Stichus.

The hard leather horseshoes rumbled out of step over the wooden Sublician bridge then took up a lighter, rhythmic beat on the stones of the Via Portuensis. Stigmus glanced over his shoulder at Bellacus and Ursus who rode behind him, and behind them the handful of praetorian cavalry. It had taken longer than he'd hoped to get them together, and then there had been the long detour through the city to the Villa Marcia: the house was quiet and dark and the two horses that had been left outside were already gone. Quistus and the Christian princess were ahead of them.

Good, no waiting about.

From Rome to the New Port was eleven thousand paces, about three hours on a horse at a fast walk. No hurry; in fact there was some danger of overrunning them up in the dark. Stigmus reined back just in case, and let an extra quarter-hour or so pass before resuming his journey.

The road was modern, with a bottle-lantern or shrine lit by a fat candle to mark the position of bends. Each distant rise was topped by a small light to reveal the continuing line of the road through the darkness, and occasional inns and houses helped show the way; otherwise the road was as black as the fields and marshes it cut through.

The navigation fires of the New Port showed for miles across the salt-marshes. *Phalusia* was moored against the harbour wall. Stigmus introduced himself to the captain, who pointed to the shadowy outline of *Pharsia* with a shake of his head. 'No one's gone aboard.'

Stigmus said, 'But they left ahead of us.'

'Probably took the old road then. The Via Campana follows the river. It takes longer.'

That explanation made sense. Stigmus settled behind the bow where he could see *Pharsia*, keeping watch. Bellacus and Ursus wrapped themselves in their cloaks and slept. The troopers played knuckles, then slept too, except for the sentry detailed by Bellacus.

Stigmus woke. He made out the broad grey waters of the harbour dotted with anchored ships. Soon the lighthouse on the island between the breakwaters was doused as the sun rose over the hills. Small busy boats ferried cargo to the seagoing ships, or returned from the ships with cargo to be unloaded. *Pharsia* stayed where she was.

Stigmus scratched his stubbled chin.

Sailors washed down *Phalusia*'s decks. Each hour of the morning felt longer than the one before. Still no new arrivals on the quayside. 'Quistus,' Stigmus muttered between clenched teeth.

Was he coming at all?

Would he even travel by ship? No, he had too much to hide.

A horrible thought had occurred to Stigmus. Somehow Quistus had taken Docilosa with him and gone another way. If the murdering slave was not tried and found guilty, none of the slaves could be, and as they were assets of the Censorina's estate her will would be frozen for months at least.

'You all right, sir?' Bellacus asked. He'd brought bread and wine, hoping to hear scraps to barter with Ursus and the lads, or at least make himself look good.

'Order your men to saddle up, Bellacus.'

'Very good, sir.'

'Quickly, man!'

Quistus would use the murderer as his servant. She was pretty for a cunning murdering bitch. She'd make herself useful. He'd enjoy her company, she'd make sure of that. He'd take her as his lover. Stigmus imagined them.

But most important of all was the British princess. He felt his mouth go dry like ash.

He ran for his horse. 'Back to Rome. The bastard's gone by road.'

But by which road? All roads led from Rome; hundreds of them. The Via Aurelia, obviously, was *the* road for Gaul. Well maintained, following straight lines between the low hills, then running perfectly straight to the wide horizon as it reached the coastal plain.

The race back to Rome had taken little more than an hour at a hard canter, but now the horses were tired, stumbling on the harsh stones of the Aurelia. Stigmus, unused to horseback, was appallingly saddlesore. The sun swung low over the sea on their left, showing the road stretching into the distance like a piece of string pulled tight. Almost empty this late, and after the brief village of Baebiana completely deserted. No one would expect to reach the town of Caere before sunset.

'There!' Stigmus strained to see, but Bellacus had eagle eyes. 'It's a cart, sir.'

Quistus had at least two women with him, possibly three, if he'd kept his black-and-gold slave. (No doubt, Stigmus thought savagely, she was his concubine too – obviously he slept with her.) Yes, definitely they'd be in a cart, possibly even a long-distance *carpentum*. He slowed the troop to a walk, keeping out of sight of anyone who looked back; the Emperor's orders were very, very clear.

'You.' He nodded for a trooper to ride ahead alone. 'Keep it casual.'

Keeping the brow of a rise between them and the cart, only their heads showing, they watched the trooper close with the vehicle. He rode ahead of it for a short distance as though scouting in a general way, then turned back. 'It's a four-wheeled *carpentum*, sir.'

'That's them.' Stigmus tried not to show his relief.

'Just the two men driving, sir,' the trooper said.

'Two *men*?' Stigmus cursed and galloped his horse forward, catching up the lumbering vehicle, which was pulled by only a couple of stringy-looking mules. He reined in, staring across.

Two young men sat on the driving seat, one with a white streak in his hair. The other smiled toothlessly.

Eleven

At the Villa Ciminia

As always, Quistus preferred to do things his own way. It was safer.

The two-wheeled *carpentum* trundled onward as it had all night, and all the next day, all night again and now into the second day. By now, its wheels guided by deep ruts cut in the road, it was no more significant than any other slowly moving speck in the huge landscape of tiny brown fields, bare orchards, olive trees sack-wrapped against frost, bald vineyards. He looked over his shoulder until he got a crick in his neck, but no one followed them. There was no real reason why anyone should, only his own curiously suspicious nature – and the feeling that if *he* were the Emperor and he'd sent a self-exiled, possibly renegade, potentially Christian ex-senator to accompany three noisily arguing women to a far province on a throw-of-the-dice mission where the odds against success were surely astronomical – *he* would want to keep an eye on him, wouldn't he?

The Emperor had eyes everywhere, of course, every way-station, every *mansione*, every town, every municipal border. But those watchful eyes slept at night, while the *carpentum* kept up its steady trundle, and during the day they were easily blinded by friendly words and a few pence.

And with every mile that passed further from Rome, eyes were fewer, and news slower.

Quistus owned small country estates at Baebiana and on the Incitaria headland, both of them westward on the Via Aurelia, the first places anyone – anyone like Stigmus, for example – would look on the road to southern Gaul. But Quistus hadn't gone west on the Aurelia. From the Flaminian Gate, he'd headed north.

Only for a couple of miles though. At the Mulvian Bridge where the Flaminian turned east, he kept north along the Via Cassia. Instead of following the course of the Tiber winding upstream, the Cassian climbed a long north-leading ridge overlooking villages but passing through few of them. Way-stations were easily avoided using local lanes, *diverticuli*, or farm tracks. Few of the slaves clearing ditches and repairing stock-fences even looked up, and he was sure none would remember them. Most were like animals, hardly able to speak.

There were few streams on the ridge but Quistus paused to let the horses drink from culverts that drained the road, and once from a rippling aqueduct carrying water to Rome. Sometimes he walked on the footpath beside them with one hand on the harness, trying to keep awake, letting them eat from the nose-bags, singing softly so they would know and trust his voice.

Yawning, he swung back into the seat. The rear door banged again, and he sighed. Docilosa walked behind the vehicle with a face like thunder. 'I hate them,' she called, now fully recovered from whatever calming drug Locusta had given her. 'They're horrible.' She put her hands to her eyes and wept. 'It's horrid in there. There's no room. We can't make it homely and Omba makes me sit up all the time, but she's just a slave, it's not fair.'

She walked beside the *carpentum* for a way, glancing up at him for sympathy. 'Can I ride up there?' He nodded, making room, and she swung up next to him. 'Can I hold the reins?' She took hold of the tough leather in her slim white hands, looking entranced. 'How do I make them go faster?'

'Just slap the reins lightly along their backs.'

She slapped the reins and the horses pulled forward. He told her, 'Now back, easy, to slow them down again. Mostly they know what to do better than us.'

They trundled in silence for a while. Gaining self-confidence, she eyed him critically. 'You look tired. You do. You look awful. You look old.'

'I've been cat-napping.'

'You should put aloe vera on your eyes to soothe them but we haven't got any. It's all a mess in there and Claudia said I didn't pack away properly. She's always swearing, she's rude. Then Omba packed it all up but it's all fallen down again and Claudia blamed her. Now they're both blaming you because you won't stop.' She put her head on one side. 'When are we stopping?'

'At a safe place. At least, I think safe. Amanda Censorina had country estates around here, didn't she?'

'Oh, she had *hundreds*, we were dragged everywhere all summer. The sea for cooling breezes, the hills when it was really hot.' She frowned, thinking. 'You mean up at the Villa Ciminia?'

'The very place. The slaves there couldn't have a better reason for sheltering us and keeping their mouths shut about you, if they want to live.' He looked back along the road.

She dropped the reins, forgetting them, trembling. 'Do you think Stigmus will come after me?'

'That's his job. Plus he doesn't like you.'

'What if he catches us?'

'He'll take you back to Rome to be examined.'

After a while she said, 'You mean tortured with fire.'

'We both know you're a murderer, Docilosa. We all heard you confess. Don't play the innocent.'

'But that old woman was *horrid* to me. I told you, she—'

'It's still murder.'

Her eyes widened. 'You don't care about me at all! You just care about Narcissus and – and all the others—'

'Hardalio,' he supplied. 'Little Tempus. Yes, all those others. I do care about you, Docilosa, but you're guilty and they aren't.'

She sulked. 'So you're saving me just to save them. Thanks.'

'Many owners would have beaten you half to death by now for speaking as insolently as you do. I'd say you're getting a good deal, wouldn't you?' He sighed. 'Hardalio was – still is – in love with you. He risked his life trying to lie for you. But you don't care, do you?'

'He's such a pest.'

'Why do you hate everyone so much, Docilosa? You're so

114

angry and you think of yourself all the time. I don't think even Protia was your friend, really, was she?'

'Protia was a slut.' Docilosa's dark eyebrows drew together under her by now rather greasy blonde curls, which were uncurling, but she was still lovely enough to make any man draw a breath; even lovelier the dirtier and smellier she became. 'Protia was out for what she could get. That's why she stole that jewellery. It's obvious, isn't it?'

'I wonder why she didn't just clear out the whole box. She could have, any time, she had the key. But she took just the one piece. And then she drew attention to it being missing.'

'Stop it. Omba's been so horrid to me. Now you.' Docilosa sounded tearful. 'So's Claudia. I'm *not* lazy.'

Docilosa had a way of changing the subject from something she didn't want to talk about. He reminded her, 'To her own people Omba's no slave, she was a princess in a vast proud land.' He added, 'And I thought we were talking of Protia. You wouldn't be trying to distract me, would you?'

'Protia was just a slave!' Docilosa said. 'A slave born to a slave. Not me. I wasn't born owned, I was found. There's a difference. I could have been someone really important. I *should* have been.'

Quistus took back the reins; the horses were cantering, lathered, as if catching the girl's mood. He reined them in gently. 'Well, Docilosa? Who should you have been?'

But by way of an answer she just jumped down, and he heard the door slam as she rejoined the others.

The Villa Ciminia overlooked, down a gentle slope, a clear lake filling an ancient volcanic crater. It was late afternoon before the *carpentum*, turning aside up the little-used Via Ciminius, broached the top of the long uphill climb and picked up speed, trundling downhill between hazelnut trees towards the shallow pink roofs of the white lakeshore villa. It was almost dark before they arrived, but lamps burned in the windows and a bare-headed man wearing a brown robe hurried out. They were expected. 'I am Apollodorus.'

Claudia, Omba and Docilosa clambered stiffly from the *carpentum*. 'Welcome.' Apollodorus flicked his fingers, tutting for a boy to hide the vehicle in the yard, another to water the horses.

'Bad news travels quickly.' Quistus stretched his legs.

'We learned of our mistress's sad death yesterday afternoon. A traveller told my brother, who oversees the slave-gang on the Alsietina aqueduct.'

'We saw them, perhaps six or seven hundred souls.' So many that the hillside had itself seemed to move from all the muddy bodies toiling in mud.

'Indeed, sir. My mistress didn't detract from her obscene wealth by letting her property snore in slave-dormitories. My brother saw your vehicle from the bridge – the coincidence of such a luxurious conveyance on such a narrow road must be significant at such a time as this – and sent word of your coming.' He stared at Docilosa with mingled fascination and disgust. 'So this is the murdering creature who has done us such a great service, and yet may be the death of us all.'

'We need two days to rest,' Quistus said. 'Time enough for any alarm to pass us by, but not so long that this unlikely place is remembered.' He reached into his cloak, pulling out a parchment with a heavy wax seal. 'You are compelled to give us every assistance. No harm can come to you from this action.'

'I see the Emperor's protection does not mention the girl Docilosa.'

'Great harm will come to you from *me* if you say her name again,' Quistus said levelly. 'If a man called Stigmus comes here and asks about her, you never heard of her.'

'Who?'

'Exactly,' Quistus said.

Apollodorus gave a deep servile bow, tutted for Docilosa and the boys to carry whatever would be needed for tonight, and led them into the house.

Dinner would be served late. Rather than sleep for an hour Quistus kept himself awake with a swim in the icy waters of the *frigidarium*. He returned to his room where Omba, finding no male clothing in this house built for women, had borrowed one of Apollodorus's long Greek gowns for him, high-necked, Attic red, gold-trimmed, in the formal style the Censorina had insisted on for her staff. She dressed him in silence, an event which was not so much unusual as unheard of. 'Long two tiring days, Omba?' he teased.

She said grimly, 'One more like today and there may not be survivors.'

'That happy, eh?'

'Claudia swears like a trooper. It's not her fault, in prison she was separated from the other Christians, she expected to die for so long that it's made her brutal and callous, she gives no thought to the pain she gives others. As for Docilosa . . .' Omba took a deep breath then shook her head. 'She sulks. She cries. She has a temper.'

Quistus straightened his gown, a little tight around the shoulders. 'A real temper, or a calculating temper?'

'Calculating. She uses words to hurt. No scratching. She pinches.'

'Poor Omba.'

Omba oiled his hair, muttering, 'They both accuse me of taking up all the room.'

'I see.' He frowned seriously, his finger over his lips to hide his smile. 'We're going to be living close together for several weeks at least. It's essential that we learn to be friends.' He thought for a moment. 'You'll all dress for dinner.'

She said, 'Master, we've no clothes!' But her face lit up.

His smile showed. 'Amanda Censorina had wardrobes full, didn't she? I'll speak to Apollodorus.'

He met Claudia in the corridor. She was returning from the cold pool with her dirty cloak wrapped around her, her hair hanging in tails. She ignored him. As she passed he said, 'Omba's bringing clothes. We're having a dinner party.'

She turned. 'What? What the fuck for?'

'Everyone's invited,' he said pleasantly. 'While you're being dressed, Claudia, give some thought to which tongue you're going to use.'

'Tongue?'

'Your Roman Christian tongue or your British tongue.' He smiled helpfully. 'In other words, whether you're going to bring the manners of a Christian lady to the table, or those of a fucking barbarian.'

He felt her staring after him as he went downstairs. Her door slammed.

Apollodorus was waiting by the low dining table in the *triclinium*, tutting while boys arranged the couches and the candlesticks were lit. 'More,' Quistus ordered. 'More light.' He mentioned clothes and Apollodorus clapped at once, sending several little girls running; obviously the wardrobes were extensive. Quistus beckoned Apollodorus to follow him on to the balcony. The new moon rode above its own slim crescent, mirrored in the bowl of the lake. 'Your mistress came here often, Apollodorus?'

'At least twice a year, sir. This house is always kept open and ready.'

'She entertained here? It's such a remote spot.'

'Indeed, sir.'

'Mostly women guests, I expect.'

Apollodorus maintained a diplomatic silence.

'I expect they were pretty wild parties,' Quistus said.

'Not in that sense. Men were not invited, sir.'

Quistus put back his head. The night was clear and he counted the seven planets, finally even seeing Mercury where the sun had been. 'You're not a man, are you, Apollodorus?'

'Not for many years, thank you, sir.'

'Do you miss it?'

'Who would, sir? I've never known anyone, and I never will.'

'You see, I've learned quite a lot about the way your mistress's mind worked.'

'They were indeed wild parties, sir.'

'Ladies didn't always behave like ladies, did they?'

'Well, sir,' Apollodorus said, 'that depends on your point of view of how ladies behave.' He raised one eyebrow.

'So, scandalous behaviour. Any scandals?'

Apollodorus said diplomatically, 'No sir. None that saw the light of day.' He lowered his voice. 'About Narcissus, sir, and the others. Are they well treated?'

'They're as happy as anyone under sentence of death can be. They've been treated well enough so far.'

'And us?'

'You'll be taken to Rome in due course, I expect.'

'Surely the Emperor will have mercy? He knows we're innocent.'

Quistus shrugged. 'He enjoys a show, and executions are good theatre. But while I have Docilosa with me your cause is not hopeless.'

'Then I wish you well in your journey, sir.' They heard footsteps on the stairs. Apollodorus turned to commence his duties, but Quistus called him back.

118

'I suppose your mistress wore her finest wigs and jewellery for her parties?'

'Indeed, sir. The girls attending her were highly trained at turning old wine into new, if you'll forgive the expression.'

'Especially Docilosa and Protia. Was Protia a good girl?'

'Yes sir, she excelled in debauchery and—'

'Not what I meant. Was she good in the sense of honest, truthful?'

'No girl was ever more honest and truthful than Protia, until she was given a cup of wine.'

'Did you ever see your mistress wear a brooch in the shape of a bird?'

Apollodorus shook his head at once. 'No.'

'Not something called the Phoenix? An Indian bird. Perhaps from even farther. The Spice Islands, the Molukus?'

'Never, sir.'

'A bird that lays no eggs, reborn in fire. It's a legend from that part of the world.'

'No sir, I'd remember.'

'Thank you, Apollodorus. We'll eat now.'

A note on the triangle signalled that dinner was ready.

Quistus congratulated himself that the meal – almost a party, really – was a great success. Naturally none of his guests resisted the chance to dress up, though Claudia wore only a plain white gown from the Censorina's 'respectable' wardrobe, but allowed her gleaming new-washed hair to be kindled like flame by Docilosa's skill. Omba had found a skirt made of thick tongues of black leather, a Roman corset in Tyrian purple – Nero's prerogative, women were fined for wearing the colour – and a glossy cloak of gold. Candlelight glinted on her shaved, polished, gold-tattooed skull; no work for Docilosa there.

Last of all Docilosa stood on the stairs, very slim and quite tall, looking both proud and shy at the same time. She was dressed in a long gown of cinnabar red, her own choice. She'd refused to let Omba dress her, so the gown was a hand's-width too lengthy, wrinkled slightly below the knee. Her blonde hair sparkled where she'd expertly woven semi-precious stones into her curls.

'You all look wonderful,' Quistus said. 'We'll eat together as equals and friends, as we will for the rest of our journey.' He held out his arm and they reclined with him at table to be served, except Claudia, who remained primly sitting up.

119

She bowed her head as the food was brought, clasping her hands. '*Benedictus.*'

Quistus noticed that neither Apollodorus nor the serving-girls reacted to the blasphemy; the household gods had been insulted, not a single mouthful sacrificed to them, and instead the Christian deity had been thanked in their place for the meal. Quistus nodded for Docilosa to be given wine and added water to it himself, a very little. 'Was your mistress a practising Christian, Docilosa?'

'Why ask me?' She drank. 'You already know she was.'

He nodded and let the conversation pick up speed at its own pace. Mostly it concerned dresses and hair. Omba still pretended to be offended by Docilosa's refusal to allow herself to be dressed. 'Girl's a prude,' she grinned, flicking chick-peas across the table.

'Not, not,' Docilosa said.

'Yes, yes.'

'Docilosa's quite right to be modest about her body,' Claudia said. 'We females are taught we must wear veils to speak in worship. But when the End comes and Jesus returns to earth in the flesh, there will be no more female or male, and men will be one with women.'

'I don't know whether to look forward to that or not,' Omba complained. 'What, no more men?'

'Yes, and no more rape, or brutality, or violence. Heaven will be on earth.' Claudia nibbled quietly on tuna, sliced egg, olives. Quistus watched her thoughtfully. Her sudden devout manner at table was a complete change from her earlier tough, assertive, foulmouthed personality. Merely by washing off the dirt of the cells and arena and donning a clean gown, she'd reverted to the prissy high-class Roman Christian lady her husband Pudens would have recognized. Quistus congratulated himself on the success of his warning before dinner.

'I could do with a man,' Omba said. 'Any kids, Claudia?'

'No.' Claudia frowned. 'Pudens and I were not blessed.'

'Want any?'

'No. Not in Rome.' Claudia finished her cup. Quistus nodded for it to be refilled.

Omba leered at Docilosa. 'What about you? You going to play little miss virgin all your life?'

Docilosa looked down. She shook her head. 'I've never been in love.' She was hiding her eyes; she must be looking at Quistus. Claudia and Omba swapped glances. Omba gave a bellow of laughter.

Claudia noticed her full cup. She drank. 'You know, Amanda Censorina never worshipped at my husband's house? She never joined our discussions in Paul's group. She would have been welcome.'

Omba helped herself to a plate of grilled sausages, then saw another platter. 'Dormice!' She poured generous helpings of honey sauce.

Docilosa drained her cup. Quistus refilled it with his own hand. 'Thank you, sir,' she whispered. 'You honour me.'

'Claudia, you must try these. Whoops.' Omba spoke with a full mouth. Docilosa laughed. Her eyes sparkled. Omba dribbled sauce down her chin. Claudia reached across and wiped it away. Quistus nodded and the little serving-girl made sure everyone's cup was full.

He said cheerfully, 'Protia called her mistress *Sanctus*. Why was that?'

'Saint,' Claudia said. 'Maybe she was. Was she?' Serving-girls brought the main course, a pike freshly caught from the lake, a spiny silver perch in its toothy mouth, and in the perch's mouth, a minnow.

'No,' Quistus said, 'not a saint.'

'Amanda Censorina was a saint of the other sort,' Docilosa said loudly. 'She was from the black side. She was a saint of Hell. She was a devil.'

'Docilosa, that's a terrible thing to say!' Claudia sounded shocked.

'It's true.' Docilosa drank. 'She worshipped the dark god. She worshipped Satan. Like Nero. Worse.'

Quistus said quickly, 'And Protia?'

'Give Protia a couple of cups of wine and she didn't know or care what she worshipped, God, the Devil, or the private parts of a wicked old woman.'

Omba ate a sow's bladder with dates. She belched.

Claudia stared at her cup seriously. 'The Devil does exist. My cup's empty.'

'Quick, fill it up!' Omba lay back. 'Oh I'm so full. Look at my belly. I'm huge.'

'There's a place round the corner.' Claudia staggered to her feet. 'Show you.'

Docilosa gazed at her cup, realizing it was full. She tapped her finger against her nose. 'I know what to do about this,' she said, and drained it. She rested her head against Quistus's shoulder. 'Aren't they enjoying themselves?' They heard Omba and Claudia throwing up in the *vomitarium*. 'They're not so bad you know, even in the *carpentum*, they're quite fun when they're happy,' she told him very seriously, looking him in the eye. 'Your head's spinning round.'

'That's your head,' Quistus said, although it felt as though his own was spinning too. 'Listen, you know those paintings the old woman had on her bedroom wall?'

'The gods.' Docilosa swallowed. 'Going be sick.'

'Watching her in bed. The gods watching everything that happened in her bed, her big bed. She was insulting them. She didn't like any gods, did she? Everything she did in public, temples, gifts, it was all hypocrisy. All a lie. The real Amanda Censorina was only ever seen in private—'

Docilosa clutched her stomach, lurching to her feet. Quistus called after her, 'There was only one woman painted on that wall among the gods. Amanda Censorina wearing a black cloak and a ruby necklace, with a cherub at her knee. That was how she dressed to worship Satan, wasn't it?'

Docilosa turned. 'She worshipped herself! Her own black heart.' She clapped her hands to her mouth and pushed past Claudia and Omba who were coming back.

'Best meal I've had since the harvest feast at Kefa,' Omba said. 'What's for seconds? Let's start again. Look, boned chicken stuffed with goose eggs. Garlic snails!'

Much later Docilosa returned. Her cup had been refilled. She gave Quistus a meek, watchful look and took only one sip.

'That's enough serious talk for one evening,' Quistus said. 'Let's enjoy ourselves. Who can sing?'

Omba drained the wine flagon. 'Me!'

'*Benedictus*,' Claudia said with great concentration, '*benedicata*,' and fell off her chair.

Quistus woke late. He lay under a linen sheet on the single bed in his room at the top of the Villa Ciminia. While he slept the shutters had been quietly opened to show the view of the lake, grey behind veils of dawn rain. His clothes were already neatly laid over the leather seat of a chair. Omba never did this without deliberately knocking something over to wake him, or booming news about the weather, or asking him what he wanted for breakfast. He looked round for her, one hand reaching down to grip the sword Apollodorus had given him, hidden under the bed.

'She's still asleep. Sleeping it off.' The slim figure of Docilosa stood in the shadows, her cloak dark with wet over the shoulders, sand clinging to her sandals, raindrops in her hair. She must have been walking alone along the lake shore while everyone slept, then come quietly up here. He had the feeling she'd been standing like this for quite some time, watching him sleep. Of course; her life, literally, hung by a thread from his goodwill.

'I wanted to put out your clothes for you, otherwise no one would have.' Docilosa gave him the meek, watchful look he'd learned to recognize, then turned and left the room.

Twelve

The Road to the Mountains

Farm tracks led around the side of the volcano, so many, and with so many twists and turns, that Apollodorus rode as their guide for the first three hours of their journey. 'Farewell, my friends,' he called after them from the junction with the wide Cassian beyond the spa village, Aquae Passeris. The *carpentum* was pulled by two fresh plough-horses from the estate, slow but strong, while the other pair walked tethered behind the vehicle with nosebags and a bucket of water to drink. By changing round every couple of hours they should be able to keep going all day, and even part of the night as the quarter-moon grew.

Quistus called over his shoulder, 'You never saw us!'

Apollodorus shut his eyes tight. The Villa Ciminia was

123

lighter by a hunting-spear as well as the sword. When Quistus next looked round, he was gone.

The day settled into the usual routine of days, one after the other, each little different from the one before; soon they could hardly remember any other life before travelling. Each of them drove for an hour then passed their time off walking beside the grumbling, thumping wheels, or foraging for food, or riding inside trying to sleep despite the jolting. The *carpentum* had no suspension, and rocked fore and aft with the motion of the horses, but the couches were surprisingly soft and comfortable once Omba covered them with extra cushions from the Villa Ciminia. The outside of the vehicle was hung with sacks of nuts and beans, plucked chickens that would keep fresh for a week if the cold dry weather held, and unplucked Ciminius pheasants strung by their necks from the door, which would keep good even longer.

The volcanic hills fell behind them as the horses plodded deeper into Tuscia, hauling up the long slope past Clusium to Arretium. Here the road turned gently downhill along the valley of the Arnus river. The hilltops wore slushy grey caps of snow, and Omba wore two cloaks and fur boots. 'I wish it was summer.' She fell in step with Quistus beside the slowly turning wheel, letting the spokes rattle the stick she held.

'Too many people in summer,' he said. These huge graded roads, built with bridges and embankments at such enormous cost to join the major towns and regions of the Empire, were almost empty. Most journeys were local and the countryside was crisscrossed with lanes, often busy; main roads were for the hectic long-distance transport of armies and imperial messengers, not travellers. In summer rich families used them to reach their country estates, but way-stations were for official use only. Inns were little used, dirty and run by thugs, and robbery was called tax.

'I've lost weight,' Omba told him proudly. 'I think it's turned to muscle. Even my feet don't hurt any more.'

The road angled left. Docilosa drove expertly now, geeing the horses on the shallow hills, letting them rest on the way down. Through the hooked-open door Quistus saw Claudia reclining with her nose buried in a book, one of her little Christian notebooks, probably a gospel by some apostle or other. Jesus had been virtually unknown in his lifetime apparently, but suddenly these eyewitness accounts were popping up everywhere in little notebooks that could be easily concealed. He often saw Claudia praying and was glad she took her mission so seriously.

That evening they stopped off the road as usual, a little before sunset, to collect firewood and water by twilight. Omba usually cooked a chicken on a greenwood spit but they'd finished the last the night before. Quistus returned with firewood to find her pulling the feathers from a pheasant – the meat was gamey enough by now and plucked easily. He added dried beans, water, garlic and pepper to a pot. 'Where's the others?'

'Claudia's found a pool.' Omba nodded where the stream flowed round some bushes. 'Says Christianity's next to cleanliness.'

Quistus stirred the beans. 'She's practising what she's going to tell the Brits.'

'Is it really possible to convert a whole people?' Omba reached beneath her furs for her thigh-knife, gutting the naked bird with one sweep of her fist.

'Gaul was converted to the Imperial Cult,' Quistus pointed out. 'They swear to sacrifice to the new gods before the old gods, that's all. Some of the tribes cling to the old ways, but mostly their leaders just want to be fashionable.'

'She says I'm a heathen. I think she's trying to convert me.'

'Yes, I've heard her. Not a hope, eh, Omba?'

'She just wants you to hear how big a Christian she is.'

'I know.'

Omba skewered the pheasant on the spit, balancing it on crossed sticks over the fire. 'She's not getting me in that freezing water,' she said. 'Even if I do smell ripe.'

Docilosa came back shivering, wrapped in thick layers of cloak wet to the knee; she hadn't stripped to wash, only splashed water over her face, which glowed. 'That looks good.' She glanced at him, letting him see her shiver.

'Sit close to the fire if you're cold,' Quistus said, but she shook her head. He said gently, 'You're afraid of fire, aren't you?'

'We're going to need a second bird,' Omba decided. 'Pull one down, Docey, I'll show you how to pluck it without tearing the skin.'

Docilosa fetched the bird and watched Omba's expert fingers.

'Aren't you,' Quistus said forcefully. He was used to Docilosa forgetting questions she didn't like.

She gave a little nervous giggle. 'I know, I'm silly.' She tried to avoid an answer. 'I don't know why I—' She shrugged. 'I just don't know.' The firelight gleamed wetly in her eyes. She could deliberately make herself tearful. He'd seen that in the Censorina's bedroom, when she'd wept for Stigmus's sympathy.

He tasted the beans, added a pinch of celeriac, then turned back to her patiently. 'Yes, you do know. Tell me.'

Docilosa said, 'I saw a girl once. One of the slave-girls, in the kitchen. She leant too close to the flames. She had lovely long hair. Her hair caught fire.'

'That's awful!' Omba said. 'Was she all right?'

Docilosa shook her head. 'I still remember the smell. The smell of burning hair. And her pretty face.'

Omba moved the pheasant a little further from the fire; the skin was crisping too fast, dripping little oily splashes of fire. 'Poor Docey,' she said. 'I suppose you were young. It must have made a big impression.'

'It's my first memory.'

'Poor thing!'

Quistus listened without saying a word. The women often talked like this among themselves, as openly and emotionally as children, about secret things men would never talk about, feelings they would never admit to. Docilosa turned to him. 'What's your most powerful memory, sir?'

'What?' He jerked out of his daydream. 'Me?'

'I just asked what your strongest memory was, sir, with respect.'

'Oh, I don't remember. You wouldn't want to know.'

Docilosa laughed, 'But you must remember—'

He stood. 'No, I don't.'

'Surely you—' She looked eager, the firelight flashing in her eyes, trying to see what he was really like.

Quistus got up and walked away, still shaking his head, until the bushes hid him. Just getting away from her.

Docilosa whispered, 'What did I say that was so wrong, Omba?'

'It's not your fault, Docey.' Omba opened the second bird with a quick slash, picking out the best bits to flavour the beans. 'Men. They're like children. Moody. Sometimes they just won't be talked to.' She looked at Docilosa sympathetically; she'd grown to like the girl a lot, because best of all she was a good listener. 'I'll tell you about *my* most powerful memory, eh? I'll never forget it. The first tickle, it was. The first ant. Just the one at first, the scout, climbing the rope to my ankle where I was staked out over the anthill. I could see this ant, right, long as my finger? Then I could feel it tickling from side to side on my leg, up my body, following the scent of honey. I arched my back, I twisted, I shook, but I couldn't shake it off. It went tickling up my neck, my chin, straight to my wide-open mouth.' She added, 'Which due to the thorn through my lips I couldn't shut.' She finished, 'And then it bit my tongue. And thousands of others came . . . came marching . . .'

Quistus heard Omba talking but not what she said. He stood among the trees. He was shaking but he couldn't put his feelings into words. He'd seen that flash of fire in Docilosa's eyes, her moment of realization – in that flash he'd seen himself exposed in her thoughts. She thought he was weak. 'You're the only man in Rome who isn't afraid,' she'd said once. Now she knew the truth. He was more afraid than any other man in Rome. He was afraid of himself; what he'd done. What he might do.

'Are you all right?'

He stared, blinking.

Claudia said, 'Quistus? It's just that you were looking at me in the most odd way.' She'd been swimming in the cold waters. She stood on the pool's grassy edge, wearing a pale shift, barefoot, her hair wrapped in a towel.

'Was I? It's nothing.'

'Wait a minute.' She called him back. 'Now I've got you alone for once, I want to say something important.' She sat on a rock. 'I need to apologize, actually. I've never thanked you for all you've done.'

'Don't. It's fate, that's all. Don't thank me.'

'But I need to thank you.'

'Oh, no, it's nothing.' He still sounded shaken. 'I'm doing this for Nero. For Rome.'

'Both you and I know that's not quite true. You don't have a family, do you?' Claudia waited, interested. She wanted to know all about him, all the private personal details. They all did. Loved them.

'No. I don't. Not now.'

'That explains it!' She looked pleased with herself. 'So, obviously you're doing all this for the girl. You're in love with her, aren't you?'

'Docilosa?' He sounded shocked. 'No, that's not true.'

Claudia sighed. Docilosa was at least twenty years younger than him but that wasn't unusual between a master and slave in decadent Rome. 'You know she isn't really a Christian,' Claudia said.

'She's a survivor.'

'Anyway, I owe you an apology for my own most un-Christian behaviour. I've been unforgivably boorish and, well, not at all myself.'

He was seeing her Roman side, he knew. If there was anything Brit – anything Gladis – about Claudia, it was completely gone, except her red hair, of course. And even that was coiled into a bun in the popular motherly Roman style called a *tutulus*.

'Apology accepted,' he said.

'One more thing.' He watched her suspiciously. 'The deal you did with the Emperor,' she continued sweetly. 'What was it exactly?'

'To escort you to Britain. To introduce you to well-connected people. To come home.'

'But, my dear Quistus, my point is: why you?'

'He believes I'm a Christian sympathizer.'

'You're not. Not once have you joined with me in prayer or giving thanks. You haven't even bothered to make a sham, as Docilosa does.'

He shrugged. 'Nero trusts me, that's all.'

'Trusts you to do what? The right thing? The Roman thing? And what would that be?'

'Loyalty to Rome above all else.'

'I know. You struck a deal with him. I watched your lips. I want to know what you said, Quistus. What could you possibly have asked for that would amuse and captivate the monster so completely?' She leant forward, sharp-eyed. 'What was your price?'

'My price is "Whatever the Emperor least wishes to give."'

'That's all?'

He nodded.

She said, 'Docilosa? To let Docilosa live? To give her to you?'

128

'Well, he certainly wouldn't wish to allow that, don't you think? He'd have to let all the other slaves live, and free them, and pay them as free people according to the terms of the will, and lose the imperial treasury a fortune. I'd say that's pretty high on any least-wish-to-give list.'

But she'd hardly heard. 'You'd have me take Christianity to Britain just for . . . your lust, lust for that silly girl?' She shook her head. 'There's more to it. There must be.'

'You don't care about slaves much, do you?'

'I believe you also made a bet with the Beast.'

'Ten thousand sesterces you'd die a Christian, in the arena. You didn't. I lost.'

'You wouldn't be asking for forgiveness of the debt . . . ten thousand's small change to you . . .' He sensed her mind racing.

'The truth is, Claudia, I don't know what reward I'll ask, yet. Neither does Nero. That's why it fascinates him. The open-endedness of it. The Emperor is the all-giving god of Rome. He's married to Rome. He gives Rome her water, her bread, her shows. He can't even imagine what he would *not* want to give. That's what amuses him. And that's why he agreed.'

She thought about it. 'There's another explanation, Quistus. He never expects you to return to claim your reward. He expects you to be dead.'

'That crossed my mind. But it would mean your mission to Britain had failed. Why should he want that? Why go to all this trouble in the first place?'

Claudia thought for a while. By now she was little more than a shadow in the dark, but there was no mistaking the excitement in her voice when she said: 'The one thing he did not expect was Docilosa!'

'I know. Without her we would have gone by sea aboard the *Pharsia*, and made our way up the Rhodanus towards northern Gaul.'

'And there's only one road inland, at least as far as the city of Lugdunum.' Her lilting British tongue softened the word to "Lyon". 'We'd be so easy to follow.'

'But because of Docilosa,' Quistus said, 'everything's different.'

Claudia sniffed. 'I do believe I smell roasting pheasant. The others will be wondering where we've got to.' She stood, then

129

touched his elbow in warning. 'Let's not talk about these secret matters in front of them.'

'I trust Omba with my life.'

'Of course she's lovely and impressive, and Docilosa is a terribly sweet girl, too, but I think it's safer to keep important decisions to ourselves, don't you? After all, they're just slaves.' She towelled her hair. 'There, I feel so much better.'

He followed her between the trees to the firelight. 'Where have you two been?' Docilosa asked. 'Made an In-Dweller of him yet?' Claudia gave her an irritated mistressy look.

'Tuck in.' Omba, firelit, sweating, slid joints of smoking meat on to a platter and they helped themselves. She poured the bean stew into bowls. 'When do we move on?'

'As soon as we've eaten.' Quistus pointed his spoon. 'Let's make the best of the moonlight, after moon-set it'll be too dark to keep going. We'll stop for a couple of hours' rest before dawn.'

Claudia nodded at the tiny sprinkling of lights in the moonlit distance. 'A close village, or far town?'

'Florentia. A big town. From there the Via Quinctia cuts west to the coast, joining up with the Aurelian again, and the mouth of the Rhodanus eventually.'

'I don't want to go that way, it's too dangerous!' Docilosa said. Quistus watched Claudia. He was sure she hid a quick smile.

'Surely,' Claudia said, as though the thought had just occurred to her, 'there's a better way. Don't forget, my father and I travelled to Rome through Gaul. I know parts of it quite well.'

'The Rhodanus is the key to the whole province,' Quistus told Docilosa. 'The valley runs north from the sea, deep into the mountains.'

'But Nero's boat was going to take us there.' She stopped eating, worried. 'Stigmus might be waiting for me.'

'You're not *that* special,' Quistus said. 'He's gone home by now. He'd be mad to travel all that way just on the chance of picking you up, he's a busy man. He's got better things to do than spread all his nets to catch one tiny fish.'

'But there's another road, isn't there?' Claudia was attentive, not eating the pheasant leg she held to her mouth. 'A mountain road that runs north from Florentia, going another way to join the Rhodanus upstream at Lugdunum?'

130

'Yes, and no one will expect us to go that way – not that I expect anyone to be watching out for us. But just to keep Docilosa happy we'll take it. And I think you have an opinion, too, Claudia?'

'Oh, whichever way you like, it's nothing to me.' Claudia shrugged, nipping the flesh daintily between her teeth, wiping her lips. 'Oh! I forgot to say grace!' She took a deep breath.

Omba and Quistus exchanged a look. They had both rather liked Claudia the barbarian.

Quistus nodded at the twinkling lights. 'We'll cut north round the town and join the road through the Apennines. It'll be cold. But beyond that's the Ligurian plain. Farmland. The easy life.'

'And then?' Docilosa asked.

'And then,' Quistus said, 'it gets tough.'

The road north from Florentia had no name that they ever knew. It wound interminably between the snowy hilltops, following grey valleys full of rain. At night Quistus wrapped himself in thick sodden furs and stayed in the driving seat, keeping watch for bear; several times they heard wolves, and once found their sack of nuts torn open and looted while they slept deafened by the storm, and the horses with blood on their legs. Nothing in the *carpentum* was dry, everything stank. No one talked, only complained, and tried to sleep.

Then the road came winding down into the great green broad plain of Liguria, and they saw the mighty Via Aemilia crossing the landscape like a line drawn with a ruler. They turned left and the sun came out.

The Imperial City of the Taurini overlooked the River Duria meandering through the last flat farmland before the Alpes. As always Quistus avoided towns by using farm tracks, but these farms were owned by retired veterans and several times they were noticed and spoken to. He knew these professionals would remember them if asked; two hundred and fifty years ago Hannibal's army had poured down these valleys pointing into the Roman heartland. Everyone knew that could never happen again, but the shock had been burnt into Rome's collective memory. Forts still dotted the green hilltops though the reason for them was long gone.

131

'Let's sleep,' Quistus said. They hid in a barn for a day, disguising the *carpentum* with moss and branches, letting the horses graze on thin winter grass; they'd need their strength. At sunset they harnessed up and set out along a dim confusion of paths and tracks. The high moon that had guided them through the long Ligurian nights had fallen into darkness but he navigated by the stars to keep to the line he needed, the river on his right hand and the lamp-sprinkled city on his left. They were through into the Duria valley by dawn.

The rising sun lit the mountains rose-red at first, then brilliant snow-white, throwing black shadows across the winding road, the foaming river.

Omba slept in the *carpentum*, Claudia read, Docilosa drove, and Quistus walked beside the horses with one hand on the neck-harness. Docilosa liked using the whip and the wagon made good time up the shallow grades from the farmland. He looked back for the last time at the green Ligurian plain laid out like a map so far behind and below them, then turned and faced the white peaks ahead.

'I told you,' he said. 'Now it's tough.'

At first the weather was good, the sun striking hot in the cold air. 'Don't whip them so hard, Docey,' he called. The road steepened and the horses threw back their heads, breath whistling as the collars tightened against their throats, strangling them if they pulled too hard. He swapped pairs every hour, pushing the harness as low as it would go to help them breathe. 'Everyone out,' he called. 'Not you, Docey.'

'Are you giving me special treatment?' She liked him to pay compliments.

'You're the lightest.'

'Is that all,' she sulked, and cracked the whip.

Omba and Claudia pushed behind the vehicle on the steepest sections while Quistus pulled the collars from the front, trying to ease the strain on the horses' windpipes. The leather horseshoes skidded backwards on the broken stones. Everything they could spare was thrown out to lighten the vehicle, all the meat and vegetables they'd bought in Liguria (which seemed so long ago now), even the last of the hazelnuts from the Villa Ciminia. Every evening they searched for a place to camp off the road, the river roaring past them in waterfalls, and slept exhausted. Each night the moon grew brighter. At Segusio

132

they risked sleeping at an inn, woke crawling with fleas, and swore not to repeat the experience.

The day came when the Duria, by now no wider or louder than a chattering street-gutter, flowed towards them for the last time. They'd reached the narrow pass of Summae Alpes. From the snowy crest they stared into the valley of the Druentia falling between the peaks to the crossroads at Brigantio. Claudia glanced at Quistus to make sure he was watching and dropped to her knees. 'Thank you, Lord, for giving us Your strength and guidance to lead us this far.'

'My master led us,' Omba said. 'It's him we should thank. Your God didn't think to push down those collars, Claudia.'

'The air is so thin here.' Docilosa leant against Quistus. 'I feel so weak.'

He touched her cheek. 'Are you all right?'

She held his finger, looking earnestly into his eyes. 'I will be.'

Quistus nodded and went to check the brake for the long descent. Omba gave Docilosa, who was grinning, a shove. 'Keep your hands off him,' Omba warned, deep-voiced. 'He's not your sort and he doesn't even like you. You're a murderer and you're a thief too, *I* think.'

Docilosa gave a small victorious smile. 'I didn't know you cared.' She gazed after Quistus. 'And I don't care what *you* think, you fat old African bitch. Keep your sad dreams about him to yourself.' She went to help him with the brake.

Omba turned to Claudia. 'Who are you looking at?'

'I couldn't help overhearing what you said.' Claudia drew Omba behind the wagon. 'Do you really believe Docilosa is a thief as well as . . . you know?'

Omba was still angry. 'Yes, I think Docilosa shoved a pin up the old woman's nose, maybe for some very good reason like she says, maybe not, who knows the real right and wrong of it? But then she took her chance to steal that Phoenix brooch off the old woman's body, and she let Protia take the blame for it, the cold-hearted bitch. That's what *I* think.'

'An interesting theory. So our lovely Docilosa murdered two people, not one. The first by the sin of commission, the second by the sin of omission – she didn't admit the truth to save Protia from being executed by Ursus.' Claudia shrugged. 'No doubt Stigmus has found it by now.'

'Anyway she's what you Christians call a damned soul and when justice comes for her and chops her, she'll scream for ever in the fires of Hell.'

'Unless your master has his way. Or she has her way with him.'

Omba thumped the wagon with her fist. 'My master believes in justice. She won't catch him like that. He knows what she's up to – she knows her life hangs by a thread from his knowing what's right and proper. Of course she wants to make herself safe in his bed. But he won't let her.'

'Won't he? Allow me to give you a small, bitter piece of advice from my own experience.' Claudia put her mouth to Omba's ear. 'I've never known a man let a beautiful girl die before he's had her.'

Omba stared, shocked by Claudia's ice-cold tone. Claudia, smiling, pretended to hear someone calling her name and went to help with the brake.

The horses pushed back, their rear hooves sliding into their forelegs, as the wagon's overbalancing weight knocked them forward. The brake, a curved leather pad on one end of an ashwood pole bolted to the vehicle's side, squealed and smoked against the wheel's rim. Coming downhill was, in many ways, a greater challenge than going up. Omba walked at the wagon's back with a rope looped behind her shoulder-blades, stamping her feet into the rutted ice.

At Brigantio – nothing but a deserted way-station and a pile of stone – they took the right turn along a narrow valley. Heavy-laden carts came down against them from the gold mines, shoving them off the one-track road, and they had to wait while slave-gangs trudged by. Neither sun nor moon illuminated the depths of these deep valleys where the road wriggled by the river, shrouded in gloom by day and night.

And then the snow found them, just a flake or two at first drifting from the strip of lead-coloured sky between the rock walls. Soon the road was hidden by whirling snowflakes, the roar of the river lost in the roar of the storm. Docilosa huddled in the driving seat, a mound of snow, while the wind cracked the whip around her. Quistus trudged head-down beside the horses. He tried to see back to Omba walking beside the wheel. She waved, the wind pulling white scraps of breath from her

134

mouth. She was shouting. *Stop, stop.* He shook his head. Once they stopped he feared they'd freeze to death inside, or the wagon would be blown over the edge.

The road turned upwards. The wagon fell back, sliding. The brake-pole bent, then broke clean through. Claudia and Omba pushed with their shoulders, Quistus hauled on the harness. But the horses were skidding, dragged backwards. Claudia shouted, falling aside with a sprained ankle. Docilosa jumped down and put her shoulder to the wheel in Claudia's place.

The wagon balanced precariously, then inched forward towards the final crest.

Thirteen

The Phoenix

Quistus stood on the top balcony of the Taverna Lugdunensis, admiring the view. The morning sun shone winter-bright and the clear sky forced blue into even the brown silty curve of the Rhodanus. Green islands in midstream were dotted with stores for wine and river-processed flax for linen, and even the white-toothed mountains seemed far away across the flood-plain.

Lugdunum covered the headland where the Arar poured into the Rhodanus, each wide river crossed by a stone bridge to the walled city between them. The streets were the usual neat grid lined with temples, a theatre, a forum, markets, impressive public buildings. Best of all were the public baths. Already, with hardly time to do more than throw down their few possessions in their rooms, Quistus saw Claudia and Omba hurrying out along the street, travel-stained, ragged, Omba with one boot torn and Claudia limping, but all their weariness gone at the thought of hot water, oiled skin, washed hair, a relaxing massage, manicure, pedicure, depilation. They'd talked of nothing else for days. He remembered Claudia, limping beside the *carpentum* down the valley from

Bergusium, getting her first sight over the swamps to distant Lugdunum shining on its hill, swearing an oath. 'If I don't have a bath, Quistus, I'm going to mutiny.'

'Me too,' Omba said.

Quistus had looked to Docilosa, who nodded.

'We mean it,' Claudia said. 'No more detours.'

'A bath it is,' he agreed.

They'd parked the *carpentum* in one of the stables outside the east gate, paid for a watchman, and strolled with the morning crowds into the town. Docilosa worried about Stigmus finding her where so many roads met, but Quistus repeated for the tenth time, 'You're not that important to him, Docey.' She'd developed an answer, however.

'You don't *know* how important I am. You *don't.*' When pressed she never said anything more, just locked eyes with him, making him look at her. Their harsh journey through the mountains had hardened her; she was no longer so meek and withdrawn, she behaved like his equal. She was growing up. If anything her edge made her even more attractive. He stayed on the balcony looking for her hair in the crowd but didn't see her, and was sorry. He felt he knew them all so well by now. They were a team. They'd been through so much together that their gender seemed irrelevant.

But, he reminded himself, men didn't mutiny over a bath.

He threw his furs in the corner, dragged off his boots, and walked to the public baths dressed only in his filthy tunic and sandals. Women had their own entrance at one end of the building, men at the other. Street traders worked the queues selling hot dainties, honey-cakes, nuts, their cries echoing off the walls. A procession made its way to the temple of Cybele, horns blowing.

A child ran in front of him, laughing excitedly.

He heard more laughter. A girl's gentle, throaty laughter. Her laugh hadn't changed. Some young men were laughing too. Docilosa was standing by a stall selling steaming food from urns. Steam from the urns blew over her. She wore a cream woollen cloak he hadn't seen before, a hood of the same colour thrown back on her shoulders, and her hair was different, longer, darker, not so curly. He couldn't see her face. She was looking away. He bumped into the child, almost falling.

The child gave a startled cry. The girl turned, pale, perfect, beautiful, unmistakable.

'Lyra,' he said.

Lyra saw him. She was nearly twenty years old. Her eyes widened, green-grey like the Tiber, recognizing her father. Her eyes hadn't changed.

'*Lyra,*' he whispered. Shock stole his voice.

She turned away with her hand coming up, sweeping her hood over her face, dropping her food, pushing between the young men, gone. Steam blew where she'd been standing.

He ran after her, tripping. The young men scattered. Steps, a row of pillars, a dark temple. At the firelit altar priests cut a ram's throat over a copper dish. White-bearded, shocked, they stared at him.

He ran back shouting her name. He found the stallholder. The man shrugged warily, lifting his tongs from the steam, offering something, shellfish.

'You know that girl?' Quistus said. 'You know her. She was here.' He tried to describe her but couldn't, tears were pouring down his cheeks. 'The girl in a cream cloak?'

The man shrugged, waving him away if he wasn't buying, then snatched the handful of coins Quistus held out.

'Eh, what girl?' he said.

Quistus stared at the ground. He knelt. On the cobbles lay a small freshwater lobster, one claw cracked where she'd taken the flesh. The iron pincers she'd used lay beside it, where she'd dropped them. He hadn't imagined her, she was real, living. He held them tight, still warm from her hand. He'd held her when she was born.

Lyra. 'Lyra's alive,' he whispered.

He pushed through the crowds, ran to the baths. He turned round and round in the steam, trying to see her, shouting her name. He saw Omba. He saw Claudia. He shook them off.

'Docilosa isn't here,' Claudia said. 'It's her you saw, don't you understand?'

'Master, you're frightening us,' Omba said. He pulled away from her.

'She ran away when she saw me!'

Which way did she go? He ran downhill, knocking people aside as he came to the east gate. Dull faces, slow traffic. The fishermen on the bridge assured him they'd seen no cream cloaks today, unless he wished to pay for them to see cream cloaks, when they would gladly see all the cream cloaks he wished. 'And as for beautiful girls, sir, they are ten a penny in this town, and each of us is married to one.'

Quistus held his side as he ran towards the west gate, then walked. He knew he wouldn't find her. She'd gone. The fishermen assured him that the fish to be caught on this river were bigger, but they would be lying if they told him they had seen a girl of about twenty years of age, with green-grey eyes and hair of a slightly reddish blonde. A lad wearing wooden shoes called, 'I saw her, true as my name's Viridorix.'

Quistus held his side, wincing. 'How much money do you want, Viridorix?'

'I'll tell you for free, I saw that woman ride past me on a white horse. Riding as though the Furies chased her.'

One of the old fishermen tousled the boy's hair. 'A woman riding a horse!'

'I saw a woman riding a white horse,' the lad said. 'I saw her ride like a man, legs astride, no lady, riding like the wind, whipping.' He pointed across the bridge where the roads split. 'North-west, along the Bormonis road.'

The old fisherman said, 'Tell him, Viridorix, tell him about the lickerfish you caught last week.' The old man held his gnarled hands a foot apart, then two, then as wide as they would go, and all the fishermen laughed at young Viridorix.

Quistus turned back to town. He knew they were mocking him, except Viridorix, who believed the nonsense he spouted but was a young fool. None of it mattered. Not at all. If only Lyra was alive.

He knew he'd made a terrible mistake, a trick of the mind. His family was dust, smoke. She'd seemed so real, but dreams did. He hardly remembered his children really. Go on, put faces on them – no, living faces. He'd seen her because he needed her alive in his heart: his soul needed to believe in her.

Why had they died? Some very good reason, but he'd never know. They were the past. They had no answers. They were the dead.

Lyra was dead. He needed to accept that. He couldn't. It was impossible.

'Thank you, Viridorix,' he said, and walked away.

Viridorix called after him, 'But I did see her.'

Quistus knocked into someone smelling of greasy cloak

and travel, pushed the man away. He walked faster now, half-running. He'd seen Docilosa. It was the only explanation that worked. Docilosa hadn't gone to the baths. She'd stayed in her room – yes, always washed in private, didn't she? The mysterious Docilosa. Pretending to be Lyra to draw attention to herself. Why? To get on her own with him. That fitted. He ran, holding his side, the stitch jabbing him, his face swollen with anger.

He pushed past the tables in the busy taverna, took the steep steps two at a time to the upstairs corridor, stopped at her door. He knocked with his fist, once.

'Who is it?' came her voice. 'I'm busy.'

He kicked the door in.

She turned her bare back at once, elbows crossed in front. Her hair hung over her shoulder-blades, already wet, she'd washed it in the steaming bucket she'd set on the table. Her tunic, unstrapped from her shoulders, hung from her waist. Her head turned slightly, watching him in the brass travelling mirror.

'Are you going to close the door?'

He slammed the door. He shouted, 'Why did you pretend to be Lyra? *Why*?'

'How could I do that? I've never even seen her.'

He stared at her, swallowing.

She murmured, 'Where are the others?' She saw his wild eyes and purred, thinking she understood. 'They aren't here, are they. We're alone.'

He stepped towards her. 'No more lies. I've had enough. I can't take any more. Give me the truth.'

She turned, crossed arms rising and falling with her breathing. She took a deep breath. 'This?' she said, and held her arms wide.

He ignored her body. 'You stole the Phoenix. Protia died for it. I want it. Give it to me.'

She looked at her breasts. 'I don't see it here, do you?' She raised her head, putting back her hair, staring him in the eye, but still he didn't take her in his arms. Her mouth opened in genuine surprise. 'You're afraid of me, aren't you?'

'I saw Lyra. That frightens me.'

'What's it to do with me?'

'I thought she was you.'

'That's disgusting.' She looked interested. 'Do you want to?'

139

'I want the truth.'

She rested her hand on her hip. Disbelieving smile. She knew her power. 'I don't know anything about her. I hope she was a good girl. Was she?'

'You did it in front of the old woman, didn't you, Docilosa,' he said. 'With men.'

She shrugged. 'Often,' she said.

'How often?'

'Since I was twelve. She liked it. It reminded her of her own childhood.'

'Oh, Docey,' he said.

She said, blank-faced, 'Then it moved on. I had to watch her and Protia.'

'Amanda Censorina loved *you*, not Protia. I think she loved you from the start, when she found you as a baby. She saw the beautiful grown-up in the child's face. At the crossroads, wasn't it?'

'Yes, my mother left me at the crossroads.'

'Amanda Censorina brought you up as her slave, her property, so she could do anything she liked with you. The little girl she loved who grew up. But then her love went too far, even for you, and you killed her with the hairpin.'

'Yes. It just slipped in. It was so easy. She didn't even die. She just stared at me and we both knew what I'd done. I had to twist it from side to side. Her arms and legs went mad. Then she died.' She spat. 'She *deserved* to die. I hope she burns with Satan.'

'Give me the Phoenix.'

Her face tightened implacably. 'No.'

He grabbed her. She pressed her breasts against him. He tore the tunic from her waist. She wore kidskin leather knickers. Around the top of her thigh burned a glittering line of fire. 'So that's it,' he murmured. 'That's why you wouldn't wash even in the company of other women. Not prudery. Greed. You had a lot to hide.'

She bit him. He held her down by her throat and pulled the necklace from her leg, holding it beyond reach of her grasping hands.

He heard footsteps on the stairs. Omba came in. 'Master!' she said. She didn't ask what he was doing. 'I'll come back later.' Docilosa spat at her.

140

'Stay, Omba.' He looked past her. 'You too, Claudia.'

He pressed warningly on Docilosa's throat, then stepped away. She lurched to her feet. 'Thank God you came, Claudia!' she wept. 'It was awful – he – I tried to stop him—'

'Shut it, Docey,' Omba said.

Claudia looked shocked. Quistus backed from Docilosa as a man backs from a dangerous animal that might attack again. He picked up her tunic, threw it to her. 'What's this about?' Claudia said. 'As if it isn't obvious.'

Quistus said: 'I saw Lyra. I *did* see her. She's alive.'

'Master, don't,' Omba said.

'No more lies. I'll take the truth from Docilosa, nothing but the truth.' He held up the necklace, showing them. 'This is the Phoenix.'

They stared at the fire curled around his fist, its glittering silver-ash embers swinging down his arm to the elbow. 'She let us think the Phoenix was a brooch. It isn't. It's a carcanet, this special kind of necklace. These aren't rubies – they're diamonds, worth a hundred times as much. Fire diamonds from India, probably, that's where the best are found. That's where Annius, the Censorina's first husband, made his money. Protia never stole this wonder from the jewellery box, it wasn't there. The old woman was wearing it when she died.'

'Yes, you said she wore it in the painting of her,' Claudia nodded. 'For her infernal rites. A black cloak, a carcanet of fire diamonds, a cherub at her knee.'

'I saw it,' Omba said.

'Docilosa stole the Phoenix from her body,' Quistus said. 'Maybe she even took it while the old woman was still alive. Maybe that's why Docilosa had to kill her. I think so. Not because of her touching story that she was too proud and pure to indulge the Censorina's pleasure. No. Just simple brutal theft.'

'It wasn't theft,' Docilosa said. 'I didn't steal the Phoenix.' She wouldn't wear the torn tunic Quistus had thrown to her; she swung a travelling cloak from her shoulders. Her face was calm now. She faced them with dignity. She said, 'I *can't* have stolen it. The Phoenix is mine.'

Quistus said, 'That's a lie. Docilosa, I—'

'It's the truth. My mother left me at the crossroads just as a thousand other babies are left every week in Rome. My father had just died. My brothers too. Perhaps that very night.

Around my little body she wound the Phoenix, so that whoever found me would be well paid for taking me in.'

Claudia said, 'Ironic, then, that the richest woman in Rome found you.'

'No,' Docilosa said. 'The richest woman in Rome left me there. But she came back. You see, I was her only daughter. All her other children were sons, all dead. I was her only girl, the only child who survived. A girl, the only one she could love.'

They stared at her, thinking the unthinkable.

Docilosa shrugged. 'You wanted the truth,' she said. 'Amanda Censorina was my mother.'

Quistus poured a cup of wine and drank it. He followed Docilosa's eyes, refilled the cup until it slopped over, and handed it to her.

'My God,' Claudia said. 'You slept with your own mother and killed her.'

Docilosa sipped the wine. 'Thank you,' she told Quistus.

He sat. Docilosa, Omba and Claudia looked calm, but he was shaken.

'You were the cherub in the painting,' he said without looking.

'Yes, I was her cherub.'

'She loved you.'

'She was evil. Does that count?' Docilosa took another sip. 'What are you going to do with me?'

'Put you in chains!' Claudia said.

He rubbed his face tiredly. 'No, nothing's changed. It's true that Docilosa's committed the most monstrous crime and I should hand her over to the authorities, but that was always the case, and all those innocent slaves do not deserve to die.'

'Listen to me.' Docilosa knelt, begging. 'Yes, I killed her. Anyone would. But I didn't steal the Phoenix. It's my inheritance. Give it back to me.'

'What?'

'She left it to me, along with the bulk of her estate.' Docilosa gave a small excited smile. 'You see, I'm the richest woman in Rome, really.'

'You're a murdering bitch,' Omba said.

Quistus said, 'But Longinus fetched her will from her desk, and he never said—'

'That wasn't her will,' Docilosa scoffed. 'Longinus is the sharpest legal brain in Rome, Nero's hatchetman in the courts. He *said* he'd found it, but did you check?'

'No,' Quistus admitted. 'I believed him.'

'Her real will is deposited with the Vestal Virgins. She was an honorary Vestal, you remember? No man's allowed even to touch her will. You'll find it's just as I said. Freedom to all her slaves and a legacy of a thousand sesterces each. The rest to me, her daughter.'

'But you'll be dead and so will they.'

She clasped her hands. 'Quistus, I'm begging you. You can get me off it somehow. You can find a way. I'll do anything.' She put her lips close to his ear. 'We could do it together.' She whispered: 'I'll be Lyra.'

He jumped to his feet. Claudia said calmly, 'This girl's a demon, Quistus.'

'I'm starting to feel sorry for the old woman,' Omba said. 'I wonder which the worst of the horrid pair really was?' She left the room.

Quistus stood at the window.

'Well, sir?' Docilosa said meekly.

He shivered. 'I'd like to tell you to get lost, disappear, but that wouldn't stop the executions.'

Omba returned, holding something. 'She doesn't care if they die, master. She doesn't care who dies.' She held out a piece of shaped wood. 'Even if it's us. Just as long as it isn't her. Look at this.'

Quistus examined it. 'What is it?'

'The brake-pole. The one that broke.' Omba pointed at the splintered end. 'Except it didn't break. It was cut half through.' She rubbed a smooth angle of knife-sawn wood with her finger. 'You remember, when the wagon was sliding backwards on the mountain? It was meant to run free and crush us to death. She was unlucky, we took the strain, and the only thing that got hurt was Claudia's ankle.'

'No.' Docilosa looked horrified; or perhaps just mortified at being caught. 'She's lying, they hate me!' She followed Quistus back to the window. He stared out, ignoring her. She spoke to his broad shoulders. 'I swear I never did it. I swear to you I'm innocent.'

'That's news,' Omba said. 'Docey's innocent again.'

He slipped the necklace into his clothes. 'I'm keeping this. I'll hide it. It's our assurance that she won't run away.'

'We're lucky to be alive,' Claudia murmured. 'God looked after us.'

'She could cut our throats while we sleep,' Omba said.

Quistus said without turning, 'Bind her hands.'

The trooper stood in the square looking at the top window. 'It's him, sir,' he told the man hidden in the alley.

'You're certain, trooper?'

'Yes sir, that's him all right. That's the one who knocked me over on the west bridge.'

'How many with him?'

'Just the three grown women, sir, like you said.'

'Adults? You're quite sure of that? No fourth, no child?'

'No sir, they're grown-ups, I can see 'em from here.'

'Excellent,' Stigmus said.

Fourteen

The Oak Cathedral

While the *carpentum* crossed the west bridge Quistus looked for Viridorix, but it was raining hard and the lad wasn't fishing this morning. On the far side he reined back seeing that four main roads, and half a dozen paved tracks, led from this place. Claudia claimed to know Gaul; he called through the speaking-hatch, 'Which way, Claudia? Go north, up the valley?'

She stuck her head out. 'No, and not Augustonemeton, it's too far west. Head north-west, to Aquae Bormonis.'

'Bormonis?'

'Yes.' The road Lyra had taken – or, rather, the road that the stranger who looked so agonizingly *like* Lyra had taken. Claudia gave him a cool stare. 'That's right. The way you want to go.'

Quistus pulled the right-hand rein and the horses swung on to the Bormonis road. The pair tethered behind the vehicle kept their heads buried in nosebags filled with fresh hay. As before, he'd swap the pairs round every few hours to keep them strong. From the hilltop he turned to look at the empty road behind, the rainswept bridge and their last sight of the city, then cracked the whip.

Docilosa sulked on the couch. Her hands were tied. She let the wagon jolt her from side to side, drawing attention to her plight. Claudia read a book. Omba slept. 'I'd never hurt any of you,' Docilosa said. 'You've got to believe me. I never cut that brake.'

Claudia glanced up. 'Who did, then?'

'I don't know. I just don't know. We're friends, aren't we?'

Claudia closed her book. She sat looking out of the rear door. Docilosa said, 'What's so interesting?'

Claudia ignored her, then said, 'Nothing.'

'It's just a road. There isn't even anything to see. People have got more sense than to come out in this weather.'

Claudia closed the door and lay down. 'Right as always, Docilosa.'

'My hands are hurting. They're tied too tight.'

Omba yawned. 'Shut it, Docey.'

Docilosa said: 'Quistus could get me off, couldn't he. Off death.' They sat up, staring at her in disbelief. 'He could if he really wanted. I'd pay him, I'd have lots of money. He could go to the Emperor – you said he did that deal – and he could say to the Emperor, I did my part, I got Princess Claudia to Britain for you, and now I want my reward. Docilosa's life.' She clenched her bound fists in desperate hope, pleading. 'He *could*.'

Claudia laughed. 'Even the Emperor can't overturn the whole legal system of Rome just for you. Not even Nero. Besides, he wants to steal your murdering inheritance for himself.'

'You're going to burn,' Omba said.

Docilosa said in a small voice, 'Burn?'

'No, it's not burning,' Claudia said. 'Crucifixion.'

Docilosa watched her steadily while the cart jolted. 'I renounce Satan. I want to be a Christian. Will you show me the way, Claudia? Please?'

'Your first convert, Princess!' Omba hugged Claudia's

shoulder. 'A mother-murdering thieving Satanist. After this the Brits should be easy.'

'I'll think about it,' Claudia said. 'You have to show remorse. And love.'

'I'll do anything,' Docilosa said tearfully.

She watched the two older women settle back, dozing, then got out and walked for a while. The rain eased, half drizzle, half fog. The horses steamed. Quistus sat up there bundled to the chin in dripping cloaks. She called, 'Can I sit with you?' When he didn't respond she climbed up. An hour passed. 'Shall I drive?' He shrugged and handed her the reins. She did her best for a while. 'I can't hold them properly.' She showed him her bound hands. He saw the sense of it and retied the knots to her wrists with about a foot of rope between them. After that she didn't ask for any more favours, just talked. When he changed horses she helped him. Darkness fell and the moon was in the last quarter, hidden behind thick clouds, so they camped overnight in the forest. She even cooked supper, her ladle-hand that stirred the hare stew jerking her other hand from her lap at the limit of the rope, pathetic-ally. Quistus sighed and reached out to lengthen it. At that there was a second mutiny, and from the least likely source.

'No, master.' Omba held his arm. 'She might cut our throats in the night.' She growled at Docilosa, 'Stir small, you.'

They lay half-sleeping all night, listening to the trees drip, and Docilosa's soft weeping. Omba had bound her hands tight and they'd cramped. Quistus sat up, ready to strike camp before dawn.

He walked by the horses' heads talking to them gently. Omba drove, then Claudia. The road turned downhill by the headwaters of the Liger. Light rain started, then sleet; no one looked at them twice plodding through snowy Rodumna, then back into the trees again, by the roaring waters. Omba walked beside him. 'She's looking for it, you know. Docey's been ransacking everything inside all day, then trying to put it back as it was, but I can tell. Where did you hide it?'

'The Phoenix? Where it won't be found.'

'Not in your clothes? You'll wake up naked.'

'Don't be nosey.'

'Just don't go soft on her, master.'

Aquae Bormonis, a spa town, was almost deserted at this

time of year. Quistus looked around him alertly but saw only steam drifting from the hot springs under the snow. Geese ran at them, wings raised in alarm, cackling, and a caretaker came to watch sleepily from a doorway. His dog barked. No other sign of life. Quistus handed the reins to Docilosa and called over, 'Anyone stopped here? A girl in a cream cloak, with a white horse?' He tossed a coin.

'No one stops here.' The caretaker scratched his beard, kicking his dog to make it shut up. 'No one's ridden through.'

Docilosa cracked the whip, clumsily. Quistus lengthened the rope between her wrists. The wagon rattled and bumped in the woods. A new river joined the Liger and brown floodwaters foamed beside the road. Lyra had disappeared as quickly and thoroughly as a dream, impossible to recall by day.

'You. Shut your bloody dog up. Seen anyone?'

'Me?'

'Make him ask you twice.' Ursus drew his sword.

'A wagon, that's all. A man driving, a young girl beside him. Bound hands.'

'Bound hands?'

'Maybe she's been a naughty slave, eh?'

The horsemen rode on, purple cloaks flapping, scattering the geese. The bearded man watched until they were gone. He spat.

Villages all looked the same. Quistus stopped at the crossroads. 'Which way, Claudia?'

She found an old woman collecting sticks and asked her the name of the place. 'She says it's Decetia,' she called.

'There's a bridge over the river,' the old woman gossiped proudly. 'It's a fine road to the left. Everyone goes that way.'

Claudia returned to Quistus. 'She seems to know what she's talking about. She says straight on.'

Quistus nodded. 'Straight on.' The wagon rumbled into the forest, following the great slow curve of the river from north to west.

The cavalry troopers milled around the cottage, coughing in the smoke that leaked through the thatch. These primitive folk – these lands still belonged to the Carnute tribe, for all the

147

good it did them – had no idea of chimneys. Stigmus called to Bellacus, 'Well? How long ago did she say?'

'Between the first meal and the second. She says they went the wrong way. She's angry because the red-haired woman told them wrong.'

First meal to second; breakfast to lunch. They'd passed through maybe four hours ago, short winter hours too, and it would be dark before long. 'We're catching up too fast,' Stigmus decided. 'Make camp. Maybe that old crone's got some chickens.'

Ursus opened his cloak, showing them hanging by their necks from his belt. 'Not now,' he grinned.

That night Stigmus stared into the firelight. 'So, Princess Claudia,' he murmured, holding a conversation with the flames, 'you're taking them the wrong way already. How very interesting.'

The sun melted the snow, showing the green shoots beneath. The Liger was very broad now but shallow, easily leapt from time to time by long wooden bridges as the road smoothed the river's twists and turns. Quistus allowed Docilosa to have her hands free during the day. Still he saw that hungry, possessive light in her eyes, and knew she was wondering where he'd hidden her birthright, as she called it, the Phoenix. She'd found the long, narrow secret compartment under the seat – the seat itself was the lid – and probably she thought it was locked in there. He refused to tell her if that was the truth or not, and the lock was stout. He didn't make the mistake of wearing the key on a string around his neck: Omba thought Docey, despite her ravishingly innocent appearance and helpful manner, perfectly capable of cutting his throat, and Omba was usually right about women.

One night he'd heard Docilosa trying to scrape a hole in the underside of the compartment, but the wood was hard. He'd grinned in his sleep and turned over.

Claudia walked ahead of the horses, as she often did now, as if fearful of losing the way. She seemed excited, striding ahead for hours sometimes, unwilling to make camp, first to rise before dawn. Quistus stood on the seat, shadowing his eyes with his hand, peering ahead. 'Claudia!'

She turned, smiling, walking backwards. He pointed across the treetops. 'What's that town?'

She swung up beside him. 'Ah. It's Cenabum. We cross the river there and strike north-west, cross-country, to Carnutia.' She corrected herself, using the Roman name. 'I mean Autricum.'

Quistus spoke to an innkeeper near the town. 'He says we're only ten days from the port people use to get to Britain. He says all we have to do is take the road to the City of the Parisians and head north.'

Claudia said coolly, 'I'd rather stick with the way I know, if you don't mind.'

'Don't forget,' Docilosa smiled with sweet malice, 'Claudia is the word of God.'

'That's good enough for me,' Quistus said.

'Whoa.' Stigmus reined back, cresting the rise. For the first time he could actually see the wagon in the distance, trundling even slower than he'd thought. Too close. Even so, they couldn't risk losing them now. He twisted in the saddle. 'Praetorian!'

A trooper rode from the orderly phalanx of five men behind Bellacus and Ursus. 'Sir!'

'You saw him before. Take off your uniform.'

'Do it, soldier,' Bellacus ordered.

Stigmus tossed the man his own brown cloak. 'See that wagon? Make sure it's them. Follow them in the town, see which road they take.'

The man fisted a salute and rode ahead.

Bellacus cleared his throat. 'Surely they'll take the road to Britain, sir?'

Stigmus snorted. It was happening just as the Emperor said it would; a little sooner than expected if anything, but that was the nature of the game. 'All I require from you, Bellacus,' he said, 'is that you obey orders. Without question.'

North of the river, clear of the town, the road forked into five different roads. Claudia pointed unhesitatingly. The road to Carnutia plunged immediately into the deep forest that still covered the Carnutian region. At first a few glades had been cleared, miserable affairs ringed with turf huts and fences woven from saplings, where ribby livestock roamed and muddy children threw stones. Larger clearings even had a few field-strips for crops, but they were few and far between. Soon there were none at all, and silence fell. Occasionally they saw

149

pigs rooting for acorns and truffles far from human habitation, the trees so thick and heavy that the sunlight seemed driven upward by shadows. Quistus looked back.

'You have the same feeling,' Claudia called, walking. 'We're being watched.'

'How friendly d'you reckon these people are?'

'People?' She shrugged, looking at the tree trunks that hemmed the road. 'This isn't a place of people. It's a place of the Old Faith.'

'Druids? I thought we'd killed them all in Gaul.'

'We?'

'We Romans.'

'Old religions don't die, even when their priests do. Folk have long memories. The songs live on, and trees, and the sun.' She reached out, pressing her hands to a gnarled trunk. 'And immortal spirits.'

He said, 'Are spirits watching us?'

'I believe so.' She explained, 'Quistus, a Christian does not mock other religions. We're not as intolerant as you Romans believe.'

He let the horses plod for a while, glancing behind at the road shrinking between the tree trunks. '*We* Romans,' he corrected her.

'I do apologize.'

'You came through here with your father into exile, didn't you, Princess Gladis?' He pretended a slip of the tongue. 'I mean, Claudia.'

'That was long ago. I *was* Gladis then. I thought I'd be executed in Rome. I thought I'd never see this place again.' Claudia walked quickly to a crossroads. 'Here we are. My father and I rested near here. There's a villa.'

She hesitated, remembering the way, then chose the smaller track. He urged the horses to a trot. Claudia laughed as she ran.

'A villa with hot food?' Omba called. 'Slaves? Hot baths?'

Claudia just laughed. 'You'll see, Omba!'

Quistus looked back as the muddy lane climbed the valley but saw nothing, only Claudia's footprints in the mud and their wheel-tracks, and tangled boughs crossing the setting sun. On the other side, the full moon rose out of the dark.

Claudia pushed a gate shadowed with ivy. 'Welcome to the Villa Ambia.'

The hinges squealed. The wagon bumped over dimly seen shrubs and saplings that had grown up. Nettles flourished in the ruin of the villa. 'This is it?' Quistus looked round the echoing rooms, his boots crunching on roof-tile. Once it had been a grand place. Now creepers grew up the pillars and cracked the once-fine mosaic floors, and the bath-pools were empty except for leaves. He drove the wagon into the draughty entrance hall and they made camp where King Caractacus and Princess Gladis had been welcomed in grand surroundings. The statues were broken; Claudia said a smaller room to one side had been the library. 'We'll sleep in there,' Quistus said. They broke up shelves and one of the room's three doors for firewood, and lit a bonfire beneath a hole in the roof. He pulled shutters across the windows. Omba set about cooking, pleased because the wood was dry and made little smoke.

Claudia remembered a herb garden and returned with lovage and garlic that had run wild, sprouting as spring warmed the soil. Quistus gave Docilosa the bucket and told her to fetch water. 'You'll find a well in the courtyard,' Claudia called. He tethered the horses outside to graze, then watched from the patio over the treetops of the valley below. Altogether four threads of smoke rose into the twilight, showing where farms were, he supposed. Behind the villa, near the hilltop, he made out a broader haze fading into the dark and stars. It was a fine clear night. As he turned to go back inside a fifth fire sparked briefly down the valley. When he looked again the spark he thought he saw was gone, obscured, any smoke made invisible by darkness.

Quistus woke. He lay motionless except for his steady sleep-breathing, eyes closed. He heard Docilosa's usual low cries in her sleep but that hadn't woken him, nor had Omba's snores. The soft hiss of a cloak's hem across the mosaic floor, then footfalls. One person, barefoot. The crackle of a leaf. A nervous pause. Movement again, going away. He opened one eye. A shadow slipped out through the library doorway.

He rolled to his feet. The fire's dull embers showed Claudia's dropped blanket. He found his sandals and padded silently across the entrance hall, then waited holding his breath, seeing her one-legged on the step in the moonlight, pulling on her boots. There was nothing sleepy about her actions. She moved quickly, furtively, a shadow slipping into the woods.

151

He tied his sandals and followed. The moon shone high and round above the net of boughs. He glimpsed her like a will o' the wisp between the trunks as she climbed, following no path he could see. He kept to one side, trees between them, thinking she'd look back. Anyone would. But she didn't. Not once. Whatever her reason for coming up here, it was driving everything else from her mind. Single-minded obsession. Claudia gave up all attempts to move quietly, striding faster now, half-running, dry leaves swirling behind her cloak. He heard her panting breaths as the hill steepened. He gave up caution and came after her in full view, only a hundred paces behind.

Firelight flickered ahead, showing turf huts around a clearing. He stopped too late to hide. The place was a natural bowl in the hillside, almost perfectly hidden from below. He turned, amazed, and made out the moonlit rooflines of the Villa Ambia. Hidden except from that one direction: he remembered closing the shutters, but Claudia must have re-opened one. A candle burned in the empty window.

She was expected.

In front of him her shape showed against the fire as she moved into the hollow, then her shadow moved across firelit thatch – only four or five huts, hardly enough to call a village even by Carnutian standards.

A woman, bent, obviously old, wearing a shawl, shuffled from a doorway. She dropped her stick and embraced Claudia. The old woman wept with happiness, groaning with joy. She wouldn't let go. Finally she sank to her knees in front of Claudia and kissed her feet until Claudia lifted her. They embraced again and he overheard garbled words, Carnutian perhaps, or British.

Quistus watched the old woman step back, half-turning with unmistakable pride. A white-haired, white-bearded man emerged into the moonlight. His face was savage with woad-blue symbols, runes and, Quistus supposed, ferocious curses. His gown was a blue so dark it seemed black; once tall, he was so crippled in the joints that he was bent over no taller than the child at his side.

She was about thirteen years old, he guessed. She wore a short linen shift. Her hair fell unbound over her shoulders as fire-red as Claudia's, her eyes as blue by moonlight. It was impossible to mistake the two for anything but what they so obviously were.

Claudia held out her arms, and mother and daughter ran together as one.

Quistus walked forward slowly. It was important not to show the surprise he felt. Someone moved in the nearest hut, watching him. Filthy shabby women, half-guessed shapes, retreated from the doorways as he passed, or stared with slack faces. He saw no other men, no other children. The women fell in step behind him as he passed. Claudia saw him come into the firelight. Her eyes gleamed, tearful with joy. She squeezed the girl's shoulder, then looked back to Quistus and held her finger to her lips. He stopped, silent. The girl watched him with serious intensity, looking to her mother to learn if he was a danger.

A ragged woman fetched the old man's long oak staff. She laid it across her wrists, its head heavy with pale beads of mistletoe, offering it to him. The women gave a low moan as he accepted the burden – perhaps, Quistus thought, this act of acceptance was also one of relinquishment, an acknowledgement of a time past, a duty done. 'Baltharnoux,' they moaned. Quistus stared, astonished. A Druid survived in Gaul. Everyone thought the last was killed a hundred years ago.

Baltharnoux led the way slowly uphill, painfully slowly. The small procession wound after him through the trees, step by step, never quite stopping. Quistus bowed his head like theirs. The women were weeping now, a lonely terrible sound in the shadows and bright slants of moonlight. Each held a short fat candle cupped in her hands. One of the women pressed a lit candle into his hand; Claudia had spoken for him. The moon's eye settled towards the west, holding them in level fingers of light as they came to the hilltop. A *cathedrus* of twelve oaks, ancient, lightning-struck, stood in a mighty circle among lesser trees that had grown to conceal them.

Baltharnoux sang. The song sounded very sad. He held out his right hand to the young girl, then his left. She was crying. The wind fluttered the candle flames. One by one the eleven women walked forward and touched the girl's face, all of them weeping as they backed into the dark. The candles went out one by one until all were gone. Step by step Baltharnoux backed down from the hilltop, sinking into the darkness as though he walked down invisible steps into the hill, becoming part of the slope and the trees, no longer to be seen.

Quistus stood without moving. The dawn wind blew out his candle. In front of him the moon set and behind him the sun rose, throwing his shadow across Claudia and the girl. 'You owe me an explanation,' he said.

Fifteen
Fire at the Villa Ambia

'He's a Roman,' the freckled girl complained in perfect Latin. 'You mean you *trust* him?'

'He and I have been through many adventures together, Tara,' Claudia said. 'His name is Severus Septimus Quistus and yes, I do trust him.'

'But a *Roman*.'

'You see, Tara, I'm a Roman too now,' Claudia explained. 'I've had to be.'

'Why?' Tara said.

'To survive.'

'*Why* have you survived?' Tara said. She was a very rational child, Quistus thought. They were walking down between the trees. Five thin streamers of smoke drifted from the distant forest but nothing showed uphill, the huts now deserted. He saw Omba watching them from the window. He waved. She nodded.

'We survive to do our duty,' Claudia said. 'Quiet now, Tara.'

The girl fell instantly silent, walking without a sound.

Docilosa was fetching water. She dropped the bucket, startled. Quistus said, 'Let's get inside. There's been a . . . development.'

'Sir, I don't want to go in the house,' Tara said respectfully.

'Why?'

'Spirits get trapped between walls.'

He gestured for Docilosa to go first to show it was safe. 'You have to do as I say, Tara.'

'Sir, I'm Princess Tara.' She gave him a very blue, very direct gaze.

Claudia commanded briskly, 'You must go into the house at once, Tara. Come with me.' She strode into the entrance hall where the wagon was parked, Tara following after her with absolutely no sign of fear. But Quistus noticed, as she passed him, that she was holding her breath, almost unconscious with suppressed terror; what an amazing child. 'Here,' he said kindly, leading her into the ruined library. 'Sit by the fire. Be comfortable.'

'I'd rather stand.'

'Who's the brat?' Docilosa leant in the doorway. 'Digging us deeper into the shit, are you, Quistus?'

'Here, love,' Omba murmured to Tara. 'Nice cup of wine, eh?'

'I don't drink wine!' Tara said. 'It is the blood of our Lord.'

'A herbal infusion would be acceptable to her,' Claudia murmured. 'She's been very . . . precisely . . . brought up.'

'Already got a drop on the boil for myself.' Omba poured steaming water into a bowl, held it out. Tara took the bowl in her cupped hands, with reverence.

Claudia cleared her throat. 'My friends, as you must know, Tara is my daughter.'

Nobody said anything, then Omba spoke: 'That explains a bit.'

Quistus gazed from the sunlit window, then turned back to the darkened room. 'For a moment, just for a moment, I'd thought she was Boadicea's third daughter. After all, no place in Britain would have been safe for *her*.'

'I assure you,' Claudia said, 'Boadicea died in the rebellion and so did all her daughters. There, you're the first Roman to know the truth.'

Quistus nodded. 'I was sure of it when Tara spoke perfect Latin. Boadicea's lasses were country bumpkins compared with her. And they must have been older.'

'Now you know our secret, Quistus. Nero would give anything to know Boadicea really is dead. You could be anything you wanted. Governor of Britain, anything. Tempted?'

Quistus tore a loaf in half, offered it to Tara. She shrank back, appalled. Omba whispered, 'She thinks it's Jesus's flesh.'

'I don't think Baltharnoux was a Christian,' Quistus said, eating.

'Baltharnoux was many things,' Claudia said casually. 'Probably the most intelligent man I've ever met.'

Quistus said, startled, 'Baltharnoux has been to Rome?'

'A great priest is a priest of all religions. Christianity among them. Yes, he's been to my house. I've not been ignorant of my daughter's progress.'

'Where is he now?'

'Now his task is done? Safe.'

'Where's that?'

'He's chosen a place where, after all the good he has done, he cannot possibly do harm. His life's work is complete.'

Quistus said, 'He's killed himself?'

'Life and death are different things to different cultures.'

He rubbed his face wearily.

Omba made barley porridge. 'No salt passes her lips,' Claudia said quickly. Omba returned the pinch of salt to her pouch. They watched Tara eat standing up. She ignored them. When she finished she rinsed her bowl in the bucket, then drank the water. Omba glanced at Quistus and prepared more infusion. Quistus was certain it contained coffee to loosen tongues.

He sat. 'Tara, do you know in your heart that this woman is your mother?'

'Of course she knows,' Claudia murmured. 'She knows everything.'

'Yes sir, she is my mother.'

'No need for formality, Tara, we're all friends here. You were parted when you were very young, weren't you? Have you ever seen her before, to remember?'

'Of course I remember her. How can I forget my mother?'

'How old were you?'

'I was two years old, nearly three, the last time I saw her.' Tara didn't reach out, but Claudia did. They held hands.

'Two years old,' Quistus said sceptically. 'You remember it?'

'It was raining. I remember the lightning on her face. I remember her eyes, the blue of deep clear sea seen from high up, at noon. This exact blue. There can be no lie.'

Quistus said, exasperated, 'How can she know that? Has she ever seen the sea?'

Tara looked for permission to Claudia, who nodded.

'Vectis,' Tara said. It was an island off the south coast of Britain with high cliffs. It was possible she'd seen the sea

156

from high on a clifftop, and remembered somehow, or been constantly reminded.

'Her memory's fully trained by now,' Claudia said. She sounded proud. 'Druids have no writing. The history of the Brits is memory, song, rhyme.'

'Our own lives too.' Tara asked, 'Shall I tell him?'

'Yes, Quistus spoke truthfully when he said he's my friend.' Claudia added, 'Your friend too, Tara. You and he are *familiaris*.' That didn't quite mean family; familiar spirits, entwined fates.

Tara looked at Quistus, accepting him in a new way. She took a deep breath.

'My mother is Princess Gladis, daughter of King Caractacus, son of King Cymbeline—'

Claudia held up her hand. 'Shorter.'

'During the rebellion of King Caractacus no place was safe for him,' Tara recited, unblinking. 'He gave his daughters into the care of priests. They lived in caves, in trees, in cathedrals, on hilltops, in swamps and bogs. One by one they were killed. But my mother Princess Gladis, sixteen years old, was given into the care of great Atenoux, who had been elected King of the Druids, King of Kings. All tribes paid homage to him, and gave life.'

Claudia said, 'The name Atenoux means resurrection, rebirth.'

'Shall I give all the deep meanings of *Atenoux*, Mother?'

Claudia waved her hand. 'Not now.' It was getting quite hot in the library. A fly buzzed.

'Atenoux married my mother and I was born.'

Quistus said. 'Who else knew?'

'All the British.' Claudia sounded startled. 'Oh, you mean my later husband, Pudens?' She shook her head. 'The Romans never knew. Good God, no.'

Tara said, 'Caractacus was finally betrayed to the Romans not by defeat in war but by his traitorous ally Queen Cartimandua. Princess Gladis chose to go with her father to Rome, to share his certain death, which was her duty as his daughter and *familiaris*.'

'But Claudius unexpectedly broke with tradition and pardoned them,' Quistus said.

'Exactly!' Claudia replied. 'My survival was unexpected. Our certain death was why I'd left Tara in Britain, in Atenoux's care. Death for myself, Gladis, was not important, as I was only the daughter of a king and the wife of one. But Tara's spirit flows directly from the blood-source of two mighty kings, Atenoux and Caractacus, the two greatest rulers and rebel spirits of the age, both of them now gods.'

'I was brought up in places where Romans never ventured,' Tara said. 'Places of which they'd never heard. Then, three years ago, they attacked the island of Mona. Atenoux was killed, but Baltharnoux swam with me to the redoubt on the islet of Caer Gybi. There our women made their final stand, buying time with their lives, while we repaired a boat and sailed away. The plans had long been made. Britain was far too dangerous for me. I would be hidden in the last place the Romans would ever look: under their noses.'

'I knew of this place from my journey through Gaul with my father,' Claudia said. Docilosa sat drowsy with heat, slapping a fly from her face.

Quistus said sharply, 'So all the while you were living in Rome and married to Pudens, you were still married to Atenoux?'

'I did nothing wrong. In Britain a man may have five or ten wives, a woman five or ten husbands—'

'You spent your years in Rome plotting and planning behind your Roman husband's back.'

'No.' Claudia shook her head firmly. 'I was saving my young daughter's life. That's all that matters. The power of the Druids is broken. It will never return. I know that. Tara has been brought up as a Christian.' She gripped Quistus's hands. 'I love my daughter.'

'You should have told me all this.'

'How could I? How could I endanger her life even by one word, even to my most trusted friend? I never even told my *husband*. Tara is the greatest secret in Christendom.'

Quistus sighed.

Claudia said: 'By giving her to us, God blesses us with a wonderful opportunity. Do you see, Quistus? I agreed to undertake this mission for Nero because I had no choice. Fair enough. I've done my best. But I never really thought I had more than a small chance of success. I mean, *Christianity* to the *Brits*? Living in Rome has taught me just how barbaric we are.'

He went to the window. The sun was high, giving plenty of heat. 'I'm still trying to see the wonderful opportunity.'

'Even Boadicea, remarkable woman though she was, was only a woman married to a king, she wasn't of royal blood herself. Her power was limited. Tara, however, is pure royalty, three times royal. The tribes will adore her. When she shows them something better than the old ways they'll take every word she says into their hearts. Nero's crazy plan actually, now, stands a good chance of success. Tara, not I alone, will bring them to Christianity.' She gave a smile. 'We do stand a chance, Quistus. Would you deny my people peace? Would you deny peace to Rome? Think of all the lives you're saving.'

Quistus turned to Tara. She was perfectly calm. She hadn't moved since she last spoke. She never made an unnecessary movement. Such discipline seemed unnaturally perfect in an adolescent child of thirteen. He snapped, 'When did Jesus rise from the dead?'

'On the third day.'

'Who were the apostles?'

'Peter, Paul, Judas—'

'How many days on the mountaintop?'

'Forty, of course. Forty is always a magical number to the Jews because—'

He stopped her. He was silent for a long while. Then he said, 'Maybe you're right, Claudia.'

She hugged Tara, who smiled.

Quistus knew he faced a difficult choice. It came down to one essential point: how much did Nero know? When Paulinus invaded Mona and Atenoux was killed, Caer Gybi fell, Tara escaped – how much had Paulinus, watching that sail depart, tortured from the survivors to learn of this strange child, so important that thousands died rather than give her up?

Another, chillier thought struck him. Nero had long known of Tara's existence and Paulinus's provocative attack on Mona was a desperate attempt to capture or kill her before she came of age. After his failure, and the inevitable revolt, Paulinus almost wrecked Britain searching for her, never guessing she'd been spirited to Gaul. He'd been recalled in disgrace.

Something like that. It was possible.

Quistus thought back to the arena. Nero had even asked, in his stagey way, if any of Claudia's children were watching. And nobody knew. An Emperor was surrounded by greatly rewarded people whose job it was to know everything; even

Quistus, who hardly knew her, knew Claudia Rufina was child-less. But nobody knew. Nero made a joke of it, 'I suppose Pudens was more interested in prayer than his pudendum.' Only Pudens. Claudia had been eighteen when she arrived in Rome, well into the middle years of childbearing age with marriage in Britain customary at fourteen as in Rome. Nero had been finding out how much Quistus knew.

On the other hand, Quistus thought, I'm imagining it. You had to assume the all-powerful Emperor Nero was honest because if he wasn't, Rome wasn't, everything was tainted, and where was right and wrong?

Claudia whispered, 'The Romans won't slaughter a chris-tianized people, why should they? Nero meant it to happen this way. We'll live in peace.'

Suppose Nero meant well. They would travel in peace to Britain and the plan would succeed or fail. Certainly Tara made success more likely. Perhaps Nero had intended all along that Claudia would lead Quistus to her. Quistus the discoverer.

Yes, perhaps Nero meant well.

Yet it did no harm to take precautions, he decided. Politics was rarely straightforward, neat or clean, especially in Rome. By day the woods were perfect ambush territory. Two women, a girl, a child and a middle-aged man would be easy meat. 'It's too late to start out now,' he said. 'We'll travel by night. When does the moon rise?'

Tara said instantly, 'Tonight the top edge of moonrise begins an hour after sunset. But it won't show at first because of the hills, so there will be one hour of total darkness followed by about an hour of gloom. Only then will the moon shine.' She looked from the window. 'The sky will be clear.'

'Stay away from the window,' Quistus ordered. 'Get some sleep. We'll leave as soon as we see the moon.' Then he drank some herb tea, lay down in his cloak, rolled himself in it and tried to sleep, but all he could think of were the extraordinary events of the day so far. Omba watched him for a while, sitting by the window in the shadows where she couldn't be seen from outside.

A hand scented with coffee-dust covered his mouth. Quistus woke without a sound, holding his breath. People snatched breaths when they awoke; it gave them away.

Night.

He slitted his eyes so the whites didn't show. Not total darkness, he saw shadows, outlines, dim shapes. The moon was up but still hidden by hills, just as Tara foretold. He gave one small nod. His first thought was that Docilosa had run away or perhaps, even – spitefully – raised the alarm. He shouldn't have let her hear what was said this morning.

Omba took her hand from his mouth. Her lips whispered against his ear. Half a dozen at least, outside. He nodded twice. She'd opened the compartment concealed in her gold belt and pressed her knife into his hand, its deadly dart shape no longer than his palm. He shook his head and tapped her belt for the key he'd been afraid to wear around his neck – the key to the compartment under the wagon's seat – because Docilosa thought he kept the Phoenix there.

Wrongly.

He pushed himself slowly to his feet, holding his blanket one-handed in front of him to disguise his shape, his other hand holding the key. Behind him Omba slipped out another way. Through the doorway he made out the wagon in the entrance hall. At the far end of the long room the double doors to the outside remained closed. He climbed up the wheel-spokes to the driver's seat without a sound, found the lock with his fingertip, turned the key. He lifted the seat. In the wide, flat compartment lay the sword and hunting-spear Apollodorus had given him, and Metellus's gift, the bow and quiver of arrows.

A hand gripped his heel lightly. He passed down the bow and quiver to Claudia. Wearing a dark cloak, she melted back into the dark. But Tara's tunic was almost white, and showed up clearly moving to the stairs, where Claudia was trying to get her to safety.

Quistus stared back over the wagon-top. One of the double doors to the outside moved, the draught sending a few dry leaves scattering and clicking across the mosaics. He drew back his arm and stayed motionless. Fingers appeared, gripping the door to stop it banging open. Slowly the door opened wide. No thief. This man was a soldier, cloaked, armoured, helmeted. He had a sword up in one hand but no shield. He knew there wouldn't be trouble. Bit of screaming from the women maybe, some running about, begging for mercy. You didn't bother with a heavy shield for easy meat.

161

Quistus's heart beat faster. He was holding back the light hunting-spear at full stretch, the steel point concealed against his neck so it didn't show. Good for hares, useless for armour.

The first gleam of the rising moon struck through the door, illuminating the purple crest. Praetorian. His chest-plate stamped with the silver scorpion. Quistus breathed through his mouth. The praetorian came padding beside the wagon. Something made him look up. Bellacus.

'You're Roman, you filth,' Bellacus said. 'Give her.'

There was a flat metallic sound like a coin dropped in a brass dish. The arrow through Bellacus's eye had hit the inside of the back of his helmet. His body dropped.

Quistus jumped down. Claudia ran upstairs. Tara pulled another arrow from the quiver. He lost sight of them. He crouched under the wagon, a shadow in darkness. Bellacus jerked, armour scraping on the tiles, his body didn't know it was dead. Quistus gave it a shove and it lay still. He waited, panting. A bar of moonlight swung towards Bellacus's arrow-tufted head; a couple of minutes and a blind man could see him.

Running feet outside. A scream. Shouts. Shouts and screams. A shriek of sheer terror. A man's shriek, falling.

Quistus swallowed hard. He waited.

A trooper ran in, crouching, sword glinting. 'That you?' The trooper pushed back against the wall trying to work out what he saw, then ran forward lightly. He stopped by the wagon, rested his hand on the wheel. 'Where in Hell are you?' Standing so close Quistus could smell his feet. He slashed with the sword, a foot came off, the trooper fell face to face with him on the floor, staring through the wheel-spokes. Quistus jabbed through the spokes for a joint in the armour and got the sword in. He couldn't hold on. The screaming was going to bring everyone in here. He got a grip on the sword and pulled it out and pushed in and did it again until it was quiet.

He stood, moving carefully on the slippery floor. Last thing you did was fall over.

He glanced back at the stairs. He couldn't see Claudia but Tara was a white blur sitting calmly on the top step, come and get me. He guessed Claudia had the main door covered, and he knew Brits shot arrows from horseback before they could walk. No need to go that way. He moved quietly back along the wall to the library.

A shadow moved in the corner and he struck out. He stopped himself almost too late. 'Docilosa!' The blade touched her hair. Docilosa moaned, cringing, bound hands raised to protect her head. He'd forgotten her. He sliced the blade through the knots, gestured with his eyes to the hall. Two swords out there. Her lips pulled back in a silent snarl.

He moved past the ash of the fire into the room beyond. Leaves. He slid his feet forward through them, silently. A moonlit window. He heard footfalls outside and stepped into the corner by the window. A head peered into the room. No helmet, very confident. Just some killing, maybe a rape or two and a bit of fun. Quistus waited until he'd climbed halfway over the sill, one leg hanging down each side, the most uncomfortable moment. He struck. The head came half off and the body fell outside.

Quistus stepped over the half of skull that landed inside and made his way to the corner of the building. No way out here. The fountain in the central courtyard was long dry, choked with leaves, dead growth, broken statues posing among others still standing. He crept between them. A statue moved and suddenly he was fighting for his life, thrust, parry, thrust with the short swords, falling back. A sudden sheet of sparks, some contamination in the metal, blinding. He thrust into the shadow behind, jarring his hand as the sword bent: armour. The hilt pulled from his hand as the trooper went down. Quistus couldn't get the blade out. He dragged the trooper's own sword from his deathgrip and stood gasping for breath. The fight had been short but furious.

Although the night was cool he was soaked with sweat. He leant back until he breathed calmly again, a statue among statues. From the house came the whine of an arrow, a shout. A second arrow whined. The shouter weakened. A little later he heard a gurgling cry from the same direction then silence. Claudia was busy.

Quistus slipped back into the house. About half a dozen, Omba said. How many were killed? Were some casualties their own? He made it back to the library. No one. He called in a low voice, 'Omba?' Someone rushed him from the back, the two of them staggered over the fire, fell wrestling in the sparks. Omba came from behind the door, gold tattoos shining by moonlight. The trooper shouted. She put her knife in his armpit, dropping him, and broke him over her knee.

163

She held up her finger. One more. Quistus nodded, then turned slowly, hearing voices.

'I want a word with you,' Ursus was saying in the hall. 'You're her. You're the one I want.'

He knelt by the wagon with arrows in him. Tara stood in the moonlight. She was perfectly calm, curious, radiant. Claudia called from the stairs, 'Clear the line of fire, Tara.'

Tara asked clearly, 'Who are you, soldier?'

'Death.' Ursus tensed. 'Yours.' But the sword slipped from his weakening grip.

Docilosa came round the back of the wagon. She stood behind Ursus. Quistus called, 'Wait! I want to talk to him.'

Docilosa pulled Ursus's head back by his hair and sliced a blade across his throat. 'For Protia,' she said.

Omba grabbed the sword. Docilosa shrieked and ran away empty-handed. The others stepped back from the dark spreading pool, except Tara. Quistus said, 'It's all right, don't be afraid.' In truth he'd never seen anyone less afraid than her. He picked her up and carried her to the stairs. 'I think that's all,' he told Claudia. 'Omba and I'll check the grounds. Docilosa mustn't get away.' Claudia nodded.

Quistus ran into the bright moonlight. Nothing moved but the wind in the branches, and the frantic lonely figure of Docilosa, who ran to the well. She threw stones from the parapet, weeping, hysterical. 'I hate you, you bastard,' she yelled into the hole, 'it's all because of you.'

Quistus grabbed her, pushed her away, leant over the parapet. 'Stigmus!' he said bitterly. Fifteen feet down, up to his waist in gleaming water, the *Specialis* of the dreaded *Cognitionibus et Fides* looked up, bedraggled, shivering, his forehead streaked with blood from the stones Docilosa had flung down on him. His lips moved but he was beyond begging for mercy. Stigmus was dying like a dog, unloved, alone, exactly as he'd lived his life. He looked so fearful that Quistus laughed, remembering the falling cry of terror. His laughter never touched his eyes. His face was harsh, and you could believe it was the face of a cruel man.

'Seven dead men,' he said. 'They're on your conscience, Stigmus.'

'He ran, I chased him, he fell.' Omba smacked her hands. 'With a little help. He's not so tough without his tough friends.'

164

'Pull him up,' Quistus ordered. 'Tie him securely. Make sure. Give him some of Locusta's herbs to make him sleep.'

'Sleep for ever?'

'Tomorrow morning will do.' He turned to Docilosa. 'Her too. I don't want to hear from either of them until I feel stronger.'

Quistus looked back over the wagon to the Villa Ambia. The moon rode high. They'd taken longer than he'd hoped to get the wagon out, harness the horses and fill their nosebags, heap deadwood in the entrance hall and pile the bodies on top, but by dawn no trace of the night's violent events would remain. Weapons and armour had been thrown down the well and covered with parapet stones. Omba walked behind the vehicle, sweeping away their tracks.

Fire glowed faintly through the trees, brightening as flames broke through the roof. A little later the roar reached them. From inside the wagon he heard Docilosa cry out in her drugged slumber. Later he looked back from the last high hilltop. The whole villa blazed, even the leaf-strewn courtyard, and as he watched the walls cracked and the roofs fell in.

He clicked his tongue, slapped the reins, and the horses pulled downhill.

Sixteen

The Third Princess

Stigmus dreamt he was bumping and jolting and more uncomfortable than he'd ever been in his life. Then he woke, and he really was. 'Quistus,' he muttered. 'You're a dead man.'

The next time he woke was even worse. Two resilient yet slightly bony objects rested on his head, pushing his face into the floor. He was lying stuffed between two benches in a wagon, someone's face knocking into his own. He tried to use the softness of their body to cushion him from the bumps.

The things on his head were the bare feet of some sitting person. The drug the black-and-gold fiend had forced into him made him feel sick. He passed out.

He woke being sick on the person he lay beside. Daylight glowed through the roof. His hands were bound behind his back. He got his shoulder round to rub his sick off his companion's head. A girl. Blonde curls. Docilosa. The wagon lurched, throwing their faces together.

Quistus had bound him to the self-confessed murderer. The one who'd thrown stones down on him. She was crazy. Crazy as Quistus. Her knees stuck into his belly.

At least the feet were no longer resting on his head. Everyone else must be walking outside. The wagon banged over a pothole. Stigmus cursed. The girl's eyelids fluttered, then she stared at him from a finger's-length away. 'You're awake,' she murmured. 'You weren't earlier.'

'Neither were you.' He tried to move away from her. 'Your knees.'

'Your elbows.' The wagon banged and they knocked heads. She started giggling. He could see she couldn't stop herself. Actually she had rather lovely eyes, which was something he hadn't noticed before, and in fact it didn't seem strictly relevant now. 'Ow,' she complained.

'I can't move.'

'You're as much a prisoner as I am,' she said. He saw that cheered her up.

'But my situation is only temporary.'

'Yes, I think so too,' she said unpleasantly. 'At least they're keeping me alive.'

'I'll be rescued.' Actually he had no idea if that was true.

'They'll probably cut your throat after breakfast. They don't like you very much after last night. I think Princess Claudia's gone back to being Princess Gladis.'

Stigmus said, 'They're the traitors, not I,' but he paled. Docilosa turned her head from side to side, something bothering her. She sniffed, then shook her head so the sticky strands of her hair fell over her face.

'Sorry,' he said. 'Couldn't help it.'

'Oh, worse things have happened.'

'How could things possibly be worse?'

'I was sick on you earlier. That funny taste in your mouth?'

He retched. She giggled. 'I'll move my knees if you move your elbows.'

He frowned. Negotiating with a murderer. But their situation, for the moment, was the same. 'Careful,' he ordered. She slid her knee down his belly. Her eyes were round, delightfully innocent. 'Sorry,' she said. They wriggled, pushing up until they sat opposite each other, backs hard against the wooden benches, facing each other with knees drawn up. At least their ankles had not been tied. Stigmus's left thigh cramped; he was thirty years older than this rather sweet-looking young fugitive. He tried to look stern. She said, 'What's wrong now?'

'Cramp.'

She put her legs apart, one foot on each side of him, and tried to rub his thigh with her knee. 'All right?'

'Better.'

The wagon jarred agonizingly. She pulled down a cushion with her teeth and worked it under her. He tried to get one for himself but it slipped away.

He sat watching her. 'You tried to kill me.'

'I did not.'

'I saw the look in your eyes.'

'I just threw stones, I was hysterical. *You* tried to kill *me*. In fact all five of us. Who's the bigger murderer now?'

'I was following orders.'

'Murder isn't murder when it's following orders?'

'You're just being argumentative. Be silent.'

She grinned. 'Now I've made you angry, haven't I?'

He looked round, eyes searching for a way of escape. 'Which way's he taking us?'

She nodded at the glowing linen roof. 'The sun's high, behind us.'

North. He groaned. 'Tell me, girl, what does this madman think he's doing?'

'You can call me Docilosa.'

She waited. He muttered, 'Docilosa.'

'What does he think he's doing?' She sighed thoughtfully. Stigmus reckoned she must know Quistus very well by now; no doubt they were lovers until this, her punishment for killing Ursus. A man could never trust them. 'Well, what he's doing, Stigmus, is what he always does. The right thing.'

'The right thing!'

167

'At least, what he *thinks* is the right thing.'

Stigmus struggled with his bonds. 'Help!' he shouted. 'Help, anyone out there who can hear me. I am being held prisoner in this wagon against my will—'

The back door opened. Omba leaned in and pushed the tip of a knife into his ear. Stigmus pressed his lips tight shut, eyes closed. She nodded and slammed the door.

'Now you've wet yourself,' Docilosa said. 'I wouldn't tangle with this lot if I were you. Christians.'

Quistus turned off the road north of Carnutia and set up camp early, in a grassy glade by a stream. Birds called in the trees. While Omba prepared the meal he found a pool and tried to wash the taste of blood off his skin. He found flakes of it dried in his hair. He could still hear their screams. His hands started to shake.

They'd been lucky, very lucky.

Yet that in its way was an omen, wasn't it? A sign that he wasn't doing wrong. He gripped his knees with his hands, hard, to stop them shaking.

He returned to camp by twilight. Stigmus and Docilosa lay by the fire. Omba had bound their ankles as well as their hands. Tara sat on a fallen trunk, spring flowers growing around her, her hands folded neatly in her lap. She said, 'Let's kill them now.'

'That's wise.' Claudia sharpened a knife.

'I've been thinking about it,' Quistus said. 'It doesn't feel right.'

'But they're dangerous,' Tara said. 'It isn't a matter of argument, it's just common sense, isn't it?'

Stigmus rolled over. 'He hasn't got the nerve.'

'Shut up.' Docilosa gave her fellow prisoner a stare, then looked round Omba, Claudia and Tara. 'Maybe he doesn't have the nerve,' she whispered, 'but he's the only one who doesn't. Keep your mouth shut.'

Omba chopped the head off a hare. She added the joints to a pot.

'We can't trust either of them,' Claudia said. 'Stigmus, obviously not. And Docilosa's already proved she'll pay almost any price to escape – leaving over a thousand of her fellow slaves to their fate – when she cut the brake.'

'I never did!' Docilosa cried. 'Quistus, you've got to believe me.'

He shrugged.

'Quistus is the traitor,' Stigmus told Docilosa in a loud voice. 'Not me.' She threw him a look, begging him to shut up. Quistus watched them with interest. They'd been tied together in the wagon all day, the similarity of their plight forcing them into a kind of kinship.

He returned from the wagon with the paper bearing the Emperor's seal. 'This proves I'm no traitor.' He held it up for Stigmus to see. 'Anyone must give me every assistance on demand. Nero's name, Nero's seal. You don't have one of these, do you?'

Stigmus sneered, 'You're a fool if you think—'

Quistus said forcefully, 'What were your orders?'

'When Claudia led you to the girl—' Stigmus nodded at Tara. 'Kill her.'

'Were you told her name?'

'No. Just a girl. We knew she'd be about thirteen.'

'Were you told to kill anyone else?'

'Anyone who got in our way.'

'*All* of us?'

Stigmus said flatly, 'Kill you as soon as the girl was dead and Claudia was dead. Bellacus and Ursus had the same orders in case you'd killed me.' He gave Quistus a sick, fearful look. 'You traitor. Go on, prove it. Kill me now if you dare.' But he trembled.

Quistus said calmly, 'How much did Nero know when he gave you your orders?'

'He said the girl was a legend, Boadicea's daughter, a daughter who'd survived the rebellion and been hidden in Gaul. He said the British believed in her, believed she'd rise up when the horns blew, lead them to victory against us, free Britain, that sort of nonsense.' His lip curled.

'A child of thirteen is to do this? And you believed him?'

An expression of doubt flickered on Stigmus's face, but only for a moment. 'He said Claudia would make sure you found her somehow because Claudia knew where she was hidden. Claudia's a traitor to Rome, a woman with a British heart, a Christian. And she guided you straight to her, didn't she! I think that proves Nero right, don't you?'

'I am to take Christianity to Britain,' Claudia said gently. 'Tara is my lovely daughter.'

169

'She's the third princess.' Omba stirred the pot. 'There's me, and Claudia, and there's Tara. Three.'

Stigmus admitted, 'Our political and military situation in Britain is difficult, but not so chaotic that the Emperor would consider stirring a new crazy religion into such a devil's brew.' If Stigmus admitted that much, it must be true the Governor had fled the country, the army was in uproar, and conspiracies against Nero were flourishing like spring weeds. 'The girl must die, Quistus.'

'Was your group working alone? Have others been sent after us?'

Stigmus had no idea. 'Yes. You don't stand a chance.'

'Kill him,' Claudia said.

'It didn't occur to you, Stigmus, that your orders might be illegal?'

'I assure you nothing the Emperor says or does can possibly be illegal. He *is* the law.'

'And you its faithful servant,' Claudia sneered.

'The Senate makes the law,' Quistus said. 'Even Nero must obey.'

'Poor blind Stigmus,' Claudia said. 'You've been duped. Yes, I am Christian. So is Tara. We seek only a peaceful Britain, free of servitude and slavery. I swear it in God's name.'

Quistus nodded, impressed. Impossible to doubt a woman who'd suffered so much for her beliefs. Even so, he couldn't forget she'd spoken the incomprehensible British tongue to Tara when they first met – and she'd known he was watching. Saying what? Could have been anything. Almost certainly a heartfelt exchange of greetings between long-parted mother and daughter. But it could have been, for example, a warning, advice, information.

Omba ladled food. Quistus wouldn't allow knives anywhere near Stigmus or Docilosa. Tara knelt, feeding them from a spoon. Quistus looked around the firelit faces of his companions as he ate. When it came down to it the only one of them he really trusted was Omba.

And, perhaps, Tara. She wiped the dribbles from Stigmus's chin, her face totally set with concentration. Yes, you could trust a girl of thirteen to be herself.

They were on the road before dawn.

* * *

170

'I like driving horses.' Tara held the reins with a fierce but critical attention to detail – the leather was too stiff, the whip too short – but a very light touch. 'It's relaxing. I've done it before. What are their names?'

'The one with the snotty nose, that's Mucus. The one who drinks from the water bucket every chance it gets, that's Bacchus.'

She looked pleased, then narrowed her eyes. 'You just made those names up.' She elbowed him reproachfully, then accepted his apology. 'Don't they go faster? I prefer fast horses.'

'Where have you driven fast horses?'

'Britain. Chariots.' She glanced at him. 'The Catuvellauni are best.' A Brit tribe. 'The Cantiaci used to be prizewinning but they gave up their souls and went over.'

'To the Romans?'

'Yes. The Deceangli are wild-crazy-ferocious. They have wonderful ponies.' Her freckly face lit up with remembered pleasure, but only for a moment. She pushed back her hair and held it down hard with her arm. 'Dead now. No chariots allowed.'

'You know all the tribes?'

'How can I not know them?' She frowned, trying to under-stand his mind, which must seem very strange to her. 'The tribes are all that matters. They're all you need to know.'

'You must hate the Romans,' he said.

'No.' She gazed steadily into his eyes. 'I hate the Brits. The ones who have their souls stolen by Rome. Who choose slavery over freedom.' She held up the reins expertly, between her fingertips, and clicked her tongue. At once the horses broke into an easy trot. Quistus looked back. Stigmus and Docilosa walked behind the wagon on ropes. Both preferred fresh air to being locked inside. They'd been talking for hours. The ropes tautened, pulling them into a jogging run. Omba had cut Stigmus's hair with an eating knife and dressed him in rough-cut sack like any escaped slave being sent back. When anyone noticed them Quistus explained cheerfully, 'Runaways.' He put his hand lightly over Tara's. 'Slow down. Stigmus is so red in the face he might burst, and we don't want to draw attention to ourselves.'

She laughed. Tara was such a natural child in many ways. He liked her a lot. They were good friends. But she spoke Latin, Greek, Germanian, Gaulish and half a dozen dialects

171

of Brit. She knew all the stars and their times of rising and setting, and which ones were planets. She'd read all the major poets, Brit and Greek, and recited their works for hours at a time if asked. She carried on under her breath if she was asked to stop, her idea of fun. Her memory was phenomenal, sharpened like a blade.

And there was more. Tara slept with her eyes open, bolt upright, cross-legged, with her hands resting palm upward in her lap. That was quite a sight. He'd seen a centipede crawl over her shoulders, around her neck, and back down her arm to the ground without a flicker from her wide-open eyes. She was forbidden to kill without reason. Nature-child.

'You know we're going to Londinium?' he asked. 'Ever been?'

'We call it London. London on the River Thames, not Tamesis. Of course I've been there. I'm a child. Who notices us? Children are ordinary.'

He grunted, half in amusement, half baffled by her. 'Not you, Tara. Not you.'

She gave him that steady gaze again, so difficult to see past that she could have been asleep. Then she smiled cheerfully, clicked her tongue, and the horses trotted eagerly.

The moon didn't rise until the night was half gone, giving them three or four hours of rest while it was too dark to travel. Stigmus and Docilosa slept a little further from the fire than the others; except they weren't asleep. Stigmus had whispered secrets about himself to Docilosa that he couldn't have said aloud or by daylight, things he'd never told anyone else – certainly never any woman; even that he had been his father's slave, and he told her about his mother's dreadful death, and his father's too, and his brothers. Though not the whole truth. That wasn't what you told anyone, ever.

'It's all so sad,' she whispered. She was a good listener. 'Surely you've got somebody? You must have a wife, a powerful and important man like you.'

She sensed the shake of his head in the dark, the gleam of his eyes as the fire sent up a few sparks. No. 'That's such a shame,' she murmured. They lay on their backs, bound, helpless, staring at the stars.

He whispered, 'Do you love him?'

'Who?'

172

'You know.'

'*Quistus*?'

'You're quite pretty, really. A long journey, close company. He must have thought of it.'

She thumped her bound hands. 'Would you call this loving behaviour?' She frowned. 'Or are you asking if I've had him?'

'Have you?'

'What's it to do with you?'

'I just wondered. I don't think any less of you if you haven't. I just wondered if, you know, there was some way of using him . . . us getting away together.'

'I don't think he's ever had sex. No, seriously. I mean, I know he's had children. But – like spontaneous combustion. I can't imagine him loving, like *loving*, like doing it, with anyone. He probably chose his wife for her ugliness.'

'You're bitter.'

'I'm not.'

'You aren't like most slaves.' Stigmus chuckled in the dark. 'You really hate him, don't you.'

'Why should I want you to get away?' She settled beside him, close. 'See, if you got away,' she whispered, 'that would mean the executioner for me, wouldn't it?'

He took a deep breath. 'I could put in a good word.'

'I know your sort.'

'No. Nobody knows me. Not really knows.'

'I do, don't I? After all you've told me.'

'Yes. I suppose so.'

'Listen, if you got me off, you wouldn't regret it. I'm not even a slave. Ask Quistus. I'm the richest woman in Rome. Ask him who my mother was.'

They lay still as Omba got up sleepily. She threw fresh wood on the fire then settled down again.

Stigmus put his head next to Docilosa's. She whispered her mother's name in his ear. The grass rustled as he twisted, staring at her. 'Really?' She nodded, the firelight dancing in her eyes.

'I'm not surprised,' he said. 'You look so lovely. It was there all the time. I see it now.'

'Quistus is a thief. He stole my Phoenix. That's why I'm tied up, so I can't have what's mine. That's why I hate him.' Her voice filled with tears. 'And you call me his lover.'

'I'm sorry. I apologize.'

'No man's ever loved me. I'm so afraid of dying alone, unloved.'

'Docilosa, I—'

'Docey.'

'I'm so sorry for you. Don't cry.' But she was. He could hear her. He lifted his bound hands with a groan.

She whispered, 'I'd give you anything if you could find it. We could escape. We could be together.'

Stigmus inhaled the scent of her body in the dark.

Morning. The legionaries of VIII *Bis Augusta* stood on the dusty roads in the hot sun, as they had since dawn. Their armour shone. Their grim faces stared southward. Around midday the wind stirred their cloaks. *Bis Augusta* didn't move. Towards evening the wind from the west brought rain. They stood unmoving, the rain dripping from their helmets down their long greasy cloaks.

Overwhelming force. The cohort of five hundred men covered, like a great red-brown wing, the three main roads that approached Samarobriva. To reach the great port of Bononia that linked Gaul with Britain, a traveller must pass through, or very close to, Samarobriva.

With that in mind, and given the known slipperiness of their quarry, a further five hundred troopers were stationed in line through the dense lowland forest of these parts. A phalanx was detailed to block each of the dozens of local roads, *diverticuli*, tracks, paths, culverts and, the centurions bragged, every snail-trail.

They waited.

Seventeen

Diversionary Tactics

The wagon trundled over the hill, Stigmus and Docilosa roped behind the spare horses which had their heads buried in nosebags, chewing contentedly. Stigmus halted in surprise, staring at the broad estuary winding to the sea. 'This isn't

Paris!' he shouted. 'Where's Samarobriva? Where are we? Is that the British ocean?' The rain from the west had eased and the sun shone low beneath the lifting lid of cloud, making the sea gold.

Claudia smiled nastily. 'Surprised, are we?'

Quistus said over his shoulder, 'Omba, gag him. There's a village.'

Stigmus looked wild. Omba pinched his nose until his mouth opened then knotted the cord tight. 'Quistus doesn't like doing what people like you expect him to,' she tutted. 'Didn't you guess? We took the north road out of Carnutia, not the northeast. Only eighty miles to the sea.'

'You're hurting him,' Docilosa cried loyally. Stigmus gave her a grateful look. No one had ever cared about him before. Not really cared, like Docilosa obviously did. It was a new feeling, strangely disturbing, yet not unpleasant. She was obviously falling in love with him. True, she intrigued him. Usually he could pin people down straight away. She was different. A slave, but freed. A murderer, yet so beguilingly innocent in appearance, those intoxicating eyes, golden curls, her skin like white wine. And she was rich, if she lived. And yet he must be her executioner. And yet, there was the Phoenix. But for the rope tugging him forward Stigmus would have turned round and round like the warring emotions in his heart.

Of course, he could take her, then take it. The two didn't have to go together. She was guilty. A remote villa for himself, Lusitania perhaps, to enjoy his fortune. Plenty of women there. A man with no need of a career had plenty of time for women.

'I'm not frightened of you, Quistus!' Docilosa shouted. Stigmus was pleased that she was publicly taking his side.

Quistus said, 'Gag her too.' They'd often seen slaves gagged to stop them shouting obscenities at decent folk, and Docilosa was more impulsive than Stigmus. She might even decide her interests lay with him once she knew the hiding-place of the Phoenix, if she thought she could persuade him to spare her life in return. How little she knows Stigmus, Quistus thought. The man has a stone for a heart.

'Gag me? You wouldn't dare,' Docilosa told Omba. Omba, grinning, made sure the knots were good and tight.

Quistus jumped down leaving Tara with the reins. The road crossed the last narrows of the river on a wooden bridge. The tide was out and they smelt mud. Further out the mud turned to a dried-out estuary with the river-channel winding between sandbanks. Quistus led them left off the bridge and they came to a fishing village, Loium, a few thatch cottages with boats leaning on the sand below. The women laying out seaweed to dry didn't look up. Stigmus watched carefully as Quistus approached the fishermen repairing nets. Several shook their heads at once, walking away. Finally a man with a long moustache put his hand out, nodding. Quistus paid him. The man shook his head. Quistus pointed at the wagon. The man nodded, lifting the horses' legs, then shook his head again. He pointed at Docilosa but his wife shouted from the doorway. Quistus offered him the bow instead. The man took it then nodded for the sword and hunting-spear as well. They spat on their hands and embraced. Claudia breathed a sigh of relief.

Quistus came back. 'Captain Drappes will take us to Britain. He says we're lucky. Nine days out of ten the wind blows from the west but he says an easterly's due with the tide tonight.'

'He's wrong,' Tara said. 'The tide's already turned, but the wind won't blow until dawn.' She sniffed the air. 'And then—'

'That's enough,' Claudia said. Tara was instantly silent.

Drappes's fishing boat *Squamus* was small but seaworthy-looking, with a high bow and stern, beamy, cut low amidships with holes for oars, used when the wind was foul. Instead of Roman linen Drappes used traditional Caletan leather sails like his father before him. The bow was decked in, making a small cabin reeking of fish, and there was another in the stern for the steersman to stand on. Stigmus and Docilosa exchanged helpless looks. Drappes's sons helped carry the few possessions from the wagon, then unhitched the horses to take them away. Quistus ran back. He'd forgotten something, and Docilosa stared as he took off one of the nosebags, turned it inside out, and used the tip of a knife to split open the pouch sewn into the bottom seam. Her eyes widened as the Phoenix, red as flames in the last of the sun, fell like liquid fire into his hand.

Quistus carried the necklace to the boat and turned his back, speaking to Omba, then they ducked into the forecabin. Quistus came out almost immediately, nose crinkled as if by a bad smell, and beckoned. Claudia pushed Stigmus and Docilosa across the sand. Quistus and Omba swung them aboard, pushing them into the cabin. A candle made the fish-stink even worse. Quistus cut the gags off and left the hatch half-open. 'If you try and speak to Drappes or his lads I'll throw you overboard.'

'We won't make any trouble,' Stigmus said.

Quistus sat on the rail. They were waiting for the tide. He played knuckles with Tara but she won. They played again, she won again. Omba guarded the hatch. 'Did you see that?' Docilosa whispered to Stigmus. 'In a *nosebag*. The one cursed place I didn't look.'

Omba overheard. 'When I asked him where it was,' she chuckled, 'he even told me not to be nosey.'

Docilosa didn't laugh. She sat white-lipped with rage, deceived, tricked, unforgiving.

Drappes and his two boys, lighter versions of himself with shorter moustaches, came aboard. The rising tide lifted the boat shortly afterwards but Drappes insisted on waiting for the ebb, letting it carry them downstream. The boat rolled as waves reached them. The deep-ocean wind from the west blew salt in their faces. 'You were right,' Quistus told Tara. The lads, glowering, rowed. Nothing could be seen of the rocky shores but for a while they heard surf. Drappes steered with an oar from the stern, dropping a weighted line overboard from time to time, navigating by the depth of the water and the stars.

Quistus slept, woken at dawn by the slap of the sail filling with wind from the east, behind them. 'Tara's always right,' Claudia said. They stood on the bow, listening to the surge of parted waves beneath their feet. 'Quistus, I've been thinking. You know, this wind could take us straight to Vectis.'

He frowned. 'Vectis? Why there?'

'Sheltered behind the island is Port Adurni, a wonderful natural harbour where we could be sure of landing safely.'

He thought for a while. 'You mentioned Vectis before.' He couldn't remember where, or in what connection.

'Oh, it's unimportant. It's convenient, that's all. I really think we should.'

'Volusia Faustina's in London. That's where the Christian movement is. I can't imagine there's many Cross-worshippers to be found on Vectis or some provincial seaport. It's not like Tarsus or Ephesus, Claudia, with smart Christian intellectuals like Pudens chattering round dinner tables. It's Britain.'

'God has spoken to me.'

177

'Not to me.'

'Perhaps you don't hear him. It's such a shame to waste this wind. We'd have to beat against it to get up the British Channel to the Thames. We'd make better time landing at Port Adurni and travelling overland to London.'

He sniffed the wind. 'Let's see what your God decides. He makes the wind blow, doesn't he? Let him decide which way he wants to blow us.'

Her lips tightened. 'Very well, Quistus. But you're making a mistake.'

At nightfall the wind backed to the north, pushing them back the way they'd come. 'There, I told you it would,' Tara said. Claudia nodded and squeezed her hand. 'I know,' she murmured, 'but I had to try.'

'Is the wind really God's will?'

Claudia made out Quistus wrapped in his cloak by the rail. She wasn't sure if he could overhear. 'Yes,' she said.

'That's strange,' Tara said. 'Why isn't it blowing us to Vectis?'

Claudia put her finger to her lips. The conversation was over.

By daybreak the wind had backed westerly, blowing the little *Squamus* up-Channel under its bat-wing sail. 'Excellent,' Quistus said, but during the afternoon the wind strengthened and Drappes shortened sail. The seas grew steeper, rushing the little vessel forward as each wave passed beneath. Drappes called his lads to help steer. Quistus ducked into the creaking, swaying forecabin with a skin of fresh water. It was dark in here even by daylight. He held the spout to Docilosa's lips. 'I don't want it,' she said. 'If I was dying of thirst I wouldn't take it from you.' Quistus shrugged and offered it to Stigmus.

Stigmus turned his head away. 'I won't take water from a traitor.'

'Stay thirsty.' Quistus backed out, but Stigmus called, 'How much longer?'

'I can see both sides of the Channel, white cliffs on our left. That's Britain. But it's getting dark and Drappes doesn't like it, he's heaving-to. We'll make land tomorrow morning.'

'Quistus.' Stigmus called him back. 'It's important.'

'Better be.'

'This is your last chance to make things come out right, Quistus. Listen to me. We're on the same side. You know why

178

the Emperor chose you, nobody else? He trusts your heart. You have a good heart. He knows you'll do the right thing in the end. The right thing for Rome.'

'I should take lessons in humanity from Nero.'

'Kill Tara.' Stigmus held up his bound hands. 'It's your duty. If you haven't got the guts, release me, I'll do it. I'll kill her for you, she won't suffer, I'll do it while she's asleep. I'm begging you for the last time. We can hear everything down here. I heard them.' He nodded to a gap in the planks. 'The girl and her lying mother. *Dentes Elysia*, the Teeth of Heaven. That's what she told the girl. Does that sound like Christianity to you?' He shook his head. 'I know Christianity, Quistus. I examine Christians with burning iron, whip, flail and blade. I've heard last words beyond count, I've endured forgiveness until I've screamed aloud. I've never heard of the Teeth of Heaven. Not once.'

'He's telling you the truth,' Docilosa said. 'We heard them last night.'

Quistus hesitated. 'Perhaps it's in their Gospels.'

Stigmus said, 'I promise you they aren't taking Christianity to Britain, Quistus. No peaceful cohabitation with Rome. You're chasing a dream. There's no such thing as peace or love. They'll set the country on fire against us.'

The candle had burned to a stump. Quistus lit a fresh candle from it, dripped hot tallow from the flame to set it in place, and blew out the stump. Then he backed out and closed the hatch.

He sat by the rail, thinking. The wind was cool and the mast swept across the stars. Behind him Claudia whispered to Tara, heads together, and sometimes Tara laughed. He called, 'Claudia, what are the Teeth of Heaven?'

'They're Tara's teeth,' Claudia smiled. 'Why? We were talking of them only yesterday. They're so white because she eats no meat or honey.'

'That's right,' Tara said.

Quistus turned back to the sea, nodding. 'Thanks.'

Stigmus whispered, 'Docey, I've been thinking.'

'About me?' She snuggled, obviously innocently unaware of the pressure of her thigh arousing him. Stigmus lay back with his head against the inner curve of the bow trying to think. He'd failed again with Quistus.

179

'Of course, you, Docey.' Her head was on his shoulder; he wished he could unbind his hands and stroke her hair to convince her of his sincerity. 'About you, and the Phoenix.'

'*My* Phoenix,' she teased him.

'I know where it is.'

She sat up straight, most beautiful by candlelight, her hair falling over her shoulders. 'Quistus has got it,' she said. 'I saw him. He hid it in his clothes.'

He gave a small jerk of his head. She leant down, her ear to his lips.

Stigmus whispered in her hair, 'He gave it to Omba.'

Claudia lay watching the stars move in the heavens. Dark waves jostled the boat. She knew the position of every rope, and she'd studied for hours how Drappes held the steering oar, how he used it, how much strength he pushed with, how he let the wind and waves do most of the work of steering. You didn't have to be strong.

God help me, she prayed. Let me be right about this. Give me a sign.

She waited, every sense edgy. In a while a shooting star made a scratch across the stars.

Tara sat asleep beside her, but of course she wasn't really asleep. The stars moved in her wide-open eyes.

Claudia sat up slowly. Quistus was a shadow sleeping near the stern. Omba lay stretched out amidships, almost invisible except for a few glints of gold on her skull. Claudia turned to Tara who stared at her at once, whispering, 'Yes, Princess Gladis?'

A chill ran up Claudia's back. Gladis. The child was right.

She slipped a knife from her cloak, passing it across. It was sharp enough for a man to shave himself. She'd bought it outside the baths in Lugdunum, and it wasn't the only one. The knife disappeared instantly in Tara's hand; she'd reversed it in a flash, the handle hidden in her hand, the blade up her sleeve.

'Tara, you will do exactly what I say.'

'Yes.'

'If I tell you to put your knife in a man's eye, you will do it.'

'Yes.'

'You will learn the position of all the ropes and how they are tied.'

180

'I already know.'

Claudia promised, 'I will not fail you, Tara.'

About an hour before dawn nautical twilight began, drawing a line between the darkness of sea and sky, and the stars faded. Drappes shouted. The wind had backed further in the night, wind and tide pushing them much closer to the British shore than he'd thought; they saw a broad valley reaching the sea between the chalk cliffs, which glowed on each side like protective ghosts in the glimmering eastern light. 'You see it?' Quistus called from the bow. 'I reckon that's Anderidos. That'll do.' He grinned at Claudia. 'Fifty miles to London!'

Drappes didn't like it. He didn't know these waters. Shallows, lee shore, the sea was rough, the tide was wrong. He let fly the sail so it flapped like a wing but did no work, and his lads bent their backs to the oars. Dark clouds from the south extinguished the sunrise so the day fell gloomier than the night. The first raindrops pattered, then rushed over them until they hardly saw the shore ahead. An anchored ship rose out of the gloom, a barge moored alongside loading roughcast iron pigs from the mines. Quistus made out surf ahead, then a darker break a little to the right. A river-mouth. He pointed. The barge had to load somewhere; there would be calmer water, a riverside dock.

'Omba!' He beckoned. 'Drappes won't stop long. Get Stigmus and Docilosa up.' She nodded, raindrops streaming from her cheeks, then banged the hatch open and ducked inside. The hatch closed.

There was a loud clatter. One of Drappes's lads had fallen off his seat. He grabbed his oar and threw his father an ashamed look. Everyone gave a sigh of relief that it hadn't been the boat hitting something.

In the forecabin Omba was crouched on hands and knees, Stigmus on top of her with his legs tight around her waist, the rope binding his hands hauled tight across her throat. She half stood, almost crushing him against the low beams. Docilosa kicked her in the belly and she went down again. Stigmus whacked his forehead into the back of her neck, butting for all he was worth. Her head hit the floor hard. He hauled with all his strength, finally clasping his fingers together behind her neck, levering tight. He could hear no sound from her. He gasped, 'Is she breathing?' Docilosa nodded, eyes shining.

'Not for much longer.'

Stigmus snarled with the effort. Omba's hands reached back and found his, squeezing, but her strength was going. He hauled tight enough to break her neck, then let her flop.

They rolled her big body over. The gold ornaments on Omba's broad belt moved under their frantic fingers, and some opened. A lion's tooth. A lock of hair. A mummified finger. A dart-shaped knife which Stigmus grabbed. Docilosa grinned. A Phoenix.

The heavy leather sail flapped noisily, throwing out raindrops. Quistus stood on the bow, hanging on as the last dying wave swept them into the river-mouth. The current pushed them back. 'Row!' Drappes's lads hauled on the oars and *Squamus* inched crabwise across the flow to a ramshackle wooden dock built along the riverbank. Quistus jumped ashore with a rope. The boat swung in hard, driven by the wind and the current sweeping downstream. An oar caught against the dock and splintered, knocking the Drappes boy off his seat again. He sprawled. Quistus took a turn of the rope around a post. Both post and rope creaked, taking the weight of the boat. Claudia jumped on to the sterndeck.

'Claudia!' he shouted. 'This way! Get ashore!'

Claudia didn't hear her name. The wind flapped her cloak. She came up to Drappes and threw out both arms without warning, pushing him clear over the stern into the water. He came up splashing. Calmly she lifted the steering oar so he couldn't grab hold. The current swept him away.

Quistus stared in disbelief. He shouted, 'Omba!' The hatch opened, but it wasn't Omba who came up.

Docilosa held the Phoenix in her bound hands, her eyes bright with victory. Stigmus was behind her.

'Omba!' Quistus shouted again. No answer. Probably they'd killed her. Stigmus held her knife, but it dripped with rainwater, not blood – she lived, perhaps. Stigmus reversed the blade, sawing through his bonds. His face was savage and intent as he stared at Docilosa's back. She held up the jewels, jeering at Quistus.

'Mine!' she called. 'Omba said you wouldn't mind. Farewell, Quistus, and curse you!'

The rope burned in Quistus's hands. The gap widened

between the dock and the boat as the speed of the current took hold. He hauled tight, tying the rope off on the post with quick painful jerks of his hands. The rope sprang bar-taut. Three feet of black fast-flowing water between the dock and the boat's waist, four feet. Five feet. Lowest amidships, best place to jump. Now or never. He jumped.

Docilosa yelled, 'Stigmus, stop him!' She sounded frightened. Quistus hung down the boat's side, his feet in the water.

Stigmus leant over Docilosa's shoulder. His hands were free. He slipped the knife easily through the loop of the Phoenix and snatched it from her grasp. She turned on him screaming. He said, 'Sorry, Docey. Safer this way.'

He pushed her with his free hand, and she went over the edge still screaming.

Quistus almost caught her. For a moment they were face to face. Her roped hands couldn't hang on. She slipped down his body. He reached with one hand, swinging, grabbing, but she dropped with a splash. Black water. Bubbles. Her bound hands came up as she was swept away, the only sign of her.

'Your turn, traitor.' Stigmus leant over the rail, eyes cold as stone. 'I'll be a great man for this, Quistus. It was *my* heart the Emperor trusted, not yours.' He slashed with the knife, but Quistus dropped into the waters.

Stigmus turned with a smile. Drappes would be easily persuaded to sail back to Gaul, but first there was business to attend to. 'Tara,' he called. 'Come here and help me, there's a good girl. You want to be a good girl, don't you?'

The child stood on the high bow, watching him calmly. The pouring rain made her hair hang down her body, red as blood clinging to her white tunic. Her legs were skinny as sticks, just a young child's legs. She looked past him.

Stigmus turned. Claudia on the stern held the steering oar just as Drappes had, under one arm, her other arm crossed in front of her. No sign of the captain.

Claudia nodded. At once Tara let the mooring rope fly. The boat slid downstream, turning in the current. Stigmus saw Quistus floundering ashore, dragging something limp over the mud. Docilosa. Life would have been lovely with such a gorgeous creature for a week or two, but Stigmus knew he wouldn't have survived their first blazing row. Better that justice caught up with her. Even if she really loved him – and he really did love her, yes he really did, she turned his limbs to water and his heart to joy, and he'd mourn her as she was crucified in the arena under Nero's stern judicial gaze – even so, however great her love was (and he was sure she *did* love him), she would always have too much reason to kill him. He was, after all, the only honest witness to her confession.

It wouldn't have taken Docilosa long to come to the same rational, sensible conclusion he had: in their relationship, death was safer than love.

He turned to Tara, smiling to reassure the child as he gripped the rail, hiding the weapon against his belly, balancing himself for the thrust. 'Don't be afraid.'

But it was Stigmus who screamed. Before he knew it she'd thrust a knife through his hand, fixing him to the rail. He fell to his knees screaming, trying to jerk the blade out with slippery fingers. She stepped away from him calmly, but he was too frantic about the knife and his agony to think of grabbing her.

'Tara,' Claudia called. 'Attend to the mainsheet.'

Tara observed Stigmus critically. His screams were weakening. Good, the pain would numb his intelligence. No need to fix his other hand with the little knife he'd dropped; she'd deal with him later. She picked it up and loped down to the waist of the little vessel, heading for Drappes's lads.

They saw her coming and jumped overboard.

Tara, obeying her mother's orders, attended to the mainsheet.

Quistus dragged Docilosa on to the mud. She sat streaming mud and rainwater, shrieking obscenities at Stigmus as the boat caught the wind, sail bellying, turning away. Stigmus knelt by the rail, his face contorted, clawing at one blood-covered hand with the other, tugging the blade bare-fingered in his agony. Quistus called, 'Omba.'

No reply. Rain and mist hid the boat.

He helped the Drappes lads ashore, pointing them to the forlorn figure of their father on the beach. 'I suggest you steal a boat.'

The boys grinned. 'How d'you think we got that one,' they said together.

Quistus returned to Docilosa, who'd given up curses for tears. 'Don't worry,' he told her. 'Your predicament is no worse than before.'

She gave a despairing cry, inconsolable. 'I held it in my hand,' she cried. 'It was all mine.'

'I thought you were going to share it with Stigmus.'

'I was.'

He glanced curiously. 'Really, Docilosa?'

She rubbed her arm over her face, nodding. 'He could have had it all, as long as I had him. I loved him, Quistus.' She wept muddy tears. 'Now look what he's done to me.' The rain lessened. They glimpsed the ship beyond the surf, turning west. She shrieked, 'I'll kill you!'

'Docilosa, listen to me. Is Omba alive?'

'Stigmus tried to kill her. Yes, she's alive. I heard her take a breath.'

Quistus cut her hands free and lifted her on to the dock. At the end of the road was a stable for the use of imperial couriers. He woke the startled ostler, unfolded the heavy paper, and pushed the Emperor's impressive permission into the man's face. The ink had run, but the seals hadn't.

'I'm travelling on the Emperor's command. Give me two horses. Now.'

Eighteen

The Day After Tomorrow

'You're mad,' Volusia Faustina said. They were sitting in her simple dining room. 'It does you credit. But you're undoubtedly mad.'

'No, Claudia's mad,' Docilosa said, finishing her cup of wine.

'I fear, my friends, that Claudia is all too sane.' Volusia shrugged. 'That is, if her objective is to raise the British in rebellion against Rome rather than simple submission to God. Knowing Claudia, that's likely. She has a British heart.'

Quistus said, 'She kidnapped her own daughter and sailed off with her to who knows where.'

Volusia shook her head. 'She doesn't see it as kidnapping. Neither does Tara. It's their duty. It's what they were born for. Sacrifice.' She said gently, 'Omba will die. So will Stigmus. You can't save them. No one can.'

'Omba's my friend,' Quistus said firmly. 'Do I desert my friends, Volusia?'

'You risked your life for us. You did too much.'

'Did I desert you?'

'No. You could have been killed for helping us.'

'Claudia's my friend. We've been through a lot together on the road. We know each other too well for me to stand back. And Tara – I *can't*, Volusia. I can't let a child die. I just can't. I can't believe you're giving up like this. What's wrong with you?'

Volusia said steadily, 'The Brits don't see sacrifice as death. To them, it's resurrection.'

Quistus shook his head; he'd drunk nothing, eaten only a mouthful or two. 'You're the Bishop of London, Volusia. You must believe there's hope for Christianity, or you wouldn't be here.'

'There's hope in London, perhaps. Slowly. Little by little. Perhaps York. A few other places, little nests of Christian love and peace. But not yet. Not now.' Volusia, who had put on a little weight, rose from the table and pointed at the scene beyond the window. 'This is what I have to work with. Three years ago, Boadicea destroyed most of what you see. Her women cut the breasts off collaborators. Thousands who couldn't run away were crucified. Every building was burnt. Everything Roman was smashed. We're rebuilding with amazing speed, but there's a long way to go.'

Volusia's house-church stood by the main road to the west, on a hilltop overlooking the Thames, which was crossed by an elm-wood bridge. Even though it was evening labourers still worked on the governor's palace and the baths, rebuilding in stone. Hundreds of thatch huts had sprung up along the roadsides and the markets were busy. Boats, some of them merchanters belonging to Volusia's brother Briginus, threaded between the islands. Beyond the grassy embankments enclosing the young town stretched endless forest. They'd ridden from the coast in one day, changing fast horses at each way-station with a wave of Imperial seals.

Volusia watched Quistus seriously. 'I owe you my life,

186

Septimus,' she acknowledged. 'But even we Christians believe the End will come any day. The future is short, we have little time. That's what Paul teaches us. Any day now Jesus returns among us and brings an end to time and suffering, and the joyful resurrection of the dead will create Heaven. Yes, even we believe the dead will live again. I wish there was more I could do to help. If there was anything I could do to save Omba, believe me—'

'How are you so sure she'll be killed?'

'This is Britain,' Volusia said. 'It's the way things happen.' She spread her hands. 'Beliefs can't be changed overnight, Septimus. She must die to live. Claudia will die. Tara will die. They'll be reborn infinitely greater than they are. It's uncivilized, but not so very different, is it? And it's what the British believe with all their hearts and souls.'

'Frankly I don't know what's civilized and what's not any more.'

'I want my Phoenix back.' Docilosa helped herself from the wine-jug. 'Then they can kill that bastard Stigmus. I hope they cut his liver out.'

'They won't do that.' Volusia stood decisively. 'Septimus, when you arrived I sent for your friend Cerialis, who's in from the country and quartered in the new wing of the governor's palace. We still have a little time before he arrives. There's something I need you to see.' She led them into the garden – 'my diocese', she called it – where some women kept the place tidy. They heard the voices of others washing up. 'I think these old women have lived here for ever,' Volusia said in a low voice, leading them past the usual vegetable plots and the orchard.

On the exact summit of the hill a collection of rough stone slabs had been left propped together as though they grew from the earth, or perhaps were the debris of some much greater structure that had worn away. 'A pagan shrine,' she murmured. 'We try to take over such places, adapting them to our new faith. But this—' She crossed herself. 'I think this place has been holy for thousands of years. Perhaps for as long as there have been people. The Brits call this Lud's Hill – they believe King Lud will return. Sometimes I think those old women know more than I do.'

'Guardians of the shrine,' Docilosa said soberly.

Volusia lit a lamp and ducked between the slabs, descending

187

into the shadows. Quistus followed the uncertain light. The tunnel turned steeply downward, then broadened out. The air was cold, blowing up from below. Other levels continued down. Volusia, halting, held up the lamp. 'I'm allowed no further. I think you'll find this is enough.'

Icons covered the rock walls, faces painted with fingers, stick figures, mostly red ochre. Many seemed to stare back at the person watching them, their stylized round faces open-mouthed as if screaming, childishly drawn but oddly disturbing. Red streaks rose from their spiky hair. Volusia pointed at the two largest figures which stood with joined hands, their outlines filled inside with stick people. Docilosa dropped her cup. Wine splashed. 'They're babies!' she said.

Volusia nodded. 'It's a wicker marriage. Tara and Claudia will die in flames and, reborn, ignite a fire that will set the country alight. It's Tara's duty. It always was.'

They stared at the ghastly painting, almost unable to believe such a horror could exist.

Volusia led the way back up to the surface and blew out the lamp. 'Don't say anything. Let's get back to the house.'

Quintus Petillius Cerialis was the best and worst sort of military commander: he had a streak of lightning in his brain. The enthusiasm beloved by his supporters was called reckless by his enemies, his bravery called foolhardy, and the intense loyalty he inspired led his troops to follow him heedlessly into danger. Boadicea's chaotic army sweeping forward had killed one man in three of Cerialis's legion, IX *Hispana*, yet Cerialis himself had counter-charged with a thousand cavalry and somehow got the infantry clear, avoiding total massacre. He was a lucky general. His men were no doubt eager to even the score with the Brits, but he'd succeeded in restraining them. Quistus looked at this energetic, well-connected leader the same age as himself and thought: but for good and bad luck I could have been Cerialis, and Cerialis could have been me.

Cerialis dropped his helmet clattering on Volusia's table. 'Quistus!' They embraced and exchanged pleasantries; Cerialis had two sons and his wife was well. Over the second cup of wine he got down to business. 'What brings you here, Quistus, old friend?'

'Revolution,' Volusia said. 'Trouble follows him.'

'Perhaps,' Quistus said.

Cerialis was interested. 'Brits against Romans? Romans against Romans?'

'It's that bad?'

Cerialis put his feet up, drinking. 'It's worse. Nero's lost control of Britain. Nobody likes a loser. Backstabbers everywhere. Each legion backs a different candidate for Emperor. Vitellius and Otho in Germany are on the point of throwing their names in the ring. Old Galba in Spain too, they say.' He spoke behind his hand. 'Even my own father-in-law, Vespasian.' He looked at Quistus over his cup. 'You don't care about any of this, do you.'

'My concerns are personal. Three princesses, two of them willingly, will shortly suffer ceremonial sacrifice somewhere in Britain. This event – this unbelievably horrific *spectacle* – will cement the British tribes as one and, in the likely absence of an effective Roman resistance, make Boadicea's uprising look like a dinner party. What concerns me, however, is that each princess is my friend.'

'Absolutely,' Cerialis said. 'Can't let it happen.' He added, 'The last thing that we want at this particularly delicate political moment, if you'll forgive me for saying so, is the Brits running riot.' Quistus knew that by *we* Cerialis meant the conspirators against Nero. Cerialis looked bland. 'What's the venue?'

'We don't know,' Volusia said. 'Oak groves are sacred to the Brits, the ceremonies take place there. The Romans have chopped down most of them, the Brits have hidden the rest. Perhaps an island somewhere.'

Cerialis nodded. 'Less chance of interference. Mona? Hercules? Manavia?'

'Vectis,' Quistus said. 'Claudia was all for going there. She sailed the ship west.'

'Good. I have a detachment at Port Adurni.' Cerialis drummed his fingers. 'Vectis. The Brits call the place Wight, the Isle of Wight. Wight means *warrior*. No, more than that.' He corrected himself. 'A place of supernatural powers. Supernatural warriors.'

'That fits,' Quistus said. 'That's the place.'

'Big island though. Lots of ground to cover.'

'Excuse me.' Docilosa sat quietly at the end of the table. 'Stigmus and I overheard—'

'The Teeth of Heaven.' Quistus remembered. 'When I asked Claudia she gave me some story.'

'It's a place,' Cerialis said. 'High chalk cliffs. South-west of the island. Remnants standing in the sea like a row of very sharp, pointed teeth.' He finished his wine. 'I don't suppose you want to stay here while I get all the glory.'

'I'll ride all night if I have to.'

'Better to get some rest. It's after midnight. This wind isn't helping your friends much and I don't suppose Claudia or Tara have the strength to row, or that they can force Stigmus to, especially if he's injured. I'll have one of the governor's messenger pigeons sent to Adurni with a message to my fellows to wake up and get a ship or two ready for sea. With a bit of luck we can intercept *Squamus* before they make landfall.'

'I appreciate it.'

'Only about a hundred men at first, I'm afraid.'

'Against possibly thousands on the island,' Volusia said.

'Excellent odds,' Cerialis responded cheerfully.

'No, wait,' Volusia said. 'You don't understand. This is a huge gathering of the tribes. Some will have travelled for weeks by backroads and tracks through the forest you've never heard of, from all over Britain.'

'So?' Quistus said.

'It's early morning now. Tomorrow's the end of April, the last day of the year. The day after tomorrow's Baaltane, the start of the new year.'

Cerialis frowned. 'Our festival of flowers?'

'Only to the Romans.' Volusia turned to Quistus. 'You saw the paintings. To the Brits it's Baaltane. Baal, the god of spring, of rebirth. Baal's festival of fire. That soon.'

Quistus said, 'I only need a couple of hours sleep.'

'Leave at dawn. It's a two-day ride. I'll arrange with my brother Briginus for a letter – most of his trade is with Hibernia, but he picks up cargo along the south coast. He may have a boat you can use.'

'I have orders to send.' Cerialis put on his helmet. 'I'll catch up.'

'Mad,' Volusia repeated. 'Both of you. Undoubtedly mad.'

Quistus woke. He felt warm breath on his face. 'It's only me,' Docilosa whispered. She was lying beside him fully clothed. 'Don't pull away. I'm so lonely. It's almost dawn.'

He sat up.

'Let me come with you.' Docilosa stroked his face. 'All these miles we've been together. You've never slept with me. You never even let me say no.' The lamp on the dresser lit her face down one side. She looked lovely. 'I've never been had by anyone who loved me. It's so sad. I just want what other people have. It's all I ever wanted. It's all gone so wrong. I've been misunderstood.'

'I don't love you, Docilosa. You can't come with me.'

'She's dead. Your wife died a long time ago, Quistus. Let her go. Let your feelings show. I just want you to live. I want us to be together. I can't be your daughter, but I can be your wife.'

She was wearing a dark blue gown, something very long and chaste-looking of Volusia's, with a white neck. He stood with a shudder. 'Docilosa, you'll stay here with Volusia. That's an order.' He held up the candle, staring at her closely, then gripped her wrist. Something hard; he pulled an eating-knife from her sleeve. She must have palmed it at supper.

Docilosa lay calmly. 'Stigmus has the Phoenix. To me it's more than a necklace. It's the only thing that tells me who I am. Please, Quistus.'

'Stay with Volusia.' He pulled on his boots.

'Stigmus must die,' she said. 'You know that as well as I do. It's the only way to save the one thousand three hundred and twelve. Let me kill him.'

He shook his head. 'You're a damned soul, Docilosa.'

But what she said was true. Awful but true.

'Give me the knife,' she whispered. 'You save the others, if you can. That's up to you. But when you see me near Stigmus, you close your eyes. It's the only way I can make this come out right.'

'Killing the man you love?'

'Said I loved,' she said.

Then she smiled, sending a chill up his spine. 'If you make me stay, I'll kill Volusia. I'll find a way. And then I'll follow you anyway. I'll follow you to Hell if I have to.'

He stared at the knife, then threw it from the window. 'That may be exactly what you're doing.'

*   *   *

For two days, and all last night, the wind had threatened to blow *Squamus* ashore; a southerly was almost useless at driving the bat-winged vessel westward, towards the Wight. During the darkness Claudia had swayed at the steering oar, exhausted yet determined. There was a real danger that they would not reach the Teeth of Heaven in time. This was a battle, she realized as the hours passed, between God and the gods; whichever was greater and more powerful would make the wind blow for them, and win.

Very well. There would be no shame in accepting the verdict of such an epic contest.

But she was a fighter. Win or lose, a fighter could still make her own fate. They could help themselves.

They could row.

Claudia looked from the fluttering, useless sail to Omba and Stigmus seated amidships, Tara standing between them with water and encouragement. All day yesterday Omba had rowed of her own will, concussed, passively accepting Claudia's tale that Quistus lay sleeping below, and they'd made good time. But not even Omba could row all day and all night, and as she recovered her proper thoughts she realized she'd been tricked and dropped her oar defiantly.

At once Tara had turned to Stigmus with her knife out.

'Omba,' Stigmus had begged. His hands had been cleaned in seawater then bandaged to his oar. 'Omba, *please.*'

Omba had swallowed with difficulty, had spoken in a thick voice. 'Cut him as much as you like,' she said approvingly.

Then Claudia had a brainwave. 'Omba, don't make her do it. She's only a child.'

And so Omba had rowed, and so had Stigmus.

The sweat had poured down Omba's scowling face as she rowed. She stared at Claudia constantly, her eyes unmoving despite the rhythm of the oar. She poured a bucket of seawater over her head without blinking. The muscles in her arms stood out as she pulled her oar. 'Claudia,' she called.

Claudia, half-asleep, woke.

'Claudia,' Omba said. 'It was you, wasn't it. Not Docilosa. It was you who cut our brake in the mountains. You tried to kill us all. You even let us think Docilosa did it.'

'She's guilty of other sins. One more made no difference.' Claudia justified herself: 'Don't you see? I had to get to Tara,

192

nothing else matters. Baaltane's so close. The wagon was so *slow*, and I was afraid Quistus wouldn't support me when he learned of the child.' She swayed. 'Yes, I cut the brake, I tried to kill you, it made sense. I'd do it again.'

'Then you deliberately hurt your own ankle pretending to save us, so we'd blame Docilosa not you.'

'She would've got the blame anyway, everyone knows she's a natural born sinner.'

'She's been sinned against, too.' Omba's muscles stood out with each pull of the oar but her eyes didn't waver. 'I'm going to remember what you did, Claudia. I'll remember.'

'It's a matter between my God and me.'

'No,' Omba said. 'It's between you and me.'

Claudia's eyelids fluttered, heavy, yet she didn't dare sleep. You had to suffer for what you believed in. Your sacrifice defined you: who you really are. She remembered the Christians in the arena, dying pointlessly on Nero's whim. You had to stand up and be counted, yes, but make your death count, too. Only that way could your beliefs win, your suffering prevail and do good. Tomorrow was Baaltane, Tara's fourteenth birthday. Tomorrow she would no longer be a child, she'd be a woman, old enough to be married. And she would be married, married in fire. Tomorrow they would all die in fiery pagan glory, and by their deaths light such a fire that all Britain would rise up in flames.

'I believe in God,' Claudia muttered wearily. 'I believe in God but this is the only way it works. Make our deaths count.' A single tear trickled on her cheek. It was hard to give up your only daughter, the only child you would ever have, the child you loved more than your own life. She dashed away the tear. Her face hardened.

The ship rolled, creaking. The night passed slowly.

The sun rose behind them. Tara brought the bucket of fresh water to Omba, lifting the ladle to her lips. She watched Omba drink, then leant close, whispering, 'What did you say she did?'

'Your precious mother tried to kill us.'

'But you're my friends.'

Claudia called sharply, 'Tara!'

They could see people running along the beaches. At Claudia's command Tara stood high up on the bow where she was clearly visible, a white figure with her arms outstretched.

193

One by one bonfires sprang up on the headlands, fading small into the distance.

Claudia called, 'Will the wind blow for us today?'

Tara watched the clouds drifting overhead at a different angle to the waves passing beneath. 'Not until this evening, Mother.'

Nineteen

The Teeth of Heaven

It had been a hard ride along the banks of the fast-flowing Trisanton river to the inn where Quistus and Docilosa spent the night. At first light, while fresh horses were being saddled, Cerialis reined in with a couple of staff officers in tow. They snatched breakfast, changed horses and rode onward in company. 'I sent orders ahead by pigeon,' Cerialis confirmed. 'The other legions are being informed by semaphore.' Quistus nodded; this secondary road to Noviomagus, with its spur to Port Adurni, was not large enough to warrant the hilltop semaphore stations found along the major routes connecting military towns. The horses cantered on the footpaths beside the road, making good time.

'Not enough people about,' Quistus said.

Cerialis nodded. 'I noticed.' A Roman villa dotted each clearing in the forest. Slave-barns still sent out long files of chained men and women to clear the oakwoods to make more fields, but any British villages which had happened to be in the way when the road was driven through were empty except for barking dogs. Chickens and goats had been hidden deep in the forest when the people left. 'You notice something else?' Quistus called. Not even the old had been left behind to stare from doorways, nor did the sick remain, or the usual cripples and idiots who were always to be found making do in such places. 'They've all gone. Every last one.'

'Hearing the call,' Cerialis said.

Quistus ducked into a thatch hut, drawn by the smell. An

194

old woman had been laid carefully on the floor, her head peacefully on her folded hands, dead.

'They give me the creeps,' Docilosa said.

At Noviomagus they turned to the right along the coast road. The local king had built a fine stone palace in the Roman style, but it was deserted. By the middle of the day they reached Port Adurni, clattering past the customs-house and along the silent wharves. No work was going on. Smooth-looking scribes, loading-clerks and tax officials – from Gaul or Iberia judging by their accents, Brits didn't read or write – hung about outside their offices. Cerialis rode forward to the military post.

Quistus showed Briginus's letter to a black-bearded Hibernian captain whose vessel was small enough to lay up alongside on the mud. 'Captain Tuathal, sire, at your service.' Tuathal thought the strike was an enormous joke, especially as his cargo was already loaded. 'Gone, the lot of 'em. All the Brits, upped and gone, slipped away in the night like smoke. Not one of them to be missed, in my opinion.'

'Will you take us?' Tuathal looked dubious. Quistus gave him money.

'Briginus?' the Hibernian beamed. 'Indeed, sire, my oldest friend! I'm bound for Cashel, the Wight's on our way.' He spat at the water creeping across the mud. 'Half an hour for the tide, sire.'

Quistus found Cerialis barking orders, red-faced. 'Curse falcons,' Cerialis swore. 'My bird never got here. The men are getting their packs together at the fort. I've found a trireme in the bay but it's a Greek crew, the rowers are sleeping it off ashore somewhere. It's a skilled job so they have to use free men, and of course they get drunk any chance they can.'

'Can't your men row?'

'Three layers of oars working together? Not and fight.' Cerialis glanced at the sun, then turned seriously. 'Quistus, I can't make this tide. Have you got some sort of boat?'

'Captain Tuathal.'

'Him. Tell the old thief I'll cut his head off if he lets you down. He cheats at knuckles.'

Quistus ran back to Tuathal's boat, now afloat. It creaked loudly as he jumped aboard, made of planks only below water level; the rest was wickerwork with skins stretched tightly across, only just about waterproof. 'Give way, Captain, if you please.' Four chained slaves sat on beams over the cargo of clay jars, working the oars. A couple of boys sat on the bow, balancing as the muddy waves of the estuary sent spray flying. Tuathal stood barefoot at the steering paddle in his green wool tunic, a sailors' folding knife hanging from his belt. The tide was still rising, making hard work pushing against the flow, and the wind blew in their faces, but the land slowly receded behind them while the island rose out of the sea ahead.

Quistus pointed off the port bow. A shape, hardly more than a dot, rose and fell among the waves of the deep sea. 'Recognize the cut of that sail?' He turned. 'We can get ahead of them. Captain Tuathal, tell your men to row faster.'

'Row faster! Breaking their bloody backs as they are, sire.'

'A hundred sesterces each.'

'Two hundred, and twice as much for me.'

'And General Cerialis promises to cut your head off if you fail.'

'You heard him!' Tuathal shouted. 'You two boys, on those oars, you scum.'

Quistus turned to Docilosa. 'Your eyes are good. What do you see?'

She shielded her face from the sun. 'It's them. Omba's rowing. Stigmus too, I think. They don't know it's us, they're rowing as hard as they can. Probably Claudia's told them we're pirates.'

Clever Claudia. Quistus climbed to the masthead. It wobbled alarmingly. He gripped with his knees and waved both arms. No response. The island's marshy eastern shore was about a mile on their right. The tide reached slack high water and they made better progress past the island.

'I can see her,' Docilosa called. 'Claudia, the bitch. She's hung fish-nets on the side so Omba can't see us.' Quistus worked out distances. The two boats moved like insects on the sea, their courses intersecting offshore several miles ahead. Claudia turned her course seawards a little. The wind gusted, pushing Tuathal's boat back. *Squamus* would pass in front of their bow.

Quistus called Docilosa to the steering paddle. 'Keep this heading. Captain Tuathal!' He pushed an oar into Tuathal's hands. 'Row, if you please.'

Tuathal rebelled. 'Tell your General Cerialis he cheats at knuckles.'

Quistus said harshly, 'When I take your head back to him, tell him yourself.' The Hibernian sat without a word. Quistus stood on the clay pots. 'What's in these, Tuathal?'

'Wine, fish paste, olives. The garrison commander at Cashel keeps a good table.'

'Not now he doesn't.' Quistus chucked pots over the side. One of the boys helped him, grinning. The two vessels inched closer. The sun dropped lower over the island. The tide ebbed, helping the boats equally, sweeping them quickly along the shore.

Docilosa called, 'The wind's changing.' *Squamus*'s sail flapped, hung limp, then filled again. 'It's coming from the east. We're getting close!' Her voice rose. 'Very close!'

'Ram her,' Quistus said. 'Aim.' He grabbed an oar and added his weight. 'Pull!'

He heard the splash of *Squamus*'s oars, saw the mast pass ahead of them, then the stern slid by. They'd missed by a few feet. Claudia stood tall, ignoring them. *Squamus* swept forward under a bulging sail.

'I'm sorry, Quistus.' Docilosa pushed the steering paddle. The little cargo boat turned slowly, then the wind caught the sail. The two boats were blown along the south shore of the island at much the same rate, *Squamus* a few hundred paces ahead. The wind increased, and slowly she lengthened her lead. The oars had been taken in and Quistus guessed that Omba, seeing him, refused to row. He threw more pots overboard.

Tuathal rested on his oar. He murmured in a quiet, reverential voice: 'Look at that, now.'

Along the low brown cliffs that bordered this part of the island, a blue line had been drawn. It took Quistus a moment to realize that he was seeing people, thousands of people. They lined the clifftop, men, women, naked but for the harsh dark blue of woad. Death by flogging even to wear the patriotic colour, if the Romans caught them. Patches of flesh showed white; their eye sockets were painted with circles of red ochre.

'There's a sight,' Tuathal murmured. 'Dressed for war.'

'Help me throw these pots over.' At last Quistus felt the ship move lighter in the water, no longer falling behind. Over the bow came a burst of spray, as white as the cliffs rising ahead. He made out a jagged jawline stretching from the final headland into the sea. 'That's it,' he said. 'The Teeth of Heaven.'

'The wind always drops at sunset,' Tuathal said. 'We have

to catch them before then. I'm not setting foot ashore.' He pointed, staring. 'There!'

On the highest part of the clifftop the forest had been felled, revealing the secret long concealed from the Romans by lesser trees: a cathedral of oaks. Quistus guessed there must be twelve, one for each month of the year. The ancient trees were coming into leaf, green with renewed life.

In the centre of the holy circle stood two giants, a man and a woman. The male was taller than the trees, his grotesque head formed of saplings, boughs and branches to make a face. His great body was wicker and straw, open-slatted, so that his empty insides could be seen. Beside him stood his woman, her right hand joined to his left hand in a cage of clasped fingers. The setting sun shone clear through the two figures, red as fire.

'It's a marriage.' Docilosa spoke in a trembling voice, fascinated. 'They're wife and husband.'

'Not yet,' Quistus said. 'Not until tomorrow.'

He stood on the bow. Claudia looked back. Only a few hundred feet separated them. The clear blue waters turned black as they came into the shadow of the cliff. The wind was failing. Quistus turned. 'Row your hardest. We'll catch them.' The two vessels closed. They could hear waves breaking on the pebble beach. There was a break in the cliff and people climbed down the steep chine, jumping from rock to rock as they followed the boats.

'Claudia,' Quistus said. The bow was moving so close to *Squamus*'s stern he didn't even bother to raise his voice. 'Claudia, turn away. Think. Think what you're doing. No mother can sacrifice her own child.'

Claudia shook her head. 'You don't understand. You're a Roman. You'll never understand freedom.' She pushed hard on the steering oar, turning for the narrow strip of shore beneath the cliff.

Docilosa, too, pushed hard. The ships turned together. 'You won't stop her, Quistus,' she called. 'That's not Claudia. She's Gladis.'

Fifteen feet of water separated the two vessels. Quistus saw the sea bottom sliding below. The waves steepened, lifting them, rushing forward.

Docilosa gave a shriek. 'There he is, the thief!' Stigmus looked startled. He stared from Docilosa to the blue-scrawled people running on the beach. His hands were bound by bandages.

In desperation he bit at them with his teeth to free himself.

Quistus felt a wave push forward, driving them into *Squamus*'s stern. He jumped, sprawled on the sterndeck. Claudia abandoned the oar and ran past him. She made no attempt to stop him, or take Omba with her, or Stigmus, only leapt on to the foredeck where Tara waited. Waves broke into pounding foam. Quistus tried to stand. He'd hurt his knee. He crawled to the steering oar and pushed, but it was too late. *Squamus* struck the beach, and stuck fast.

Claudia and Tara jumped from the bow.

Moments later Tuathal's boat slid alongside, scraping. The wicker sides creaked loudly, absorbing the shock. Docilosa screamed at Stigmus, who'd torn his bandages into strips that fluttered from his wrists. She grabbed the knife from Tuathal's belt, lifted her gown to the knee, and jumped the gap.

A folding knife. She stopped to open it, breaking a nail. Quistus grabbed her ankle. She pulled the blade open and slashed at his wrist.

The old scar had never healed properly. It split so easily at the touch of a knife. Blood poured out, released. Quistus clutched the wound with his other hand, holding it closed. Docilosa stared with crazy eyes. 'I'm sorry,' she said. 'I never meant to do it.' Then she was running after Stigmus, who'd freed himself from the oar. Omba stuck her foot out and Docilosa sprawled. Stigmus jumped into the surf. Docilosa leapt after him, struggling waist deep, then the foam drew back and she ran after him on the stones. Spray burst over a line of green rock. Stigmus made it first, scrambling. He slipped on the weed, sliding back to her. Docilosa stabbed him through the thigh and raised the knife for another go. Stigmus shrieked. Fire showed at his neck. Docilosa grabbed it and stared at what she held. The Phoenix.

She smiled and put on the necklace. She found a pool to see her reflection. She knelt, admiring her beauty.

Stigmus stood on one leg behind her. He grabbed the necklace at the same moment he brought a lump of driftwood down on her head, but it struck her shoulder instead. She leapt at him, knife upraised. A wave broke, sweeping him off his feet.

He tried to worm from her on his back, slipping, sliding down the weed with the retreating surf. She came after him. Spray burst over them both from the next breaking wave. When it receded only Docilosa was left standing. Stigmus struggled head-deep in the water. He looked like he couldn't swim. She gave a furious scream, running after him as he was swept along the shore. The waves dragged him over half-submerged rocks, then the tide carried him into the foaming gap between the Teeth of Heaven.

Quistus looked away.

Some blue-painted women coming round the corner saw Docilosa. They gave chase. She ran back but they caught her. They whacked her on the head with a club. She lay with one hand and one foot in the pool. Men ran past.

'Omba,' Quistus called. The naked men, their faces wild with blue runes and symbols of war, flooded over the bow of the beached ship.

'Quickly, man!' Tuathal shouted. 'It's too late for her. It's almost too late for you.'

Quistus crawled. Tuathal grabbed him, hauling him over the railing. Oars groaned. The little vessel backed away from *Squamus*. Warriors swarmed along the wreck. There was a brief tussle over Omba then the victors stood shouting on the stern. They threw a few spears, stopping when all fell short. After a while the trussed figure of Omba was dragged along the beach.

'Omba,' Quistus whispered.

'That's the end of that,' Tuathal said.

Twenty

Wife and Husband

It was dark. Only the cliff showed in front of them, a faint pallid wall with the surf-line below and stars above. 'You can't be doing this,' Tuathal whispered.

Quistus rolled his cloak tight to stop water getting in.

'You can't save them,' Tuathal said. 'You can't.'

As the boat moved closer under the cliff the bonfires along the clifftop were hidden by its bulk, though they still heard the murmur of the crowd. Tuathal sighed. 'No dancing tonight, out

200

of respect for their guests of honour. Drums, yes. And everyone will drink a skinful, because they always do. But no singing, no dancing, definitely no lovemaking. Almost no drunk fighting. That's all to look forward to tomorrow. Tonight's chastity night.'

'How long do I have?'

'If you aren't back before dawn, you aren't coming back.'

'You mean I'll be dead.'

'You still don't get it, Roman.' Tuathal chuckled. 'They won't waste you, they won't let you die, you'll live for ever. You'll burn, and somewhere a baby will be born.'

'Wait until dawn.'

'Well you've thrown all my cargo away, what else can I do but go back to Port Adurni and twiddle my thumbs and spend my money?'

'Not until dawn.'

Tuathal squeezed his arm. 'How's your wrist now?'

'It won't let me down.' Quistus stared out to sea. Darkness. No triremes. 'So much for Cerialis.' He slipped over the side holding his rolled cloak in front of him, swimming for the shore. Behind him Tuathal called softly, 'Farewell.'

A dark wave swept Quistus forward. His knees banged on stones and he held on as the surf pulled back, then waded quietly ashore. He didn't think there was anyone on the beach, unless they'd come down after nightfall. The stones hurt his feet. He tied his sandals then unrolled the cloak and fastened it, moving quietly along the beach.

Fallen chalk boulders glowed faintly, showing him where the chine rose. He climbed the crumbly mixture of chalk and earth. Voices came from above, too many now to pick out anyone in particular. There was a burst of laughter. Bonfire sparks rose among the stars. He made out the black arrowhead line of the clifftop angled back on each side of him. Bare cliff edge on his left, a tangle of trees to his right. He climbed across the centre gully, heading right. A little water trickled. A woman came down, grunting. He heard her drink. Without looking backwards she relieved herself in a warm stream by his foot, then climbed back the way she'd come.

Quistus moved forward. The cliff was too steep and crumbly to hold his weight but he found a tree root. He pulled himself up, saw no one, and crawled into the undergrowth.

Far enough from the cliff edge he stood, pulled his cloak

201

over his head to hide his shape, and came forward slowly between the trunks. From the limit of the trees he saw that the clearing – still with a maze of axed stumps sticking up – was really part of a ridge with the sea on each side. Thousands of camp fires burned on the slopes; the air stank of smoke. They were burning green wood from the newly felled trees.

He stepped forward, then stopped with his foot raised.

People slept all around him in the dark. He could smell them. He'd almost trodden on this one. The man turned over sleepily, muttering, stinking of sweet fermented honey, rotten teeth, sweat. Quistus looked round without moving his head, only his eyes. A bonfire flared. The edge of the forest, like the clearing, was carpeted with sleeping bodies, so dark with woad they were almost invisible. A small child sat up in her sleep, stared straight at him, then lay back on her mother's breast. Quistus stood on one foot, not daring to move.

A drunk stumbled across the sleeping people, followed by curses. The sound faded and peace returned.

Quistus stumbled forward swaying like a drunk, followed by curses.

No one stopped him. No more sleeping bodies now; he wondered why. From behind a thorn fence came low cries, the sound of weeping, laughter, a tuneless voice singing. Innocent vacant faces stared at the fires that had been lit for them. A cripple staggered. A man beat his head on the ground, possessed by an evil spirit. These were the sick, the stupid, criminals, the very old, the souls who would feed the fire.

Quistus moved on. He lay down near the peak of the ridge.

He was about two hundred paces from the cathedral. Over the oak-tops he made out the bride's head, the groom's savage face beyond. All the felled tree trunks, boughs and branches had been gathered at the feet of the giants. Ladders crisscrossed within each leg, and inside each torso rose platforms like the storeys of a house. Wife and husband were ready to burn.

Quistus staggered drunkenly between the camp fires and sleeping people, then dropped beside an oak-root. A couple of men stood guard, watching him. He snored, sleeping it off. They turned away.

A drum thudded softly, like a beating heart. Quistus felt the sound in his bones. Through slitted eyes he saw two strong men beat the drum. More stood ready to take over. The base of the drum was fire-hardened wood, the stump of some great tree scooped out, perfectly hollowed, ancient. The top, twelve feet across, was a single wild aurochs-skin tightly stretched.

Twelve priests, each holding a shepherd's crook, stood in a circle around the kneeling, hooded woman. Their bodies were bent, with straggly white beards hanging from their blue-scrawled faces. Every one of them looked as old as Baltharnoux. Their eyes were closed. Their lips mouthed silently in prayer.

The woman at the centre put back her hood. Claudia. Her head was bowed but he recognized her hair.

He looked for Tara and saw her at once, dwarfed by the great wickerwork toes of Wife and Husband, a thin white figure with night-adjusted eyes, sitting in a wicker bower draped with mistletoe.

She saw him. He was certain. She didn't move, but he knew.

Quistus staggered around looking for a place to pee. Trees close behind the bower, darkness. He stumbled from sight then dropped, crawling in the dark.

The creak of wicker. He whispered, 'Tara?'

After a moment she hissed, 'Quistus. I'm not allowed. Sssh.'

He saw the back of her head by firelight. He whispered, 'Are we still friends?'

She turned slightly. 'Yes. You and I are *familiaris*.'

'Yes, we are. Do you remember the horses? You liked them.'

'I remember their names.' Her voice smiled.

'We've been through a lot together, haven't we, Tara? Do you remember at the villa, the fight at the villa? You saved my life.'

'That was just arrows.' But she turned a little more. He saw the line of her nose, the gleam of her eye.

'I didn't want to die. Do you? Do you want to die now, Tara?'

'I'm not going to, silly. I'm going to live. I'm going to be married.'

'It's not marriage, Tara. It's death.'

'I'll have children.'

'The fire will hurt you terribly and it will go on and on.'

She turned her head another notch. 'Having children hurts.'

'That's a fact, Tara. But this, here, this burning, it's just belief. What these people believe to be true about sacrifice and the good it does might be fact but nobody knows. Nobody really knows. Listen to me. One day you'll have real children of your own.

Real babies. Wouldn't that be better? Wouldn't you like that?'

She looked straight at him. 'But I'd have to fall in love.'

'You will.'

'How do you know?'

'Because love happens. You know when it happens. It just does. You don't have to burn yourself alive for love, Tara. It's already in you.' He bit his lip, holding his bandaged wrist tight. 'It just *is*, Tara. Believe me, it never dies.'

She thought about it. 'Mother says you're a Stoic. She says Stoics don't know about love, or about God, or about truth, only about logic. She says they have no heart.'

He whispered, 'Then, Tara, as a Stoic, the fact is, I am a complete and utter failure.'

Her teeth gleamed, smiling. She slipped from the bower more quickly than he believed possible and lay beside him. 'I don't know Mother very well,' she whispered in his ear. 'I want to. Can she come? Shall I stay with you?'

'I need to get you away from here, Tara. I don't think it'll be long before you're missed. It's dawn soon.'

'The moon comes before the dawn.'

'Is that when things hot up?'

'Yes. The first horn of the moon, Accord. And then the second horn, Discord.'

'There's plenty of places to hide on the beach. I'm coming back for Omba, and Docilosa, and your mother, because I bet as soon as she knows I've got you, she'll want to be with you.'

'Promise.'

'I know mothers. Anyway, I expect the soldiers will arrive in time to stop anything bad happening here.'

'All right,' she said matter-of-factly. 'Baltharnoux is dead, you know.'

'Yes, I know.'

'He won't be coming back. He said he would, but I know he won't. He taught me about every religion that's known, every god there is. But death's just death, and I believe in love.'

Quistus wrapped her in his cloak and carried her in his arms into the forest like any father carrying a sleeping child. She was heavier than she looked. After a while he put her down and guided her deeper through the woods, taking the long way round to the top of the chine. Her eyes were better than his and she saw the drop before he did. She lowered herself by the tree

root, then looked up. 'Quistus? Suppose you don't come back?'
'You find yourself a good hiding-place down there. I won't
be long.' He watched her go jumping and sliding nimbly into
the shadows, then turned back into the woods. He heard footsteps. At once a knife was at his throat.

Claudia held the knife to Quistus's throat. 'Where is she?
Where is she?'
   He was so completely unafraid. She could feel it; ready for
death. It was all that stopped her. Her hand trembled. A drip
of blood trickled on the blade, lit by the first faint glow on
the eastern horizon. So little time. 'So help me God,' she
hissed, 'what have you done with her?'
   'She's safe, Claudia.'
   'You stupid bastard,' she cried, then forced herself to
whisper. 'You don't know what you've done.'
   'Kill me, Claudia.' He leant towards her against the blade,
forcing her to give way. 'You can't kill your own daughter.'
   'Where is she?' Claudia heard her voice shaking. She
couldn't stop herself. Her control was going. 'Christ, Quistus,
where? We need her. *I* need her. I have to show them.'
   'Show them what?'
   'My commitment to them. To the rebellion. To freedom.
They're my people.'
   'You can't let your people kill your only child, Claudia.
You know you can't. You're not as strong as your God.'
   Claudia's hand shook. She threw down the knife. 'Then let
them take me.'
   The first horn of the dying moon, sharply hooked, down-
ward-pointing, glimmered on the eastern sea-horizon. At once
the first great horn trumpeted between Wife and Husband and
the people stirred, waking.
   Claudia turned, jostled, surrounded by the awakening
congregation. Quistus was gone.

Quistus ran. He was too late. Everyone was running. Warriors
locked spears, holding back the crowd. The lower crescent of
the moon pulled clear of the sea and the second horn blared:
Discord. People covered their ears. The kings and princes of
the twelve tribes known to Britain led their peoples forward
around the twelve oaks. 'Iceni. Trinovantes. Atrebates.' A

blare of the horns, as long as three men, their curled ends resting on the ground, accompanied each name roared by that tribe. 'Silures.' More horns. 'Deceangli.' Others Quistus had never heard of. The horns fell silent.

The drum thumped its heartbeat. The priests chanted. The crowd murmured expectantly. Claudia was led forward by her hands by two small infants, who looked very serious. Their mothers encouraged them proudly. The two infants stopped between Wife and Husband, turned Claudia round, then ran back. The oldest priest stood behind Claudia, his curved knife of gold and ivory raised over her head.

Quistus almost shouted, thinking the knife would be thrust into the top of her head, but it was a blessing, a symbol of her authority. He covered his mouth. The thorn fences were opened. Confused-looking men and women were guided, or pulled, or carried, to Claudia. The priest blessed them. Claudia held out her left hand to women and girls and they passed to her left, dutifully helping each other up the ladders that climbed Wife's legs and body. They'd practised. Claudia held out her right hand to men and boys, who climbed the ladders inside Husband.

The crowd shouted approval to those who climbed fastest. One bald painted man reached the head of Husband first and a cheer went up. The sick and lame were accommodated lower down, or carried up by the strong. The crowd sent up a great roar, reaching out with grasping hands as each word was chanted. 'Wife! Husband! Moon! Sun!'

Beneath Moon the horizon glowed with invisible Sun. Quistus felt himself swept up emotionally, part of the crowd. He shouted too. The drum beat faster.

Enough light now to see the tears on Claudia's face. He stopped, silenced. Claudia had seen him shouting with the rest.

Docilosa was led forward. Someone pushed her to her knees. Claudia looked straight at Quistus. For three breaths she waited for a miracle.

She held out her left hand and Docilosa was led to Wife. From the ladder Docilosa saw Quistus. The ceremony's spell broke. She struggled. She screamed his name. 'Quistus, don't let me die.' She tore her dress, showing her bare neck. She clung to the ladder but she was hauled up by her hair. A tough old woman slapped her.

'I repent!' Docilosa shouted. 'Quistus, I repent! Forgive me!'

He turned his head away. People were looking at him. She screamed his name.

The light was growing. A couple of warriors with spears saw him and pushed through the crowd pointing at his Roman cloak. The crowd shoved him at the warriors. A shout went up. They whacked him with their spear-butts.

They dragged him to Claudia for a decision.

Claudia trembled. The priests waited.

The priests frowned at Claudia.

Claudia held out her right hand.

Quistus felt a ladder against his body. He was pushed up from below, pulled from above. Husband was nearly full up top, where the most honoured places were. Feet pushed on his head. A ladder collapsed somewhere and people screamed as they went down. He shoved his way to the edge of the platform somewhere high on the left leg and grabbed the wickerwork, staring out.

He saw Claudia below. Omba with her arms tied behind her back. Claudia held out her left hand. Wife was almost full, creaking with the weight. The door in Wife's right ankle was forced closed behind Omba.

A long ladder was brought forward by acolytes, its end lifted swaying into the air, and propped high up against Wife and Husband's joined hands: the sacred union, Princess Gladis's pride of place.

More importantly, Tara's place: granddaughter of King Caractacus, daughter of Gladis who was both royal princess and queen, daughter of Atenoux, King of Kings. Tara, three times royal, the third princess.

Somebody shouted. Confusion down there. Priests milled about arguing. Tara's absence had been discovered. Nobody knew what it meant. The crowd gave a moan of dismay in the red glow of dawn.

The priests came to a decision. Claudia was led to the ladder. Her robes fluttered in the dawn wind as she climbed slowly to her fate. Quistus shouted to her but she was deaf. Her face was lost, uncomprehending. Because of her child whom she barely knew but had come to love, she'd failed. Their deaths today would change nothing. Claudia had been too selfish to see that Tara was the real Christian. Claudia spoke of love but Tara believed in it.

207

The priests ringed the piles of timber with brushwood torches. Below the moon the first red crescent of the sun showed through, lighting the heads of the giants. At the same moment the fires were lit. Quistus smelled smoke at once.

That was when the screaming began. The women in Wife stuck their arms through the wicker limbs, wailing, and the men around Quistus howled and wept. But that was not where the screams came from.

The screams came from the crowd. The line of sunlight rippling down the slope showed people scattering in every direction.

Along the cliff edge helmets and armour glittered in the first rays of the sun. Swords were drawn. Cerialis had arrived. Sunlight touched the sea, revealing two triremes anchored in the bay.

The soldiers threw javelins then charged in wedge formation, cutting into the crowd with swinging swords. Panic spread.

Quistus coughed. Warm bitter smoke poured past him, rising up the leg like a chimney. Hot now. People down below tried climbing up, begging, pulling at the ankles above them. The people above kicked down. Struggles broke out. People fell down, others scrambled up. Quistus knocked his fist through the wicker thigh, shoved his shoulder through to the outside, between the giants. Someone pulled him back, shoving with their own shoulder. The wicker gave way, flapping out, and the man hung by his hands then dropped into the flames roaring from below. The weight of people held back the progress of the fire inside the leg but the smoke stank of burning hair. Quistus knelt at the hole. He twisted, sliding out backwards, grabbed hold. He swung from his hands, flames under his feet. Someone stood on his fingers, apologized. Another pair of hands grabbed his wrists, trying to pull him back up. Quistus shouted. He swung to the right, pushed hard with his feet. The man trying to help him was pulled out with him. Both fell just clear of the fire. Quistus rolled on his burning cloak. The man jumped up and ran away.

Quistus got to his feet. Thick red smoke poured past him; at once he bumped into something hard. The ladder. It swayed. He climbed, glimpsing the sky, and Claudia. She held tight to the rungs, white-knuckled. He called, 'Jump.'

She looked at him thoughtfully. She was far too calm. He knew exactly what she was thinking. She could jump head-first. He could go no higher; the rungs between them burned.

He called: 'Whatever you do, do it for Tara.'

She looked away, then nodded. She jumped feet-first, clothes fluttering. He grabbed at her but they both landed in a heap. She shouted.

'My leg!'

He gasped, dragging her. The flames drew in fresh air to make smoke; suddenly he saw clearly around him. 'Late enough for you?' Cerialis called cheerfully. His sword was bloody. 'Can't hold them, Quistus. The Brits have got over the shock, they're counter-attacking out of the forest. Devils are everywhere. Let's go.'

'Omba. Docilosa.'

'No time. They're dead. They're dead, Quistus, save yourself.'

The giants burned, wreathed in smoke and flame.

'Give me your dagger.'

Cerialis sighed, chucked the weapon hilt-first. 'Hurry.'

It was horribly dark in the smoke, as though the sun wasn't shining; everything in here was blood red. Quistus crawled, peering beneath the rising smoke. He covered one ear, trying not to hear the screams. Cool air rushed past him, drawn upwards. He saw a huge wicker leg standing in front of him, flames pouring up from the ankle. Omba lay flat where he'd last seen her, in the heel, her face pressed to the door-slats. The wood was thick, too thick to break through, supporting the weight of the structure above. She was alone. Everyone else had climbed up, away from the rising flames that came after them.

'I waited,' she said. 'I knew you'd come.' He levered off the door-pegs with the dagger and pulled her out.

He stared up at the mass of fire above, drips of burning fat falling from the smoke-clouds like fiery rain. 'Docilosa?'

Omba pulled him. 'Even you have to fail at something, master. That girl's beyond help, and always was.'

The sun struck their eyes as they stumbled from the smoke. They gasped fresh air. The body of a Roman soldier lay over a tree stump, limbs hacked off. Above the deep roar of the flames came the clang of swords along the ridge, the shouts of men facing death. Fighting heavily, the line of Romans was pressed back towards the fire. Cerialis took an arrow in his shield and another in his body-armour. A Brit leapt the others and threw a spear before he was cut down, then more poured through. Cerialis ordered his men to fall back. Quistus picked

209

up the spear. The Roman line fell back on the cathedral of oaks ready to fight to the death.

'Look, master.' Omba pointed out to sea. *Squamus* drifted into view, moved only by the tide at first, but now the bat-wing sail was raised. Quistus said: 'Stigmus.'

'They say scum rises to the top,' Cerialis said. 'Quite a survivor, isn't he?' The wind caught the sail. The boat turned away.

Quistus heard a thin, high scream.

Docilosa stood in the open mouth of Wife. Smoke and flame roared behind her. Quistus murmured, 'She was always afraid of fire.'

But Docilosa had eyes only for the little boat across the sea. Her screams were of rage, jealousy, betrayal, not pain or fear. Quistus drew back the spear. Flames licked delicately at the hem of her dress, then leapt up hungrily. Her hair burned.

'Don't bother with her,' Cerialis said. 'Here they come. Time for us all to die.'

Quistus threw the spear. It caught Docilosa where her heart was supposed to be. Still she stared through the flames at the boat. Then she fell backwards into the fire.

Cerialis strode forward. 'Steady, men. Shields up. Make every blow count.'

But the British charge faltered. Suddenly it was just a mass of individual warriors looking round. The lines parted.

The men knelt.

A thin white figure walked among them, her arms outstretched, the wind blowing her hair.

Twenty-One

Embers

The sky was a bright British blue over a sea of a slightly darker hue, the cliffs whiter than the drifting clouds. Cerialis strode along the beach. 'I ordered the chieftains to give hostages. Nearly everyone's quietly slipped away

210

to whatever boat, coracle, raft or piece of driftwood they hid in bays along the north coast. Their spirit's broken.'

'For now,' Quistus said.

Cerialis shook his head. 'We'll teach our young hostages to wear the toga, live in town-houses and ask for fish sauce in Latin. Within a lifetime they'll live in servitude, call it freedom, and fight to defend us.' He changed the subject. 'I gather from our mutual friend Captain Tuathal' – they stood by Tuathal's beached boat – 'that you asked him to take you across the Atlanticus Sinus, all the way south to Burdigala in southern Gaul. I should have thought you've had enough excitement for one day.'

'Unfinished business.'

'That bay has a reputation for the roughest waters in the known world.'

'Stigmus was heading south-east. It's calm enough today.'

'You're probably fortunate that Tuathal was too sensible to take you.' Cerialis ignored a wave that swirled around his ankles. 'Stigmus has a fair wind. He could be in Burdigala in three or four days, Narbonne by road in the same time, then a week at most gets him to Rome.' He peered into Quistus's eyes. 'Stigmus has won, don't you see? Your enemy has won. He's home first. Stay away, Quistus, save yourself. Stigmus will be whispering the truth in Nero's ear long before you could possibly reach Rome with your excuses.'

'I know. Stigmus will tell Nero that with Docilosa dead – doubtless he believes I'm dead too – Amanda Censorina's will can be executed, so can her slaves, and Nero will inherit everything. Nero will be very grateful to Stigmus. I'd say Stigmus's boss Tigellinus will soon be making way for a younger man as prefect of praetorians.'

'But you're going back to Rome anyway.'

'Yes, I am.'

'To certain death.'

'I have to go.'

'Because of you Nero almost lost Britain. Claudia tells me that together you killed seven praetorians. *Seven*. As soon as you turn up alive Nero will have you tortured and executed for what you've done, no questions asked. You'll be flogged to death like a common murderer. Your money and property confiscated. Your name extinguished. Everything you knew will no longer exist.'

'I'm already extinguished, if I have no children.'

'*If?*'

'I saw Lyra.'

'Are you insane? What do you think you're doing, old friend? Promise me you'll go into exile to Hibernia, with Claudia and Tara.'

Tuathal called from the boat, 'Happy to have you aboard. Hibernia has the best rain in the world.'

Quistus turned back to Cerialis. 'You've come out of this a hero. Give me a trireme, that's all I ask.'

'No. I need both for my men. I'm not letting you go back to Rome to die.' Cerialis looked to the others for support. 'Omba. Claudia. Tell him.'

But it was Tara who spoke. 'Quistus must do what he must.'

'But it's hopeless.' Cerialis was getting angry.

'Nothing is hopeless,' Omba said. Something had changed in her since the fire. 'Better to die well than live poorly.'

'I've done my best for you.' Cerialis shrugged. 'Quistus, I'll take you and Omba back to port. After that go as crazy as you like. Just don't involve me.'

'Thank you, old friend.' They clasped wrists. Cerialis saluted and went to supervise the loading of the wounded.

Claudia said, 'Will the Romans let us live in peace?'

'What?' Quistus turned, nodding. 'Cerialis won't mention you in his report. He only knew the rumours I told him and acted on them, to his very great credit. He never went to Volusia's house, and he never saw you here, because only embers remained when he arrived. He fought a brilliant action and took hostages, and that's all.' He added, 'And if he did talk, he knows people would hear of his conspiracy to get his father-in-law made Emperor.'

Tara said, 'Come with us to Hibernia, Quistus. You'll be safe. We'll make a good Christian of you.'

'If you can make a good Christian of your mother, that will be quite a success.' Quistus chuckled, but Tara could see his mind was already on the trireme. The rowers waited ready. 'Good fortune, Tara. Good fortune both of you, and God go with you.'

'To Rome,' Omba said, 'and your certain death and disgrace.' She added, 'I hope you know what you're doing, master.'

The trireme sped them to Port Adurni. From there it was a simple matter – with the help of the Emperor's seal waved in

212

the faces of startled but instantly respectful ostlers – to acquire horses for London, and within the day a boat owned by Briginus sailed from the customs wharf at London Bridge for Gaul.

The Bononian customs official was the first one to be unimpressed by the Emperor's seal. 'Wait a minute,' he said, not seeing Omba standing behind him. 'I'm sure this has been revoked. I've got the semaphore message right here . . .'

'Stigmus has been quicker than I thought.' Quistus stepped over the unconscious official.

They purchased horses for twice their value at the local inn, exchanging them the next morning for fresh mounts. But the road through the isle of Paris was blocked, and this time the officer shouted at Quistus by name.

None of this stopped them, but it all added to the length of their journey.

More importantly, added to the time it took.

On the west bridge at Lugdunum Quistus reined in and spoke to a boy named Viridorix for seven minutes.

At Massilia they reached the southern coast and heard the first up-to-date news of Rome from an approving tavern-keeper. Apparently the escaped slave Docilosa had died before she could be tried for the murder of her mistress, but before she died she'd confessed her guilt to the imperial *Specialis*, Stigmus. The will of Amanda Censorina could now be settled. For the public good the widely respected lawyer Cassius Longinus – also acting for Nero – argued successfully in the Senate that the murdered woman's slaves must receive neither their freedom nor money, and insisted all suffer the extreme penalty for Docilosa's crime. The vast estate would go to Nero, who promised to lavish every penny on entertainments for the people; the first would be the public execution of all one thousand three hundred and twelve guilty slaves in the Circus Maximus, the only venue in Rome of sufficient size and grandeur for such justice. It was said Nero himself would perform the first death, on a monster of depravity called the brute Narcissus. Other brutes would follow, including the brute Apollodorus, who'd apparently fled to the country before being dragged back in chains.

'Wish I was there,' the tavern-keeper said. 'Rome. Only three days off, and a special public holiday. No way to get there in time though.'

'I say it's disgusting,' his wife said. 'It's disgusting and wrong.'

'Shut up,' the tavern-keeper said. Quistus and Omba slipped away like shadows in the night, and disappeared among the boats tied at the dock.

Epilogus

Rome, the Ides of Maius, AD 64

'If they don't start cheering,' Nero said, 'I'll kill them too.' He made a face to show he was joking.

Tigellinus murmured, 'The people of Rome are fickle, great Caesar.' He was sweating. He stepped back from Nero at the first opportunity.

The podium was enormous, covered with purple and gold banners, flags, and pennants that streamed in the wind above the Circus Maximus. The marble walls were polished glass-smooth, overhanging so no one could climb up, guarded by black-cloaked *Augustiani*.

The podium was placed halfway along the immense sandy circuit, as high as the gods. You could see everything from here. This is the life, Stigmus thought, inhaling the scent of blood and dust while a buxom beauty pressed a wine cup to his lips. 'What a view.'

'Don't get used to it,' Tigellinus said.

'I rather think I will.' Stigmus wore a toga that was deliberately a little too white and new for good taste. His hands were ostentatiously bandaged in recognition of the injuries he'd received on the Emperor's service. One of the little girls fed him a grape. Sweet tasty little thing.

Nero kept his smiling face. Out there the crowd made an angry noise. A hundred thousand people made a noise that sounded very angry indeed, shaking the podium. Let them.

Even so, thousands more were barred for the sake of public order. Yesterday Nero had been obliged to admit that he regretted the necessity of the executions: 'But even I cannot change the Law.' Today when he signed the death warrants he'd claimed:

'I wish my hand had never learned to write!' Instead of condolences he'd heard sniggers. Must have used the line before.

Later his promise to perform the first execution was quietly dropped.

Incredibly the crowd sided with these stinking slaves. Each murderer would endure a different torment, over a thousand variations on a theme of death. It would be a wonderful performance. But according to the catcalls, Nero was the criminal, not they.

Stigmus had never experienced crowd politics close up before. He had yet to develop an ear for it. 'How they love you, great Caesar.'

Nero examined his fingernails. 'What do you suggest, Tigellinus?'

'As soon as the first blood flows,' Tigellinus promised, 'they will love you.'

Yes, that was always true. Nero nodded his permission for the executions to commence, but he was angry. 'My soldiers lined the streets as these scum were dragged in, Stigmus, or the mob would've set them free. My praetorians were attacked with stones and fire.' Nero's voice rose. 'Tigellinus gave orders to stand fast.'

'The blood of Roman citizens mustn't be spilled lightly,' Tigellinus said, alarmed at the mention of his name.

Stigmus said, 'I would have ordered reprisals. Show them who's in charge.'

'So would I,' Nero said. 'In fact, Stigmus, I think you should.'

'Great Caesar—' Tigellinus said, white.

'Look.' Nero leaned forward. 'Here we are.' He consulted a list. 'Narcissus. Oh, a eunuch. Not very brave I suppose. Good.' The crowd liked terror. It appealed to their humanity.

Narcissus was led forward, a big man looking rather small down there. That was the Circus Maximus for you. He fell, weak with horror, dragged by his chains to the axeman's block. Nero made a gesture, let him speak. Narcissus swayed to his feet. He pulled his torn robe around him with tattered dignity. They always appealed for mercy and paid you lots of compliments before they died.

Narcissus looked up at Nero. He opened his mouth to begin. Then he looked past Nero. His smudged eyes widened. The crowd fell silent, staring at the podium.

An Emperor could not simply look behind him just because

215

other people were. Stigmus's face was as too-white as his toga. His lips moved.

'Quistus,' Stigmus croaked. 'But you're dead.'

Slowly Nero turned. Quistus and his adamantine slave princess, true. Quistus looked stern, angry, exhausted. Nero said, 'Arrest—' then bit his tongue. Between them the pair escorted the slight figure of Aethera, high priestess of the Vestal Virgins, in chalky robes. Behind her more Vestals came forward, bare-breasted, powdered. Nero bowed his head in silent respect, thinking furiously.

Aethera moved like one unused to sunlight. Her veiled face was pale shadows, some age between twenty and eighty. In her white-gloved hands she held a scroll.

Quistus stepped forward. 'This is the will of Amanda Censorina,' he said loudly, for the crowd to hear. He added, 'Her real will.'

Nero's hand opened. He saw himself grabbing the sword of the nearest *Augustianus* and slashing both the interfering Vestal and Quistus and the black woman to bloody ribbons. He clenched his fist. 'Very well.'

'I object.' Longinus the lawyer pushed forward. 'The will of Amanda Censorina was found by me in her house, witnessed by me, examined by me. This is a forgery.'

Aethera spoke in a thin high voice. 'You are a liar, Cassius Longinus. The will of our sister was deposited with us untouched by man's hand. The forgery you speak of is your own.'

The crowd murmured, understanding. The Vestals' reputation was spotless.

Quistus, travel-stained, his face encrusted with salt, limped to the front of the podium. 'Listen to me, people of Rome. I'll tell you the truth of the death of your beloved Amanda Censorina, one of the most virtuous women who ever lived. When a loved one is taken from us, it's natural for us to search for a reason, for guilt, for someone to blame. Even when there's no reason, no guilt, no blame, we feel obliged to search for it. Fantastic stories grow from tiny seeds, lies flourish like weeds, and conspiracies ripen until everything that seemed good is rotten. But the truth is simply this. She died in her sleep.'

'That's a lie!' Stigmus cried.

'There was no murderer,' Quistus said, 'because there was no murder.'

216

'Docilosa killed her,' Stigmus said, high-pitched. 'She confessed! I heard her!'

'What confession?'

'She confessed to you!'

'I heard no confession. Where were you, Stigmus? In the next room? I was close enough to her to feel her breath on my face. I heard Docilosa speak only of her love for the woman who found her, educated her, lavished money and gifts on her. Omba was there, comforting the poor girl. Omba, did you hear any confession?'

'I heard only love,' Omba said.

Stigmus shouted, 'Docilosa was a murderer and a thief! She murdered her mistress and stole her jewellery!'

Quistus turned to the Vestal. 'Aethera, kindly read the summary of the will.'

Aethera unrolled the scroll at arms' length. 'To each—'

Quistus said, 'Louder, so everyone hears.' He turned to the crowd. 'There are no secrets between us.'

Aethera raised her voice. 'This is the testament of Amanda Censorina. To each one of my slaves I give freedom and one thousand sesterces, except to the girl Docilosa, who is my beloved daughter—'

There was a collective gasp.

'—My beloved daughter and tragically my only surviving child, lost and found, who has no need of such a small gift. To her I give my entire estate, including the piece of jewellery known as the Phoenix which is of such sentimental value to us both; except my house the Domus Censorina, which I give to the Emperor.'

'A draughty place,' Nero muttered to Tigellinus. 'The kitchens are half a mile from the dining room. What's this about a Phoenix?'

Quistus looked at Stigmus, whose face was the colour of ash. He stepped close, slipping his arm round Stigmus's shoulder. 'You've got it on you, I know. I know you, Stigmus. You couldn't bear to let it go, could you, it's worth more money than you'd earn in a lifetime. But the Phoenix means much more even than that to you. Maybe you still love her. The only girl you ever loved, Stigmus. Probably the only girl you ever will. The girl you stole it from.' He whispered: 'Shall we tell Nero?'

'There was no confession,' Stigmus said. His face set like concrete. 'I made a mistake.'

Quistus said, 'Louder.'

'The old woman died of natural causes.'

'No crime, so the slaves must be freed,' Quistus shouted down. 'Let them go!'

Nero turned furiously to Longinus, who spread his hands in dismay. Nero said wearily, 'Release them.'

'And a thousand sesterces each,' Quistus said.

'Wait,' Longinus said. 'Docilosa's dead. She can't inherit anything.'

'We're coming to that,' Quistus said. 'Standard clause.'

Aethera read, 'No beneficiary shall receive benefit unless he or she survives to the execution of this my will. Any person not so surviving shall be deemed to have predeceased me.'

'All mine!' Nero turned to the crowd, arms upraised in victory. They roared for him. Everyone loved a winner.

Aethera finished, 'In that case the benefit shall pass wholly to the God-Emperor Nero for the glory of Rome.'

'Exactly as I intended!' Nero said. 'For the glory of Rome!' He turned to Quistus, smiling for the crowd, and spoke in a low vicious voice. 'I'll never forgive you. Freeing those worthless slaves cost me a fortune.'

But Quistus looked content. 'Justice has been done. I saved one thousand three hundred and twelve lives from certain death, and I did my best to save the last, Docilosa. From the very beginning that was all I tried to do.'

'You spoiled my show,' Nero said dangerously. 'You sided with the enemy. Stigmus told me everything that happened in Gaul and Britain.'

'Not quite everything.' Quistus grabbed Stigmus, Omba put her elbow around the neck of the struggling man, and Quistus pulled the Phoenix from the folds of Stigmus's toga. He held up the necklace like flames in his hands. 'Fire diamonds. Priceless.'

'Don't,' Stigmus said. 'No.'

'I do believe you've stolen the Phoenix from the Emperor, Stigmus.'

'No.' Stigmus's face collapsed. 'I – I was just looking after it for him. It's a gift. The Phoenix is yours, great Caesar.'

Nero took it, interested. 'Oh. I love fire.' He tossed it aside. 'Loyal Stigmus, I appoint you Prefect of Praetorians. I suggest your first official act should be to arrest your incompetent predecessor.' Tigellinus shouted as he was bundled away.

'As for you.' Nero turned to Quistus. 'What punishment is great enough? You're a traitor to all we Romans believe in. Death is too merciful. I shan't kill you. However, I can take your life.' He raised his voice. 'This is my decree. All that this traitor had is mine, even his name. He is no longer Severus Septimus Quistus. His house is mine, his money, his slaves, his pathetic pictures of his wife, everything. He has nothing to live for, he is *persona non grata*. He's no one.'

Quistus turned away.

Nero called him back and spoke in a low voice. 'Naturally you'll beg me and remind me of my promise to give you whatever I least wished to give. In this case, no doubt, your miserable life.'

Quistus shook his head. 'No, Nero. I'm going to save that promise for when I really need it. You gave me this quest meaning me to fail. I succeeded. Why did you go to all that trouble? For Tara. That was all that mattered to you. Killing Tara. I led you to her. It was Stigmus who failed, not I. You should be ashamed of yourself, Nero. A certain lack of greatness of mind. An artistic misjudgment.'

'I trusted you to do the right thing. I trusted your Roman heart.'

'You were wrong about me, Nero. I don't kill children. I never have.'

Nero watched him go, then called, 'Come back.'

Quistus stopped.

'Claudia and Tara,' Nero called. 'What happened to them?'

'They died in the fire.' Quistus walked down the steps that led from the podium.

Nero leant over the rail. He shouted, 'Tell me the truth and I'll give back everything I've taken from you. Everything!'

Quistus didn't even look up. He called, 'They died in the fire.'

Nero sat. He was alone. He stared over the empty arena.

And so ended Quistus's involvement in a death by natural causes that became a murder yet was finally a death by natural causes once more. An examination of the dead had brought about, as always, an investigation into the living, and revealed in their fragile souls more lies than truth, and more darkness than illumination.

And more knowledge than was wise or safe.

And yet, love.

As for Quistus, nameless, an exile in his own city and his own heart, he was content to live in hope. For he had seen his daughter and knew Lyra was alive.